# Do It To Me

# Do It To Me

## P.F. Kozak

APHRODISIA

KENSINGTON PUBLISHING CORP.

http://www.kensingtonbooks.com

APHRODISIA BOOKS are published by

Kensington Publishing Corp.
850 Third Avenue
New York, NY 10022

All Kensington titles, imprints, and distributed lines are available at special quantity discounts for bulk purchases for sales promotions, premiums, fund-raising, and educational or institutional use.

Special book excerpts or customized printings can also be created to fit specific needs. For details, write or phone the office of the Kensington Special Sales Manager: Kensington Publishing Corp., 850 Third Avenue, New York, NY 10022, Attn: Special Sales Department. Phone: 1-800-221-2647.

ISBN-13: 978-0-7582-2272-5
ISBN-10: 0-7582-2272-6

First Trade Paperback Printing: November 2008

10  9  8  7  6  5  4  3  2  1

Printed in the United States of America

# Acknowledgments

Although fictionalized to protect the not-so-innocent, the stories in *Do It to Me* are based on the real-life adventures of sailors, a good number of them I am proud to call my friends.

These career merchant mariners are a breed apart. They sailed at a time in shipping history when the adage "men were men" rang true, and "Hello, Sailor!" resonated in ports around the world. They worked hard, played hard and stayed hard.

The female pioneers who had the courage and the strength to become part of this world deserve a special salute. To step on board a ship and work side by side with an all-male crew took grit and guts. These women had both.

It is impossible to mention everyone who helped make this book possible. But I have to give GL, RL, SR, JP, GW, and especially SC a nod and a sincere thank-you. Your stories and inspiration are at the heart of *Do It to Me.*

And, as always, ML and IK, thank you for your love and support. *Alla famiglia! Ti amo!*

# Contents

Cruise Ship Charlie   3

Southern Seaman   123

Merchant Maureen   237

# Prologue

**Why's a Ship a "She"?**

A ship is called a she because she is all decked out and usually pretty well stacked.
She has pleasing lines from stem to stern and there's generally a gang of men around her.

It's not her initial cost that breaks you; it's the upkeep.
Her rigging costs you a fortune and she always looks her best in a new coat of paint.

There's usually a lot of bustle about her, but she usually manages to show off her superstructure to advantage.

When entering the port, she heads straight to the buoys.
When you want to attract her attention, a whistle's the appropriate signal.

Once you get to know her, you never want to leave her.
On a balmy night or on a calm moonlit night, she can make men forget their troubles.

Finally she has as many tricks and teases as any woman, and consequently it takes a very capable man to handle her properly.

—Author unknown

# CRUISE SHIP CHARLIE

# 1

Charlie really needed a shower. His eight-to-twelve shift in the engine room had wrapped up at midnight. He wiped his grimy hands on his white boiler suit, now covered with grease, soot and sweat. He wasn't fit to be seen, let alone enjoy some female company. Nonetheless, he made his way to the Monkey Bar at the stern of the ship, to see if his mate Morgy had come through for him again.

As he thought would be the case, the crowd at the bar had thinned. After midnight, most passengers inclined to late-night partying drifted to the Twilight Bar, where they could disco until the wee hours. The Monkey Bar closed at 1:00 A.M.

Morgy spotted him and waved him over. Charlie could tell by the expression on his face that the barman had a bit of business to share.

"Hey there, mate. How about a pint to wash the taste of soot out of my mouth?"

"Bloody hell, what happened to you? You're filthy!"

Charlie propped his foot on the rail in front of the bar and watched Morgy draw his pint. "I had a run-in with a fan on the

number four soot blower. Fuckin' thing got stuck. I got it un-
stuck and lubed, but not before I got covered with soot and
grease." He gratefully took the glass, then looked around. "Good
thing there aren't many passengers left. I shouldn't be in here,
looking like this."

"Especially with your coveralls open to your navel." Morgy
eyed Charlie's hairy chest. "There's dirty sweat sliding down
your treasure trail."

"It's hot as Hades next to the boiler!" Charlie chugged half
the pint in one long drink, then wiped the foamy mustache on
his sleeve. He noticed Morgy still looking at him. "You're
going to burn a hole in my chest if you keep staring at it."

"You're making me wish I'd lined up a bit of company for
myself tonight."

Charlie laughed. In a low voice, he poked some fun. "What,
you couldn't find yourself a boyfriend in the crowd tonight?"

"No, I was too damn busy sorting out a sheila for you."

Charlie smiled broadly. "Which one of the ladies did you
reel in?" Charlie had given Morgy a list of candidates before he
started his shift in the engine room. He'd hoped one of them
would come into the bar tonight.

"The one I want to be like, of course." Morgy then did a
spot-on impersonation of the stacked blonde Charlie had seen
by the swimming pool that afternoon. " 'What is your name
again? Yes, of course, Morgan. I do remember seeing that delightful young man earlier today. Meet with him? Goodness, is
that allowed?' "

Charlie held up his hand to stop Morgy's performance be-
fore any of the remaining passengers heard him. "All right,
Miss Oz! I know which one it is. Sandy blond hair and a great
body. I saw her again this arvo on the Lido Deck by the pool."
He smiled as he remembered the crimson bikini she had on.
"Her togs gave me a throb in the knob."

Morgy winked at Charlie. "You do the same for me."

Charlie shook his head. "Jesus H. Sufferin' Christ, you're such a friggin' queen."

"Yes, and proud of it. Can't show it too much in here. It's bad form."

"You're shit out of luck getting a chubby from me. I like women."

"Can't blame a girl for trying. One of these days, I'll get you drunk and give you a head job." Morgy tapped his lips with his index finger. "Or maybe, you'll have your way with me."

"Not bloody likely, mate. Never have, never will."

Morgy smiled. "I've heard that before."

"Now you're hearin' it again." Charlie took another drink and waited. "Well, you going to tell me about the sheila you set up for me?"

"This one's on the prowl. You were right, her name is Petula, but she says her friends call her 'Pet.' Came in here looking over every man in the bar. Seemed happy she hooked up with someone she fancies."

"You think she fancies me?"

"I know she does. She asked me if you're married, and what you do on the ship. You'd best be finishing that pint PDQ. I told her to meet me here at one, and I'll take her to your cabin. If she sees you looking like a brown-eyed mullet, she'll turn around and go back to her first-class cabin."

"First-class? Not too shabby! Think she has money?"

"What do you care? It's not her money you're after."

"You got that right, mate." Charlie finished off his pint. "Gotta go and wash up. You got your key?"

Morgy patted the pocket on his red vest. "Right here. Don't worry, you'll have a naughty tonight."

"I know I will. Thanks, mate. I'll see what I can scare up for you next time."

"Promises, promises." Charlie left Morgy finishing his clean-up. He would be closing the bar directly, and then escort Pet to Charlie's room.

Charlie took the authorized route back to his cabin, walking through the verandah and crossing the Lido Deck to the stairs that led back to the engine room. Just as he thought they would be, the swimming pools on the Lido Deck were deserted at this hour. Again he remembered seeing Pet that afternoon in her swimming togs. His mates called this the "Libido Deck" for good reason.

From the engine room, he took the stairs that led to the crew's quarters on the starboard side of the ship. As he walked down the alleyway on C Deck toward his cabin, Charlie glanced at the locked door that separated the passengers' quarters from the crew's. In about fifteen minutes, Morgy would be opening it with his contraband key and bringing the sexy sheila to his room.

He didn't have much time. After skimming off his soot-covered boiler suit, he jumped into the shower. With a woman coming, he made sure he scrubbed all the nooks and crannies thoroughly. He paid particular attention to his nuggets, hoping this sexy lady would do some teabagging.

Once he quickly dried, he put on some black trousers and a white shirt. He didn't bother with shoes and socks, figuring he wouldn't have his clothes on for long. He straightened his bunk and unearthed his stash of gin. Just as he set two glasses on his desk, someone knocked on his door.

When he answered, a curvaceous blonde in a sexy, low-cut blue halter dress stood there. Morgy was nowhere in sight.

"Charlie?"

"You're Petula, right?"

"Yes. Morgan unlocked the door, and then pointed down the hall. He told me cabin 169. I'd hoped he wasn't mistaken."

"Nope, Morgy knows my cabin. We're best mates. He

wouldn't steer you wrong." Charlie stepped aside. "Please come in."

"Thank you." Petula came into Charlie's small cabin. He gave her a once-over from behind. He almost whistled when he saw that the back of the dress dipped open nearly to her bum, and then it flared at her waist into a full skirt. She obviously didn't have a bra on! Charlie could see most of her bare back.

He managed to get his wits. "Make yourself at home. Would you like a drink? I have some good Gordon's gin. I can make you a gin and tonic."

"That would be lovely. And please call me Pet." She laid her clutch bag on his desk and sat down on the edge of the bunk. "They don't give you fellows much room in these cabins, do they?"

Charlie smiled. "They save the good cabins for the paying passengers. We're just the hired help." He noticed Petula studying his old scratched-up desk.

"Are those initials carved into the wood?"

"Yeah. When my mates come in here for a drink, they leave me an autograph. That desk has history. Some of those initials are from other engineers who had this cabin before me."

"You're an engineer?"

"I'm a third assistant engineer. I just got off my watch. I do eight-to-twelve twice a day."

Petula took the glass Charlie offered her. "That's how you could be on the Lido Deck this afternoon. I wondered about that."

Charlie pulled out his desk chair and sat down. "I saw you this arvo." He gestured toward her with his glass. "Couldn't help but notice what a good-looking woman you are."

"How sweet of you to say that. I also picked you out of the crowd."

"Did ya now? You weren't put off by my being with the crew and not a passenger?"

"Quite the contrary." Petula checked him out as he had her. "Most of the men I've met are old, married or pansies. You aren't any of those."

"Now, how would you know that?" Charlie moved from the desk chair and sat on the bunk beside her.

"It's quite obvious you aren't old, or a pansy." She sipped her G and T before she added, "And I asked if you were married."

"Who'd you ask?"

"The lifeguard at the pool. I pointed you out today. He told me your name and said he didn't think you had a wife, but to ask the barman at the Monkey Bar."

"So that's how you met my mate Morgy. I wondered why you showed up there tonight." Charlie considered telling her more, and decided it wouldn't hurt. "I described you to him and told him to keep an eye out for you."

"It did seem quite a coincidence that he offered to bring me to your cabin without my asking."

"No coincidence. I wanted to meet you, but I had to be careful. It's against the rules for me to be socializing with the female passengers. I could get my arse in deep if anyone finds out you've been in my cabin."

"Don't worry. I won't tell anyone I know you, or that I've been in your cabin." Petula pointed to his poster of a topless dark-skinned woman, who seemed about to peel off her panties. Charlie had hung it over his desk so he could see it from his bunk. "Charming picture."

Not the least bit embarrassed by his choice of artwork, Charlie explained his fantasy sheila. "I found that picture in a small shop in Sydney and snapped it up straight away. I call her 'Yooralla.' "

"I never heard that name before."

"It's an Aborigine word that means 'love.' Knew a girl once

called Yooralla. Don't know what ever became of her, but she was even more beautiful than that sheila. I think of her sometimes when I'm alone. . . ." Charlie's voice trailed off. He hadn't meant to say that.

"That picture reminds you of her, doesn't it?"

"S'pose so." Not wanting to sound so serious, he set his glass on the floor and again pointed to the poster. "Figured she would keep me company on these long, lonely nights at sea."

"Does she? Keep you company, I mean."

"When I need her, she does. But tonight, I don't need her." Petula suddenly stood up, set her glass on the desk, and picked up her bag. Charlie got up and grabbed her arm, afraid she had decided to leave. "You aren't going, are you?"

"No, dear Charles. I have something for you in my bag."

Charlie relaxed his grip on her arm. "Bloody hell, you gave me a start. I thought I had done something to put you off."

"Not at all. Truth be told, you're the only man I've met on this long, boring trip that interests me."

Charlie grinned. "Is that a fact!"

"That is indeed a fact. That's why I want to give you this." Petula opened her clutch bag and gave Charlie a key.

"Is this what I think it is?"

"That's an extra key to my cabin. I'm on Deck B, cabin 232."

"Hell, Pet, B232 isn't a cabin, that's a suite with a balcony. Those digs cost a friggin' fortune!"

"I can afford it, so why not?"

"I know you're British. What are you, royalty or something?"

"No, not royalty, just lucky."

Charlie gave her back the key. "Don't know why you're givin' that to me. I'm an engineer on the *Ortensia*. You're a first-class passenger on her."

Petula put the key on his desk. "Your mate Morgy told me

about you, about how you know more about a ship than anyone else he's ever known. He also told me you're good at making keys."

"He told you that?"

"He told me you're the one that copied the special key that
opens the door between the passengers' cabins and the crew's.
You could copy my extra key, and then give it back to me."

"Your knowin' that could get my arse put off the ship, let
alone your being in here with me."

Petula wrapped her arms around Charlie's neck. "Getting
cold feet, Charles?"

"Why me, Pet? Why are you keen on me?"

"I could ask you the same thing."

"That's an easy one. You're a good-looking woman. You
gave me a boner this arvo, and you're giving me another one
now." Charlie cleared his throat. "I'm sorry. Don't usually use
such coarse talk with a woman."

"And I don't offer the key to my room to just anyone. I saw
you the other day. I made it a point to find out your name when
I saw you again on the Lido Deck this afternoon."

Charlie slid his hand up Petula's bare back to her neck. "I
don't remember seeing you before today."

"I was bored, so I wandered around the ship. You were busy
checking the lifeboats."

"Friggin' 'ell, you watched the lifeboat inspection? You
must have been bloody bored."

"I was. You entertained me."

"Is that what I'm doing tonight?"

"I hope so. I need to be entertained."

"I can see that." Charlie leaned over and kissed her, hoping
Petula would return the kiss. Not only did she return his kiss,
but she held on to him like a drowning woman clinging to
driftwood.

When he pulled away, she whispered, "What are we waiting for?"

Charlie reached under her hair and tugged at the string that held her halter top in place. "Not a damn thing. Let's get on with the job." The tie came loose. Just like a bib falling from a baby's neck, the halter top covering her breasts fell to her waist.

Without Charlie having to ask, Petula unbuttoned his shirt. "Do you remember how hot it was the day you inspected the lifeboats?"

"Sure I do. It was cooler in the engine room than it was on deck."

Petula pulled his shirt open. "Your coveralls were open like this, and I could see your chest. I wanted to touch it so much." She rubbed his pectorals with both hands.

"Well, Pet, when I saw your bathing togs today, I wanted to rub yours, too." He filled each hand with a soft breast. "And that's not all I wanted to rub."

"Tell me what else."

"Better to show you, I think."

He stepped backward toward his bunk, taking Petula with him. "I don't want to muss up your dress. Maybe you should take it off."

"Perhaps I should. Will you help me? You're an engineer, you should be able to manage a zipper." She turned around and waited.

Knowing his way around an engine didn't help him one iota in this situation. All he saw were folds of poofy blue chiffon. He didn't see even the slightest hint of a zipper. "Where exactly is it, Pet?"

"It's back there. You'll find it."

Charlie sat down on the edge of the bunk. He figured the easiest way to find it, and the best way to get things rolling, was feeling under her skirt. He heard her breath catch as he slid his hands up the back of her legs, but she didn't stop him.

When his fingers grazed the bare flesh of her bum, he nearly pulled his hand away, startled that she didn't have any underpants on. He paused, and got his bearings. This one wanted it as much as he did. It had been a while since he'd had a sheila so willing, and ready for it.

Letting one hand rest on her bare arse cheek, he reached up with the other to feel the inside of her dress. He felt the zipper teeth with his fingers, but still couldn't see the damn thing.

Reluctantly he pulled his other hand out from under her dress and felt for the zipper from the outside. After he traced the line of the teeth, he finally discovered the small tab wrapped in blue cloth at the waist of the skirt. He slid it down in one smooth motion to the bottom of her bum.

"Christ, Pet, it's easier to tear an engine apart than it is to open this friggin' zipper."

"That's why I asked for help. I knew you'd figure it out."

The dress hung precariously on her hips, her bum crack now partially visible. On impulse, Charlie leaned forward and licked her lower back. Petula shivered.

Not wasting any time, he pushed the dress down her legs to her ankles. As he suspected, she had nothing on underneath. He kissed each arse cheek and then reached around and tickled her pubic hair. Petula sighed.

"Pet, you shouldn't walk around the ship wearing nothing underneath your dress. My mates are good blokes, but not one of them would think twice about reaching under and copping a feel, and maybe even doing a private lifeboat inspection with you."

"Charlie, maybe that's what I've been hoping would happen."

He gently lifted each foot, took off her shoes and untangled her dress. Then he turned her around and tickled her pubes again. "You want it bad, don't ya, Pet?"

"You're the first man I've met on this ship who seems to be more than just talk. Yes, Charlie, I want it bad, and I want someone who's man enough to give it to me."

Even with his erection throbbing in his trousers, Charlie decided not to take her just yet. He wanted to make her want it even more. He pulled her closer and buried his face in the golden curls between her legs. Petula gasped when his tongue connected with her sensitive flesh, and she moaned when he sucked her clitoris into his mouth.

Charlie sucked his prize until he had Petula squirming to get away. She pushed at his head and gasped. "I can't stand it. Stop!"

When he let her go, he fully expected Petula to collapse on the bed beside him. She didn't. Instead, she knelt between his legs. Before he fully grasped what she meant to do, she leaned forward and licked his knob through his trousers. "Pet, aren't you ready to get a leg over?" He wanted to screw her, badly.

"Not yet, dear Charles. It's your turn." She tried to undo his trousers. Not wanting to get his willy nicked in his fly, he stopped her and undid it himself. He'd never had a sheila go after him like a hungry wombat. He rather fancied it.

Charlie lifted his arse so Pet could drag his trousers down and off. He doffed his shirt and tossed it onto the floor. That left them both naked.

He reached down and squeezed her tits. "Christ, Pet, you're built. You should be a model."

Much to his surprise, she started to laugh. "I used to be. I design clothes now. I designed the dress I was wearing."

"Shoulda done a friggin' better job on the zipper."

"Says you, Mister Engineer."

Then she shocked the shit out of him. She grabbed hold of

his donger and took him full in her mouth, sucking him like a vacuum pump.

"Oh, yeah, Pet, that's the way. Shit, yeah!" Petula sucked him hard, and licked him all the while. Charlie remembered he'd hoped for some teabagging. He tapped on her blond head. "Pet, do my knackers."

Without missing a beat, Petula released his cock and moved her mouth lower. First she licked his balls; then she sucked the whole sac into her mouth. Charlie thought he had died and gone to heaven. She rolled his testicles in her mouth like lollies, licking them as she would yummy sweets.

Charlie let her play with him as long as he could stand it. When he knew he wouldn't last much longer, he stopped her. "I'm ready to shag, my Pet. Let's do it."

"Wait, I've got condoms in my bag."

"No worries. I have some right here." Charlie reached under his mattress and pulled out a small package. Petula watched as he ripped open the wrapper and rolled the rubber onto his prick. "Sailors, and engineers, are always prepared."

"So are women looking to get laid."

Charlie grinned and pushed her backward onto the bunk. "Well, Pet, you're about to get it good."

With no preamble, Charlie pushed his cock deep into Petula's body. She gasped and lifted her pelvis to meet his. "Fuck, yes, Charlie, do it hard!"

She didn't have to ask him twice. He frigged her harder than he had any sheila on the ship. He had only ever fucked a woman this hard during the few visits he had made to a whorehouse in Hong Kong. Petula stayed with him, slapping her pussy against him just as roughly as he pounded her.

Charlie didn't know how long he could hold on, but she seemed close. He practically growled at her, "C'mon, Pet. Come for me, I want to feel you come."

"Jesus, yes, I'm so close."

He wiggled his fingers between them just enough to reach her nipple. Then he pinched it as hard as he could. Petula yelped and then began to shudder.

"Oh, yeah, Pet, that's it, let it fly."

Charlie continued to bang her as she shook underneath him. Before she stopped shaking, his balls clutched and he sprayed into the rubber. Petula dug her fingernails into his back and scratched him down to his arse. Another spasm gripped him and he squirted again.

He heard her whisper, "Oh, yes, you're definitely man enough to get the job done."

# 2

Charlie made his eight o'clock watch the next morning. It didn't matter how hard you partied, or how knockout gorgeous the sheila might be, you didn't let your mates down. You would show up for duty on time and do your job, even if you had to stand in a cold shower for half an hour to sober up.

He didn't need the cold shower to sober up this time, but he did need it to cool down. He woke up with a boner so hard he could've used it to pound nails. Even the cold shower didn't do it. He had to have a wank before he left for the engine room. He couldn't get Petula out of his mind.

Pet had wanted to spend the whole night with him. Charlie knew from experience he should get her back to her cabin while the alleyways were empty. Smuggling a sheila out in the morning could be done, and had been done frequently by his mates, but he preferred not taking the risk unless he absolutely had to do it.

Charlie used his personal copy of the contraband key to unlock the door to the passenger side of the ship. He didn't want

Pet wandering around the ship in the middle of the night alone, so he walked her back to her cabin. She invited him in.

As much as he hated to do it, he declined the offer. He knew he had to get some rest before his watch started at eight o'clock. They agreed to meet that afternoon. He told her he would leave the details with Morgy.

He used his key again to get back to his cabin. That key had a history. When the lock on the door broke, the Captain decided to replace it with a German lock. It came with four-sided keys, which supposedly could not be duplicated.

The Captain kept a key, and gave a few to the master-at-arms for distribution among the ship's security officers. The Chief Engineer also got one. It didn't take long before one of his mates got the Chief Engineer drunk and waited for him to pass out so he could borrow the key.

Before returning it, he asked Charlie if he could figure out a way to make a copy. Unable to copy a four-sided key the usual way, Charlie made a wax impression of all four sides before giving it back. Once he had the impressions, he used a rat-tail file to duplicate the grooves onto pieces of metal. Then he silver-soldered the four sides together.

He made several copies. He kept one, and gave one to his mate who had borrowed it. He also made copies for several other crew members, good lads he knew he could trust. No one ever suspected anyone had copies, since everyone believed the key couldn't be duplicated.

Later he gave one to Morgy. Morgy's job included overseeing the stewards for the Monkey Bar, who would often deliver food and drinks to the passengers' cabins. Many times Morgy would also help out and make deliveries, to the crew as well as to the passengers. When he would be asked to escort a woman for a late-night meeting with a crew member, no one would question his being in the passenger section of the ship.

Charlie continued his work on the soot blowers that morning, and again got himself filthy. When his early shift ended at
noon, he wanted to catch Morgy before he left his meeting with
the stewards who would be on duty in the bar that day.

Knowing the Monkey Bar wasn't yet open for business, he
saw no harm in going there, again looking crusty. Sure enough,
he saw Morgy in a huddle with his stewards, going over the
day's work. He waited in the background until Morgy dismissed his staff.

Morgy had his back turned, so he didn't see Charlie behind
him.

"G'day, mate."

Morgy jumped. "Holy dooley! What are you trying to do?
Bury me at sea?"

Charlie grinned. "Christ, why would I want to kill ya, mate?
I need you alive, not dead as a herring."

"Now, there's a comfort." As he had the night before, Morgy
gave Charlie a once-over. "Been working on the soot blowers
again?"

"Spent all morning on 'em. Tonight's watch should finish
'em off. After my day off tomorrow, I get to work on the bilge
pumps."

"Glamorous work for a ladies' man."

"Yeah, I know. I got to go clean up, but wanted to tell you,
I'll need your help again. Pet wants to hook up with me this afternoon."

Morgy put the clipboard he had in his hand on a table and
crossed his arms over his chest. "Is that a fact? Why would she
want to do that?"

"I s'pose she enjoyed herself last night."

"You think so?"

"What, you don't think she did?"

"I don't know." Grinning like a shot fox, Morgy looked past
him. "Petula, did you enjoy yourself last night?"

"I certainly did, Morgan. That's why I'm here."

When he heard her voice, Charlie wanted to crawl under a rock. "Shit! Pet?"

"Hello, Charles."

Knowing he looked like hell, he still turned around to face her. There she stood, wearing a smart flowered sundress. "What the devil are you doing in here? The bar isn't open yet."

"I know, but the door was open. I stopped by to see Morgan, obviously for the same reason you're here."

"I just got off my watch, and haven't been back to my cabin yet."

"Why don't I go with you?"

Charlie glanced at Morgy. He got the message. "You go on ahead, Charlie. I'll bring Pet along directly."

"Thanks, mate. I owe you one."

"You wanker! You owe me more than one!"

"One of these days, I'll pay you back." He winked at Pet. "See you in a few minutes, love." Charlie hurried back toward the engine room, again taking the longer route to his cabin. He had to hustle, or Morgy and Pet would beat him to the door.

He beat Pet to his cabin. Hoping to at least wash the dirt off his face before she got there, he went to his loo, pulling his arms out of his boiler suit as he walked. He then rubbed some soap and water on his face.

Before he could rinse it off, he heard the knock on his door. He quickly splashed some water on his face, then grabbed a towel and rubbed it dry. When he opened the door, both Pet and Morgy stood there.

"Didn't know you were joining us, mate." He gave Morgy a questioning look.

"No worries. Pet asked me to come with her for a few. She wants to ask us something." Morgy followed Pet into Charlie's cabin. Then Charlie closed the door.

Pet sat down on the bunk, as she had the night before.

Morgy pulled out the desk chair. Still in his dirty boiler suit, Charlie remained standing. "What's on your mind, Pet?"

When Petula looked up, her eyes stopped at his chest. "It's hard to remember, with your being half undressed."

Morgy tittered. "Oh, my dear, I tell him that every time he comes to the bar with his coveralls open. A girl can't think straight with that chest out in the open air."

Charlie couldn't believe Morgy had said what he said in front of Pet. He hurriedly put his arms back into the sleeves of his boiler suit. "You have to forgive my mate, Pet. Sometimes he has verbal diarrhea and runs at the mouth."

Morgy chastised him. "Oh, stop being such a whinge. Petula knows I fancy you as much as she does."

Suddenly concerned that Pet would think he and Morgy were more than friends, Charlie quickly added, "And Pet also knows we're good mates and that's all."

Not to be outdone, Morgy retorted, "After last night, I'm sure she knows that very well."

Pet agreed. "I certainly do, except I think I prefer him clean. Do you always get this dirty?"

Glad that Pet had changed the subject, Charlie spoke up before Morgy had a chance to say anything more. "Depends on what I do during my watch. Most days I get pretty damn cruddy."

"It's rather attractive, in an earthy sort of way."

Directing his comment at Charlie, Morgy quipped, "Oooh, I do like her."

Already feeling a woody coming on, Charlie agreed. "Yeah, so do I." He wanted to get Morgy out of his cabin, so he tried to get things moving along. "What did you want to ask us, Pet?"

"I want to host a party in my cabin, with you two and some of your mates. I have a few friends on board who would like to meet some men." Pet pointedly looked at Morgy. "Those include male friends."

Charlie spoke before Morgy could. "Pet, we can't do that. You'll get all our arses thrown off the ship—"

Morgy interrupted. "Not so fast, Charlie. We've done it before."

"Yes, but not in a passenger suite. We have parties in our cabins."

"So let's do it in here."

Petula appeared skeptical. "You've had parties in these small cabins? The three of us nearly fill it up."

Charlie glanced at Morgy. "What was the most we ever did?"

"Ten. That's our voyage best."

"You fellows crammed ten people in one of these tiny cabins? That's not possible!"

Morgy grinned. "My dear, it is possible. We've done it. It makes for meaningful relationships."

"I would suppose so!"

Curious about the friends she mentioned, Charlie wanted to know more. "Who are your friends, Pet? Can we trust them?"

"You can absolutely trust them. They work for me."

"I don't understand."

"The women are models. We just had a show in Sydney. The man is my assistant, Derrick." She smiled at Morgy. "He would definitely fancy you."

Ignoring the last comment she made, Charlie asked, "How many women?"

"Three. If Morgan pairs with Derrick, then we need three more men."

Morgy jumped up from his chair, then sat back down beside Pet. "Since he's too damn filthy to do it, let me." With that, he hugged her tightly. "The answer, my dear Pet, is yes! We can do ten."

Petula gasped for air as the bear hug squeezed the breath out of her. When she could speak, she again offered her suite. "We would be more comfortable in my cabin. I have so much room, it's obscene."

Charlie didn't have to say no this time. Morgy did it for him. "Darling, we can't do that. If anyone would complain because of the noise, or if the crew would be seen in the passenger section at night, we'd all be put off the ship at the next port."

Petula appeared mildly disappointed, but agreed. "All right, then. When?"

Charlie jumped in. "Tomorrow night would be spot-on. I have the day off. What about you, Morgy?"

"I can switch shifts tomorrow with someone, and work the early shift at the bar. That would give me tomorrow evening free."

"Pet, does that work for you?"

"It certainly does, Charles. You just have to find three more men for my girls."

"The only problem there is figuring out which three. Morgy, what do you think?"

"Let me mull it over. I'll come up with some willing blokes to show the ladies a good time."

"I'm sure you can, Morgan. I have every confidence in you. And what about food and drink? I'll pay for anything we need."

Morgy tapped his cheek. "I'll have everything delivered on a cart to your suite. No one will question that. Then we'll bring it down here when it's time." He turned around and looked at the cluttered desk. "Charlie, clean up this mess so we have a table for the food."

"My pleasure, mate. I'll just stuff it all under my bunk."

Morgy threw his hands in the air. "Heterosexual men are completely hopeless!" He got up to leave. "Shall we say tomorrow at seven o'clock?"

Petula clapped her hands. "That will be splendid. I'll tell my girls to wear something appropriate for sitting on the floor."

"And make sure what you wear is washable. You never know what might get on it," Charlie chimed in.

Morgy opened the door. "With what I expect will happen, very little would be good." With that, he went back to work.

Feeling a bit awkward about Pet being in his cabin when he needed to shower, he thought to offer her a drink. "Would you care for a G and T, or is it too early for you?"

"A tonic with no gin would be splendid."

"You got it." Relieved he had a distraction, Charlie found his bottle of tonic water and poured a glassful for Pet. When he handed it to her, he thought to excuse himself. "I need to shower before I get any closer to you. Right now, I'm not fit to be close to a dingo."

"Do you want to be close to a dingo?"

The question threw Charlie for a moment. Then he noticed the twinkle in her eyes and knew she had just yanked his chain. "I'd rather be close to you. Dingoes bite."

"Maybe I do, too. You don't know everything I might do."

Charlie's partial woody instantly became a full-blown erection. "Pet, you're playing with fire here. I don't think you want me on top of you before I shower. More talk like that, and you're about to have soot in your blond hair."

"Let me shower with you. We have time, don't we?"

"My next watch doesn't start until eight o'clock tonight. Damn straight we have time."

"Well, then, let's get you cleaned up."

Charlie could hardly believe she meant it. When Pet stood up and took his hand, he knew he had found himself one hell of a sheila. Since he'd never been with anyone so willing before, he had to ask her, "Are you sure about this?"

"I told you last night, you are man enough to do the job. I meant it."

"What job is that, Pet?"

"You are man enough to satisfy me. You have no idea how long I've been looking for a man like you. Wait until you meet my assistant. Then you may understand."

"Morgy will be happy, won't he?"

"Your friend will be quite happy. Most men in my profession prefer trousers to skirts. Even when they are sexy enough to put dew on my flower, they aren't interested in me."

"They have to be frigging crazy! How could any man walk away from you?"

"Plenty have."

"Frigging hell, I want you right now." Charlie tried to pull Pet closer to kiss her.

She put her hand on his chest and flexed her fingers in his chest hair. "My wonderful, filthy sailor, let's scrub you up."

Charlie took offense at her remark. "You best be getting this straight. I'm an engineer, not a sailor."

She laughed, a beautiful, sparkling sound. "I am so sorry, my wonderful, filthy engineer. Unless you want me to find you a dingo to frig, you'd better let me wash you."

Trying to hide his shock that a sheila of her breeding would use such language, he retorted, "I'm not frigging any damn dog when I have you in my cabin."

"I thought you might feel that way. Let's take a shower."

Pet took Charlie's hand and squeezed it. He desperately wanted to fuck her, but knew he would put her off if he didn't clean himself up. So he figured he would let her lead the way. She did, through the door to the shower.

"Your loo is just as small as your cabin!" Charlie's toilet had a commode, a sink and a shower stall. Two people could barely fit in the remaining space.

Charlie stepped away from her as far as he could in the tight quarters. "Careful, Pet, you'll get your dress dirty. I don't want you to rub up against me." He grinned. "At least not until I shower."

"That's not until *we* shower." Pet lowered the spaghetti straps on her dress. Charlie just stood there, watching her. "Do you want me to undress you? Take off your clothes!"

Charlie knew that as soon as he took off his boiler suit, Pet would plainly see his reaction to her being there. Rather than hiding it, he figured he would make the most of it. "You'd best be hanging that pretty frock in the closet by my bunk." Charlie slipped his arms out of his coverall sleeves. "I have to take off my boots, and they're covered with soot. Don't want it to get on you."

Petula took his advice. Stepping just outside the door, where Charlie could still plainly see her, she pulled her dress over her head. Once again, she had nothing on underneath. It took a considerable amount of willpower for Charlie to not have a wank staring at her naked tits and pussy. Instead, he chastised her.

"Jesus Christ, Pet. You're going to get yourself into a shit-load of trouble running around the ship like that. My mates can sniff a hot pussy at a hundred paces. Most of us were raised in the bush, if you get my drift."

Petula laughed. "Charles, you worry too much. I can take care of myself." She moved out of sight while she hung up her dress.

As he sat down on the toilet to take off his boots, Charlie whispered, "I fucking bet you can."

"What did you say? I didn't hear you?" Pet yelled from around the corner.

"I said I bet you can take care of yourself."

She reappeared in the doorway. "Of course, I can." Charlie couldn't help himself, he stared at her tits. "For God's sake, Charlie! Take off your clothes." She came back in and stood in front of him, her blond pussy now only a few centimeters from his face.

This is what Charlie wanted. Now that he had her naked, he wanted to see how far he could push her. "If you want me in the nick so bad, then I think you should help me get there."

"So you do want me to undress you."

Charlie held up his foot. "Can't get the suit off with my boots still on." He put both hands behind his head, leaned back and waited.

Exasperated, Pet put her hands on her hips, which made her tits jut out even more. "You have a set of bollocks, don't you?"

"Just got off my watch." He closed his eyes, while keeping his foot poised in the air. "I could use forty winks. Take your time." He knew he had her. His prick twitched in anticipation.

"Well, aren't you being a bloody bit of business!" Pet grabbed his boot. She was so focused on pulling it off, she didn't notice he'd opened his eyes to watch. She tugged hard and almost fell backward when it let loose. After regaining her balance, she grabbed his other ankle. "Lift your frigging foot."

Without saying a word, he obliged. All the while, Pet's tits bounced with her efforts. The view he had couldn't be beat. She tugged again and the boot came off. This time, she managed it better, but not before she got soot all over her legs.

Her hair had fallen over her eyes. Before Charlie could stop her, she involuntarily brushed it back, leaving long black streaks on her forehead and in her hair.

"You know, Pet, you've gone from being a tidy sheila to being a grub like me."

Pet looked down at herself. "Bloody hell. You did that on purpose, didn't you?"

"Look in the mirror."

Petula glanced in the mirror over the sink. "Bugger! I even got it in my hair." She walked right past Charlie and stepped in the shower. "I'm taking a shower. You can join me, or not. Up to you."

Charlie followed her into the shower, still wearing his boiler suit. Before Pet had a chance to turn on the water, he spun her around and yanked her against him. Her breasts flattened against his chest, and her pale skin took on the same dark hue as his.

Before she had a chance to whinge about his still having his clothes on, he kissed her. He dug his fingers into her bare arse and held her pelvis tightly against his groin. He knew she could feel his erection, he wanted her to feel it. Charlie rubbed himself against her leg, not caring that he got her even dirtier.

This sheila wanted shagging, and could handle it being rude. Charlie kissed her hard, forcing his tongue deep into her mouth. She sucked it the way she had his dick the night before.

Pet tried to pull his coveralls down over his hips, not realizing they were still snapped the length of his groin. When the snaps popped in one long rat-a-tat-tat, she jumped and nearly bit Charlie's tongue. He moved his head just in time.

He steadied her and whispered, "Easy, Pet."

"Oh, Lord, did I rip them?"

"Hell, these things are indestructible. You just pulled the snaps open."

"Will you please take those bloody things off?" She caressed him through his underpants. "I don't know anyone who showers with their clothes on."

"You've already started undressing me, why don't you finish it?"

Petula immediately yanked his coveralls down, taking his underpants with them. Once she stripped him bare, she tossed his soiled clothes onto the toilet floor and closed the shower door.

"Stand behind me, Pet. The water's cold when it first starts up. Don't want you getting hit with it."

"Give me the soap and the rag."

Charlie handed her the bar of soap and waited for her to be fully behind him. Then he turned on the water. When the cold water hit him straight on, he thought for sure he would wilt. But his organ stayed stiff. A moment later, he felt her hand wrap around his dick. She must have had the same thought.

"No worries, my Pet. You'll get your shag."

"I don't doubt it." As the water warmed, she slowly pumped his prick. "Let's get us both clean, then have at it."

Using the bar of soap and a washrag, she scrubbed him like a sailor swabbing the deck with a mop. Dirty water rolled off his skin and went down the drain. He wondered if she'd wash his arse the same way. Sure enough, she shoved the rag between his cheeks and rubbed his arsehole. He nearly creamed. If she touched his prick like that, he surely would.

"Take it easy, Pet. My fatty almost became a skinny."

She giggled. "Sorry, didn't mean to nearly make you shoot off."

"Let me wash you."

Charlie took the soap, not bothering with the rag. He washed her as she had done him, rubbing the bar everywhere, especially between her legs. She leaned against him and moaned. "I want to frig so bad."

"So do I." He cupped his hand and filled it with water, then rinsed the soap from between her legs. With the water pelting against them, he backed her up against the tile wall. He leaned against her and whispered into her ear, "Are you ready for it, Pet?"

"Fuck me, Charlie. Fuck me hard, like you did last night."

He spread her legs with his knees and found his mark. Then he lunged forward. Petula groaned, and squirmed against the wet tile. He had her riveted to the wall. Grabbing her wrists, he pinned her arms over her head.

Then, like a piston in an engine, he fucked her, hard, just like she wanted. He showed no mercy, pounding her pussy, slapping his pelvis against hers, driving his cock deep into her body.

With every thrust, she squealed, the sound muffled by the running water and contained in the shower stall. He grunted as he ground his prick into her. The effort to hold on until she finished took everything he had, but he knew from the night before it would be worth it.

Suddenly she shrieked, "Charlie!" and rapidly thumped her pelvis against him. He felt her pussy grab him as her muscles contracted in orgasm. On the very brink of shooting his load, he remembered he hadn't put on a condom.

He jerked his prick loose from her cunt, and it banged against her leg. Still holding her wrists over her head, Charlie leaned forward and humped her slippery thigh. He groaned when the white cream shot out of him and ran down her leg. A moment later, the water washed it away.

# 3

Pet stood beside Charlie, briskly rubbing her hair with a towel. While he dried himself, he admired the scenery. When Pet raised her head, she saw him watching her and swatted him with her towel. "Make yourself useful. Did my hair get clean?"

"Looks clean to me." He gave her a blatant once-over. "Nope, don't see any dirt anywhere."

"Thanks for the inspection."

"Hey, it's what I do. I inspect engines for dirt all the time. Your assembly is just easier on the eyes."

Pet glanced at his now flaccid dick. "Do I get to inspect your piston?"

"Anytime you want, my Pet." Charlie tossed his towel over the shower door. "Hey, I'm sorry about forgetting a rubber. Hope you don't mind how I handled it."

"No drama about getting off at Edgehill. I use condoms as a second layer of protection. I'm on the pill."

"Hell, if I'd known that, I wouldn't have pulled out!"

"Well, you'll know for next time, if we forget again."

"We?"

"I forgot, too. When I went to see Morgan, I didn't bring my bag. Didn't think I would be seeing you quite so soon."

"We should get dressed. I need to get you back to your room." Charlie went to get some clothes. Pet followed him.

"Already? I thought you said your next watch doesn't start until eight o'clock."

"It doesn't start till eight. But I don't think you want to stay cooped up in my cabin all damn day. You should have a swim and get some sun."

"Could we get some lunch in the dining room? I'm hungry."

"Can't do it, Pet. I eat in the officers' mess. The passengers' first-class dining room is off-limits."

"But the Captain eats in the dining room. I sat beside him at dinner last evening. The night before, I sat between the Ship's Chaplain and a doctor. What bores they were! At least the Captain could manage a conversation."

Charlie stared at her in disbelief. "You fucking sit at the Captain's table for dinner? Jesus Sufferin' Christ, Pet! Only the high and mighty sit at that table."

Petula's eyes sparkled. For the first time, Charlie noticed they were hazel. "I've done all right for myself. It seems the Captain must know that."

"No shit!" Wanting to end the conversation right there, Charlie abruptly bent over to pull out a small trunk from under his bunk. Then he rummaged for a clean pair of socks and underpants. Pet didn't move from beside the desk. She stood there, totally nude, with her arms crossed over her breasts. Charlie looked up at her. "Aren't you going to get dressed?"

"Eventually. First I want to know what the fuck difference it makes where I sit for dinner."

Charlie didn't pull any punches. "It's called first class for a reason. You're way outta my league, Petula. If you let anything slip at that table about knowing me personally, that's grounds for my dismissal."

"You think I would do that to you?"

"Not intentionally. But after a few drinks, who the hell knows?"

Petula squeezed past him to get to the closet. "You're being a frickin' snob!"

"I'm what?"

She pulled her dress off a hanger and clenched it in her fist. "You're being a frickin' snob! I felt the wall go up when I told you about the dining room."

"I know the rules."

"Yes, and we've broken most of them by now. This isn't about the rules, it's about class." Pet stepped into her dress and pulled it up to her breasts. "I never bloody well thought I would be on this side of the fence."

"What does that mean?" Charlie put on his underpants and then took his turn getting clothes out of the closet.

"You might like to know, my father was a merchant. He sold fruits and vegetables. When I first went to London to model, some restaurants wouldn't serve me because of my accent."

"I didn't know that."

"Of course, you didn't. No one does. I've spent years making my accent posh so no one could pinpoint my hometown. Going to Sydney as much as I have has helped. I've got enough Aussie in my speech now to really make them wonder."

"Why are you telling me this?"

"Because I like you. Without a doubt, you're the most interesting person I've met on this ship, and that includes everyone at the Captain's table."

"When I saw you yesterday, I really thought you might be upper-crust, a duchess or something. I still had Morgy bring you to my cabin."

"But the British monarchy isn't your world. In your world,

the Captain is king, and I know the Captain. I sit at his ridiculous table every night, and am bored to tears." She adjusted the spaghetti straps on her shoulders. "What did you say? I'm way out of your league? Why is that true now, and it wasn't last night or earlier today?"

Charlie didn't know what to say, so he focused on putting on his clothes. "I have to get you back to your suite."

"You didn't answer me."

"I don't have an answer."

"Then maybe you'll have an answer for this. Come to my suite with me. I'll order us a late lunch, and then leave word I'm dining in my cabin tonight. I want to have dinner with you. If we can't do that publicly, we'll do it privately."

Charlie knew he should say no. Everything in him shouted, *Say no!* But he couldn't bring himself to do it. This sheila had something special. It didn't surprise him that she had made something of herself. He had never known anyone with such unbridled spirit.

She reminded him of the brumbies Yooralla had told him about. She claimed the name "brumby" for the wild Aussie horses had come from the Aborigine word "*baroomby*" for "wild," just like her name had come from the word meaning "love."

Charlie didn't know if that was true, but he felt more than a little bit of something when he connected something Yooralla had told him to Pet.

Pet broke him out of his reverie. "You aren't answering me. I suppose that means no." He could hear the disappointment in her voice.

He went to his desk to retrieve his special key. "I have to be back here by seven o'clock to get ready for my watch at eight."

"Does that mean you'll do it?"

"That's what it means." Petula's smile warmed him like sunshine. Charlie didn't embarrass easily, but Pet's unabashed delight that he had agreed made him flush. "If we're doing this, let's go."

"Yes, sir!" Pet saluted, and then hugged him. "Don't worry, Charlie, we'll be careful."

"We have to be, or I'll be helping you design boiler suits after they kick me off the ship."

Petula poked him in the side. "Could be a new fashion trend, you never know."

"C'mon, you. Stay behind me."

Charlie cracked the door and peeked out into the alleyway. Pet hunkered down behind him. She whispered, "Is there anyone out there?"

"No, it's empty, and it's a straight shot to the door." He took her hand. "Once we're on your side, we have to hustle to your suite."

"With you dressed in your regular clothes, the other passengers will just think you're one of us."

"It's not the passengers I'm worried about."

Charlie quickly led her down the hall to the door. Thanking his lucky stars that he had it, he used his custom-made key to unlock the barrier between her world and his. He cracked the door open. Again, Pet whispered, "Is anyone there?"

"Just an old couple going toward the stairs. The coast is clear. Let's move." Charlie and Pet hurried through the door, which Charlie quietly closed and locked.

"Charlie, I'm not sure I remember how to get to my suite from here."

"I know the way. We have to follow those folks up the stairs to the B.Deck." He took her hand again and deftly guided her down the long alleyway toward the stairs. Once they climbed the staircase to the upper deck, they continued down the hall.

He paused at an intersecting passageway. Before making the

turn, he peeked around the corner. He jerked his head back. "Wait. One of Morgy's stewards is delivering room service."

"Let me watch. If he sees me, it won't matter."

Charlie switched places with Pet. He heard the steward talking to the passenger receiving the delivery. Then he heard the door close and the steward whistling as he walked away. Charlie whispered, "That's Joey. He's always whistling. Drives Morgy nuts."

"I know where we are now. That's the hall to my suite down there."

"Give Joey a few seconds to get ahead of us. Then we'll make a run for it."

"This is so cool!"

"Yeah, right."

Pet leaned against him, her arse pressing into his groin. He couldn't believe it when he felt his dick getting hard. Pet also felt it, and wiggled her bottom against him. "I could go again, too."

Charlie squeezed her arse cheek. "Let's get to your cabin and we'll see to it."

Charlie heard Joey's whistling receding as he left the deck. Pet grabbed his hand and yanked him forward. "It's empty now. Let's hit the road, Jack."

"My name is Charlie. You know that."

As Pet dragged him down the alleyway toward her suite, he heard her mutter, "That's a song. You really need to spend more time off this ship!"

As they approached the door to B232, Charlie realized he didn't bring the key Pet had given him to copy, and Pet didn't have her bag. "Where's your key?"

"I don't have it. I left my door unlocked."

"That's a fucking stupid thing to do!"

"Why?"

"It isn't safe."

Pet's laughter echoed in the empty alleyway. "What, do you think some sailor on the ship will come in and molest me?"

"No mate of mine would do that, but some crusty old gent who hasn't had any for a time might."

Pet opened the door to her cabin. "I'll take my chances. If someone does come in, you'll protect me, won't you?"

"Depends on what they intend to do. I might fancy watching."

Charlie followed Pet into her cabin and closed the door behind him. He knew the suites were spacious, but Pet's was especially so. It had two rooms, a sitting room and a separate bedroom. The heavy golden drapes on the glass balcony doors were open, and the sunshine streamed into the room. A large spray of fresh flowers sat on a small oak table next to the wine-colored sofa.

Pet unexpectedly turned around. He had been checking out the cabin and nearly bumped into her. "Do you like that sort of thing?"

"What sort of thing?"

"Watching."

"Depends."

"On what?"

"On what I'm watching."

"Would you fancy watching two women together?"

"Frigging shit, yes! I wouldn't be a man if I didn't fancy that!"

Pet trailed her finger down his chest. "How much would you fancy it?"

"Plenty." Charlie wrapped his arm around her waist. "Are you just being a tease, or do you have something in mind?"

"Depends."

"On what?"

"On how much stamina you have."

"What the fuck does that mean?"

"That means you have to be able to do us both."

Charlie considered the proposal. "How much time between?"

"Half an hour?"

Charlie knew he could manage that. "That's good enough. Who is she?"

"One of my models. She's coming to the party tomorrow night. Her name is Jennifer."

Charlie suddenly put two and two together. "You like girls, too?"

"Sometimes. Jennifer is special. She's a good friend. We help each other when men are scarce."

"Well, now, isn't this a kick in the arse!" Charlie stared into her hazel eyes. "You're a wild one, aren't you?"

"When I have the opportunity, I am."

He held her tightly. "Just how wild are you?"

"Wild enough to make you remember me for quite a long time." Pet pushed away from him and walked to the other side of the cabin.

"Where are you going?"

"Before anything happens, I'm calling for some food. I haven't eaten since nine o'clock."

"I haven't eaten since seven. That's not stopping me."

"Considering how peckish I am, it's stopping me. I'll call for some food to be delivered now, and order dinner for three at six o'clock. It would be lovely if Jennifer would join us."

"Where's Jennifer now?"

"I have no idea!"

"Maybe you should find out. She could come now, and we could have some lunch together before things heat up."

"That's actually a good idea."

"Yeah, I have one every now and again."

"So do I." Pet picked up the phone and dialed. Rather than

calling room service, Charlie heard her say, "Hello, Jen? I'm glad I caught you in your cabin. Could you come to my room? I have someone here I'd like you to meet." Pet paused for a moment, then said, "Great. See you in a few minutes."

Charlie tried to sound cool, even though his blood boiled at the thought of having two sheilas at the same time. "She's coming?"

"She'll be here directly." Before Pet put down the phone, she called and ordered sandwiches and beer, and also requested the dinner menu. Then she called the main dining room to offer her apologies that she would not be joining the Captain for dinner that night and would be taking dinner in her cabin.

Charlie wandered around the suite. They could easily divide this space into four of the crew's cabins, and have enough left over for a tidy galley to share.

"Quite a cabin you have here. I've only been in the first-class digs a few times, when we've had the *Ortensia* docked for repairs. Had some time to kill, so I had a look around."

"I let them know well in advance when I'm traveling, and ask for this suite. I usually get it."

"You travel to Sydney often?"

"At least once a year."

"Why every year?"

"I have a house in both cities. I divide my time between them."

"You live in both cities?"

Pet laughed. "You could say that. But I'm talking about my business, not my home. I own Petula Kinlan Fashions, and have a house in London and in Sydney. That's where the clothes I design are made, shown and sold."

"Sounds pretty fucking posh."

"Wealthy women must think so. It seems no matter what I charge for Pet originals, they are willing to pay what I ask."

"That's how you can afford this?"

"Absolutely! This trip's a working vacation for me. I get so bored with nothing to do, I sit and sketch. Some of my best designs have been done in this cabin." Pet went to an oak cabinet with glass doors in the corner, where she had several bottles of liquor. "Would you like a drink while we're waiting?"

"I'll have a G and T if you're offering."

Pet turned around to mix the cocktail. While watching her, Charlie had an almost uncontrollable urge to lift her skirt. His erection had become damned uncomfortable. A good rub against her bare bum truly appealed to him. Before he could act on his impulse, she turned around and handed him a glass.

"Do you see how much space I have? We would be so much more comfortable having the party in here."

"Sorry, Pet. Can't do it."

"But you're here now."

"Yes, and I bloody well shouldn't be. I told you, we'd have our arses in a sling if we're caught."

"You won't budge on this, will you?"

"Nope. We're having a party in my cabin tomorrow night. You're welcome to come with your friends. If that's not good enough for you, then my mates will find us some women in tourist that don't mind the close quarters."

"That's a bit harsh, isn't it?"

"No more than you not taking into account we could lose our jobs. I won't be responsible for my mates being put out because of a sheila."

"All right, I surrender." Pet sipped her drink. "You don't take any hostages, do you?"

"I speak my mind, always have."

"I like that. And I like you." Someone knocked at the door. "That's probably Jennifer."

"Find out for sure. I'll duck out of sight if it's a steward with the food."

"Who is it?"

"It's Jen."

Petula answered the door. Before Charlie saw her, he heard her say, "Why all the mystery, Pet? What's going on?"

"Come in. I have a friend for you to meet." Pet led her inside and formally introduced them. "Charlie, this is my friend Jennifer. Jen, this is Third Assistant Engineer Charles . . ." Pet paused, then said, "I'm sorry, Charlie, I'm afraid I don't know your last name."

Charlie didn't answer immediately. His voice left him when he saw Jennifer. She held out her hand to shake his. "Hello, Charles. How very lovely to meet you."

He took her hand. "Nice to meet you, too." He glanced at Pet. "It's Weston, if you want to know."

"I do want to know." Pet went to get Jennifer a cocktail. "Jen, Charlie has a poster in his cabin with a woman who looks like you. You'll see it tomorrow night."

"That's quite a coincidence. Who is she?"

Still holding Jennifer's hand, Charlie replied, "Don't know who she is. I call her Yooralla."

Pet added, "Charlie knew someone named Yooralla. It's Aboriginal."

"I know the word. My mother is an Aborigine."

Charlie smiled broadly. "I knew you had to be! If you don't mind my asking, are you mixed?"

"My father is British."

"By God, that is a coincidence! Yooralla had the same mix. She was nearly as beautiful as you are." Jennifer's uncanny resemblance to Yooralla held Charlie spellbound. She had the same dark eyes, tawny skin and full lips. Except for Jen being several inches taller and having longer hair than Yooralla, Charlie would have had trouble telling them apart.

"Why, thank you. That's very kind."

Pet brought Jennifer a glass. Charlie reluctantly let her hand go. "Let's sit down and talk. The sandwiches should be here soon." Pet poked Charlie in the side as she walked by. "I knew you'd fancy Jen." Pet had no idea how much.

Pet sat down on an armchair, leaving the sofa free for Charlie and Jennifer. Directing her question to Charlie, Jen asked, "How did you meet Pet? I've been trying to get to know a few of the crew members for ages, and can't seem to manage it."

Charlie glanced at Pet, and Pet nodded. Charlie understood he could trust Jennifer. "I saw Pet at the pool and asked my friend Morgy to keep an eye out for her at the Monkey Bar."

Petula offered, "And I saw Charlie inspecting the lifeboats, and made it a point to find him."

Charlie continued, "One thing led to another, and here we are."

Jennifer studied them. "So you two have . . ." She trailed off, but her question was understood.

"Have we, Charlie?"

"We've shagged, if that's what you're asking me."

"Brilliant!" Jennifer raised her glass to both of them in a toast. "Here's to shagging. Cheers!" She belted back a healthy swallow of her G and T. Charlie and Pet echoed her sentiment with their drinks.

"We're having a party in my cabin tomorrow night. You're invited if you'd care to come," Charlie offered.

"But I understood we're not allowed in the crew's part of the ship."

"We're not, Jen. But Charlie has found a way to smuggle us in."

"Splendid! Will there be other men there?"

"I expect a few of my mates will come."

"Dear Pet, you've found yourself a diamond in the rough."

"I know I have." Pet gave Jennifer a pointed look. "And I'm sharing my treasure." The two women seemed to speak without words for a moment. "Are you in?"

"You know I am!" Turning back to Charlie, Jennifer smiled. "This will be delightful!"

"Pet here says you two help each other out when pickings are scarce?"

Jennifer appeared confused. "I don't understand."

"Jen, I told Charles we've had to depend on each other when there isn't a man around."

"Oh!" Jennifer put her hand on Charlie's leg. A surge of heat moved in his groin. "Pet and I have known each other forever. We have what could be called an 'intimate friendship.'"

"I figured that much out."

"I expect you did." Jennifer slid her hand a bit farther up Charlie's thigh, enough to make him involuntarily shift his position. He wanted her to touch his business, and had to force himself to sit still. If Jennifer noticed his discomfort, she didn't let on.

He pulled his attention away from Jennifer and glanced at Pet. It took him aback when he saw her staring directly at his crotch. Jennifer might not have realized what she did to him, but Pet sure as shit did!

Not that he minded two gorgeous sheilas eyeing him like a couple of hungry Tasmanian devils, but he knew they had real food coming any minute. No doubt one of Morgy's mates would be delivering it. He removed Jennifer's hand from his leg and stood up. "Ladies, lunch is on the way. This is dessert."

Petula also stood. She wrapped her arms around Charlie's neck and deliberately rubbed her pelvis against him. "What do you think of him, Jen?"

"You tell me, Pet. Did he make you happy?"

"He made me quite happy. I'm still smiling."

"Then I think he'll do the same for me, won't you, Charles?"

Charlie never once backed down from a fight, no matter what the odds. In this case, he knew these two sheilas could kill him. He smiled, figuring what a way to go. Without responding to Pet's advances or Jennifer's question, he matter-of-factly asked, "Where do I hide when the food comes?"

"What?" He could tell Pet had forgotten about being peckish.

"Remember, you ordered sandwiches and beer? The steward will wheel the cart in here. He can't see me."

Pet stepped back and looked around. "Yes, of course. I suppose you have your choice of the loo or the closet."

"I'll take the loo." He stopped for a moment and listened. "Do you hear that?"

"Hear what?"

"Whistling in the corridor. It's Jocy. Let me know when he's gone." Charlie went to the toilet and closed the door.

He listened at the door. Within seconds, he heard the knock, and then heard Pet answer. Sure enough, he recognized Joey's voice.

While Pet took care of receiving the delivery, Charlie splashed some cold water on his face. While drying off, he noted with some amusement Pet also had a bathtub. He couldn't remember the last time he soaked in a tub. The crew only had shower stalls.

He had calmed himself enough to be able to have a piss while he had the chance. The old saying "when it rains, it pours" really applied to this one. He had two gorgeous sheilas waiting for him. As attractive as he found Pet, it was Jennifer who really had him by the knackers. She had the same exotic features as Yooralla, complete with the smoldering pout that drove Charlie crazy.

He hadn't told Pet that Yooralla was why he went to sea. After Yooralla broke off with him to go with some bloke who had money, he'd decided to get licensed and sign on with a ship. He applied on the *Ortensia*, and they took him on. He'd been sailing on her now for three years. He had no idea what had become of Yooralla.

But now seeing Jennifer, he felt his fascination with the striking woman in his past bubble to the surface again. It might not be Yooralla, but he could still enjoy her company. He fully intended to do just that.

Charlie went back to the door and listened. He heard Pet ordering dinner for three in her cabin, and she asked Joey to have it delivered at six o'clock. He glanced at his watch. They had several hours before he had to leave. Plenty of time.

Jennifer knocked on the toilet door. "It's all right, Charles. The steward is gone."

Charlie came out and immediately saw the roll-in cart, set as a table for three, complete with chairs already arranged around it. The sandwiches were on plates and the beer poured into mugs. "Did Joey question why you had three places?"

"Not at all. I simply said someone else would be joining us momentarily and would be staying for dinner."

Jennifer threaded her arm through Charlie's and led him to the impromptu table. "How long can you stay?"

"My next watch is at eight. I told Pet I should be on my way by seven."

"Let's eat, and then we can get to know one another better."

Wanting to make sure Pet didn't mind Jennifer coming on to him, Charlie winked at her. "I already know Pet pretty damn well, but I expect there's more to find out."

"Oh, yes, dear Charlie, I can assure you, there's more coming." Charlie could see the now-familiar sparkle in her hazel eyes and knew everything was spot-on.

It surprised Charlie when these two lithe women attacked their sandwiches with the same gusto as he did. He hadn't realized how hungry he was until he started eating. The beer washed it all down nicely. All the while, the ladies continued to flirt with him. The afternoon promised to be a memorable one.

They had nearly finished eating, when someone knocked on

the door. Charlie looked at Pet, and she shrugged her shoulders.

He whispered, "Find out who it is."

In a surprisingly calm and pleasant voice, Pet called out, "Who is it?"

"It's Captain Driscoll, Miss Kinlan. May I come in?"

Charlie jumped up and exhaled, "Jesus Christ!" Then he bolted into the loo.

# 4

At the last moment, Charlie remembered not to slam the toilet door. He closed it with barely a click, then locked it for good measure. He hoped to hell the Captain hadn't gotten wind of him being there.

Not usually prone to listening in on others' conversations, this one he strained to hear. With his ear pressed to the door, he heard Pet greet the Captain.

"Well, hello, Captain Driscoll. This is an unexpected surprise. To what do I owe the pleasure?"

"Pardon the intrusion, Petula. When I saw tonight's dinner list, your name wasn't on it. When I inquired at the dining room as to why, they told me you had canceled. I feared you had become ill."

Charlie would have laughed, had he not been so bloody pissed off. *"Petula? . . . I feared you had become ill?"* He muttered to himself, "That son of a bitch." He wondered how the hell Pet would handle it.

He heard her laugh and quite naturally explain, "Oh, no, I'm not the least bit ill. I have work to do. I'm working on designs for my new collection and preparing for a show in London at the same time. The scheduling for the show is brutal. It happens practically as soon as I step off the ship."

"Surely, Petula, you could take some time to have a meal with me."

Charlie figured the Captain wouldn't give up easily. He hoped Pet could say no to him.

"I've already arranged to take my meals in my cabin, with some of my staff. That's the joy of being the boss. I can arrange working dinners and no one can complain. Isn't that correct, Jennifer?" He heard Pet pause, then say, "Oh, I am sorry, Captain Driscoll, this is Jennifer. She's one of my models."

Charlie heard Jen respond, "It certainly is a pleasure to meet you."

"And it's a pleasure to meet you, Jennifer. Can't you please talk some sense into your boss for me?"

"I'm afraid, Captain, there's no talking her out of it. We have to get ready for the show. What's left of this trip is the best opportunity we'll have."

Before the Captain could say anything, Pet went for the jugular. "Perhaps I can arrange for my seat to be filled this evening by another of my models. Jennifer, don't you think Suzy would enjoy meeting the Captain?"

"Let me ring her up and ask if she's available."

Just when Charlie thought the ladies had the situation in hand, he heard the Captain ask, "I see you've also had your luncheon here. Seems I missed meeting another member of your staff."

"That would be my assistant, Derrick. I sent him back to his cabin to gather some sketches I left with him. He'll be back in a bit."

"Excuse me, Captain Driscoll. I have Suzy on the line. If it wouldn't be an intrusion, she would be delighted to take Petula's seat this evening. Would that be acceptable?"

"Yes, indeed, it surely would."

"Splendid." Charlie heard Jennifer give Suzy the news, and then add, "Captain, Suzy wants to know if perhaps you could show her the bridge after dinner?"

"I don't see why not." Charlie could tell that the Captain, just like the rest of the crew, wanted some female company. Pet giving him a substitute did the trick.

"Captain Driscoll, I do appreciate your concern. I am so sorry I will miss dinner, but as you well know, duty calls."

"Perhaps before the voyage ends, you will do me the honor of sharing dinner with me privately."

"Thank you, Captain. I will certainly remember you made the offer."

Charlie murmured, "Yeah, so will I."

He waited for the all clear from Pet before emerging from the loo. When he came out, Pet had another G and T waiting for him. "Here, you look like you could use this."

Charlie took the glass, but didn't drink. He gestured toward the door with the glass. "You know that son of a bitch wants to get laid. He had his eye on you."

Pet held her ground with Charlie. "Well, he's too frigging late, isn't he? You beat him to it." Then she turned to Jennifer. "Jen, ring Derrick and make sure he knows he had lunch with us this afternoon. While you're at it, let him know he's invited to an exclusive party tomorrow night. Tell him there will be someone there who wants to meet him, and that if he tells anyone, I'll personally cut off his knackers and feed them to him."

Charlie had a good swallow of his G and T before he asked, "What about the other two girls? Do they know about tomorrow night?"

"I'll call them, too, and tell them what's what," Jennifer volunteered.

Charlie asked Pet, "Can we trust them to keep their mouths

shut? If Suzy ends up shagging the Captain tonight, loose lips can really sink this ship."

"Don't worry. They travel with me frequently. They know how to keep a secret, don't they, Jen?"

Jennifer laughed. "Working for Pet, they have to, professionally and personally."

While Jennifer rang up the others, Charlie whispered to Pet, "I don't want to rush things along, but we should get going soon. Dinner will be delivered in a couple of hours, and then I have to leave."

Pet trailed her finger down the crack of his arse and whispered back, "Understood."

When Jennifer finished making her calls, she reported back to Pet. "Derrick values his knackers and won't breathe a word. He also knows to cover for this afternoon if it comes up. Suzy understands the whole thing now and is cool with it. Tess has a request."

Pet seemed bemused. "And what would that be?"

Jennifer spoke directly to Charlie. "Do you know someone named Sparky?"

"Sure I do. Why?"

"Tess has been seeing him. She's spent the last few nights in his cabin. She said she won't come to the party unless he's invited."

Charlie had just sipped his G and T and practically blew it out his nose. "Are you shitting me?"

"No, that's what she said."

Pet interjected, "Does he have a key?"

"Sure he does. He's the one that gave it to me to copy."

"Then we can invite him, can't we?"

"We absolutely can. Morgy may have already told him. I'll call him now and make sure."

"Brilliant! Then Tess will come."

While Charlie called Morgy, Pet wheeled the lunch cart into the hall and put the DO NOT DISTURB sign on the door.

When Pet returned, she caught Charlie whispering something into Jennifer's ear. Jennifer giggled. "Go ahead, ask her. I dare you."

"Ask me what?"

"How many pairs of knackers have you cut off?"

"Enough to earn the respect of the men who work for me."

Charlie covered his balls protectively. "Are mine safe?"

"For now."

"Tough, isn't she?"

Jennifer giggled again, something Yooralla never did. "She can be. To do what she's done, she has to be." Then Jennifer shocked the shit out of Charlie. She pulled her dress over her head. She only had panties on underneath. Next, she peeled those down her long bronze legs and kicked them off. "Pet, should we get Charlie warmed up?"

"Oh, yes, Jen, I think that's what we should do."

Jennifer walked right past Charlie. As Pet took off her dress, she kept her eyes riveted to Jen's tits. Jennifer waited until Pet tossed the dress on the floor; then she knelt in front of her. Charlie about pissed himself when Jen buried her face in Pet's blond curls.

Pet moaned. She squeezed her own tits, one in each hand. When she looked directly at Charlie, he held her stare. They were doing this for him. There was no question about that. As quickly as he could, he shed all of his clothes. Hell, why not? These ladies knew what they wanted, and so did he. Charlie wanted both of them, and fuck, yes, he would have them both.

Charlie knelt beside Jennifer and slid his hand between her legs. Jen squirmed, then moaned into Pet's pussy. In turn, Pet whispered, "God, Jen, that is so good!"

Charlie looked up. With no inhibition about him watching her, she pinched her nipples between her thumbs and index fingers. Their eyes met again. As he always did, he spoke his mind. "Let's go into the bedroom. I want to shag Jen while she licks you."

Pet put her hand on Jen's head. "No, right here, let's do it right here." She sat down in the armchair and propped her right leg over the arm. "Do me, Jen, eat me till I come."

Charlie's view of Pet's pussy spread wide nearly made him spurt. He took a couple of deep breaths as Jennifer crawled like a panther toward Pet's open legs. Again she buried her face in the deep, blond crevice. Pet lifted her arse off the chair as Jen lapped at her.

As he positioned himself behind Jen, memories of Yooralla flashed in Charlie's mind. Rather than dampening his arousal, the thoughts of what they had done together poured gasoline on his fire.

He had wanted for years to fuck her again. The wildness in her had driven him to do things he had never done with anyone else. Now, as he entered the first dark pussy he'd had since Yooralla left him, the surge of untamed power she'd triggered in him overtook him once more.

Somewhere in the haze of his own arousal and memories, he heard Pet hiss at him, "Fuck her, Charlie, fuck her until she begs you to stop. You know you want to make her scream."

And he did want to make her scream. He lunged forward, driving his prick into Jennifer until it would go no farther. Jennifer groaned and pushed backward, but she didn't lift her head. She never broke contact with Pet, sucking and licking all the while.

Even with his balls about to explode, he remembered to ask, "Pet, is she on the pill, too?"

"Of course, she is. All my girls are!"

When Charlie heard that, he cut loose. He banged Jennifer's ass with everything he had, his cock sliding in and out of her like a steam-powered piston. Her cunt gripped him, and he could feel the Aborigine in her, just as he had Yooralla. He knew how to fuck her to make her come. She needed it hard and fast. As his momentum increased, so did hers, her ass thumping his pelvis with every thrust.

He had been so focused on Jennifer, he hadn't noticed Pet go over the top. When she squealed, "Motherfuck, yes!" Charlie saw her writhing in the chair. The intensity of Pet's orgasm affected Jennifer. She rubbed her cheek against Pet's inner thigh and dragged her chin across Pet's clitoris.

He reached under Jennifer and squeezed her breast as hard as he could; then he said with a grunt, "You're so fucking ripe. Come for me, baby, come hard for me."

Jennifer braced herself, one hand on each of Pet's thighs. She pushed herself back on Charlie's cock so hard, she nearly knocked him onto the floor. Like two dingoes humping in the bush, he rode her and she took him in.

Suddenly her cunt gripped his prick, and spasms rippled through his balls. With a passion he hadn't felt since going to sea, he trembled as scalding liquid shot out of his penis. He ground his pelvis into Jennifer's arse, letting her pussy drain his balls dry. Thanks to Pet, Charlie had himself another hot Aborigine lover.

Before he pulled out of Jennifer, he caught Pet's eye. He winked at her and she blew him a kiss. She was one hot sheila, all right. It amazed him she didn't seem to mind him shagging Jennifer, and, in fact, she appeared to have enjoyed it as much as he did.

Still feeling randy, he wrapped his arm around Jennifer's waist and fell backward onto the floor, taking her with him. She squealed in surprise as she landed on his chest. Then she dissolved into a fit of giggles.

She rolled off him, still trying to get her breath. "Flippin' 'ell, why did you do that?"

"Felt like it." The afterglow of a good fuck had settled in on Charlie. He'd begun to feel damned sleepy.

Pet noticed and practically pounced on him. "Oh, no, you don't, Mr. Third Assistant Engineer. You don't get a nap. There's not enough time. Jen, help me keep him awake."

"I'd love to!" The next thing Charlie knew, he lay sandwiched between two naked women, both of them feeling him up.

Pet whispered into his ear, "The clock is ticking, Charles. You've already had five minutes. You have twenty-five more to get it up again. The agreement was you'd do both of us before dinner."

Charlie smiled a contented, sleepy smile. "I did say that, didn't I?"

Pet squeezed his balls, hard enough to get his attention. "You bloody well did!"

Jennifer pinched his nipple. "Don't hurt him, Pet—at least not too much."

Charlie raised himself up on his elbows. "If you ladies kill me, you're going to have one hell of a time explaining what happened!"

Pet leaned over, licked his neck and whispered into his ear, "And you'll die a happy man."

Charlie shivered, the unexpected rush of warm air in his ear gave him chills. "Jesus Christ! You are trying to kill me." He pushed himself up with his hands and stood. "If I'm going to die, at least let me die in bed."

Leaving Pet and Jennifer on the floor in the sitting room, he went into Pet's bedroom and made himself comfortable on her bed. He knew they would eventually follow him. In the meantime, he drowsily closed his eyes.

He really didn't mean to doze, but he must have. He bolted awake when something wet and cold hit his chest. Pet stood over him with a gin and tonic in her hand. She had just poured some of it on him.

"What the frigging hell are you doing?"

"Waking you up."

He looked around and didn't see Jennifer. "Where's Jen? Did she leave?"

"No, she's in the loo cleaning up. You gave her quite a ride. It left her a bit sticky."

Charlie stared at Pet's matted blond curls. "Looks like Jennifer did the same to you."

"She did. Jen knows what she's doing."

"Seemed to enjoy doing it, too." Charlie pointed to the glass in Pet's hand. "Are you going to offer me that drink or just pour it on me?"

Pet took a sip, but she didn't offer the glass to Charlie. She looked him over, slowly studying his entire body. "You know, you're really quite well built."

"I'll say he is!" Jen had just come into the bedroom. "He'd look like a bodybuilder if he shaved his chest."

"The tousled brown hair and matching brown eyes set off the muscles nicely. He should model men's clothes. There's a market for that look." Pet handed her drink to Jen. "Want some?"

"Thanks." Jennifer took the glass and had a healthy swallow.

Charlie eyed Jen, and then Pet. Both women were still naked, and both were getting under his skin, in more ways than one.

Suddenly, and unexpectedly, he grabbed Pet's hand and pulled her onto the bed beside him. "Let's get this straight. I'm not shaving my chest and I'm not strutting down some runway like a bloody twink! Got that?"

Pet reached between them and closed her hand around his prick. "Oh, yes, Charlie, I've got it. And it's getting deliciously hard."

Pushing his advantage, Charlie dared her. "Why don't you suck me like you did last night?"

Charlie's challenge didn't go unnoticed. Jennifer offered her support. "Go ahead, Pet. Blow him. I'll work the other half." She put her glass on the night table and crawled into bed beside Charlie.

Pet still had her hand on him, but she had not moved otherwise.

Charlie chided her. "Well? Are you going to suck me like I asked you?"

"You're enjoying this, aren't you?" Pet didn't move a muscle.

Charlie put his arm around Jen. "Why the hell shouldn't I? In bed with two beautiful sheilas, already shagged one, gonna shag the other. Of course, number two might not get hers, if she doesn't give me some oral attention."

"Blackmailing me?"

Charlie caressed Jennifer's breast. "Whatever it takes." He could see Pet wasn't used to being on the receiving end of orders. "Well, boss lady, what's it going to be?"

"Jen, could I have my glass back, please?"

"Sure, Pet." Charlie could hear the question in Jen's voice. It was the same question he had. What the fuck?

Jen gave Pet the glass. She took a sip and held it in her mouth, all the while watching Charlie. Then she raised the glass high in the air and tipped it, pouring a thin line of her drink down the length of his stomach to his groin.

Charlie jumped. "Jesus Christ!"

Before he had a chance to act on impulse and get off the bed, Pet barked, "Jen, keep him still." The tone seemed to need a "Yes, ma'am" to punctuate it.

Just like they had rehearsed it, Jennifer lurched forward and practically threw herself across his chest. Too stunned by this performance to react, Charlie missed his chance to free himself.

Pet set her glass on the floor and proceeded to crawl onto his legs. He found himself pinned to the bed by two naked women.

Now more perturbed than aroused, Charlie growled, "Petula, I don't know what the fuck you think you're doing, but I didn't sign on for this bullshit." He figured if he put all of his weight into it, he could throw them both off. But he thought better of it, for fear he might hurt one of them. He chose the more civilized approach. "Let me up. I'll get dressed and go." He meant it.

"Don't be silly! You can't leave now. I'm about to deliver the goods."

Pet leaned down. Jennifer, lying across his chest, blocked his view. He couldn't see Pet's head at all. He braced himself, not knowing what to expect. When he felt her lapping at the gin on his stomach like a cat drinking milk, he closed his eyes and moaned.

She followed the trail she had poured down his stomach to his navel, pausing there to lick out the pool that had collected inside his innie. Then she continued her agonizingly slow journey down to his groin. By the time her chin bumped the tip of his penis, he had a full-blown woody.

Charlie still couldn't see her head, but he heard her speak to Jennifer. "Jen, are you okay like that?"

"I'm fine, Pet. Feels kind of good, actually. He's hard as a rock."

"He is down here, too. Why don't you scoot up just a bit, so he can feel your tits and your ass while I suck him? That should really get him revved up."

Charlie had been so preoccupied with Pet, he hadn't been aware of Jennifer's breasts pressed into his chest. When she slid across him as Pet suggested she do, the sensation of her hard nipples rolling over his skin was right out of a wet dream.

He closed his eyes and tried to take a deep breath. Jennifer's weight on his chest prevented him from inhaling too deeply.

While trying to calm himself, he suddenly realized he didn't need to fight this. He could just relax and enjoy it.

In a matter of seconds, Pet would be sucking his dick. Jennifer had just positioned herself so he could squeeze her tits and rub her ass. This wasn't just a wet dream, it was a frigging porn movie! His mates would think he was full of shit if he ever told them. They'd never believe it!

Jennifer's breasts draped over the side of his chest, hanging heavily like ripe tomatoes on the vine. He filled his hand with one and squeezed. Jennifer sighed. With his other hand, he stroked her ass. To his delight, he discovered he could reach between her legs, which he did with considerable satisfaction.

He noticed Pet had raised her head, and had apparently been watching him make a move on Jennifer. "I see you're finally getting into the spirit of things."

Charlie chuckled. "Don't know if I am or not. But I do know I'd have to be dead not to cop a feel. Isn't that right, Jen?"

Jen's arse undulated as she humped his hand. "Charles, being felt up never felt so good. Cop away."

"Pet, I'm still waiting for you to suck me off. Oh, and by the way, my legs are numb. Think you could shift a bit?" Even in his immobilized state, Charlie still felt as though he had regained the upper hand in this unusual standoff.

"Spread your legs apart."

"Isn't that what I should be telling you?" Charlie countered.

"Not this time, you bugger. By the time I climb on it, your nuts will be ready to crack open." Charlie finally understood what she meant to do. He wondered what the Chaplain would say when they buried him at sea.

As he had done with women on many occasions, Pet now did to him. She forced his legs wide open with her knees. He resisted the impulse to protectively close them, reminding himself that this would be a shag to end all shags. Hell, everybody had to die sometime. He could think of worse ways to have it all end.

First she fondled his balls, gently squishing the soft sacs in the palm of her hand. "Charles, even your testicles are picture-perfect."

"And what kind of pictures have you been looking at, Petula?"

"Models send me their portfolios. I use men, too."

"Fuck, I figured that one out already."

"I expect you have." She looked him in the eye when she asked, "Do you regret getting involved with me?"

"Hell no! Never met a woman before as strong as you are. And you introduced me to Jen." He pulled his hand out from between's Jennifer's legs and swatted her arse.

"Ouch! That hurt." She didn't give him time to apologize before she said, "Do it again."

Happy to oblige, he slapped her lovely chocolate arse. "You like that, sweetheart?"

Jennifer squirmed against him, attempting to rub her pussy on his chest. "I quite fancy it, thank you."

"Maybe you'll like this, too." Charlie slid his middle finger inside her vagina.

Jennifer moaned. "Oh, yes, darling, I fancy that, too."

Without warning, Pet's mouth closed over his prick. He involuntarily lurched and jammed his finger deeper into Jennifer than he had intended. She yelped.

He muttered, "Sorry" as Pet once again sucked him harder than anyone ever had.

Jen giggled, as she seemed to do often. "That's all right. Just watch the fingernails. Keep doing what you're doing. It feels bloody wonderful."

Charlie barely managed to say, "Will do." Pet's ministrations had him breathless.

Wanting to please Jen as much as he could, he again wiggled his middle finger inside her cunt and caressed her breast. She responded as he'd hoped she would, with a squirm and a sigh. As long as he massaged her, she would be fine.

Pet had him right where she wanted him. Part of him resisted the idea of a sheila besting him, and part of him relished it. He'd never known a woman like this, someone so used to being in charge that she also gave the marching orders in the bedroom. He wondered if Pet would take to having her arse swatted the same way Jennifer did. That's something he hoped to find out before the voyage ended.

Charlie remembered how Pet had reacted to watching him shag Jennifer. If Pet mounted him as he expected her to do, he knew what would get her going the same way she had gotten to him. He had a plan. This would certainly be a good one.

He couldn't see Pet, but he sure as hell could feel her. She had stretched out between his legs, and had his boner in her mouth. Jesus, could she suck dick! Her jaw muscles were strong enough to play a trumpet. She either did this frequently, or she really did belong in the brass section.

Charlie tried to focus on Jennifer, even with being eaten alive by Pet. For his plan to work, he had to get Jennifer close to the edge. He fingered her cunt with one hand and pinched her nipples with the other. From the way she tried to hump his hand, he knew she was getting close. So was he. Pet had better get to it soon, or she would be shit out of luck.

"Hey, boss lady, can you hear me down there?" Pet didn't respond. She just kept lapping at him. "Well, you'd better listen up. You're going to have to swallow soon, and you won't get laid."

That got her attention. Pet lifted her head. "All right, then. I'm ready."

Jennifer raised herself on her hands, meaning to get up. Pet stopped her. "No, Jen. I want you to stay there, if you're all right with that."

"Christ, yes, I'm all right with it. What he's doing to me is fucking brilliant!" Jen settled back on top of Charlie's chest.

"Aren't you going to ask me if I'm all right with it?"

"I know you are, Mr. Third Assistant Engineer. Just like you'll be all right with this."

Pet straddled him, keeping eye contact with him as she did. Charlie held her stare. He instinctively knew this was a showdown between them. He wouldn't be the one to surrender.

He knew Pet meant to ride him until he exploded inside her. It was about time he let her know she had met her match.

He needed Jennifer's help. "Jen?"

"Charlie?"

"Sweetheart, I want to take you over the top. What do you need to get there?"

While he spoke to Jennifer, Pet had positioned his prick at her wet opening. He gritted his teeth, trying not to shoot.

Jennifer directed him. "Charlie, rub my clit hard. I need that to finish."

Never taking his eyes off Pet, he found the small nub between Jennifer's legs. He rubbed it hard, just as Pet lowered herself onto his boner. He groaned, but held on.

Jennifer humped his hand as he rubbed. "Fucking 'ell, that's good. Harder, Charlie, harder!"

He obliged. Pet rode him with everything she had, bobbing up and down like a buoy in rough water. They were in a dead heat, racing to a photo finish. A betting man couldn't have called this one. With the three of them all close, the climax could not be predicted.

Jen took the prize. She squealed and thumped her pelvis against Charlie's chest. Gathering all of his willpower, he finger fucked Jen as she orgasmed, and lifted his arse off the bed at the same time, driving his cock deeply into Pet. The sensation, along with Jennifer's orgiastic release, proved too much for Pet. She shuddered and slammed herself down on Charlie's prick.

Again he thrust upward, making sure he sent Pet over the top. Only then, did he ejaculate, allowing the steam in his balls to vent, and the scalding liquid to spill.

Yes, sir, the boss lady had definitely met her match.

# 5

Charlie glanced at his watch. Seven-fifteen. He had time to catch Morgy before he had to be in the engine room. He stepped into his fresh boiler suit and snapped it, not bothering to shower first. Hell, he could still smell the women. Why wash that off? He'd shower after his shift ended.

He had left Pet and Jennifer at seven. They'd all finished dinner and were having coffee when he got up to leave. They asked him to stay a few more minutes, but he didn't want to risk being late. Considering what had happened earlier, he thought he'd best escape while he could.

Fortunately, most of the passengers were at dinner. He didn't see a single person as he went back to his cabin. He quickly changed his clothes. Pet said she wanted to talk to Morgy to-night. Charlie wanted to get to him before she did.

He remembered to tuck Pet's key into his pocket, so he could copy it. He had been ambivalent about doing it this morning. Tonight, everything had changed. If she had this same cabin every trip she made, he definitely wanted a copy of that key.

Once again taking the sanctioned route out of the crew's quarters, he followed the maze of alleyways back to the Monkey Bar. As he expected, Morgy stood behind the bar, keeping an eye on everything and everybody. Being dinnertime, the place was quiet. He could easily chat for a few minutes and not be a bother.

"G'day, mate."

"Well, hello! Haven't seen your hairy arse all day today."

"Been a bit busy."

Morgy pretended to wipe the bar, but actually leaned over and sniffed. "Chanel Number 5. No, that's not it." He sniffed again. "Chantilly? Or is it Eau de Been Laid?"

"Fuck you!"

Morgy lowered his voice. "Love to. How many times can you go in one day?"

In an equally low voice, Charlie replied, "I'm at three today, and hope for one more later. And, mate, you sure as hell aren't on the list."

A gentleman interrupted from the other end of the bar, wanting a refill on his pint. Morgy delivered a tall one, and then came back to where Charlie stood.

Picking up where they'd left off, he asked, "All those with Petula?"

"Two with her, one with Jennifer."

"Who's Jennifer?"

"One of Pet's friends. She joined us this afternoon."

Morgy unloaded a tray of clean glasses while they talked. "No shit! Seems like that smell really is Eau de Been Laid."

"Didn't have time to shower. My watch starts soon." Charlie considered having a quick pint, but figured he'd better not before going on duty. "Is everything good for the party tomorrow night?"

"Sparky is in. He didn't know Tess had friends on board. He

wants to meet them. Did you know Sparky and Tess have been an item for the last week?"

"Not till today. Jen told me."

"I pride myself on keeping tabs on who's doing what. That one got past me."

Charlie grinned. "You're as bad as an old woman spying on the neighbors."

"Thank you, darling. Compliment accepted."

"Who else is coming?"

"How about Dazza and Stevo? What do you think?"

Charlie knew both men well, and knew they could be trusted. But he had to make sure of a couple of things before giving Morgy a thumbs-up on the guest list. "Will Dazza do the pineapples?"

"If I ask him, he will. And I'll have Stevo bring his red light-bulb and his reel-to-reel."

Charlie glanced around to make sure no one could hear him. "Jennifer is part Aborigine. Make sure that isn't a problem for these blokes."

"We'll hook her up with Dazza. His brother married an Aborigine. He's fine with it all."

"I didn't know that."

"I told you, I make it my business to know."

"You make frigging everything your business."

"I listen, and I keep my mouth shut. That's what barmen do."

"Well, here's another one for your treasure chest. Miss Petula's business is Petula Kinlan Fashions. She's damned rich, from what I can tell. Works out of Sydney and London."

"Fuckin' 'ell, Charlie! She's Petula Kinlan? I didn't make that connection before."

Charlie checked the time. He had to go in a few minutes. "You know who she is?"

"Bloody right I do! Her clothes are all the rage in London, and the fire has caught on in Sydney. She's hot!"

"You're not telling me anything I don't already know, mate." Charlie still wanted that pint, but asked for some tonic water instead. "Could you give me some T without the G? I'm damned thirsty."

"Sure, mate, coming right up." Morgy gave him a full glass, loaded with ice. "You ate some dinner, I hope."

Charlie knocked back the whole glass in one long drink. "Yeah, I ate with Pet and Jennifer in Pet's cabin."

Morgy raised an eyebrow. "You went to *her* cabin?"

"Sure as hell did. Spent the afternoon there."

"That's fucking dangerous, isn't it?"

"You don't know the half of it. She has dinner at the Captain's table. He showed up and wanted to know why she wasn't on the guest list for tonight. I hid my arse in the loo until she got rid of him."

"Shit!"

"Exactly! Oh, and he's got an eye for Pet, too. Wants a private dinner with her before the end of the voyage."

"Think she'll do it?"

"Don't know. Anyway, I gotta go. If she shows up here tonight, tell her what you told me about the party. I'll leave it to the two of you to figure out the food situation. After all, it's her shout."

"Am I taking her to your cabin again?"

"You got the key. Let her in if she wants to go."

"Will do, mate. See you tomorrow." As Charlie turned to leave, Morgy groused, "You didn't ask if I can come."

Without missing a beat, Charlie retorted, "I'll let Derrick ask you that tomorrow night."

Charlie left Morgy stewing in his own juices. He patted his pocket, making sure he had Pet's key. He would make a copy tonight, and decide how to use it later.

It didn't take long to finish up the remaining maintenance

on the soot blowers. He tried not to get so dirty tonight, hoping that Pet would be waiting for him when he got back to his cabin. Of course, maybe seeing him sweaty and dirty appealed to her.

Remembering the key, he set about making the copy. He found a suitable piece of metal and clamped it with the original in a vise. Then he proceeded to hand-file the copy from the original pattern. Charlie had copied keys many times, and could manage it fairly quickly. This key didn't present any problems. It had a simple set of ridges that he duplicated easily.

Once he tucked the two keys safely in his pocket, he finished his watch by puttering around for a bit, taking care of a few other minor maintenance jobs. When he left the engine room, he didn't bother going back to the Monkey Bar. He headed straight for his cabin. He figured either Pet was there, or she wasn't. If not, he could get some much needed sleep.

Charlie opened the door to his cabin. The light wasn't on. He muttered to himself, "Guess this root rat won't get any more tonight." He closed the door and snapped on the light.

"Hello, Charles."

Charlie nearly dirtied his knickers. "Bloody hell! Jen?" Jennifer was in his bunk, covered with the sheet. She appeared to be naked. "Where the fuck is Pet?"

"She's knackered. Said she had to get some sleep, and then asked me to go see Morgy for her."

"Pet told you to do this?"

"Not exactly. I went to see Morgy about the party. Pet told me to leave a message for you with him, that she would see you tomorrow. He told me you expected Pet to be in your cabin after your watch. I certainly didn't want you to be disappointed. Neither did Morgy."

"Won't Pet be pissed off if she finds out you're here?"

"Maybe, but I doubt it. If she minded, she wouldn't have

asked me to her cabin this arvo. Anyway, she knows you fancy her."

"I fancy you, too."

Jen pointed to his poster. "Is that why?"

"Partly. But you're more beautiful than she is."

"Do you really think so?" Jennifer threw back the sheet. Charlie's palms started to sweat. Just as he suspected, she was in his bunk, naked.

He took his time looking her over. "Oh, yeah, Jen, I really do. You're one hot sheila."

"Do you fancy Aborigine women?"

Charlie cleared his throat. He didn't know how to answer that. "I'm keen on all women, especially if they are as gorgeous as you and Pet."

Jennifer glanced at his poster. "Fess up, Charlie. You like the color of our skin, don't you?"

Seeing the exotic beauty of this naked woman in his bed, he couldn't deny it. "Jen, I always have. Yooralla sealed it. Christ, all I had to do was look at her, and I could come in my knickers."

Jennifer slowly slid her hands over her body, seductively caressing herself. "What about me, do I make you cream in your pants?"

"I'm ready to. I'd rather do it inside you."

"Take off your clothes. I want to see your skin, too."

"I need to shower. I just came from the engine room."

"No, you don't. You were sweaty today, in the bedroom. The smell made me crazy."

"It did?"

"I'm Aborigine, remember? My mother's family still lives among our people, even though my mother left the clan."

Charlie slowly unsnapped his boiler suit. "Have you done a Walkabout?"

"You know about that?"

"Yooralla told me about the Dreamtime, and the Walkabout to the Belonging Place. Told me the ceremonies they do are secret."

"Some are secret, some aren't. I went on a Walkabout with my grandmother when I was sixteen, to learn how to connect with our ancestral spirits. My father objected, but my mother wanted me to know the ways of our clan. It's something you never forget."

"I reckon not. Don't suppose you would tell me about it?"

"I can't. It's sacred and meant to be experienced, not explained." Without meaning to, Charlie caught himself staring into Jennifer's eyes, as if trying to see a vision of the Dreamtime. Jennifer saw him do it. "But I don't think I have to tell you. You feel it in me, don't you?"

Charlie stepped out of his boiler suit, then took off his underpants. Jennifer licked her lips and continued to touch herself as she stared at his erection.

"You have the same wildness about you that Yooralla had, like you grew up in the bush."

"I grew up in London, but spent enough time with my mother's family to make me more wild than tame."

"Is that why you get on with Pet so well? She's a wild one, too."

"I've known Pet for years. We were roommates in school. That's when we discovered we could keep each other happy. We still do, when we can't find a man that can handle it."

Charlie went to the edge of the bunk, but didn't get in. He stood over Jennifer, his erect cock dangling from his groin. He wanted to look at her, the way he looked at his poster night after night. Without thinking about it, he took his cock in his fist and wanked. "You are so frigging beautiful."

"And you are the only man who has ever taken Pet and me on at the same time, and has come back for more."

Charlie grinned. "Hell, you ladies tried to eat me alive. But it'll take more than the two of you to best me."

Jennifer held her arms open. "Then we'll have to keep trying, won't we?"

"S'pose so." Charlie accepted the invitation, and the challenge of keeping pace with these two hungry women. He crawled into bed beside Jennifer. "Tomorrow night, at the party, you know I'll be with Pet."

"I know. Who did you find for me?"

"His name is Dazza. He's another Aussie, and a good mate of mine. Wouldn't hook you up with just anyone."

"Think he can handle me like you can?" Jennifer threw her leg over Charlie's. He could feel the damp heat from her pussy on his thigh.

"He'll give it what he's got. If he can't manage it, you, me and Pet can always go again."

"We will anyway. Pet told me after you left that she wanted to, before we reach London."

Charlie squeezed the soft flesh of Jen's breast. "Is that a fact?"

"That's why I came here tonight. I wanted at least one time with you alone."

"Pet likes to run the show, doesn't she?"

"It's what she does. Her being the boss doesn't bother me. But I have to tell you, it tickled me silly today when you turned it around on her."

Charlie raised himself up on his elbow and looked into Jen's dark eyes. "I didn't piss her off, did I?"

Jen reached up and threaded her fingers through his hair. "Not at all. In fact, she told me she wants to keep seeing you, even after this trip."

"No shit!"

"She's got it all figured out. When she's not on the ship, she'll arrange to meet you when you dock."

"What about you?"

"Depends."

"On what?"

"On you, and what you want."

"Right now, I want you." Charlie bent over and pressed his lips against Jen's lush mouth. He pushed his tongue inside and kissed her. She returned the kiss, wrapping her arms around his neck and holding his face to hers.

Charlie felt her rubbing her pussy against his leg, the slippery moisture coating his thigh. As much as he wanted to prolong being in bed with her, the impulse to roll on top of her overtook him.

When he pushed her back on the bed, Jen spread her legs wide and raised her knees up. Charlie lowered himself between her legs and positioned his cock for entry.

He raised his head and again looked into those glorious dark eyes. "Are you ready, Jen?"

"Bloody 'ell, yes! Frig me, Charlie."

He entered her slowly and deliberately, watching her face as he did. She closed her eyes and gasped as his prick pierced her. Then she did something he had never seen a woman do—she arched her back, bared her teeth and growled. He had the unsettling sense that the "Gippsland Phantom Cat" had somehow found its way on board and ended up in his bed.

Charlie wasn't about to hurry with this one. He had all night to ride her, and having already shagged three times that day, he knew he could hold on for a bit. Jen had a different idea. She squirmed underneath him and arched her back again, trying to force him to hump harder.

He leaned down and whispered into her ear, "Jen, I'm going

to fuck you slow and easy, maybe even for the rest of the night."

"You bloody drongo! Frig me like you did this arvo!" Jen tried her best to increase the rhythm, but Charlie had control.

His pelvis lifted and lowered like an engine in low gear. "Slow and steady, Jen. That's what we're doing tonight. And, my beauty, you'll love every minute of it."

Jennifer struggled and squirmed underneath him. He knew she wanted him to jackhammer her, but he didn't have the inclination, or the energy. This unhurried pace suited him just fine, and felt damn good.

Considering how much bigger and heavier he was, Jennifer had no choice but to let him have his way. He didn't have the advantage of being on top earlier. Now he did, and he intended to make the most of it.

"Work with me, Jen. Relax and enjoy it, like I am. You'll be better for it."

When he told her to relax, he honestly didn't think she would. However, her whole body softened underneath him, then joined with his in a syncopated rhythm.

Once her movement blended with his, they danced a dance as Australian as "Waltzing Matilda." With each stroke of his penis inside her, Jen's pelvis met his with a purposeful tempo, meant to slowly escalate the sensation.

Charlie could feel the pressure building in his balls. Even with the impulse to pick up the pace, he sustained the slow simmer. "How're you doing, love?" He hoped she might be getting close.

In a dreamy, almost sleepy voice, Jennifer said, "I'm wonderful. This feels so good."

"Yeah, it does to me, too." He wanted to finish, but he also wanted her to get there. "Don't go nodding off under me."

Jennifer giggled. "Oh, dear Charles, I'm not going to sleep. I'm waiting for you to put the pedal to the floor."

Even as he answered, he thumped her harder. "And what will happen when I do?"

Jen stayed with him as he rode her. "I'm going to make you forget Yooralla."

Taking her at her word, Charlie cut loose. He banged her just as hard as he had Pet the night before. Her pussy stayed tight even with the slippery juice that flowed between her legs. All the while, he looked at that beautiful brown face and those gorgeous dark eyes.

Jennifer clung to him as he humped her. Even with his determination to have her finish first, when he thought of the chocolate-colored skin between her legs he was pushed over the top. Not believing he could come so hard after all the fucking he had done that day, he grunted and quivered as he shot his load inside her.

With barely enough breath to speak, he apologized. "Christ, Jen, I'm sorry. I tried to hold on, but you're too damn hot for it."

"Roll over, and let me finish against your leg."

Charlie didn't quite understand what she meant, but he obliged. He rolled off her, then found himself wedged against the wall. She quickly sat up so he could lie in the center of the bunk. Then she straddled his leg.

It didn't matter that he was fucking exhausted, watching this gorgeous sheila rub against his thigh nearly made his eyes pop out. Her tits jiggled just centimeters from his face as she masturbated against his leg.

In what may have been one of the hottest moments he'd ever witnessed, this Aboriginal nymphet had an explosive climax right in front of his face. She threw her head back and hissed as she rubbed her soaked pussy against his leg. Her entire body shook for several seconds as her orgasm consumed her.

When she finally quieted, she fell forward onto his chest, gasping for air. He shifted to the outside edge of the bunk so she could squeeze in by the wall. Charlie stroked her hair. "Jen, are you all right?"

"I'm bloody fine. I just need to sleep."

He knew he should get her back to her cabin, but no way in hell could he drag himself out of bed to do it. What the fuck. He had the day off tomorrow. Jennifer had already drifted off, and a few minutes later, so did he.

# 6

It seemed to Charlie that he had just closed his eyes when he felt Jennifer shaking him. He muttered, "I have the day off. Go back to sleep."

Jennifer whispered, "Charlie, wake the fuck up! Someone's at the door!"

Charlie's eyes popped open like they had springs attached. "Jesus Christ!" Again, someone knocked. Gesturing for Jen to stay quiet, he yelled, "Yeah, who is it?"

"It's Morgy. Let me in."

"Just a minute."

Jen grabbed his arm. "Should I hide in the loo?"

"Don't bother. He knows you're here." Charlie glanced at her exposed breasts. "But you might want to cover yourself up before I open the door." To emphasize his point, he tweaked her nipple.

He fished his underpants out of his boiler suit, then kicked the suit from in front of the door. After he stepped into his pants, he opened the door for Morgy.

Morgy cheerfully greeted him. "G'day, mate. And how are you this beautiful morning?"

"What the fuck time is it, and what the fuck are you doing here?"

"It's eight-thirty." Stepping inside, Morgy eyed Jennifer sitting on the bed, holding the sheet against her chest. He grinned. "Grumpy today, isn't he?"

Charlie slammed the door shut. "Morgy, you'd better have a frigging good reason for being here."

"Oh, I think I do." He didn't say anything else.

Jennifer spoke up. "Charlie, are you going to punch him or should I?"

Morgy laughed. "You're as much of a cracker as Pet is! Charlie, you got yourself a couple of grouse birds with these two!"

Knowing Morgy would drag out his reason for being there as long as possible, Charlie played his hand. He knew he held four aces. "Jen, did you know Morgy fancies men more than women? Maybe you should show him why he should change his mind about that."

Charlie stood behind Morgy, so Morgy didn't see Charlie wink at Jennifer after he made the suggestion. Jennifer picked up her cue and ran with it. "Morgan, is that true?" She threw the sheet aside and gestured for him to join her on the bunk. "Come here. Let's see if I can win you over to our side."

Morgy turned beet red. The sight of Jennifer stark naked on the bunk, ready to have a go with him, did the trick. "Save it for Charlie, Jennifer. I like my side of the fence, thank you."

He turned back to Charlie and spilled the beans. "Pet rang me up a few minutes ago. It seems she was supposed to have breakfast with Jennifer at eight o'clock, and Jennifer is nowhere to be found."

"Oh, Lord Almighty! I forgot she asked me to meet her for

brekkie. She wanted to go over the menu so we could get the food order in for tonight."

"Does she know Jen's here?"

"She certainly suspects it. That's why she called me. She wanted to know your number. I told her you don't have a phone in your quarters, only the crew's intercom. I volunteered to come and tell you about Jennifer being MIA."

"Where is Pet now?"

"I suppose in her cabin. That's where she called me from."

"Did she sound pissed off?"

"Couldn't tell. She sounded all business."

"Jen, you know her better than we do. Are we in deep shit?"

"I'm in deep shit, you're not. She hates it when we're late for anything." Jennifer crawled out of the bunk. "I'd better get dressed and go talk to her."

Charlie sounded incredulous. "Are you telling me she'll be more pissed off about your missing breakfast with her than spending the night with me?"

"That's what I'm telling you."

Morgy cackled. "Guess she has her priorities straight, lover boy!" He went to the door. "Gotta go. I'm doing the early shift today so I'm free for the party tonight, in case you're interested." Over his shoulder, he said to Jen, "Let me know when you have the menu ready. I'll make sure the food gets done right."

"Thank you, Morgan. We'll see you later, I hope."

"No worries. I won't let her cancel the party, even if I have to promise her my firstborn."

"Always knew I could count on you, mate. Don't let the door hit you in the arse."

When Morgy left, Jennifer went straight to the closet to get her clothes. "You have to get me back to my cabin, Charlie. Pet may be as mad as a cut snake. Like Morgy said, it's hard to tell with her."

"Give me five minutes to shower, and then we'll go." Charlie wasted no time. He jumped in the shower, lathered up and rinsed off. By the time he came out, Jennifer had dressed. He grabbed some clean clothes and got himself together.

He picked up the boiler suit from the floor. Pet's keys were still in his pocket. He made sure he had his own, and the one to return. While he showered, he had an idea, and he hoped that Jennifer would agree.

"Jen, I have a suggestion. Let me talk to Pet alone and smooth things over. I don't want there to be a problem between the two of you because of this."

"Charlie, I've known Pet a long time. It's better if I face the music myself and get past it."

Charlie stood his ground. "In this case, I don't agree with you. If she's pissed, it doesn't matter why. I want to make it right."

Jennifer shrugged her shoulders. "All right, if that's what you want to do. But don't say I didn't warn you. She can be a bitch when she wants to be."

"I have no doubt about that. But I don't work for her. You do. The odds are in my favor of coming out on top." Charlie grinned.

Jennifer definitely got his meaning. "Beauty! If anyone can bring her around, you can."

"That's the plan. Let's go."

Charlie followed his established route back to Pet's suite, with Jennifer behind him. He paused only once, so a couple just leaving their cabin could get a head start.

As they approached Pet's door, Charlie whispered to Jen, "Can you get back to your cabin from here?"

"Sure can. I know where I am. My cabin is around the corner." Jennifer gave him a kiss on the cheek. "Good luck." She stifled a giggle, so as not to be heard, then added, "You need to shave before the party."

Charlie held her close and rubbed his cheek against hers.

"I'll try to remember." He spun her around and whacked her bum to send her on her way.

He waited until Jen rounded the corner to her cabin, then pulled the two keys out of his pocket. Charlie chose the key he had made the night before, to make sure it worked. After quietly slipping the copy into the lock, he gave it a turn. The satisfying click meant the cylinder properly turned. He had made a good copy.

Pet wasn't in the sitting room, as he expected she would be. For a moment, he thought she wasn't there at all, and then he heard water running in the loo.

He made himself comfortable on the sofa and waited. She had to come out sometime. A glass sat on the floor beside him, half full of ice. He picked it up and sniffed. Definitely gin, and fresh red lippy on the rim. She'd already put most of it away, and it wasn't nine o'clock yet. In spite of Jen's take on it, Charlie guessed Pet was spitting chips at both of them.

Charlie's stomach growled. He hadn't eaten anything since dinner last night. There was no sign Pet had eaten anything, either. Having Jen not show up apparently had put her off food. Maybe once he calmed her arse down, he would ask her to call for room service.

The water he'd heard running stopped. A few seconds later, the door opened. Where he'd expected a tongue-lashing as soon as she saw him, he got silence instead.

He turned to look at her. "G'day, Petula." He couldn't read her expression.

"What the fuck are you doing here? Who let you in?"

"You did, my Pet. Seems you forgot about this." He put her original key on the stand beside the sofa. "I copied it last night. The one I made works."

"Where's Jen?"

Charlie told her the truth. "In her cabin. She spent the night with me. Said you were too tired, so she stepped in."

"How generous of her." Pet picked up her glass and went to refill it.

"Having G and T for brekkie? I prefer scrambled eggs and sausage."

"Is that what you and Jen had, eggs and sausage?" Pet poured more gin than tonic in the glass, stirred and then raised her glass. "Cheers!" Pet sipped her drink before she said, "I expect Jennifer found the sausage fucking brilliant."

Charlie could see the explosion coming. Pet was spewin' under the surface. "We didn't eat, at least not food." He intentionally goaded her.

Pet glared at him. "Why did you come here? If you're protecting Jennifer, don't bother. She can take care of herself."

"I came here to see you. I know you're pissed off."

Pet spit back, "You don't bloody well know anything about me! You don't even know who I am."

"What, that you design clothes? I could give a shit about that."

Pet slammed her glass down on the oak table. "Maybe you fucking should!" She stormed into the bedroom. Charlie followed her.

He stayed in the doorway. Pet had disappeared into her oversized closet. He yelled at the open closet door, "What's the matter, boss lady? Not used to someone standing up to you?"

She came out of the closet and tossed her swimming togs on the bed, the same crimson bikini that made Charlie crack a fat two days before. "I'm going for a swim. I would ask you to join me, but it isn't allowed, is it?"

"Depends on which pool you use. The crew has a small pool on the foredeck, not nearly as posh as the first-class pool you use."

Pet pulled her dress over her head, leaving her in her bra and panties. "I thought we weren't allowed to socialize in public."

The boner in Charlie's pants thickened. Nonetheless, he remained by the door, choosing not to approach the bed. "We're not. But our pool sometimes gets the overflow from tourist class. No one cares if there's an occasional sheila from tourist doing the backstroke in the crew's pool, as long as we don't touch her."

Pet unhooked her bra. Her breasts tumbled free of the cloth. "And what if a first-class sheila uses it?"

Charlie kept his voice steady, even as Pet pulled down her panties. "Then I expect my mates would figure you were slumming." Charlie blatantly looked her over. "Is that what you're doing with me, Pet, going slumming?"

"Is that what Jennifer thinks?"

Pet stood naked, making no move to pick up her togs lying on the bed. She obviously wanted him to see her nude. Charlie stepped into the bedroom, but stopped before he reached the bed. "No. That's what I think. What we're talking about has nothing to do with Jennifer."

"Oh, I think it does. You won't accept me for what I am, but you'll accept her for what she is, an Australian, same as you. She's been in the Aussie bush with her Aborigine family. That makes you hot, just like her bush does."

Charlie pointed to the blond curls between Pet's legs. "Yours is making me bloody hot right now, and that has nothing to do with what you do or where you're from." Charlie moved closer and picked up Pet's bikini. He handed it to her. "Here. You should put this on and go for your swim." Then he turned to leave.

"Where are you going?"

"To see Morgy and tell him the party's off."

"Excuse me?" Pet dropped the bathing togs on the floor. "Where the fuck did that come from?"

"Why would a first-class sheila come to my cabin? Don't want my mates feeling like you're looking down on them, like you are me. Call the Captain. He'll cream when you tell him you'll have dinner with him, privately. He knows who you are, and you won't be slumming when you're with him."

"Charles Weston, you're a goddamned hypocrite! I told you yesterday I thought you were being a snob. That goes double today. You think you're better than me, not the other way around."

"That's bullshit."

"Like hell it is!" Pet's whole body had turned pink. Absolutely furious, she walked over to where Charlie stood. She didn't seem to notice or care that she had no clothes on. "You're running hot and cold. One minute you want me, the next you're telling me to go fuck myself. Make up your frigging mind!"

"I wouldn't be here if I didn't want you. I had to make sure I didn't throw a spanner in the works by sleeping with Jen. She's hot, all right, but nothing like you."

"What the hell does that mean?"

"That means I frigging want to keep seeing you. Bloody hell, what do I have to do, write it in diesel oil on my forehead?"

Pet wasn't so easily swayed. "Why?"

"Why what?"

"Why do you want to keep seeing me? If it's not my money or my name, then what is it?"

Charlie stared at this blond bit of dynamite. Here she stood, stark naked, having a knock-down-drag-out with him, and she didn't know why he wanted to keep seeing her? "Fuck, Pet, if you don't know, nothing I can say will explain it."

"Then you're just as full of shit as the rest of them. And I honestly thought you were different." Charlie thought he saw her eyes well up before she turned around. Her voice cracked as she said, "Go ahead, tell Morgy the party's off. There's no point in continuing this."

Pet walked over and picked up her togs from the floor and tossed them back on the bed. Then she disappeared into the closet. Charlie stood there for a few seconds, unnerved by her obvious emotion. He muttered, "Jesus Christ!" Then he went after her.

She didn't hear him come up behind her as she rifled through the rack of clothes. "Pet?"

She jumped, then quickly wiped her face. "Frickin' 'ell! I thought you left."

"I'm not ready to leave."

"Well, I am!" She yanked a dress from a hanger. "I have to see the Captain."

Charlie gripped her shoulders and turned her around. "I've heard he has a small dick, if you're interested." She had tear tracks on her face, which she couldn't hide.

"I'll find out for myself, thank you." Pet tried to wrench herself free. Charlie didn't let her go.

"You want to know why I want to keep seeing you? This is why." Charlie held her tightly against him and kissed her. More accurately, he devoured her. She was more than a bit of dynamite. She was a frigging powder keg!

He kissed her mouth, her salt-stained face, her neck, and then bent her backward to kiss her tits. Pet lost her balance. Before he could catch her, she fell back into the rack of clothes. She grabbed the dresses, trying to stay on her feet, and managed to pull most of them off the hangers.

The dresses hit the floor first, and Pet fell on top of them. Rather than helping her up, Charlie went down with her. Stunned by both Charlie's voracious attack and the fall, Pet tried to speak, and couldn't.

Not giving her time to regroup, Charlie buried his face between her legs. The impulse to suck her and lick her overwhelmed him. He might not be able to tell her what she did to him, but he sure as hell could show her.

Pet writhed on the pile of dresses as he ravenously feasted on her clit. She reached down and pulled his hair. He was too far gone to care. He had never wanted a woman like this before. The intensity of his lust overpowered every thought in his mind. He wanted to fuck, and nothing would stop him.

When he raised his head, he saw Pet clutching the clothes in her fists. She had her eyes closed. Her chest had speckled with a deep rose rash. He opened his trousers and pushed them down to his knees. His prick bobbed from his groin when he released the hard rod from his underpants.

Pet opened her eyes. She rasped out, "Charlie, let's move to the bed. I don't want my dresses damaged."

"Fuck the dresses!" He fell on top of her. "Open your legs, Pet, or I'll open them for you."

Pet clamped her legs shut. "I'd like to see you try, Mr. Third Assistant Engineer."

"All right, then, have it your way." Charlie stood up, and quickly doffed his trousers and shirt. "I know what you need, my Pet, a good walloping!"

"You frigging wouldn't dare!"

"Oh, yes, I would."

Charlie grabbed her arm and pulled her to her feet. Before she could put up a struggle, he picked her up and took her back into the bedroom. Without the least thought of gentleness, he dumped her on the bed and rolled her over. Then he straddled her legs so she couldn't move.

"What the bloody hell do you think you're doing?" Pet tried to free herself. The effort proved pointless.

"I'm protecting your precious frocks and giving you what you deserve at the same time." He wedged his knee between her thighs and opened them just enough to squeeze his hand between her legs. She squirmed against his fingers when he found her clit.

"Who the frigging hell are you to tell me what I deserve?"

"I'm the one you said was man enough to do the job." He shoved his middle finger into her vagina. "I've decided you're right about that."

"Fuck you!"

"No, love, fuck you!" He rammed his middle finger in and out of her cunt several times, until he felt her push back on it, trying to make it go deeper. Then he pulled his finger out and whacked her arse with the palm of his hand. She yelped.

Charlie's hands were large and calloused. When he saw his handprint on her smooth pink ass, he smiled. He slapped her bum again, with the same effect. The third one, he heard a moan instead of a yelp. "You like that, don't cha, Pet?"

She didn't answer. He gave her another one. "I asked you a question, my beauty. I want an answer. Do you like it?"

"You ratbag, yes, I like it!"

"How many more, Pet?"

Again she didn't answer. The rosy mounds were quickly becoming red. "You'd better tell me, or I'll decide. We could be here all day."

"All right, you win. Five more."

Charlie chuckled. "That's brilliant. I would've only done three."

He gave her five hard whacks, which made her arse cherry red. After the fifth one, he again slid his finger between her legs. "You're even slicker than Jen was last night." If she hadn't been lying on her belly, he suspected she would have spit at him.

Charlie flipped her over onto her back. "Now, Pet. Let's try this again. Spread your legs for me, or . . ."

He didn't have to finish the sentence. Her legs opened like the wings of a swan. Charlie fell on top of her, his prick separating her lips. With one thrust forward, he popped into the slippery hole and slid into her body.

Pet clutched his back and lifted her pelvis, making him sink in even deeper. While he had her pinned underneath him, he whispered into her ear, "This is why I want to keep seeing you."

She whispered back, "And this is why I want to keep seeing you, even after this trip."

She made him feel like more of a man than any other woman ever had. He rode her like an Aussie roughrider, and she bucked like a wild horse. As much as he enjoyed being with Jen, Charlie sensed that Pet had an aggressive strength that challenged his own.

He had corralled the boss lady, and he knew what she needed.

# 7

"You could help me pick these clothes up. It's your fault they're on the floor." Charlie had come into the closet to pick up his own clothes. He found Pet on her hands and knees, still naked, threading hangers through the sleeves of dresses.

"Bloody hell, Pet. I thought you came in here to get dressed. Those frocks will wait until later. We need to get some brekkie. I'm starving."

"These frocks, as you call them, are Petula Kinlan originals. What you nearly used as shag padding are worth thousands."

"No shit!" Charlie surveyed the dresses still on the floor. "These frocks are worth thousands of pounds?"

"Assistant Third Engineer Weston, you haven't a frigging clue who I am. I'm torn between being grateful for it and being royally pissed off by it."

"Yeah, I figured that out, too." He bent over and picked up a dress. "This is the one you wore the other night, when you came to my cabin. How much is this one worth?"

"Three thousand pounds, give or take."

"Even with the mucked-up zipper?"

Petula snatched the dress from him. "The zipper is not mucked-up! It's invisible! That's a selling point, not a flaw."

Charlie chuckled. "Tell that to the bloke who tries to get it open for a shag." He knelt down beside her. "Hand me those hangers."

"Be careful. They're already wrinkled. I don't want them torn."

Charlie picked up the dress lying beside him. "If these are so posh and expensive, what are they doing hanging in here with everything else? Shouldn't they be under lock and key?"

"If you must know, these are for my next line. They will debut at a show in London, and the originals will be sold. Then the designs will be copied and mass-produced. I don't want anyone to see them, so I keep them with me."

"But you wore that one. I hate to be the one to break this to you, but people will see them if you wear them." He picked up a few more to hang.

Pet pointed to the adjoining rack, on the other wall. "Those are my personal clothes, the ones I wear every day." She gestured to the rack of originals. "I only wear these on special occasions. When I have one on, nobody knows it's an original, unless I want them to know."

"You wore one of them to meet me."

"Exactly."

"Why were you looking for one now? Seems you meant to wear one this morning."

Pet didn't mince words. "I was upset. I was going to dress to the teeth and go ask the Captain to have dinner with me, since I thought you had walked out."

"You still planning to have dinner with him before we dock in London?"

"Probably not. We'll see." She picked up the last dress. "By the way, how do you know he has a small dick?"

"Because a lovely lady who slept with him told me."

"Was it a fair comparison?"

"If you're asking if she slept with me, too, yeah, it was a fair comparison."

"I'll keep that in mind." Pet took the hangers from Charlie and stood to put them back on the rack.

"Morgy says you're all the rage in London, and now in Sydney. S'pose that means you're famous?"

"Depends on what you call famous. In the fashion world, I am. I can go to my local butcher or chemist, and no one will recognize me."

"They might not recognize you, but they sure as hell will notice you. Pet, you're one good-looking woman!"

"Thank you." She straightened the clothes and made sure all was in order. Then she turned and asked him a direct question. "Tell me something, Charlie. Do you care that I'm famous, or that I have money?"

He answered just as directly. "No, doesn't matter to me at all. What I do care about is that I could lose my job if I'm caught with you."

"You could work for me."

"And do what, Pet? Doubt you have many engines in your business. Anyway, I love my job, and being at sea. I'm not ready to give it up yet." Charlie paused for a moment before he added, "I'm glad you don't think less of me 'cause I earn my living getting my hands dirty." Charlie scooped his clothes off the floor and put them on, while Pet still hadn't decided what to wear.

"You're an exceptionally capable man, Charles. Morgy told me that first, but now I've seen it for myself." She studied the rack of her daily clothes, and finally selected a colorful Catalina patchwork playsuit. "It's not your job that has me so upset. It's all these damn rules! I should be able to socialize with whomever I choose. It shouldn't matter that you work in the engine room and I design clothes. If we fancy each other, it shouldn't be anyone else's business."

"Yeah, well, tell that to the Captain." Pet gave him a peculiar look, and he realized she could well tell the Captain. "On second thought, forget I said that."

She stepped into the playsuit and turned around. "Could you tie this for me?"

"Lift your hair." She did, and Charlie tied a perfect bow.

"Are we going to have to sneak around like this every time I'm on the ship?"

"If you want to keep seeing me, we will. Sorry, Pet. That's just the way it is."

"The trip between London and Sydney usually takes about a month. That's two months out of the year when I rest and work on new designs. Now I can also spend time with you."

"Sounds good."

"But that's not all, Charlie. I want to see you off this damn ship, somewhere that we don't have to tiptoe around the rules."

"What about Jen?" Charlie smacked his forehead with the palm of his hand. "Jesus, one of us should call her. She's probably wondering what the fuck is going on."

"I'll call her, then call for food." Pet smiled. In the playsuit, she looked like she should be on the cover of a magazine. "I expect we can work something out with Jen, as long as you keep me informed when the three of us aren't together."

She didn't have to draw Charlie a picture. "You want to know what we do together, don't you?"

"In great detail, Mr. Third Assistant Engineer. Let's just say I would enjoy hearing what you do with her."

"Why?" Charlie already knew why, but wanted to hear her say it.

"Because I'm kinky, and I want to know what you do with other women, especially with Jen."

"Then you don't care if I sleep around?"

"Of course not. You wouldn't be the man I think you are if you didn't!" As an afterthought, she added, "I hope you understand that I'm not taking a vow of monogamy because I'm involved with you. And if you knock up some bimbo sheila, I won't be happy."

"Yeah, that wouldn't make me happy, either." He put his arm around her shoulders. "Let's go call Jen. She's worried you're cross as a frog in a sock."

"I was, but I'm all right now."

"Good. And the party's still on?"

"It absolutely is. Let's hope it's not too late to order the food."

"No worries. Morgy will take care of it."

Pet called Jen. After Pet reassured her that all was well between them, she invited Jennifer to come have breakfast with them. Over some scrambled eggs and sausage, which Pet had ordered with a wink at Charlie, Pet and Jen hashed out an appropriate menu. Not particularly paying attention to their conversation, Charlie sat back and drank champagne, which Pet also ordered with the food.

Once they had figured out what they wanted, Pet called Morgy to arrange the party buffet. The food would be delivered to Pet's suite during the dinner hour, when the alleyways on the passenger decks were the least traveled. Then Pet's group would bring the trays to the locked door, where Charlie and his mates would be waiting. They would take the trays to Charlie's cabin and get everything set up.

Morgy gave Pet a message for Charlie, which she delivered with conviction. He had to clean his pigsty of a cabin before the food arrived. With considerable reluctance, Charlie left Pet and Jen in Pet's suite, and made a discreet exit back to his quarters. As well as cleaning his cabin, he also needed to shave.

It wasn't even six o'clock when someone knocked at his

door. Charlie knew who it had to be. He yelled, "G'day, Morgy. It's open."

Morgy opened the door. "Help me with these." Charlie saw several bags sitting in the hall.

"What the hell is all of this? I thought the food was going to Pet's suite."

Morgy handed him a couple of the bags. Charlie heard bottles clinking. "The food is. I brought the beverages."

Charlie glanced in the bags he held. "Jesus Christ, Morgy. This is Bombay Sapphire gin."

"Yeah, I know. I gave Dazza two more bottles to use in the pineapples." He handed Charlie another bag. "Here's the tonic water. Stevo's bringing another bagful. I couldn't carry anything else." Morgy held up a final bag. "And this, mate, is the VSOP cognac."

"You're shittin' me." Charlie took the bag and looked inside. "I didn't hear Pet tell you to bring this. I heard her say throw in a few bottles of Gordon's gin, nothing else."

Morgy collapsed on Charlie's freshly made bunk. "I'm exhausted! She's a real ballbuster. Called me after the lunch rush and changed the liquor order midstream. I had everything ready to go, and had to redo the order."

"Like I said, it's her shout." Charlie carried all the bags into the loo and set them in the shower, where they'd be out of the way.

"Don't kid yourself, mate. She has enough money to buy this ship if she wanted."

Charlie yelled, "You think so?" He played dumb.

"Hell yes. I asked a few questions today, and got some interesting answers. Seems she won an award last year for being the most influential designer of the season."

"Who told you that?" Charlie stopped short and stared at Morgy sitting on his bunk. "What the hell do you have on?"

Morgy looked like a neon sign in his white linen pants, hot pink shirt and mauve scarf.

"To answer your second question first, fashionable clothes, darling. According to Derrick, this color combo is the latest rage with the East End crowd."

"You met Derrick?"

"That's the answer to your other question. He came into the bar today and introduced himself. Pet had more party details she wanted handled, and Derrick volunteered to work them out with me. We got on famously. He's luscious, and I expect delicious, too. I hope to find out later." Morgy licked his lips.

Charlie chose to ignore Morgy's suggestive comment. "What did he say about Pet?"

"He's been her assistant for three years. Says she's tough as nails, but fair, and good to the people who work for her. He has no complaints." Morgy grinned. "He also says she's hot for you, mate, big-time."

"Don't spread that around. We're trying to keep it quiet."

"Are you keeping it quiet about Jennifer, too? Seems Derrick got an earful from her, as well as Pet."

"Why don't I just turn on the intercom and you can friggin' broadcast it all over the goddamned ship!"

"Touchy, touchy! You know your secret's safe with me, lover boy. I just wish I had your stamina. Must be the Aborigine in your genetics."

Charlie shot him a dirty look. "Christ, I'm sorry I ever told you my grandmother is Aborigine. No one on this ship knows that, and I want to keep it that way."

"It's nothing to be ashamed of, Charlie. Why do you hide it?"

"My grandmother left her clan and never looked back. It's hard enough that I have family in the bush I'll never know. I don't want to advertise it."

"You never told Yooralla. You should at least tell Jennifer. She would understand."

"Maybe I will, someday." He checked his watch, then changed the subject. "When will Dazza and Stevo get here? I want Stevo to get the reel-to-reel set up before they bring the food."

"I told them to be here at six-fifteen, and I told Derrick to do the buffet relay at six-thirty. We have a few minutes yet."

"What about Sparky?"

"Tess is with him. They'll be here by seven. He's bringing the paper plates, cups and silverware. I also packed the straws and napkins in his bag."

Charlie looked around to see if he'd missed cleaning anything. "Does the cabin pass inspection?"

Morgy got up. He ran his finger across the top of the now-empty-and-scrubbed desk. "I left the white gloves in my cabin, but it looks clean."

Charlie poked some fun. "You have time to go back for them. White gloves would match your trousers."

"Your fashion sense is questionable. White gloves would take the focus away from the mauve scarf. That is the focal point of the *ensemble*."

Charlie grinned at Morgy's French pronunciation of the word. "Sorry, mate. Guess I should leave it to the experts."

"They'll be here directly. You can ask them."

At 6:15 sharp, Dazza and Stevo knocked on the door. They were spit and polish clean, wearing civilian clothes and had combed their hair. Stevo could only do so much with his tangle of curly blond, but it was obvious he tried. Dazza had his thick brown hair slicked back. Charlie noticed he had even trimmed his sideburns.

"Here, mate, take this, so I don't spill anything coming in." Dazza handed Charlie an ice chest, which Charlie knew to handle carefully. It held the gin-filled frozen pineapples, which were Dazza's specialty. He took it straight into the loo, where it would be safe until the guests arrived.

As usual, Dazza had to duck to get in the door. After whacking his head enough times on the ship's door frames, it sunk in that he stood taller than they made the doors. Charlie hoped Jennifer liked 'em big, since she would be paired with Dazza tonight.

Stevo followed and gave Morgy the second bag of tonic water. Then he immediately set up his reel-to-reel inside the closet. They had all learned to maximize the space they had. By putting the music in the closet and leaving the door open, they could hear it without the box taking up any people space.

Once he had that under control, he pulled out the desk chair and stood on it. He unscrewed the regular ceiling lightbulb and put in his red one.

"Turn it on, Charlie. Make sure it still works." Charlie flipped the switch and the room glowed like a brothel. All the men were satisfied they had successfully completed their bit of preparation.

At 6:30, Charlie took his key and went to wait for the others at the dividing door. Morgy watched for Charlie's signal to go down the alleyway and help carry the food back to the cabin.

He only waited a few minutes before he heard a soft knock at the door. "Yes, who is it?" He had to be certain before he used his key.

"Charlie, it's Pet."

Charlie waved at Morgy, then unlocked the door. When he opened it and saw what was waiting, all he could say was "What the fuck?"

There stood Pet, balancing a stack of hatboxes, and Jennifer, with a long garment bag draped across her arms. Behind them stood two other people, which Charlie took to be Derrick and

Suzy. Derrick had a leather portfolio and Suzy had what looked like a narrow writing-desk drawer covered with a towel.

Pet shook him out of his bewilderment. "Don't just stand there! Let us in. And take these before I drop them."

Charlie stuffed the key back in his pocket, then relieved Pet of the boxes. He stepped aside so they could all get through the door. "Is this the food?"

Jennifer giggled. "We disguised it so no one would notice us carrying it."

Charlie eyed Pet. "You really thought no one would notice this parade? You have to be joking."

"Yeah, well, it seemed like a good idea at the time. Luckily, no one saw us."

Morgy, Dazza and Stevo had joined the crowd. Morgy went right to Derrick. "Don't tell me. That's the platter of cold cuts, right?"

"Of course, it is, dear. I just had to convince Petula that protecting the meat was worth removing her drawings." Charlie saw the chemistry immediately. Morgy and Derrick already appeared smitten with one another.

Morgy took the leather-covered tray from Derrick, then addressed Petula directly. "You, of all people, should know nothing is more important than protecting the meat." He then led Derrick down the hall to Charlie's cabin.

Petula watched as Derrick leaned over and whispered something into Morgy's ear, which caused Morgy to erupt with laughter. She poked Charlie in the side. "Do you get the feeling this is a match made in heaven?"

"Seems it might be, doesn't it?" Not forgetting his manners, he turned to Jennifer and Suzy. "Ladies, let me introduce my mates Dazza and Stevo. Dazza is the ship's first assistant engineer, and Stevo is the ship's second mate." Nodding toward Jennifer, he said to Dazza, "This is Jen. She's your date." And to Stevo, he echoed, "This is Suzy. She's with you tonight."

Dazza attempted to take Jennifer's garment bag. She stopped him. "Wait, you have to hold it straight. There's smoked salmon, prawns and caviar on this tray."

"Yes, ma'am!" Dazza carefully took the tray, making sure it didn't tip. "Charlie didn't mention how pretty you are. You're even prettier than my brother's wife. I'll have to tell you about her."

"And Charlie didn't mention to me how big you are. Good heavens, you're tall as a tree!" Jennifer threaded her arm through Dazza's as they walked toward Charlie's cabin. Again, Charlie recognized the rapport. He didn't know if he felt relieved or jealous.

Then Stevo approached Suzy. "What's in this one?"

"All sorts of goodies. Wait till you see." Suzy's Irish brogue set off her red hair and freckles nicely. "I can't wait to get to dessert."

Stevo grinned. "Neither can I. Let's get on with the party."

That left Charlie and Pet standing by the door, which still stood ajar. "You either have to take these boxes back so I can lock the door, or get the key out of my pocket and do it yourself."

"I don't mind locking the door." Pet reached into Charlie's pocket, but she didn't immediately take the key. She had him by the balls, in more ways than one. Holding all the boxes, he couldn't do a damn thing when she blatantly fondled him through the cloth of his trousers. Only then, did she take out the key and use it.

With the ridge in his trousers already becoming uncomfortable, he didn't give her a chance to put the key back in his pocket. "Let's go, Pet, before someone sees us." He hurried down the hall to his cabin, with Pet close behind.

# 8

When they got to the door, Dazza had it completely blocked. He still held the garment bag filled with fish. Jennifer stood in front of him, trying to unzip it. Charlie stated the obvious. "Dazza, I can't walk through you."

"Sorry, mate. Jen is having a bit of trouble here."

"Yeah. The plastic wrap is caught in the damn zipper. It's stuck."

Morgy came to the rescue. "Come over here and let me try. If it's one thing I know, it's zippers."

Charlie laughed. "You and Pet need to talk. Maybe you could teach her a thing or two about how a zipper should work."

Pet wasn't amused. "The only zipper you need worry about is the one in your trousers. It would be a shame if anything should accidentally get caught in it."

"Mate, sounds like you'd better be careful. Could be painful." Dazza stepped to the side, allowing Charlie and Pet to squeeze past. When Charlie put the hatboxes on the desk, he saw a white linen tablecloth covering it. "What the hell is this?"

"Derrick brought it. Picked it up in the dining room this afternoon. It adds a bit of panache, doesn't it?" Pet smiled.

Derrick added, "I gave Tess the flowers and candles. Make sure you leave some room for them."

"I thought we were just doing sandwiches and desserts. My cabin is hardly the place for a posh buffet!"

"Derrick helped me arrange it, didn't you, love?" Pet pulled the tablecloth forward a bit, covering the initialed desk drawers.

"With exceptional pleasure. I spent the afternoon with Morgy, and we got it sorted."

"Not the least of which is this masterpiece." Morgy had opened the garment bag zipper and extracted a beautiful platter of caviar, surrounded by the smoked salmon and prawns. "Pet, are the blinis in one of the boxes?"

"The one on top, with the crackers. The rolls are in the next one, and the stuffed figs are in the bottom one."

Dazza cocked his head, as though he hadn't heard correctly. "Stuffed what?"

"Stuffed figs." Pet unstacked the boxes and opened the bottom one. "See."

Charlie looked inside. "What the hell are they stuffed with?"

"Some have chicken liver pate, some have goat cheese with walnuts and some have brie wrapped with prosciutto."

"Caviar, blinis, stuffed figs? Jesus Christ, Pet! Who do you think you're feeding here? The sandwiches would have been plenty. You aren't entertaining royalty tonight."

"I hope you don't expect us to pay for all of this," Stevo chimed in.

Morgy answered for Pet. "No drama, Stevo. It's all paid in full. Pet took care of it. This is her shout."

"I hope somebody remembered the mustard," Charlie muttered.

"And the peanuts," Dazza added.

Jennifer surprised Charlie when she quipped, "You blokes have enough nuts to keep me happy. I don't need any peanuts."

"I'll second that." Suzy helped herself to a stuffed fig and took a bite. She smiled as she chewed. "Shit the bed, these are brilliant!" She popped the rest of it into her mouth.

"With an endorsement like that, who could resist?" Pet reached in and tried one. "Damn, they are good, aren't they?"

Derrick arranged the blinis on the fish platter. "I had Morgy double the fig order after I tried one. They are heaven, aren't they?"

Someone knocked on the door. Charlie waved everyone quiet. "Yes, who is it?"

"It's Sparky."

Charlie unlatched the door. Sparky came in, followed by a tall girl with waist-length shiny black hair. "G'day, mates." He handed Morgy the bags. "Here's all the stuff you asked me to bring."

"And here are the candles and flowers." Tess gave Derrick her contribution, then turned to Charlie. "Thanks for asking us to come."

"It's good to have you." Charlie proceeded to introduce Sparky to Pet's group, explaining he operated the ship's radio and telegraph, among other things. Then Pet introduced Tess to Charlie's group. Morgy and Derrick set about finishing the buffet; then everyone filled a plate.

Charlie played bartender, until Morgy relieved him of the duty. Then he crawled across his bunk to get to the closet. After he snapped on the reel-to-reel, he reached up and took a large tin can off the shelf. He plunked a king-sized can of peanuts down next to the platter of caviar. "Hey, Dazza, here's the peanuts."

Dazza's face lit up. "Good onya, mate. Now it's really a party!" He took a handful and tossed them onto his plate.

Stevo flipped the light switch and the room glowed red.

Suzy approved of the effect. "You're on the ball with that one, lad. It's feckin' spot-on."

Stevo picked up his plate and sat down on the floor beside Suzy. "That's a new one. The last one I had burned out. Had a helluva time finding another one."

"You can say that again." Sparky handed Tess a full plate, then went back to make one for himself. "The damned wanker had us looking all over Sydney for one before we sailed. Charlie finally found one in the same shop where he got his poster."

Charlie settled in beside Pet at the far end of the bunk. She poked him in the side. "What kind of shop is it, the gift shop at a local brothel?"

He feigned indignation. "No fucking way! It's a novelty shop in King's Cross."

Jennifer giggled. "A novelty shop in King's Cross? Did you pay her by the hour in the back room?"

Dazza took that one. "He bloody well wanted to! But we had to get back to the ship before she sailed without us."

Charlie retorted, "You dickhead. You're the one we had to drag out of there." Directing his rebuttal at Jennifer, he continued. "Dazza met a sheila on the street that fancied him. She followed us into the shop. We'd paid for the bulb and went looking for him. Found 'em in a far corner, copping a feel. If not for the *Ortensia* sailing that day, we surely would've lost Dazza for the duration."

Tess finished the food Sparky had given her and took another stuffed fig off his plate. Suzy stopped her before she could eat it. "Wait! Save some room. We still have dessert!" Suzy asked Stevo to do the honors and pass around the tray of sweets.

Before eating the éclair she'd selected, Tess asked Sparky, "Do you fellas pick up girls on street corners often?"

Sparky laughed and looked to the others for help. "Mates, do we pick up sheilas on street corners often?"

Stevo answered first. "Not me. I usually find 'em in a pub." He put his arm around Suzy's shoulders. "Unless I get lucky on the ship, like I did tonight."

"You haven't gotten lucky yet, Stevo. But the night's still young." Suzy cuddled closer.

"I'm usually the one saying, 'Hello, Sailor.' " Morgy winked at Derrick. "That's why I work on a ship."

Pet picked up the ball. "Dazza obviously does. What about you, Charlie? Do you pick up women often?"

"As often as I can, Pet. But I'm not telling you anything you don't already know."

"Morgy told me I won the lottery for this voyage. Interesting how you select companions." Pet glanced at Suzy. "By the way, Suzy confirmed what you told me earlier."

It took Charlie a moment to get her meaning. Then he grinned. "I warned her, Suzy. Don't think she believed me. Thanks for proving me right."

"Right about what?" When Charlie didn't answer him, Stevo looked at Suzy. "What the hell is he talking about? Or is he just blowing hot air out his arse again?"

Pet encouraged her. "Go ahead, Suzy, tell them."

Suzy hesitated. "They have to swear it won't leave this room."

Charlie answered for the group. "We'll swear on a stack of Bibles! Tell them what you found out."

"I took Pet's place last night, and had dinner at the Captain's table—"

"You have a seat at the Captain's table? Aren't we upper crust!" Dazza interrupted.

His jibe didn't faze Pet. "I had a better invitation yesterday, just like I did today. Isn't that true, Charlie?"

"Bloody right it is." He nodded toward Suzy. "That's why she asked Suzy to take her place. The Captain wasn't happy when she turned him down."

Suzy continued her story. "After dinner last night, he took me on a tour of the bridge, and, well, he got a tiny bit frisky."

"And . . . ," Charlie spurred her on.

Suzy held up her pinky and wiggled it. "I discovered he's got a wee willy winkie."

The room exploded with laughter. Sparky choked on his drink and forcefully coughed. Tess slapped his back and scolded him. "You can't die on me, at least not until we get to London."

He managed to say, "At least if I do die, I know you won't be sleeping with the Captain."

Pet pointedly said, "From the looks of things tonight, none of us will."

Charlie leaned over and whispered into her ear, "Do you mean that?" Pet squeezed his thigh and nodded yes. He kissed her neck and then whispered, "We'll talk when everybody leaves."

"Hey, hey! None of that." Charlie raised his head and saw Dazza stand. "Morgy, help me get the pineapples set up, before Charlie and Pet start feeling each other up over there in the corner."

Morgy and Derrick had commandeered the other end of the bunk, beside Charlie and Pet. The other three couples sat on the floor. Morgy put his hand on Derrick's leg. "Trust me, darling, you'll want to sit this one out with me."

"Sit what out?"

"You'll see." Morgy slid off the bunk and joined Dazza. He then announced, "I volunteer to be the master of ceremonies. Derrick will be my assistant."

Dazza laughed. "Bloody coward. Don't want to get your togs mucked up. I can see that plain as day." Dazza went into the loo to retrieve the cooler.

"Dazza, has anybody ever told you you're smarter than you look?" Morgy yelled at the door. Then he held out his hand to help Derrick stand up. "Come, dear. You'll thank me for this in a few minutes."

"Charlie, what did Dazza mean about Morgy not getting his togs mucked up? What is this?"

"Remember when I told you not to wear your posh clothes tonight?"

"Yes, and none of us did. But I thought that was because we would be sitting on the floor."

"That's only part of it. You are about to find out the real reason."

Dazza handed Morgy the cooler, then ducked underneath the door frame to come back in the cabin. "What do you think, Morgy? We don't have a table. Will the two bowls sit on top of the cooler?"

"I think so. Let's give it a go."

Jennifer tugged on Dazza's trousers. "I want to help. Give me something to do." Charlie could tell she wanted an excuse to stay close to him.

Dazza opened the cooler and took out a bowl. "Here, hold one of these, and don't let it tip."

"What is it?"

"It's a hollowed-out pineapple."

"Feckin' 'ell, I can see that. What's in it?"

"Gin." Dazza handed Morgy the other bowl for safekeeping before he closed the lid. "Jen, set the one you have on top of the cooler first."

Jennifer carefully bent over and put the bowl down. The top of her dress gapped as she leaned over. Charlie got a good look, and noticed Dazza doing the same. Pet whispered to Charlie, "What is this, strip pineapple?"

Charlie put his arm around her waist and discreetly rubbed the underside of her breast with his thumb. Then he quietly said, "That's up to you ladies. If you want to strip, no one here will mind." He corrected himself. "Of course, don't know if Morgy and Derrick would."

Pet smiled. "They can always leave if it gets to be too much for them." Charlie already knew enough about Pet to appreciate her lack of modesty. He couldn't predict what she might do.

Morgy set his bowl beside the other one. In his best ringmaster voice, Morgy announced, "Ladies and gentlemen, please assume your positions around the bowls. We'll need two couples per pineapple, alternating male and female."

Tess asked Jennifer, "Do you know what this is all about?"

"Nope. I have no idea." Jen threaded her arm through Dazza's. "All I know is I'm sitting next to him."

Charlie grabbed Pet's hand. "C'mon. I want to make sure I'm sitting between you and Jen."

Once everyone settled in, Sparky, Tess, Dazza and Jennifer were around one bowl, and Charlie, Pet, Stevo and Suzy were around the other. As he hoped to do, Charlie sat between Jennifer and Pet.

"Derrick, be a love and get me the box of straws from that bag beside you." Morgy took the box and then said to Derrick, "Now, for your own safety, step inside the door of the loo."

Morgy quickly gave each of the eight participants a straw, then joined Derrick in the toilet. "Now, boys and girls, when I say, 'Heads down and suck,' you dip your straw into the pineapple and drink as much gin as you can."

Jennifer shouted, "That's brilliant!"

"Quiet, dear. I'm not finished."

Jen smiled sheepishly. "Sorry, I didn't know there was more."

Morgy continued his instructions. "Then, when I say, 'Heads up and clear your straw,' you will blow the contents of your straw onto the person to the right or to the left of you, as I tell you to do. This will continue until the pineapples are empty, or until you pass out, whichever comes first."

Pet looked genuinely surprised. "He can't be serious."

"Sure he is." Charlie grinned. "Why do you think I wanted to sit between you and Jen?"

Derrick yelled from over Morgy's shoulder, "Dear Petula, you've never had a problem being marinated in gin before."

Charlie agreed. "You even had some for brekkie today."

Pet shot back, "So did you, Mr. Third Assistant Engineer."

Sparky rubbed his hands together, as though warming them over a fire. "Bloody 'ell, this is already getting good!" He held his straw over the pineapple. "Let's get the ball rolling, Morgy."

Before he started the first round, Morgy asked Dazza to reach behind him and grab a couple of cups from the stack on the desk. He passed them around the circle to Sparky, who gave them to Morgy, who handed them off to Derrick.

Jennifer asked, "Are those part of the game, too?"

"Heavens no, dear. Those are so Derrick and I might enjoy the VSOP while the rest of you are being soaked in gin."

Dazza said to Jennifer, "Never thought of this as a game. It's more of a ritual."

"Sounds like an Aborigine initiation ritual. Do we all get to bathe together afterward?"

Charlie answered Jennifer before Dazza could. "The shower is small, but we could manage it, if you're inclined."

Rather than responding to Charlie, Jennifer spoke to Dazza. "I might be. We'll see."

Charlie felt Pet's hand on his leg. He glanced at her and realized she had noticed Jennifer's brush-off as much as he had. She leaned over and whispered softly into his ear, "Don't let it bother you."

He put his arm around her waist and murmured, "No worries."

"All right, group, listen up." Morgy had returned to his position just inside the door of the loo, cup in hand.

Sparky yelled, "Hey, Morgy, save some of that for the rest of us!"

"By the time you're done with those pineapples, you won't

know the difference between plonk and VSOP. It would be a waste of good brandy."

Derrick agreed with Morgy. "It takes a refined tongue to appreciate the bouquet."

Morgy fanned himself. "Be still my heart."

Stevo muttered, "Bloody 'ell!" Then he shouted, "Keep it in your pants, Morgy. The pineapples are melting. The bowls are filling up with gin."

"Derrick, the natives are getting restless. We'd best get them drinking." Derrick retreated farther into the loo. "Straws in the air. On the count of three, one, two, heads down and suck!"

With that command, everyone stuck their straws in a pineapple and sucked. Morgy gave them about five seconds, then yelled, "Heads up! Clear your straw on the person to your left."

Charlie blew his straw right into Pet's cleavage before she had a chance to turn to her left. Jen hit him in the side of the face with hers. One after the other, every person blew gin onto the person next to them. Morgy barely gave them all enough time to clear their straws before he said, "Heads down and suck."

When he again told them to blow, he instructed them to turn to the right. This time, Charlie blew on Jen. He aimed for her breasts, too, but he hit her neck when she turned to blow on Dazza. It still had the desired effect, when he saw the liquid trickle down her chest.

Pet blew on him. He felt something cold soaking into his trousers. She had emptied her straw on his dick. Rather than cooling him off, it gave him a boner.

Morgy again called "heads down." His next "heads up" went back to the left. Charlie forcefully shot the contents of his straw at the front of Pet's dress, hoping to soak it even more.

With each round, Morgy gave them a bit more time to drink

before a "heads up" call. Their clothes were streaked with gin, on the verge of being doused.

Suddenly Jen started to hiccup, and stopped drinking. Then she started to giggle. The more she giggled, the more intensely she hiccupped.

Dazza stopped drinking and tried to help. "Jen, hold your breath."

"I can't frigging"—she hiccupped again, then continued—"... hold my breath."

"Get a bag and put it over her head," Tess volunteered.

Sparky sniggered. "She's not nearly ugly enough for that."

In the meantime, Pet lifted her head and blew her straw right in Charlie's face. It startled him, and he jumped, bumping into Jen. Now, well beyond giggles, she fell down on the floor, laughing and hiccupping. Dazza went over with her, massaging her belly. "You've got to relax your diaphragm. It's spasming."

Stevo and Suzy had continued to drink through Jen's hysterical hiccupping. When he heard what Dazza said, Stevo had to throw in his suggestion. "Give her an orgasm. That'll stop them."

Charlie could hardly believe Stevo had suggested such a thing. "Shut the fuck up, Stevo. You're drunk."

Ignoring Charlie, Stevo put his arm around Suzy. "My Irish lass, wouldn't you like to see Dazza give Jen an orgasm? I know I sure as hell would."

"Maybe. It's up to Jen what she wants to do." Jennifer still lay on the floor, hiccupping. "Jen, honey, do you want Dazza to get you off?"

Jennifer didn't hesitate. In between hiccups, she said, "Bloody 'ell yeah!"

Before Charlie could object, Pet interceded. "We're all grown-ups here. If Jen doesn't object, I see no reason not to try that hiccup cure." She looked around the circle. "If anyone isn't into it, speak up now. You can leave, and no one will mind."

Sparky asked Tess, "Do you want to leave?"

"No fucking way! This is so hot, it's totally cool!"

"Beauty! You're my kind of woman." Sparky put his arm around Tess and settled in for the show.

Morgy spoke up from the doorway. "Derrick and I will sit this one out. Hope you'll have as much fun out there as we'll have in here." He stepped inside the loo and closed the door.

"Anybody else?" When no one answered, she looked directly at Charlie. "What about you, Mr. Third Assistant Engineer? Are you in?"

Charlie looked at Jen. He didn't have to ask Dazza if he wanted to participate. He had moved his hand from Jennifer's belly to her breasts. She still had the hiccups, but Charlie could see her already responding to Dazza rubbing her tits. Her skirt had crept up her thighs. She reached down and pulled it up even more.

He had a flashback to when they had all gone to the brothel in Hong Kong. They had watched live sex acts before each man had hooked up with a girl and went to a room. With the red light and the willing women, this had the same effect on him. Without taking his eyes off Jen, he nodded and said, "I'm in."

# 9

It seemed to Charlie that for Dazza and Jennifer, everyone else had disappeared. Jen had her eyes closed, and Dazza remained focused completely on Jennifer.

Charlie could feel the effects of the gin, as he supposed the others could. They were all more than a bit stonkered. Somehow the hazy buzz made this whole business even hotter. If Jen didn't mind providing some adult entertainment, why the hell should he?

Dazza tugged Jen's skirt up higher. Just before her panties could be seen, Pet interrupted. "Dazza, take her dress off. Jen won't mind, will you, Jen?"

Jennifer's answer to Pet's question was obvious to everyone when she sat up and tried to pull her dress over her head. Dazza intervened and helped her pull it off. She had nothing on underneath except her underpants.

When her tits tumbled free, Charlie heard a guttural rumble come from Dazza's throat, just before Dazza said, "Fuck, your tits are good ones."

Charlie had to admit, Dazza nailed it. Jen did have beautiful breasts. Sparky and Tess scooted closer to Stevo and Suzy to have a better view. Stevo said out loud what every man in the room wanted: "Make her come, Dazza. Make her come hard."

Pet leaned over and whispered into Charlie's ear, "She's naturally an exhibitionist, that's why she's such a brilliant model. She loves it when people look at her. If the people are men, all the better."

Jennifer definitely wasn't shy. From what he'd experienced with her the last couple of days, including her flashing Morgy that morning, Charlie knew Pet hit it spot-on.

Charlie glanced at the closed toilet door. He would no doubt get a report from Morgy about his time alone with Derrick. He shook himself out of considering what might be happening in there. He figured, *To each his own.* Morgy deserved some companionship, just like the rest of them did.

Pulling his attention back to Dazza and Jennifer, he saw Dazza whispering something to Jen, and then she nodded. She still had the hiccups, but she appeared too far gone to care.

Dazza propped himself up on his arm beside Jennifer and stretched out. He nearly kicked the cooler with the pineapples. Charlie signaled to Stevo to get it out of the way. With Suzy's help, they pulled the cooler back by the closet door.

The three couples sat in a semicircle around Dazza and Jennifer. Jen opened her legs wider as Dazza stroked the cloth of her underpants. Her leg bumped into Charlie's. She either didn't notice, or didn't care, as she made no attempt to adjust her position. Neither did Charlie.

As Dazza caressed her, Jen touched up her own breasts, first massaging them, then pinching her nipples. Charlie didn't want to break contact with her leg, but he had to shift his position. His erection was uncomfortably bunched in his trousers, and he had to do something about it.

He moved closer to Pet, hoping to discreetly straighten his

boner as he moved. Not only did Pet notice, but Jennifer shifted with him. Hopelessly wedged between the two women, he had no more space to move.

Charlie stifled a groan when he felt Pet's hand on him. Pet understood his difficulty. She gently adjusted him, then began stroking him. He had two choices, allowing her to wank him, or disrupting the whole scene and standing up.

He glanced at Sparky. Even in the dim red light, he could see Tess working him. Stevo and Suzy were behind him. He couldn't see them, but he could hear them. The sighs and whispers told him plenty. Damn straight his mates weren't paying any attention to him. They were otherwise occupied.

Jennifer twitched against his leg, and Charlie again focused on the sex show in front of him. Dazza had slipped his hand inside Jennifer's underpants. It startled Charlie to see Dazza had unzipped, and Jen had her hand inside his trousers. She still had her other hand on her breast.

Watching this Aborigine beauty and one of his best mates together took the prize as the hottest sex scene he had ever witnessed. He wondered how far they would go. Truth be told, he hoped they would fuck. That would be a real ripper, all right.

He felt Pet tugging at his zipper; then he heard her say, "Open it." He didn't want to be the only one with his donger hanging out, but, hell, Dazza had already unzipped. So Charlie obliged.

As soon as he opened his trousers, Pet reached in. She wasted no time. After untangling his dick from his undershorts, she completely exposed him. He also felt movement behind him. Stevo and Suzy had claimed his bunk. Sparky and Tess took advantage of the extra space and stretched out their legs.

Charlie slipped his hand under Petula's skirt as he quietly said, "This really is turning into a bloody orgy!"

"Isn't it frickin' brilliant!" With that enthusiastic comment,

Pet pulled her dress over her head. She had nothing on underneath.

Charlie couldn't believe it. He grabbed her dress and gave it back to her. "What the fuck do you think you're doing? Put this back on!"

Pet tossed the dress aside. "I'm getting into the spirit of things. Don't be so stuffy."

Dazza noticed first. "All right, Pet! Charlie, this is one ripsnorter of a party!"

From behind him, Charlie heard Stevo agree. "Bloody hell, you can say that again. Maybe the best one ever. Well done, mate." Sparky and Tess were too involved in each other to notice.

Pet continued to fondle him. "If we slide back a bit, we can lay on the floor."

Jennifer shifted as Dazza pulled her underpants off. Now both Jen and Pet were naked. Dazza lowered his trousers to his knees. Charlie knew what he meant to do. He said to Pet, "Wait. I want to see this."

"Well, now, Charles! You are inclined to watching, aren't you? I'll tuck that one away for future use." Pet unbuttoned his shirt. He didn't stop her.

"Never thought of myself as a Peeping Tom, but, fuck, this is hot!"

"I know it is, and so are you." As Charlie watched Dazza mount Jennifer, Pet opened his shirt and caressed his chest. "Frigging hell, Charlie! I want to eat you alive."

Pet's hands were all over him. She rubbed his chest and his belly before she again wrapped her hand around his prick. Charlie couldn't help it. He groaned, the sound mingling with Dazza's grunts. He'd seen enough. Now he wanted to fuck.

"Move back, Pet. Watch your head when you lie down. Be careful you don't whack it on the wall."

Pet slid backward. Charlie knelt and lowered his trousers, as Dazza had. He could see Stevo's bare arse as he humped Suzy. Tess had Sparky in her mouth. Charlie muttered, "Jesus Christ, looks like a frigging whorehouse in here."

He didn't care. His balls were about to pop. He needed a good fuck, and he knew Pet would give him one. Charlie practically fell on top of her. She wrapped her arms around his neck and pulled his face to hers.

"See anything you like, Sailor?"

"I'm not a sailor. I'm an engineer."

"Mr. Third Assistant Engineer, you're more of a man than any other I've ever met."

With that, Pet pulled his head down and kissed him, her smoldering heat enveloping him like a cloud. She spread her legs wide and Charlie entered her. He had himself a sheila to shag that stood head and shoulders above any other he had known.

For several minutes, the sounds of sex filled the room—groans, grunts, sighs and soft murmuring. Somewhere in the fog of his own arousal and the cloud of gin, Charlie heard Sparky tell Tess to take off her underpants, and to get down on her hands and knees. Since there wasn't enough room for her to lie on the floor, they went at it doggy-style.

Dazza and Jen finished first. Charlie heard Jen hiss like a spitting cobra, the same way she had with him. Then Dazza growled, "Fuck, yes!" Dazza's long legs bumped Charlie as Dazza thrashed with his ejaculation.

Pet heard it, too. Her hot breath singed his neck when she said, "Sounds like Jen took your mate over the moon. I'm going to do the same for you."

Charlie raised himself up on his hands and looked right into Pet's eyes. "No, my Pet, I'm going to do it to you."

Their eyes remained locked as Charlie fucked her. Pet's

pelvis rocked more than the ship did in rough surf. She grabbed his upper arms and held on, giving him total control over her body.

Charlie felt Dazza roll off Jennifer. A moment later, Dazza said, "Ride her, mate. Fuck her real good. These ladies love it!"

"We do when blokes like you feckin' horse it into us!"

Even when he heard Suzy's comeback, Charlie didn't slow down. He hadn't realized Stevo had finished, too. Maybe Sparky and Tess had as well, he didn't know. Charlie didn't care if they all watched him fuck Pet. At least his mates would know he could hold his own with a wild sheila.

Pet said what he already knew: "I think we have an audience."

"I don't give a shit. Do you?"

"Not at all. Let's show them how it's done." Without the slightest concern about the others watching them, Pet raised her knees to her chest. She pulled her legs back so much that he almost popped out of her. "Get up on your knees, Charlie. You'll fuck me deeper that way."

Sure enough, when he raised himself up on his knees, his prick slid back into her. "Shit, Pet, that's good." He placed his hands on the backs of her thighs, and leaned into her, pressing her legs against her breasts. Putting all his weight into it, he pounded her.

Pet reached between her legs and rubbed her clitoris while Charlie continued to fuck her. She suddenly arched her back and moaned. Charlie felt her pussy grab his cock as she lost herself in her orgasm. Forgetting about the others listening, he murmured, "That's right, my Pet, come for me. Fuck, yes! Baby, that's good!"

Charlie's knackers burned with his own need to come, but he held back until Pet had peaked. Then he cut loose, and banged her with everything he had. His balls boiled over, the hot liquid spilling into Pet.

No one said anything for a few minutes, which gave Charlie time to catch his breath. He pulled himself out of Pet, and quickly tucked his business back into his trousers and zipped up. Pet's dress was under the desk. He grabbed it and tossed it at her.

"You might want to put this back on before Morgy and Derrick come out. You'll give them a heart attack."

"Thanks, stud."

"You're welcome, party girl."

Once everyone had themselves together, Sparky knocked on the toilet door. "Hey, Morgy. I have to take a whiz."

From inside the loo, Morgy yelled, "Is everyone decent out there?"

Sparky looked around. "No naked women, if that's what you're asking."

When Morgy opened the door, the bright light from the loo made everyone squint. Morgy and Derrick came out, both looking totally together. "Bloody hell, it reeks of sex out here."

Sparky went into the loo. "It does in here, too, mate." He closed the door, and once again, only the red light lit the room.

There wasn't much food left. Everyone filled a plate of leftovers to finish it off. Morgy promised to pick up the trays in the morning. Stevo also left his red lightbulb and reel-to-reel for tomorrow.

All the men had to report for duty the next day, and they needed to get some rest. Sparky and Tess were the first to leave, followed by Stevo and Suzy. Charlie knew they would get the ladies safely back to their cabins. They knew the drill.

Morgy didn't want any of the leftover food. He only wanted a bottle of brandy to take back to his cabin. When he left with Derrick, Charlie figured their party would continue in Morgy's cabin.

That only left Dazza and Jen. It surprised Charlie when Jennifer hugged him and gave him a kiss on the cheek. "Thank you, Charlie, for a glorious night, and for a great hiccups cure. It's a party I'll surely never forget."

"I'll second that, mate." Dazza came over and shook Charlie's hand. "Don't know how you found these sheilas, but bloody glad you did." He then turned to Pet. "Charlie has watch at eight o'clock. I'm his boss. He'll catch hell from me if he's late."

"And I'm Jen's boss. I expect her to be at my cabin at eight o'clock to plan our social calendar for the rest of the voyage. She'll catch hell from me if she's late."

Dazza grinned. "Is that true, Jen? Pet's your boss."

"Fuck, yeah! She's Petula Kinlan."

"Who?"

The belly laugh came out of Charlie's mouth before he could stifle it. "That's brilliant! He doesn't know who you are, either!"

Pet put her arm through Charlie's. "If you all are allowed off this ship for an evening, once we dock in London, I'll have my girls give you a private show. Then you can see for yourselves what I do."

Dazza looked at Jen, then at Pet. "Your girls? What are you, a madam?"

Charlie grinned. "Is that what you are, Pet, a madam?"

"Fuck you both! I have to use the loo." Pet stormed into the toilet and slammed the door.

"Shit, Charlie, she's pissed off again!"

"No worries, Jen. I'll take care of her."

"All right, then. If she's in a good mood by morning, I'll know why." With that, Dazza and Jennifer took their plates and left.

While Charlie waited for Pet, he stacked the trays and the hatboxes on the desk. He hadn't had any dessert, so he helped himself to a pastry from the batch Morgy had piled on a plate.

Pet took her good, sweet time coming out of the loo. When she finally did, he couldn't read her frame of mind.

"Jen and Dazza left?"

"Yup, a few minutes ago."

Pet sat down on his bunk, seemingly in no hurry to leave. She glanced at his alarm clock. "It's only eleven. The night's still young."

"Some of us have to work tomorrow."

"You don't think what I do is work, do you?"

Charlie leaned against his desk and studied Pet. "Why are you so frigging worried about what I think?"

"Because I'm as proud of my work as you are of yours. Just because I don't know anything about engines doesn't mean I don't respect what you do."

"You think I don't respect what you do?"

"Do you?"

She had him there. Whatever thought he had given to it, which wasn't much, had been along the lines of drawing pretty pictures and playing dress-up. He'd never considered it to be actual work. He answered as honestly as he could. "Don't know if I do. You earn a good living at it. I guess it must be a decent job."

"In all seriousness, when we get to London, would you let me show you what I do? I'll take you all on a tour of my business, and have Jen, Suzy and Tess model some of my clothes."

Charlie considered the offer. "We'll be docked for a few days. I expect we can all get shore leave. But we have to keep it quiet what we're doing."

"I promise we will."

"Is Morgy invited, too?"

"Of course, he is! Derrick is already arse over kettle for Morgy. He'd never forgive me if I didn't include him."

"I can't promise Dazza, Stevo and Sparky will want to come along."

"If you tell them Jen, Suzy and Tess will be their dates for the night, I think they will."

"You really care about what I think of you, don't you?"

"I really do. If we're going to keep seeing each other, it has to be as equals. That means you can't trivialize what I do. I don't want to be above you, or below you, unless we're in bed."

"You're an interesting sheila. If you weren't so frigging sexy, I'd think you were one of my mates."

"Precisely! That's what I want, to get the same respect from you that you have for your mates. I want to be part of your inner circle, not just another sheila."

"Pet, I knew from the first time I saw you that you weren't just another sheila." Charlie glanced at his alarm clock, thinking about having to get up in the morning. "Do you want me to take you back to your cabin?"

"I'd rather spend the night with you and go back in the morning."

Charlie went and sat beside her on the bunk. "That can be arranged, if you don't mind waking up at seven."

"I don't mind." Pet put her hand on his thigh. "Are you good for one more before we go to sleep?"

"Depends."

"On what?"

"On you lying across my lap."

"I don't understand."

"Let me spell it out for you. I want to hike up your skirt and paddle your arse until I get hard. Then I'll think about fucking you again."

Pet laughed. "Paddling my arse will make you hard?"

"Sure as hell worked this morning. But I have to make sure it wasn't a one-time deal."

"Do you know how many men would love to be in your shoes, and smack my arse?"

"No. How many?"

"Plenty."

Pet stretched out across Charlie's lap like a cat settling in for a nap. He pulled up her skirt, her bare arse pink and inviting. Using his hand, as he had that morning, Charlie slapped her bum. Pet yelped and squirmed against his leg. His prick thickened with the second smack, and it rubbed against her side with the third.

Charlie glanced at his poster. Maybe Pet would let him replace it with a picture of her. If anyone asked, he could tell them Petula Kinlan gave it to him personally.

Bloody hell, Petula Kinlan wanted to be his sheila! That was more than a bit of all right.

# SOUTHERN SEAMAN

# 1

As Buck followed his shipmates down the gangway, he wondered what he had gotten himself into. His buddy Sam had asked if he'd ever had a Frenchwoman. When Buck told him no, Sam decided he needed an education.

Buck had never been to France. In fact, he'd never left Savannah, Georgia, until he signed on with the Blue Star Line and went to sea. After he got his promotion to the rank of Able Seaman, they had transferred him to a new ship, the *Halifax Star*.

He had only been on her two months, when she had to be docked at a repair yard in Marseilles. They would probably be there for a week to ten days, to have a bent cargo derrick fixed. That's when Sam decided they had time to indulge in some local entertainment. He had asked Buck to come with him. Being the First Mate, Sam had the authority to get Buck a shore pass.

When they reached the dock, there was a disagreement between Sam and the older Chief Engineer on where to go. Both Sam and Pete had been to Marseilles before, and each had a favorite place. Sam angrily defended his choice.

"Buck needs some entertainment before we end up at the goddamned whorehouse. This cabaret strip club I went to a year ago is the best fucking show I've ever seen. I'm telling you, the girls are hot." Sam winked at Buck. "Last time I went, they did the cancan topless, with nothing on under their skirts."

Pete tugged at his crotch. "Yeah, well, I haven't had any for three months. My balls are about to bust. I need more than watching some French babe flash her pussy at me."

Sam wouldn't back down. "Hell, Pete, I'll pay one of the dancers at the club to jerk you off. They do that there, if you know who to ask."

"You know who to ask?"

"Yeah. The waitress will arrange it, if you slip her something."

"I'd like to slip her something." Pete closed his large fist and pumped the air. "But, if you're paying, I'll settle for a hand job until one of Madame Séduisant's girls can give me a ride."

Buck said nothing while the other two sailors wrangled about where to go. Whenever the conversation turned to women, he usually sat quietly and listened. He loved hearing the old sea dogs tell stories of their adventures in brothels and bars. A girl in every port seemed to be a way of life for them. Truth be told, he really hadn't had much experience with women, but he didn't want them to know that.

From day one on the ship, Sam had taken Buck under his wing. Sam was also from the South. He hailed from Charleston, South Carolina. Sam was the only one who had figured out Buck didn't know much about women.

Buck agreed to go with Sam, not knowing the burly Chief Engineer would also be going with them. There weren't many Americans on board. Pete lived near Houston, and often latched onto Sam, and now Buck, because they also were Americans. Buck didn't like Pete, and tried to avoid him when possible. He decided that might be his best choice now.

"If y'all don't mind, I'm gonna pass on this one." Buck took off his baseball cap and stuffed it into his back pocket. Then he turned and headed back up the gangway. Sam grabbed his arm.

"Hey, where the hell are you going? We're doing this for you."

"Yeah, well, it seems like the engine's runnin', but nobody's driving. I'd just as soon sleep tonight." Buck again turned to leave.

This time, Pete stepped in. "Buck, didn't your daddy ever tell you excuses are like backsides? Everybody's got one, and they all stink. Now get your stinkin' ass back down here. We're going to find us some women!"

Buck glanced at Sam. He knew if he didn't go, Sam would be stuck alone with Pete all night. He reluctantly turned around and joined the other two men on the dock.

Pete slapped him on the back. "Now that's more like it! Son, we're going to get you a Frenchie tonight, and give you something to write home about."

Buck put his cap back on and muttered, "Can't wait." He really didn't want to go. Not giving him a chance to change his mind again, Sam headed across the dock toward La Canebière.

Pete hustled after him, with Buck following. "Jesus, Sam, where's the fire?"

"In my shorts. Don't want to miss the beginning of the first show."

"Where're we going, anyway?"

"Le Club de Plaisir. It's up yonder a little ways, right off Can o' Beer."

"How far up Canebière?"

"Not far. It's about a ten-minute walk."

"Madame Séduisant's is close to the train station, on Rue Lafayette."

"That's a few blocks from the club. I know the street, but don't remember seeing a whorehouse on it."

"For Christ's sake, they don't advertise it! You gotta know where it is to find it."

"You've got a nose like a frigging bloodhound. You probably sniffed it out."

Pete grinned. "In Texas, they teach you two things, how to fight and how to find a whorehouse. Never forgot how to do both."

"Well, buddy, I'll go to the whorehouse with ya, but I don't have a mind to fight. I'd rather fuck."

Sam had a way with Pete. Most of the time, Buck felt like he was about three steps away from getting beaten up by Pete. Sam could get him to act civilized with a joke and a friendly slap on the back. Buck sure as hell didn't want to fight. He would follow Sam's lead tonight, and try to keep things light. So he decided to tell a story.

"Did I ever tell y'all about my Uncle Bubba winnin' a ham?"

Sam lit a cigarette as they walked along La Canebière. "Don't think so."

"Well, Uncle Bubba and Aunt Minnie went to the county fair last summer. A bunch of Uncle Bubba's drinkin' buddies were crowded round a booth that was auctioning off hams. When Uncle Bubba asked why all the excitement over some hams, they told him Jimmy, the guy who owned the pig farm, would give his biggest ham to the man with the longest donger.

"Uncle Bubba told Aunt Minnie he wanted to enter the contest. When Aunt Minnie told him she didn't want him pulling his pecker out in front of all those people, Uncle Bubba smiled and told her, 'Not all of it, honey, just enough of it to win us that big ham.'"

It surprised him when Pete guffawed. "Son, if it runs in the family, you'll have the mademoiselles fighting over you tonight. You can give the ones you don't want to me."

Sam grinned. "Pete's right. They'll be crawling all over you like fleas on a dog."

At least, Buck had them believing he could hold his own in a whorehouse, even if he didn't think he had a snowball's chance in hell of doing it. Maybe if he got drunk enough at the club, he'd pass out, and they'd just carry him back to the ship.

Buck thought to ask his companions what he considered to be an important question. "I sure as shit hope one of you can communicate with these folks. I couldn't talk my way out of a paper bag in French."

"Pete cut his teeth in Cajun country. Met him in New Orleans, before we sailed together. He can get by on his Creole French."

"Hell yeah. If I can't find somebody who speaks English, I can get my meaning across. If you know how to say 'toilet,' 'beer' and 'women,' you'll get what you need."

It surprised Buck to hear they had known each other so long. "Then you two go back a ways?"

"I met Sam here about six years ago, at the Port of New Orleans, rounding up stevedores to unload containers full of coffee from his ship."

Sam grinned. "After Pete helped me find the manpower we needed, we went to the French Quarter. Ended up in a whorehouse that night, too."

"Those ladies know how to fuck. There's nothing like a French Quarter whore to clear your sinuses."

Despite Pete's abrasiveness, Buck had to laugh. "Is that what y'all pay a whore to do, clear your sinuses?"

"Junior, she can clear all my pipes, and I won't complain."

Sam agreed. "I'll second that. Being with a lady who knows her way around the equipment makes getting laid hotter than a firecracker on the Fourth of July."

"You fellas been to a lot of whorehouses?" Buck had to admit, he was curious.

"Sure, haven't you?"

"Only had 'em off the street, never in a bunch." Buck didn't lie. He had paid a hooker once for a blow job. "Must be a real kick in the ass to have a room full to pick from."

Sam elbowed him in the side. "It's like havin' the pick of the litter. You want one that's friendly and willin' to please."

Pete added, "Yeah, but make sure her nose is dry and her pussy is wet."

Even though Buck knew Pete's vulgar mouth followed him everywhere, he still had a hard time putting up with it. "I hope you don't say shit like that to them. No matter what, they're still women."

Sam again diffused the tension. "Hell, Buck, when he walks into a house, he's polite as a preacher on Sunday."

Buck pressed his advantage. "That true, Pete?"

"My mama raised me to treat women right. Don't matter to me how they earn their livin'." Pete ran his fingers through his hair, then stuffed his hand in his pocket. "Thing is, they don't look down on sailors. That's my kind of woman."

Buck had to agree. "Yeah, I know. The women I knew back home took a hike when they found out I signed on with a merchant ship."

"Damn, that's the truth." Sam flicked his cigarette butt in the gutter. "All the women I knew in Charleston are married and have kids now."

Buck muttered more to himself than to his buddies, "Gets kinda lonely, doesn't it?"

Pete answered before Sam did. "Sure as hell does. At least you boys will probably go ashore and get married someday. No respectable woman would want an old dog like me."

Sam laughed. "Don't be too sure about that, Pete. My mama has some widow friends that might warm up to you—that is, if you take a bath and shave once in a while."

Buck had the impulse to duck, in case Pete took a swing at Sam for that crack. Instead, Pete seemed interested.

"Are you shittin' me, or are you serious?"

"I'm serious. Mama has asked me a couple of times if I know anybody that wanted to meet some of her friends. Didn't think you'd be interested, or I would've asked you before."

"I might be interested. We'll talk before we get back to Charleston." Pete stared up the street. "Where the hell is this place, Sam? Don't see nothing up ahead that looks like a club."

"Don't get your dick in a twist. It's right up here, around the corner."

They walked quietly for a few minutes. Buck took the opportunity to look around a bit. There was still enough daylight to see the old buildings, most between four and six stories high. The only things taller were the church steeples, jutting against the skyline ahead.

The street seemed to run straight as an arrow into the heart of Marseilles. Lots of folks passing them had shopping bags. If Buck could get Pete to translate for him, maybe he could get some souvenirs before they left port.

Sam abruptly turned the corner. Buck had been gawking around and overshot the turn. He hurried to catch up with Sam and Pete, who already stood in front of the club.

"Christ, Sam, don't you believe in turn signals?" Buck tried not to appear flustered, but he didn't quite manage it.

"Can't help if you weren't paying attention." Fortunately, both Sam and Pete were more interested in the club than his awkwardness. Sam asked Pete, "So what do you think, my friend?"

Pete eyed the pictures of the scantily clad dancers on the sign. "They strip?"

"Oh, yeah, they sure as hell do. I'll put cash on the table to see that cancan again."

Buck slapped his pocket where he kept his wallet. "Shit, guys. I didn't change any money. I don't have any francs."

Pete laughed and slapped his back. "Damn, boy, you're so green I bet your pecker looks like an unripe banana."

Sam grinned. "He'll ripen up after tonight." Sam took out his wallet and checked inside. "Don't sweat it, Buck. I brought enough to cover both of us. You can pay me back later. Anyway, I'm sure they can change money at the places we're going tonight, if we need more."

"What about me?" Pete crossed his burly arms across his chest.

"I said I'd pay for a hand job, and a few beers. You're on your own for whatever else."

"Good enough. I brought enough to cover whatever else."

Sam led the way inside. He paid the cover charge to get them in, telling Pete he would pay for him, too, if he would keep his mouth shut during the show. Pete agreed.

The hostess, who spoke some English, led them to a table close to the stage. Sam ordered a round of beer. Buck didn't know what to expect. He stuffed his cap back in his pocket, settled in and had a look around.

Le Club de Plaisir looked like a burlesque house his brother had taken him to in Atlanta. It had the same gaudy decorations. Big artificial flower arrangements lined the walls. The stage curtains looked like the kind they had at the funeral parlor back home, except these curtains were fire engine red. Buck considered telling the undertaker he should consider the red curtains instead of the dark green ones. They sure as hell would brighten up the place.

The waitress brought their beer. Buck tried to ignore the fact his prick came to attention when she bent over to set his glass on the table. Her breasts practically touched his face, and her cleavage, Lord Almighty, it was so deep a man could drown in it.

He could smell her. She smelled like his grandma's flower garden when all the flowers bloomed at once. She had a pretty face, too, and nice eyes, which lit up when she smiled at him. Buck shifted in his chair. He definitely had a hard-on rubbing against his leg.

Pete noticed her chest, too. He watched her walk away and muttered, "She has great tits. Maybe I should follow her and see if she'll jerk me off."

Buck flared. "Fuck that shit, Pete. She's a waitress. Sam said the dancers do that, not the waitresses." The idea of having her hands on Pete made Buck's stomach roll.

"So what is she, your sister?" Pete took a swallow of beer.

Buck held his ground. "Let's wait and see the dancers. My daddy always said to throw the first one back. It always brought him luck."

"Buck's right, Pete. Let me talk to the waitress. She spoke English when she took our order. Don't want you getting us thrown out of here."

Before Pete had a chance to argue with them about the waitress, a loud drumroll announced the beginning of the show. All three men looked toward the stage as a swell of music filled the room.

When the curtain went up, a single dancer stood in the middle of the stage. All she seemed to have on were feathers, and just enough of them to cover the indecent parts. She even had feathers on her head. Buck thought she looked like a giant peacock.

There were wide, empty stairs behind her. Opening her arms in a welcoming gesture, she greeted the audience. "*Bon soir. Bienvenue au Club de Plaisir.*"

When she turned around, her bare ass cheeks jiggled like Jell-O as she walked up the stairs. Buck again had to shift in his chair, his erection already becoming damned uncomfortable.

Sam tapped Buck's shoulder and whispered, "Wait until you see this!"

As Buck watched, the stairs seemed to fill with white feathers. Huge, billowing birds seemed to float toward the stage. Except these birds had legs—long, beautiful legs.

Sam again whispered to him. "This is the fan dance. Nearly made me come in my shorts when I saw it last year." Buck again adjusted his position, wondering if he actually would.

The dancers on the stage all opened their fans at the same time. They wore the same minimal plumage as the first dancer. Buck only caught a quick glimpse of the nearly bare women before they again covered themselves with the feather fans.

He braced himself for when they turned around. Sure enough, they wore the same G-strings, and their bare bums were as round and full as the first dancer's. Buck considered excusing himself. He needed to find a toilet and jerk off.

As the women swayed and dipped to the music, fanning themselves all the while, Buck tried to distract himself. He glanced at Pete, who hadn't said a word since the curtain went up. Buck saw Pete's arm moving ever so slightly, and realized Pete wasn't waiting for after the show. He was jacking off under the table.

He wondered how Sam could handle it. When he turned around to ask him, Sam wasn't there. Buck hadn't heard him leave. He looked around and spotted him at the bar, talking to the waitress that had served them. Buck saw Sam gesturing to their table and making a circular motion with his hand. Figuring Sam had just gotten up to order another round, Buck again focused on the dancers.

Small piles of feathers lay on the stage. Buck missed how they got there. When the dancers waved their fans from side to side, he realized what he had missed. They were all topless! He had never seen so many bare tits at the same time.

Like swans floating on water, the dancers flapped their wings, each time showing their breasts a bit longer. They suddenly stopped in a single line and dropped their feather fans on the stage. Buck murmured, "Jesus Christ!" as they intertwined their arms and started doing high kicks in unison.

Wearing nothing but flimsy feather G-strings and feathers in their hair, a dozen women kicked and squealed in a burlesque chorus line, the likes of which Buck had never seen. He didn't know where to look, with so many legs lifting and boobs bouncing.

He heard Sam yell, "Oh, yeah, mama!" and then whistle. Other men in the theatre joined Sam, clapping and whistling. Even with the music and raucous noise, Buck heard Pete grunt. Without thinking twice about it, Buck handed him a napkin. Pete had just finished his first round.

The dancers kicked for several more minutes, before bending over to pick up their fans. As they stood up, they simultaneously took off their feather G-strings and stood stark naked for a moment, before covering themselves with their fans. Then they turned around, wiggled their bare bums at the crowd and took off up the stairs. They disappeared into the wings at the top of the stairs.

Pete turned around and asked Sam, "Is that it?"

"Fuck, no, man! They're just getting warmed up. Last time, a couple of women came out and stripped before they did the cancan number. I really liked one act where a clown watched a woman undress and got all hot and bothered."

Sure enough, Sam called it. A woman came out dressed like a French streetwalker, in a short black skirt and a striped midriff shirt that didn't completely cover her tits. Buck could see garters attached to black stockings. A stagehand wheeled out a lamppost for her to lean against.

What Buck didn't see coming was what she would do with the streetlight. A man walked by. To get his attention, the stripper lifted her skirt. When he didn't seem to notice her, she lifted her skirt higher and wrapped her legs around the lamppost. She wasn't wearing any underwear.

In rhythm to the sexy music, she undulated against the pole. Buck couldn't believe it when the man came up behind her and pulled her shirt off. Then he yanked her skirt and it came off. That left her only in spike heels, her garter belt and black stockings.

She continued to rub against the pole as the man fondled her. Buck couldn't help it. He reached under the table and stroked himself while he watched the couple's provocative act.

Buck had never actually seen a woman have an orgasm. When the woman started to quiver and shake, she shouted, "*Je jouis!*"

Sam muttered, "Fuck, yes! She's coming!"

Buck watched, totally mesmerized. The Frenchwoman rubbed the pole like his dog used to rub against his leg. The man behind her bumped her ass with his groin and squeezed her tits. Suddenly he growled, "*Mon Dieu!*" as he, too, appeared to come. Then the stage went dark.

In the dark, Buck heard Sam say, "Shit, never saw that one before!"

Pete echoed, "The only thing he didn't do was stick it in!"

Buck remained silent. When the stage lights came back on, the clown act Sam had described came on. In this one, a hobo on the street saw a woman undressing through her bedroom window. Behind him, a woman standing in an empty window frame slowly undressed. The hobo was beside himself, watching her.

Once she was completely undressed, the nude woman sat on the windowsill to brush her hair. The hobo hid behind the same lamppost left on the stage from the scene before. As he watched the woman, he pretended the lamppost was her, and he began to make love to it, kissing it and caressing it.

When she saw him, she played along, acting the exhibitionist to the hobo's voyeur. She gave the man on the street a show, caressing herself and doing nasty things with the hairbrush. The hobo clown dropped his baggy pants, revealing polka-dot boxer shorts with a huge bulge inside.

Buck had been watching intently, and jumped when Pete guffawed and slapped the table with his palm. He muttered under his breath, "That's how my prick has felt all night!" Buck had to admit, he felt the same way.

When the houselights went down again, Sam leaned over and whispered, "The cancan number is next. We'll hook up with a few ladies when it's over."

Buck didn't know how much more he could take. He picked up his beer and downed it in one long chug. His boner throbbed against his leg. The chances of his making it through more naked women on the stage—without creaming his skivvies—were slim to none.

The same line of dancers from the fan dance came back to the stage. This time, they were already topless, wearing colorful floor-length skirts. Buck recognized the music as the band played the cancan for the dancers. The women lifted their skirts, revealing the petticoats underneath. Just as Sam had said, they had nothing else on.

Buck had to close his eyes for a moment. The sight of a dozen bare naked women flashing their pussies nearly pushed him over the edge. He gritted his teeth and hung on, trying to think of anything but naked women.

The women started to squeal. He opened his eyes just in time to see them, one right after the other, doing full splits on the floor, with their skirts up around their waists. Sam again whistled and shouted, "Spread 'em wide, girls, that's how we like it!"

Pete clapped loudly and added, "Bring it on home, ladies. Let's see some heinie!"

Just as the last dancer hit the floor in a full split, the first dancer got up, turned around and threw her skirt over her head.

With her legs spread wide, she mooned the audience and squealed. The rest of the dancers followed suit, until all twelve had their butts in the air, and their pussies open wide.

"Jesus Christ, I want to fuck one of them." Pete pushed his chair back. Sam jumped up and grabbed him before he could get up.

"Whoa, Pete. Hold your horses. You're getting the one on the end, and I'm getting the one next to her. I've already paid for it."

Pete settled down. "They damn well better do it soon. My dick's about to split in half."

Buck's prick felt the same way, and Sam hadn't said anything about getting him a dancer. He squelched the urge to ask, "What about me?"

# 2

When the show ended, the three men sat at their table and waited. Buck still hadn't asked what Sam arranged for him, if anything. Part of him didn't want to know, one way or the other.

Sam kept glancing toward the bar. "The waitress said she would give me a signal when the girls were ready."

Buck finally found his voice. "Where we going, anyway?"

"See that door by the bar? There's a bunch of little rooms back there. That's where the girls go after the show." Sam turned and grinned at Buck. "By the way, you get the waitress."

Buck couldn't hide his disbelief. "Y'all are shittin' me, right?"

"Hey, I'm not lyin' to ya! I tried to get you one of them." Sam pointed to the stage. "But the waitress said no. Don't know what the hell she sees in *y'all*, but she wants you for her-self."

"Damn!" Buck picked up his glass to have a drink, but he had already drained it. In fact, he had two empty glasses. He didn't even remember getting the second one, but he must have. He drank it.

Pete chuckled. "Well, boy, I hope she's not your sister. Don't think that's legal, even in France."

Sam coached the other two men. "Now let's get this straight. We'll have half an hour with the girls. And remember, they don't fuck here. The bouncer will throw your ass out on the street if that's what you try to get. I paid for a hand job for you and me, Pete. Buck's is on the house."

Buck couldn't believe his ears. "What did you say?"

"The pretty mademoiselle offered. I took her up on it. Didn't think you'd mind."

Pete took that one to the bank. "Jesus Christ, son. Maybe I should rub your dick like a rabbit's foot. Maybe some of whatever you got will come my way, too."

Buck shot back, "You touch my dick, I'll kick your ass so hard you'll have to take off your shirt to shit!"

Pete chortled. "Now that's more like it. Good to see your daddy didn't raise no sissy boy." He put his arm around Buck's shoulders and leaned in close to his ear. "I'm bettin' your daddy also didn't raise no fool. We both know I could whup your ass, if ever I had a mind to, that is."

Well beyond being scared of Pete tonight, Buck turned his head so his nose almost touched Pete's. "If you got yourself a can of whup ass, bring it on over, 'cause I got the can opener."

Sam pushed them apart. "Nobody's whupping anybody's ass. C'mon, Mademoiselle Waitress is waving us over to the door."

Pete was up and on his way to the bar before Buck got out of his chair. Sam took the opportunity to speak quietly to Buck. "Buddy, don't let Pete get under your skin. He's blown hot air out of his asshole ever since I've known him. When he tries to get a rise out of you, joke with him, like I do. He'll back off."

"Don't understand how the two of you are friends, Sam. You ain't nothin' alike."

"I'll explain it sometime. Right now, we got us some women waitin'. Let's go."

Sam and Buck caught up with Pete at the bar. Buck didn't see the waitress. "Where'd she go?"

Pete pointed to the door by the bar. "She went in there."

Sam led the way, and Pete followed close behind. Buck waited until they went in; then he brought up the rear. His companion introduced herself.

"*Bon soir, messieurs.* I am Giselle. You are?"

Sam introduced them. "My name is Sam. This is Pete. And this is Buck."

"How lovely to meet you. My English is good enough, I hope?"

Sam smiled. "It's fine, mademoiselle."

"Have you visited Le Club de Plaisir before?"

"I have. My friends haven't. In fact, this is Buck's first time in France."

She asked Buck, "You are on holiday?"

Buck cleared his throat before he answered. "No, ma'am. We're sailors. Our ship is docked for repairs." He tried not to stare at her cleavage.

"While you are at Le Club de Plaisir, you are on holiday. Come, let me show you to your rooms."

She led them down a hall to a series of rooms. She spoke to Pete first. "Monsieur Pete, this is your room. Antoinette is waiting inside." Pointing to the next room, she said to Sam, "Monsieur, Desirée is waiting there for you. *Amusez-vous!*"

Just before Sam disappeared into his room, he grinned and said, "I'll meet you both out front when we're done."

"See you later." Both Pete and Sam left for their French rendezvous, leaving Buck alone in the hall with Giselle.

"Monsieur Buck, follow me, please." Giselle led him to a room farther down the hall. She held the door open, directing him inside. After closing the door, she sat down on a love seat, just big enough for two people to sit closely together. Buck remained standing.

Giselle patted the seat beside her. "Sit, *s'il vous plaît.*"

Buck nearly turned tail and left. But she patted the seat again, and smiled. Something about that smile bolstered his confidence. He cautiously sat down beside her, sitting as though the cushion were covered with tacks.

"Monsieur Buck, you must relax." Giselle took his hand.

Buck had to ask. He couldn't do this unless he understood. "Giselle, why me? You're a waitress. You don't have to do this sort of thing."

Giselle put her other hand on his thigh. "You are correct, monsieur. I do not have to do this." She slid her hand closer to his groin. "But I saw you are not like the others that come to Le Club de Plaisir."

"How do you know that?"

"Your cheeks flushed when I served you. You wanted to look inside my dress, but instead, you looked into my eyes, and you smiled."

"I did?"

"Yes, Monsieur Buck, you did."

"You smell good."

Giselle laughed. "The smell of a woman pleases you?"

"When they smell like you, it does."

Giselle's hand moved again. Buck tensed. "Monsieur, if you do not want to be touched, I will honor your wish."

Buck closed his eyes and took a deep breath. His prick had been rock hard for over an hour. If Giselle didn't do it, he would have to do it himself. He quietly said, "I want to be touched."

Giselle lifted his hand to her breast. *"S'il vous plaît,* touch me while I touch you."

Buck looked at this kind woman in utter disbelief. "You would let me touch your tits? God, I'm sorry, I mean your breasts?" His face burned like he had been in the sun for days.

Giselle didn't answer. Instead, she untied the small string that held the front of her dress closed and tugged it open. Her bare breasts tumbled out.

Buck looked into her eyes and saw the same gentleness he had seen when she served them. He slowly tilted his head, so he could really look at her tits. As he stared in wonderment at the most glorious breasts he had ever seen close up, he whispered, "Giselle, you are so beautiful."

"Monsieur, touch them. I want you to touch me."

Buck stroked her breast with his fingertips, then cupped the weighty flesh in the palm of his hand. At the same time, Giselle reached for the zipper on his pants. He didn't stop her as she opened his fly and slipped her hand inside.

She touched him so gently, he wasn't sure she had touched him at all. Then she closed her hand around his erection. Buck squeezed her tit and moaned, the feel of her hand on him nearly as heavenly as the softness of her breast.

Buck noticed Giselle's chest moving under his hand as her breath deepened. Reacting to his instinct, Buck leaned over and kissed her breast. She didn't push him away. He kissed her again, then found the dark pink nub of her nipple. He sucked it into his mouth.

She somehow managed to untangle his cock from his skivvies and pulled it out of his fly. She pumped him as he suckled her. Even though she spoke in a breathless whisper, Buck still heard what she said. "Monsieur, touch under my skirt, the excitement aches me."

Even though her English didn't quite make sense, Buck still

understood. She was hurting just like him, and wanted to come. He'd never brought a woman off before, but that didn't seem to matter now. He lifted her skirt and slid his hand up her bare thigh until he touched her panties.

Without any hesitation, he pushed the crotch aside and slipped his finger into the damp crevice. Giselle moaned, just as he had when she touched him.

Buck had nearly reached the point of no return as Giselle rubbed against his fingers. But more than wanting his own orgasm, he wanted to make her come.

His buddies called the middle finger their fuck finger, and said they used their thumb to rub the love nub. Gathering as many wits as he could muster, he deliberately pushed his middle finger deep into Giselle's body and massaged her clitoris with his thumb.

She thrashed against his hand, and scraped her nipple between his teeth. Suddenly her grip tightened on his cock and she grunted. Her cunt squeezed his finger as she lost herself in her climax.

Sucking her tit like a newborn calf, he held his finger inside her and cut loose. He ejaculated into her hand, spilling semen onto his pants and splashing her leg. Never in his whole life had an orgasm felt as good as this one did with Giselle. The tingles went on and on as his prick finally got some relief.

Buck released her nipple from his mouth, and rested his head on her bare breast. He needed a few minutes to get his wind back, as did Giselle. She stroked his hair, then murmured something he didn't quite hear.

He lifted his head. "I'm sorry, Giselle, I didn't hear what you said."

"It is I that am sorry, Monsieur Buck. The time is nearly gone. I must go back." She picked up a towel from beside the love seat. "You should clean yourself."

"Damn, I made a mess, didn't I?" He took the towel. Before he cleaned himself, he took Giselle's hand and wiped it, then gently dabbed her leg. Only then did he rub the white drops on his pants.

Giselle stood and closed her dress. "Monsieur, I hope you have enjoyed your holiday at Le Club de Plaisir."

Buck also stood. He knew what he wanted to say, but couldn't manage it. All he could get out was, "*Merci*, Giselle." Then he leaned over and kissed her on the cheek.

"Your friends are probably waiting for you." She turned to leave.

"Giselle, wait."

"Yes, Monsieur Buck?"

"Is there any chance, I mean, would you consider . . ." He took a deep breath and blurted out, "Can I please see you again before our ship leaves port?"

Her smile said it all. "*Oui*, monsieur."

"Can we meet outside this place?"

"*Oui*. Come, I give you the address."

Buck followed Giselle back to the bar. He noticed the rooms where Sam and Pete had been were now empty. She quickly scribbled something on a piece of paper and slipped it into his pocket.

She whispered, "Tomorrow, monsieur. I write the place and time on the paper."

Buck grinned and whispered back, "I'll be there."

Sam and Pete were waiting on the street outside the club. "Hey, partner! 'Bout time you came up for air." Sam offered him a cigarette. "Want one of these?"

"You know I don't smoke."

"Thought maybe you'd start, after being with *Giselle*."

Buck tried to deflect the conversation away from Giselle. "So how was it with Desirée and Antoinette?"

Pete did take the cigarette Sam offered. "Woulda been better if I could've fucked her. But, I gotta say, she wasn't shy about anything."

Sam offered Pete a light. "Neither was Desirée. She latched onto me like a flea on a dog. Knew what she was doing, too." Sam took a long drag on his cigarette, then blew smoke out his nose. "So what about Giselle?"

Buck really didn't want to talk about her, but knew he had to say something. "She's hotter than Georgia asphalt. I left that room hummin' a happy tune."

"Just wait, junior. Madame Séduisant's is next."

"Why don't y'all go on without me? I'm good for tonight. I'll head back to the ship and get me some shut-eye." Buck turned to leave.

Sam stopped him. "No fuckin' way, José! You're comin' with us for the main course—"

Pete interrupted. "You can go back to the ship on one condition."

"What's that?"

"If the sign on the whorehouse door says, 'Beat it—we're closed,' we'll all go back together."

Sam chuckled, then winked at Buck. "C'mon, pal. You don't want to miss this. It's like being a kid in a candy store."

Buck knew he'd lost this one. No way would Sam and Pete let him off the hook. He reluctantly agreed, but he decided he also had a condition. "All right, I'll go if you do something for me."

"Name it."

"Get me a day pass for tomorrow."

"What the hell for? There's nothing happening here during the day."

"Never mind why I want it. Will you get me one?"

"Shit, Sam! He's got himself a girlfriend."

"Goddamn! Is he right, Buck? Are you hooking up with Giselle?"

Buck again felt his face flame, but he still looked Sam in the eye when he answered. "We're meeting tomorrow afternoon, if I can get that pass."

"All right, buddy! You got it." Sam started walking toward Madame Séduisant's on Rue Lafayette. "Why the hell didn't you just say you wanted to see Giselle?"

"Don't want y'all bustin' my chops about it, that's why."

Pete sniggered. "Now, why the fuck would we do that? Just because you got yourself a Frenchie? Think she'll have some wine and cheese waiting when you get there?"

Before Buck could react to Pete poking fun at him, Sam again intervened. "Did I ever tell you fellas the one about the two old farts that went to a whorehouse?"

Buck recognized Sam's maneuvering immediately and helped it along. "Don't think so. What about 'em?"

"Well, these geezers hadn't had any for years, so they decided to go to a whorehouse. When they got there, the madam took one look at them and decided she wasn't going to waste any of her girls on these two. So she thought she could get away with blow-up dolls. She put the dolls in their rooms and told 'em to have at it.

"After they were done, they started for home and got to talking. The first man said, 'I think the girl I had was dead. She didn't move or make a sound. . . . How was it for you?'

"The second man answered, 'I think mine was a witch.'

"The first old guy asked, 'How's that?'

"'Well,' his friend said, 'when I nibbled on her breast . . . she farted and flew out the window!'"

It worked. Pete laughed and slapped Sam on the back. "That's a good one. How about this one?

"This drunk goes to a whorehouse, but he has to take a piss

before he goes to his room. He finds the toilet. A few minutes later, everyone hears a loud, bloodcurdling scream. A few minutes after that, there's another scream. The madam goes to see why the man is screaming. She yells through the door, 'What's all the screaming about in there? You're scaring my girls!'

"'I'm just sitting here on the toilet, and every time I try to flush, something comes up and squeezes my nuts.'

"The madam opens the door, looks in and says, 'You idiot! You're sitting on the mop bucket!'"

In spite of himself, Buck had to laugh. "Don't suppose that's ever happened to you, Pete?"

"Hell no! That's why I piss standing up!" Pete punched Buck's shoulder. "All right, Bucko, you're up. Give us a good one."

Buck thought for a minute, and remembered one he'd heard from a Texan. "This one's for you, Pete.

"A sailor walks into a whorehouse, finds the madam and says, 'I want to get laid.'

"The madam says, 'Let's see what you got.' So he pulls down his pants and shows his dick to the madam and her girls.

"They start giggling when they see his dick. It has *Shorty* tattooed on it. The madam says, 'Okay, Sally, you take him upstairs.'

"After an hour, Sally comes downstairs looking exhausted. The madam says, 'What happened with you and Shorty?'

"Sally says, 'After Shorty gets hard, it spells out, *Shorty's Bar and Grill, Houston, Texas.*'"

Pete practically choked, he laughed so hard. Sam gave Buck a discreet thumbs-up. Between them, they had reeled Pete in. He had forgotten about Giselle.

All the joke telling made the walk to Rue Lafayette a short one. When Sam saw the street sign, he said, "Okay, Pete. Where is Madame Séduisant's?"

Pete studied the row of buildings. He pointed down the block. "It's that one. It used to be a boarding house before Madame Séduisant took it over. She keeps a Christmas candle in the window so men know which house is hers."

Sam and Buck followed Pete as he hauled ass down the block. Sam said under his breath to Buck, "He's been coming here for years. Says he's slept with the madam herself."

"Damn! That must have cost him."

Sam grinned. "Maybe she gave him a discount for being a good customer."

When they caught up to Pete, they found him checking his wallet. "Just making sure I brought enough to get what I want." He eyed them both. "Don't wait around for me. I plan on spending the night."

Sam called him on that one. "You have to be on the ship tomorrow morning. The guys from the dockyard are coming aboard to start working on the derrick."

"Fuck, Sam, why don't you make like that derrick and get bent?" Pete stuffed his wallet back in his pocket. "I'll be on the ship in time for breakfast. Is that good enough for ya?"

"As long as you aren't falling-down drunk when you get there, it's good enough."

Pete went up the wide stone steps and rang the bell beside the double doors. Buck and Sam waited on the street. An older woman, about Pete's age, opened the door. "*Bon soir. Que désirez-vous?*" She stopped and looked at Pete for a moment. "Monsieur Pete, is that you?"

"*Bon soir, Madame. Ça va?*"

"*Ça va bien, merci. Et vous?*"

"Can't complain. Good to see you again, Madame Séduisant."

"And you as well, Monsieur Pete." Madame Séduisant put her arms around Pete and kissed one cheek, then the other. "Please come in."

Pete gestured for Sam and Buck to follow. Buck whispered to Sam as they went up the steps, "Shit, Sam, she recognized him."

"And she didn't slam the door in his face. Who woulda thought? Seems he's been telling the truth about her."

From the street, Buck couldn't see the design on the entry doors. When he got closer, he saw the heavy oak doors had angels carved on them. Even the milky frosted windows had small cherubs frozen in the glass.

When they followed Pete into the foyer, another surprise greeted him. On a pedestal inside the door stood a plaster statue of a male angel holding a human woman. The angel had wings worthy of Gabriel. He wore nothing else. His genitals were clearly visible. The woman was also naked. They seemed about to make love.

There was a small plaque attached to the stand. Buck tried to read it, but the inscription wasn't in English. He poked Sam in the side and pointed to the plaque. "Do you know what that says?"

Sam glanced at it. "Nope, can't read French. We'll ask Pete if he knows."

Before Sam could ask Pete about the inscription, Pete turned around and introduced Madame Séduisant. "Madame, these are my friends. This is Sam, and this here is Buck. It's their first time at your place."

"*Bon soir*, messieurs. Welcome to my home." Just as she had with Pete, she kissed Sam on both cheeks, then did the same with Buck.

More curious than shy, Buck asked Madame Séduisant, "You live here, ma'am?"

"*Oui*. It has been my home for many years. Those who work for me also call it home. It is a big house."

This woman wasn't anything like what Buck had expected. Her warmth and friendliness drew him in immediately. He felt comfortable talking to her. "If you don't mind my askin', what does this say?" He pointed to the plaque.

Madame Séduisant smiled. "You are the first in some time to ask." She gestured toward the statue. "That is the guardian of my house. This angel loves women, as all men should." With near reverence, she touched the statue. "It is called *Immortal Love*. The plate reads, *The Sons of God Saw the Daughters of Man that They Were Fair.*"

"That's real nice, ma'am."

Pete cleared his throat. Buck could see his impatience. He wanted to get on with his evening. "Madame, could we take Sam and Buck into your parlor?"

"But, of course, monsieur." She again smiled at Buck. "We will find you a special one." Then she went down the hall toward another set of doors, with Pete right behind her.

Sam grinned at Buck and said softly, "Goddamn, these Frenchies like you! I'm gonna start callin' you butter. You're on a roll!"

Thankfully, Sam went ahead and caught up with Pete. Buck didn't want to draw any more attention to himself tonight. Determined to stay in the background, he brought up the rear. He followed Sam and Pete into the parlor.

Buck wasn't prepared for what waited for him in the parlor. He'd thought he'd seen it all at Le Club de Plaisir. What could be more indecent than topless cancan dancers flashing their naked behinds at the audience? He realized that couldn't hold a candle to this.

There were at least ten girls sitting around the large room. Two had male companions. The others were either alone or casually talking among themselves. Most of them were topless. A few had on only bustiers. One young woman in the corner wore a black lace see-through robe and nothing else. As Buck glanced at her, she stood and opened the robe. He quickly looked away.

Pete had taken Madame Séduisant aside. Buck saw him point to one of the girls in a bustier. The one he pointed to didn't have underpants on. Her dark pubic hair matched the lace trim on her lingerie.

Madame Séduisant gestured to the girl. She came over to Pete and wrapped her arm around his waist. Pete looked her over like a man buying a new car. He nodded and took out his wallet. He handed Madame Séduisant a wad of bills.

He held up one finger, indicating he wanted the girl to wait a minute. Then he came back to where Sam and Buck stood.

"Fellas, I'm going upstairs and don't plan on coming back down until early tomorrow morning. Madame will take care of you boys." He slapped Buck on the back. "Son, you can bet your bottom dollar your dick won't be green tomorrow. These girls will ripen it. You can count on it."

With as big a smile as Buck had ever seen on Pete's face, Pete collected his female companion for the night and left the parlor.

Buck felt more at sea here than he had on his first trans-atlantic voyage. He looked to Sam for some sense of what to do. Sam seemed preoccupied checking out the available girls. Again he considered slipping out. With Pete gone, he might manage it.

Before he could turn tail, Sam grabbed his arm. "Buck, look. Madame Séduisant is talking to those two girls over there and pointing to us." The girl in the sheer black lace robe was one of them. The other one had on a miniskirt and nothing else.

Intending to leave, Buck took his ball cap out of his pocket and put it on. "Sam, I'm going back to the ship. Y'all have a good time tonight."

"Jesus Christ, Buck! You can't just leave."

"Yes, I can."

"Why the hell do you want to leave?"

"I'm like a fish outta water here. I can't do this."

"I think she might not agree with you."

The next thing Buck knew, someone snatched the baseball cap off his head. "What the fuck? She took my cap."

Sam laughed. "That's what they do here. If a whore picks you out of a crowd and wants to do business, they steal your hat. Now you have to go after it."

"Like hell I do. She can have it." Buck turned to leave. Sam stopped him.

"What are you so frigging afraid of, Buck? Are you a virgin?"

"No more than you are, Sam. Are you a virgin?"

Madame Séduisant interrupted the exchange. "Pardon, messieurs, is there a problem?"

Buck apologized. "Sorry, ma'am. There's no problem. I just decided to leave."

Madame Séduisant glanced at Sam, who shrugged his shoulders. She pointed to the girl in the miniskirt. "Monsieur Sam, that is Yvette. Does she please you?"

"Yes, ma'am, she does."

"*Très bien!* She speaks English and is most happy to escort you this evening." Madame gestured Yvette to come over. "Mademoiselle, Monsieur Sam would enjoy your company."

Before Sam left, he took out his wallet. He handed Buck a wad of bills. "Here, if you do stay, this should cover an hour here. You can pay me back later. See you back at the ship. I'll meet you in the mess room for breakfast." Without saying anything else, he left. Yvette took him out the same door Pete had gone through a few minutes before.

# 3

Buck really wanted to get the hell out of there. He stuffed the money Sam had given him into his pocket. "Ma'am, if you'll excuse me, I think I'd best go. The mademoiselle can keep my hat."

Madame Séduisant slipped her arm through Buck's. "Before you leave, monsieur, tell me why you wish to go."

Buck had never been so uncomfortable in his whole life. "I think I bit off more than I can chew with this, ma'am." Not knowing why he admitted it to her, Buck added, "I ain't never been in a place like this before."

"Have you been with a woman before?"

"'Course I have!" He couldn't help sounding indignant. "I've just never been in a whorehouse!" He wanted to bite back the words as soon as he said them. "Sorry, ma'am. Didn't mean to be disrespectful."

"No disrespect taken, monsieur. Please, stay for a time. Sit in the parlor and talk to Simone." She called to the girl who had taken his hat. "Simone speaks better English than Yvette."

The young woman who had taken his cap put it on her head, then took his hand. The black lace robe gapped open, leaving nothing to his imagination. Although her breasts were smaller than Giselle's, they were still perfectly shaped globes. Her light brunette hair perfectly matched the hair that peeked out between her legs.

Not wanting to make a scene, Buck let Simone lead him to an empty sofa. When she sat down, her robe fell completely open. Buck's cock twitched in spite of his nervousness. Simone tugged his hand, urging him to sit down beside her. "Monsieur, please sit with me."

"I will, miss, if you close your robe. It's mighty distracting seeing you in the altogether."

Simone smiled an absolutely beguiling smile. "Monsieur, it is meant to be more than a distraction. I do not please you that you wish for me to cover myself?"

Buck sat down. Not wanting to insult her, he tried his best to be complimentary. "Miss, you're prettier than a speckled pup under a red wagon. You bet you please me."

Simone still held Buck's hand, and made no attempt to close the robe. "Then why do you not want to see me?"

"Because seein' y'all makes it mighty hard to leave, that's why."

"Then perhaps you should stay, and we will spend some time together, no?"

Buck's resolve to leave diminished as his hard-on grew. "Let me think on it. Maybe I'll stay."

Just then, Madame Séduisant reappeared. She carried a tray with an open bottle of Bordeaux and two glasses. "Ahhh, Monsieur Buck, you are still here. *Très bien!* I have brought you some wine. It will help you to be calm."

Simone squeezed Buck's hand. "He is doing well, Madame. He is calmer now."

She set the tray on a table beside the sofa. After pouring the wine, she handed Buck a glass. "This will quiet you more. Simone will help you along. She knows what to do."

Buck glanced at Simone's bare chest and muttered, "She's already doing it."

Before she left them alone, Madame Séduisant told him, "You are welcome to stay as long as you are comfortable. If you decide to leave and not enjoy Simone, there will be no fees."

Buck drank most of his glass of wine in a few gulps. Simone quickly refilled his glass. "Monsieur Buck, you are better now?"

"Getting there." She still hadn't closed that damn robe. He really did want to touch her breasts like he had Giselle's. He glanced around. "What are we allowed to do in here?"

"What do you wish to do, monsieur?"

He belted back some more wine before he answered. "Your breasts are beautiful. I want to touch them."

"You may certainly touch them. You may kiss them as well, if you would like."

Buck glanced around the room again. No one was paying them any attention. He gingerly reached out and brushed her bare breast with his fingertips. He felt the ridges of gooseflesh raise under his hand. He quickly pulled his hand away.

"Sorry about the goose bumps, ma'am. Didn't mean to give you a chill."

She picked up his hand and put it back on her breast. "Monsieur, my skin rippled because it felt good, not bad. Do more, s'il vous plaît."

Buck finished his wine and handed Simone the empty glass to put back on the tray. He cupped a breast in each hand and squeezed. Her flesh was soft as taffy on a hot summer's day. Even as they sat in a room filled with people, Simone opened her legs wider.

"Simone, I don't want to break any rules."

"Monsieur, we can have privacy if you wish, or we can do more here. No one will mind."

"Are you sure?"

Simone moved one of his hands to the smooth curve of her belly. "I am quite sure, monsieur."

The wine had quieted his nerves, and quelled his self-consciousness. He remembered how Giselle had touched him and he had touched her. Gathering up all his courage, he asked Simone, "Do you like it when men touch you between your legs?"

"*Oui*, monsieur, if they do it the right way."

Buck didn't know there was a right way. He thought all you had to do was rub. "What's the right way?"

"Gently, with a light touch." He couldn't believe it when she moved his hand from her belly to the moist slit between her legs. "Let me show you."

With no inhibition, she opened her legs wide and placed her hand over his. She guided his hand to her most forbidden place and pushed his fingers inside. "Do you feel *la praline*?"

"Do I feel what?"

"*La praline*, my sugared almond." She massaged her clitoris with his finger. "If you touch like this, in small circles, it will become *la praline en délire*, a delirious sugared almond, and will burst with pleasure."

Buck smiled. "That's how to make a woman come, right?" He thought of how he had massaged Giselle earlier. He wanted Simone to show him the right way—so he would know how to do it when he saw Giselle tomorrow.

"*Oui*, monsieur. Women wish to climax just as men do."

"Will you show me how to make you come?"

"Perhaps it is best we go to my room, and I will show you all you wish to know." Simone picked up the bottle of wine and the two glasses. When she stood, the lace robe closed. Buck had the sudden impulse to pull it open again.

"That lacy robe is real pretty, ma'am."

"*Merci.* Monsieur, you may call me Simone."

"If y'all will call me Buck, we have a deal."

"Buck, follow me."

Buck didn't mind following her, not at all. Her behind jiggled inside the black lace like the steps in the fun house at the county fair. He thought about what Pete had said, about one of Madame Séduisant's girls giving him a ride. As Buck watched Simone's ass, he expected the ride she would give would be better than any carnival ride he'd ever been on.

Simone led him down a hall, and up a wide flight of stairs. They walked past a series of closed doors. Buck heard male and female voices coming from those rooms. From a few, he heard moans. He wondered which rooms Pete and Sam were in.

Now more curious than nervous, he again focused on Simone's well-shaped bottom. She suddenly stopped. He came within an inch or two of bumping into her.

"We are here, Monsieur Buck. This is my room." She took his ball cap off her head and put it back on his. Then she put her hand on her hip, the robe opening like a curtain. In a pose worthy of a French lady of the evening, she asked, "Are you ready to go in, monsieur?"

Buck took a moment to look at her before answering. With the negligee pushed back, her fully exposed breast nearly touched his chest. With unabashed admiration, he whispered, "You are so fucking beautiful."

Simone smiled. "Then you are ready?"

"I'm ready. Let's go."

Simone held the door open and Buck went inside. The room had a bed, a few chairs and an oddly shaped stool. A large oval mirror in a wooden frame stood beside the bed, and a picture of a naked woman lying on a sofa hung on the wall over the dresser. An open box of rubbers lay on the nightstand alongside a long leather stick with a flat end.

After she put the wine and glasses on the dresser, Simone said, "There is a toilet there if you have need." She pointed to a closed door in the corner.

"Is this where you live? I mean, is this actually your bedroom?"

"No, Monsieur Buck. Where we sleep is on the other side of the house. This hall is where we bring our guests."

"But you said it is your room."

"For tonight, it is. Tomorrow night, I might have another room. They serve the same purpose."

"I s'pose that's true." Buck picked up the leather stick. "This looks like what we use with horses back home."

"It is a riding crop, monsieur."

"You use this in here?"

"Sometimes, if it is desired. There are men who ask for it."

Buck tried to imagine Simone whacking him across the ass with the crop. It surprised him when his cock twitched at the thought. He quickly put it down. Then he nervously took off his cap and stuffed it into his back pocket.

"Maybe I'd better use the toilet."

"Monsieur, before you go, might I ask you . . ." Simone went to the dresser and took out a black garter belt with black stockings. She held them up for Buck to see. "Perhaps it would please you if I wore these with my robe? The black against my skin would excite you?"

Buck had never been asked such a question in his life. It took a moment for it to register. When it did, he blurted out, "Ma'am, if y'all put those underthings on, you bet your bottom dollar it'll excite me." Whistling a soft wolf call through his teeth, Buck went to take a piss while he could still manage one.

When he came out, Simone had her back turned, pouring them each a glass of wine. She still had the robe on. Buck thought he saw the stockings, but couldn't be sure.

Not knowing quite what to do next, he made small talk.

"That toilet is better than what we got on the ship. Those old fixtures look like the ones my granddad had in his house. They were put in just before the Depression, in 1928, I think."

"Everything in this house is old. Madame says they built it in 1919, just after the Great War."

"I'd believe it. The house kinda looks like a museum from the outside."

Simone handed him a glass. When she turned around, Buck saw she had put the stockings on. He tried not to stare. "Is it like a museum on the inside?"

"Depends on what you're lookin' at." Buck sipped his wine.

Simone held her robe wide open. "What about when you are looking at this?"

This woman had no bashfulness at all about being naked. She reminded him of the way dogs sniff each other, with no sense of modesty or shyness. Hound dogs only know what their instincts tell them. They don't think about any of it, they just do it. It comes naturally to them.

The same thing seemed to be true of Simone, and even of Giselle. To them, what happens to a man when he's with a woman didn't make them embarrassed at all. In fact, they accepted it just like gravy took to biscuits.

That being the case, he decided to take a good look before he answered. The more he looked, the hotter he got. He didn't care that his prick pushed against his fly. This lady would know what to do with it when the time came.

Simone stood like a statue for several minutes while he eyeballed her. "Ma'am, I hope you don't mind my sayin', you're like a twelve-pound bass I caught once. I didn't know if I should eat her, or mount her!"

Even with the language difference, Simone got the joke and grinned. "Monsieur, in this house, you do not have to choose." She took his hand. "Come. Let me teach you how a woman wants to be touched."

Buck set his glass on the nightstand. Remembering he only had half an hour with Giselle, he thought to ask how long he had here. "Simone, I don't know how this works. My buddy Pete is stayin' here all night. Sam intends to leave. Exactly how much time do I get with you?"

"Madame told me not to rush, as it is your first time in her house. It is also a slow night, and there are many girls available. For the price of an hour, you will get much more."

"Well, doesn't that just beat all! I didn't expect special treatment."

"Monsieur Pete has known Madame for many years. She is fond of him. She asked that his friends be treated well."

"Damn! No wonder he wanted to come here first thing. I'll have to thank him."

Simone sat down on the bed and patted the spot beside her. "Tell me what you want to know."

With his prick throbbing in his trousers, Buck sat down. "I want to know how to make a woman hot." He self-consciously fidgeted. Then he picked up his glass and drank some more wine, hoping it would slow down his pulse. His heart thumped in his chest.

"Monsieur Buck, a woman likes to be touched, not just between her legs, but everywhere." She set his glass back on the table, then covered her breast with his hand, just as she had downstairs. "You saw my flesh ripple when you caressed me. Those are the tingles a woman wants."

Buck lightly caressed Simone's breast, as he had earlier. He again felt the gooseflesh. "Does that always happen?"

"When the touch is right, it happens. Yours is the right touch."

Buck had the overwhelming impulse to kiss her breast. Not wanting to move too fast, he asked, "Do you like to be kissed, I mean all over?"

"*Oui*. When a man kisses a woman everywhere, it says he adores her."

"Would y'all let me kiss you like that?"

"Oh, monsieur! It may cause *la praline* to burst with pleasure!"

"Hell, isn't that what we want it to do? What did you call it, the delirious sugared almond?"

"You learn well, Monsieur Buck."

"Simone, just call me Buck. In the States, we use first names, 'specially when y'all are in bed with someone."

Buck had a sudden impulse to push Simone back on the bed. He wanted to kiss her, and touch her, and fuck her. A surge of lust moved through him like a dam bursting. He had always been timid with women, never knowing exactly what they expected of him. But he knew Simone wouldn't judge him or criticize him. He could cut loose with her, and not be afraid she would slap his face.

He pushed her backward, more forcefully than he'd intended, nearly knocking the wind out of her when she hit the bed. His sudden ferocity startled Simone almost as much as it did him. She gasped, "*Mon Dieu!*"

Instantly ashamed of himself for possibly hurting her, Buck pulled back. "Simone, I'm sorry. I didn't mean to be so rough."

Simone smiled reassuringly. "Monsieur, it is all right. You only surprised me with your strength."

Buck wasn't convinced. "Are you sure I didn't hurt you?"

"*Oui. Je suis très bon.*"

"'Scuse me?"

"Buck, I am good." Simone opened her arms. "Come, give me kisses."

Simone opened her arms, and her legs, wider. He knew he had to fish or cut bait. His prick made the decision for him. He hadn't been with a woman in a long time, except for Giselle jerking him off earlier. Buck knew he couldn't get up and walk away from Simone. He wanted her, real bad.

Buck slowly, and gently, pulled Simone's robe open. Then he leaned down and tenderly kissed her breast. She wrapped her arms around his neck and held him close. "Your kisses are sweet, Buck. Give me more."

With Simone's encouragement, Buck relaxed. He covered each breast with moist kisses. The ridges of gooseflesh made her silky skin rough. He had kept enough wits about him to know that reaction meant it felt good to her.

Simone twisted just enough to make her nipple poke his face. He lifted his head. She ran her fingers through his hair and said, "Suck."

He got the message. Without any hesitation, he caught her nipple between his lips and sucked it full into his mouth. He heard her murmur, "Mmmmmmm, *très bien*." Once he started, he didn't need to think about what to do. Buck teased her nipple with his tongue. He sucked, licked and nibbled, taking his time with each breast.

Without her having to tell him, he trailed kisses down her belly. Before he made his way any lower, Simone stopped him. "Monsieur Buck, I wish to kiss you now."

Buck tensed. He figured honesty was his best chance at saving face. "Simone, I am so hot. If you touch me, I'm going to cream."

"Then perhaps you will allow me to make you more comfortable before we continue." She began unbuttoning his shirt. "We have all night. We need not hurry."

Buck didn't know what she meant by making him more comfortable, but he did know his undershorts were about to take his load. He gritted his teeth and took a deep breath. "Simone, I'm frigging close."

"I will take care of you, monsieur."

Simone knelt, took off her robe and tossed it on the floor. If Buck had any doubts this woman was a pro, she quickly wiped those suspicions from his mind. Using nearly as much force as he had, she pushed him backward. She had his fly open and his dick in her mouth before he understood what she intended to do.

Buck thrashed on the bed as she sucked him. He had paid for this before, but Simone took the prize. The suction of her mouth, combined with the lapping of her tongue, made him a wild man.

No question this woman knew how to make a man come. She took him over the edge within minutes. As Buck lost himself in his climax, he imagined having Giselle there, too. For the first time in his life, having two women in bed didn't seem like a pipe dream.

Buck floated in a dreamy haze for several minutes after he finished. Simone remained beside him, and waited for him to come around. When he opened his eyes, Simone simply said, "Good?"

"Good" didn't begin to describe the pleasure Buck had experienced. Not having the words to explain all he'd felt, he answered just as simply. "Damned good, mademoiselle."

"Then we will continue?"

"You bet we will!" Buck raised himself up on his elbows, not caring that his fly was open and his business still hung out. "Are you sure it's all right, I mean, that I stay here longer? I only have enough to pay for an hour."

"I am sure. If Madame says an hour, no matter how long, then that is what you pay."

Buck lay back down. "Dang! I owe Pete one for this. He didn't let on we would be treated special here."

Simone unbuttoned the last two buttons on Buck's shirt and rubbed his chest. "Madame says Pete usually comes alone. She sees him whenever the ship comes to Marseilles. You and Monsieur Sam must be good friends, or Pete would not have brought you here."

Buck put his arm under his head. "Well, ma'am, Pete's friends with Sam more than me. I've only been on this ship two months. I know Sam more than I do anyone else."

"But is it not true that Monsieur Pete must trust you to bring you to Madame's house?"

Simone slid off the bed so she could take off his shoes. Buck didn't object. "I s'pose it's true. I didn't think about that."

"Perhaps you should." Simone tugged at his pants. "These must come off."

"Yes, ma'am!" In the aftermath of his orgasm, Buck relaxed even more. For some unknowable reason, he felt just as comfortable with Simone as he did with Giselle. He'd have to remember to ask Sam if that happened to him, too. He grinned. Maybe he should ask Pete. That would be a kick in the ass.

Buck let Simone strip him naked. When he sat up so she could take off his shirt, he again eyed the riding crop. An image of Simone whacking him with it flashed in his mind. His flaccid prick began to harden.

"Ah, I see monsieur is ready for more." Simone noticed him looking at the riding crop. She lightly stroked his semierect penis. "You would like to know how it feels to have the crop across your buttocks?"

Buck didn't immediately say no. "Never did anything like that before. Can't say I know if I do." Buck took another good look at Simone. He'd only ever seen a woman wearing nothing but black stockings in the girlie magazines they passed around on the ship. "Do a lot of guys ask for it?"

Simone picked up the crop. "Many do." She trailed the tip of the crop down Buck's chest and tickled his erection. "Some say I am the best at using it that Madame has."

"No kidding!" Buck couldn't hide his reaction to what Simone had told him. His prick bounced against his belly.

"*Oui*, monsieur. It is true. Do you wish to try?" This time, she tapped his leg. "Some want to lay facedown, others want to kneel or bend over."

"Do you ever tie them up?"

"*Oui*. But not the first time. That is for the more experienced."

"Damn! I didn't mean I wanted to be tied up, I just wondered if y'all did that, too."

"*Oui*. We will do what men pay to have done." Simone again tapped his leg. "What do you wish, Monsieur Buck?"

What Simone told him sunk in like water into dry soil. "Y'all will do *anything* a man will pay for?"

"*Oui*, as long as no one is hurt."

Buck's mind raced with the possibilities. "What sort of things do they ask you to do?"

Simone held on to the riding crop as she crawled back onto the bed beside him. She again tickled his erection with the flat leather end. "You would like to know what is on the menu?"

Buck hesitated, then answered honestly. "Yeah, I guess I do."

"Monsieur Buck, men ask for what they cannot find otherwise. Some want my mouth on them, some want intercourse, some want the crop. Others come for special services. They like sodomy or panties or spanking or other *fétiches*."

Buck shook his head. "Lord sakes, I'm happy just lyin' here next to you dressed like that. Y'all are purtier than any of the girlie pictures the fellas have on the ship."

Simone smiled a smile that curled Buck's toes. "Monsieur, you are a gentleman."

"Hell, I ain't no gentleman! Look at me. I'm lyin' here next to a lady, buck naked, and I have a boner. In Georgia, I'd be arrested for this."

"There are no police in Madame's house. You can do whatever you wish."

Buck followed the trail Simone traced across his groin with the riding crop. "Ah, hell, Simone, I might as well tell you the truth. A neighbor woman took a stick to my backside once for riding my bicycle through her flower garden. Walloped my ass good. She didn't know it, but I got a boner from it, almost as hard as the one I have now."

"You see, the memory of what you like returns. You will try the crop?"

"Yeah, I'll try the crop. Tell me what to do."

Simone lifted his erection with the end of the crop, then let it fall against his belly. "It is not yet leaking. You will last for the crop."

Buck didn't know how to say it, but he had to be sure. "If I try the crop, I can still have sex with you, can't I?"

"But, of course, monsieur. The whipping is the appetizer. I am the main course."

"Y'all sure as hell will get some whipped cream for dessert."

"I am quite sure we will, monsieur. Now, if you please, kneel on the bed."

Not knowing what to expect from this, Buck obediently knelt on the bed. He had his back turned to Simone. He couldn't see her, but he felt the crop tickle his balls.

"I think it is better if you are on your hands and knees, with your legs spread. I want to see your sacs hang like church bells."

With some trepidation, Buck got on all fours and spread his legs. Simone slid the edge of the crop between his ass cheeks. Buck shuddered.

"Now, monsieur, you are ready." Simone punctuated that sentence with a crack of the crop across his rear end. Buck grunted and lurched forward, but remained on his hands and knees. Simone whacked him again. It stung like hell, but in a peculiar way, it also felt good.

Buck involuntarily spread his legs a bit wider. He could feel the weight of his erection hanging from his groin. Simone lightly tapped his penis with the crop. "Monsieur's church bells have a hard clapper."

Buck muttered, "Yeah, ding-dong." He braced himself for the next smack. When Simone again connected with his ass, the sting moved through his balls like wind whistling through the sails of a ship. Buck half moaned, half whimpered.

Simone struck again, this time catching him a bit lower and grazing the edge of his balls. Searing pain ripped through his groin. Rather than stopping her, he gasped. "Jesus Christ, that hurt! Do it again!"

She did. The unbelievable sensation about sent him over the edge. He shouted, "Stop, Simone! I'm close. I don't want to come like this."

Simone tossed the riding crop onto the floor. Without Buck having to ask, she lay down beside him and spread her legs wide open.

Any sense of inhibition had long since passed. Buck wanted to fuck her, and fuck her hard. Before he had a chance to roll on top of her, Simone pointed to the table by the bed. "Monsieur, you must wear one."

Buck reached over and grabbed a condom. He quickly tore open the package and rolled it on. Then he did what sailors for generations had done before him. He fucked a whore in a brothel, and claimed his right to be a true seafarer.

# 4

Buck spent the rest of the night with Simone. After ejaculating three times in one night, he didn't know if he could manage another. He asked Simone to continue his education, and show him more ways a woman wants to be touched. She did.

After she explained how best to use his mouth on her, he gave her an orgasm by sucking and licking her clit. Then he gave her another one using his fingers. By the time she had finished a second time, they both needed to sleep. Buck dozed beside Simone, resting his hand between her legs.

A car horn on the street woke him up. It took a minute to get his bearings. Simone slept beside him, the room dimly lit by the rising sun. He bolted upright in the bed.

"Shit! Simone, wake up. I gotta get back to the ship!" He gave her a shake. "Simone, it's morning. I have to leave."

Simone stretched. "Monsieur Buck, is that you?"

"Yeah, it's me. And I gotta go." He crawled off the bed and gathered up his clothes. "Hope you don't mind if I use the bathroom first." Without waiting for an answer, he darted into the toilet and closed the door.

After having a piss and then splashing some cold water on his face, he quickly dressed. He'd left his shoes by the bed. When he came back out, Simone sat on the edge of the bed, wearing her sheer black robe.

His prick didn't care about the time. It twitched at the sight of her, and began to harden. He muttered, more to himself than to Simone, "I can't. There isn't time."

Simone stood. "But you will come back to Madame's house before you leave?"

"Don't know, sugar. I'll try, but can't promise." He dug into his pocket for the wad of bills Sam had given him. Without asking the cost, he stuffed the money into Simone's hand. "I hope that's enough to cover all night."

"It is enough, Monsieur Buck. If I could, I would give it back to you."

"Oh, no, ma'am. This is your livelihood. You deserve to earn a decent living just like anyone else."

"You are a gracious man, monsieur. I hope you will return and ask for Simone."

"If I come back here, sweetheart, y'all can bet your bottom dollar I'll ask for you." Buck moved closer. "Simone, I really have to go." He leaned forward, meaning to kiss her on the cheek. But the compulsion to hold her seized him. He impulsively grabbed her and kissed her, as a man kisses a mistress when leaving. Buck hugged her tightly. "Thanks for everything. I'll never forget last night."

"Nor will I, monsieur." Buck felt her hand on his ass as she grabbed his cap. Simone yanked it out of his back pocket, stepped backward and put it on her head. "I will keep this, monsieur, to make sure you come back and ask for Simone."

Buck grinned. "Ma'am, I intend to get that ball cap back. Keep it safe." Then he left.

Buck retraced his steps from the night before and found the stairway. It was barely dawn. He made sure he walked quietly down the stairs so he wouldn't wake anyone. It surprised him to see Madame Séduisant and Pete standing in the hall.

When Pete saw him coming down the stairs, he came to meet him. "Well, it's about goddamn time you got your ass down here. Madame said she didn't think you'd left. I was about to send her up there after you."

Buck held his ground. "I'm not late. We'll both be back in time for breakfast."

"We sure as hell will, son, but we have to shake a leg." Pete went back to Madame. It took Buck by surprise to hear him address her casually. "Aimee, it was good seeing you again. I hope next time we can spend more time together."

"Next time, Monsieur Pete, perhaps I will take you to my room."

"Madame, I'm gonna hold you to that one." Then Pete kissed Madame Séduisant, tenderly, even sweetly.

Following Pete to the door, Buck stopped to thank his hostess. He did kiss her on the cheek, and then thought to do both cheeks, as is the French style. "Madame, thank you."

"You enjoyed Simone, monsieur?"

"You bet I did. I want to see her again, when I can get back here." In a conspiratorial whisper, Buck added, "She kept my cap to make sure I ask for her."

"*Très bien!* You are welcome at my house whenever you are in Marseilles. Do not forget the address."

"Don't worry. I won't."

Pete stood on the stoop, waiting for him. Without having Sam as a buffer, Buck wondered how this would go. He reminded himself to keep it light, and not let Pete get under his skin.

Buck took the initiative to get the ball rolling. "Thanks for bringing us to Madame Séduisant's, Pete. Never been to a place like that before."

"Son, I've been to plenty of whorehouses. Madame Séduisant's is a cut above the rest. Her place is the best I've ever been."

"How long y'all been going there?"

"I s'pose about ten years, give or take. Happened to be walking by one day, looking for a place, and saw some girls sitting on the steps. When you've been around as long as I have, you learn to know what's what."

"You knew they were whores?"

"Hell yes. The way they were dressed, and the way they were trying to get the attention of any man walking by, gave it away."

"Did they take your hat?"

"Didn't have one." Pete stepped back and looked at Buck's back pocket. "I see yours is missing."

"Simone kept it."

"Fuck, you ended up with Simone?"

Buck tried not to sound like he was boasting, but he couldn't help it. "Spent the night with her."

"Is your dick still attached?"

"Damn right it is." It suddenly hit Buck. "You've been with her, haven't you?"

Pete gave him a peculiar look. "Once. She does something special."

"Yeah, I know. She's the best Madame has with the riding crop."

Pete burst out laughing. "No damn way in hell your dick's still green if she took the crop to your ass."

Buck's curiosity outweighed his sense of territoriality. "She did it to you, too?"

"About a year ago. I asked Madame for something a little different. She said she had a new girl, and she hooked me up with Simone. I could tell from what Aimee told me this one had to be a real firecracker. I'd never done the crop, and thought what the hell."

"Did you like it?"

"Did you?" Pete shot Buck a look that should have intimidated him. But for some reason, it didn't.

"Yeah, I kinda did."

"You've got more balls than I gave you credit for having. That's serious shit."

"My first time for anything like that. Next time, maybe I'll have her tie me up for it."

"Frigging hell! No way do I want it again."

That surprised Buck. "Why?"

"I go there for a good time, not to have my ass strapped."

"Fuck, Pete! All she had on was black stockings when she did it. Hottest damn thing I've ever done."

"I'll take the black stockings, but forget the rest of it. My daddy took the belt to my ass one too many times for me to want any more of it."

Buck almost told Pete about the hickory-stick licking from his neighbor and the hard-on he got from it, but he decided that wouldn't be a good idea. Obviously, the memories of his daddy weren't ones Pete wanted to dig up, so Buck changed the subject. "You and Madame are friends?"

"We've known each other ever since I started coming here. Yeah, I guess we're friends."

"She thinks highly of you. Simone told me so."

"She is one classy lady, better bred than any other woman I've known. Surprised the shit out of me when she took a liking to me."

Buck wanted to say, *Me too*, but held his tongue. Instead, he said, "Simone told me Madame treated us special 'cause we were with you. She told me you don't often bring anyone with you."

Pete kicked a beer bottle lying on the sidewalk into the gutter. "You and Sam are different than the rest. I knew you would like the place, and wouldn't bust my chops for going there."

"Why the hell would we do that? Madame Séduisant's house is great."

"It's too hoity-toity for most of the crew. If word got around, and anyone gave me any grief, I'd have to take the sons of bitches out."

Buck grinned. "Me and Sam would help y'all."

Pete slapped Buck on the back. "That'd be worth writing home about." The ship had come into sight moored at the dock. They would soon be back on board. "You still got that date with Giselle."

"Sure do. I have to find Sam and get my day pass."

"Depending on when we sail, think you'd want to go back to see Simone again?"

"I might. She has my ball cap. I'd like to get it back."

"Come find me when you get back from seeing Giselle. We'll see if Sam is interested. Maybe I can talk Aimee into giving us a good rate." Buck didn't tell Pete he'd spent the night and only paid for an hour.

Buck and Pete didn't waste any time. They headed straight for the mess room to hook up with Sam and get some breakfast. They saw Sam sitting at a table by himself. He waved them over.

"So you fellas made it back."

Pete grabbed a bottle of ketchup and smothered his hash browns in it. "Told you we'd be back for breakfast."

Sam paused with a big chunk of sausage on the end of his fork. "You said you'd be back for breakfast. Buck didn't say he'd be spending the night. When I left him, it looked like he wasn't going to stay at all."

Buck could hear the edge in Sam's voice. He tried to smooth things over. "I did almost leave. Madame Séduisant talked me into staying."

"I guess so." Sam stuffed the sausage into his mouth.

Pete picked up the ball. "Hell, Sam, they broke in Buck real good. Madame paired him with Simone."

"So? Madame said she got us girls that could speak English."

Pete slapped Buck on the back. "Tell Sam what Simone did to *y'all*."

Buck's face warmed as he glanced around to see if anyone heard Pete. No one had. Sam stared at Buck.

"What the hell did she do to you?"

Buck took a deep breath before he answered. "She whooped my ass with a riding crop."

Sam actually dropped his fork. It clanked as it hit the plate. "You're fucking kidding me!"

Beaming, Pete confirmed. "Sam, he's not kidding. I know what she does. Our man Buck wants to go back for more."

It surprised Buck to hear Pete's tone. He almost sounded proud. It surprised him even more to hear Pete call him a "man." Since Buck had transferred to the ship, Pete had always called him "son" or "boy." Without trying, Buck seemed to have won Pete's respect.

Sam pulled him back into the conversation. He whispered, "Shit, Buck! How was it?"

Buck took a swallow of coffee. Both Sam and Pete were waiting for his answer. He put his cup down and looked Sam in the eye. "It was hotter than a goat's ass in a pepper patch."

Sam grinned. "I bet your ass was even hotter."

"I had it once. It stung like friggin' hell! Getting my ass blistered doesn't get me off," Pete chimed in.

"What about you, Buck? Did it get you off?"

Before Buck could think of an answer for Sam, Pete answered for him. "He stayed all night, didn't he?"

Buck ate some eggs. He mulled over how much to tell Sam, especially with Pete sitting right there. He swallowed his food and thought to add, "Hell, Sam, I have to go back. Simone kept my ball cap. That's my lucky hat. She won't give it back unless I let her whoop my ass again."

Sam agreed. "Shit, yeah, you have to go back. You can't let her keep your lucky ball cap! Maybe Pete and I should go with you."

Buck winked at Pete. "I don't know, Pete, waddya think?"

"I have work to do. But I think I can squeeze it in."

Sam laughed. "What? Are you saying you're hung like a frigging horse? You have to squeeze it in?"

Without missing a beat, Pete retorted, "Hey, buddy, I wear a size-twelve shoe. That should tell you something."

"Yeah, it tells me you have big frigging feet."

"Hey, Buck, when you see Simone again, ask her if I had to squeeze it in."

"Maybe I will." Pete didn't seem to mind that Buck meant to ask Simone. Maybe he really was hung like a horse.

"Hey, Sam, did you get me that day pass?"

"How many women can you do in one day?" Sam reached into his pocket and pulled out the pass. "You gonna have Giselle smack your ass, too?"

Buck took the pass. "Don't know. I'll see what she wants to do in the time we have."

Sam pushed back his chair, getting ready to head back to the deck. Before he got up, he smirked at Buck. "Sweet Jesus, it's always the quiet ones you have to watch out for."

Pete got up to go back for seconds. "You got that right, Sam. I'll see you later. Lover boy, look us up when you get back. We'll see what's doin' then."

"Yeah, I will. Oh, and, Sam, I'll pay you back later."

"I'm not worried. I know you're good for it."

Pete took one last shot before he left. "Simone and Giselle know he's good for it, too."

Buck flipped Pete the bird. "Up yours, dickhead." Pete laughed as he walked away. Before today, Buck wouldn't have spoken to Pete like that, for fear of being knocked through himself. Things had changed.

Sam still sat across the table, staring at him. "What the fuck's gotten into you?"

"What are y'all talking about?" Buck shoveled another forkful of eggs into his mouth.

"Talking to Pete that way could get you killed."

"Don't think so. He knows I was poking fun."

"Yesterday you didn't want anything to do with him. Today you're best friends. What the fuck's going on?"

Sam's tone didn't sit well with Buck. "Wasn't that the idea? Y'all invited him yesterday. I didn't."

"Yeah, and I came back to the ship last night. The two of you made it a night."

Buck finished his eggs in one large bite and picked up his tray. "Is that the bug up your ass, Sam? That I didn't come back last night?"

"I would've liked to have known you intended to stay. When you didn't come back, I thought you might've gotten yourself into some deep shit."

"Well, I didn't." Buck looked to see if Pete was on his way back to their table. He spotted him sitting with the other engineers. "When Pete came downstairs this morning, Madame told him I hadn't left yet. He waited for me, figuring he'd haul my ass out of there if he had to."

"Did he have to?"

"Hell no! I saw the sun coming up. I knew I had to get back to the ship and check in."

"You gonna tell me what really happened with Simone?"

"I already did."

"Like hell you did. I had a couple of hours with Yvette and thought I was doing damn good. You spent the night with Simone. I don't expect you got much sleep."

Buck grinned. "Some. Being tired never felt so good."

"Did Pete arrange it?"

"No. Madame Séduisant did. We got special treatment because we're Pete's friends."

"For Christ's sake! I didn't know that."

Buck took his tray to the bussing area for cleanup. Sam followed. "I didn't see Madame Séduisant when I left. Did you?"

"Yeah. She was with Pete. Surprised the shit out of me when he called her by her first name."

"What is it?"

"Aimee. Coming back to the ship, he called her that a few more times. Before we left, she said she might take him to her room next time."

"And here I thought he was bullshitting about knowing the madam so well."

"He says he's known her for about ten years."

Sam and Buck left, and made their way to the deck of the ship. Sam wanted to check on the dockyard crew. They walked quietly for a few minutes. Buck could tell Sam still wanted to talk, and figured he would eventually say something, which he did. "When you meeting Giselle?"

Buck remembered the piece of paper Giselle had slipped into his pocket. "She wrote it down. Let me look." He found the slip of paper. "She says one o'clock." He handed Sam the paper. "Can you make out that address?"

"Yeah. She's on Allées Léon Gambetta. That's the street we walked down to get to Madame Séduisant's from the club." He handed the paper back to Buck. "Maybe you should stop for a quick cropping on the way back to the ship."

"Don't knock it if you haven't tried it." Buck folded the paper and put it back in his pocket. "Speaking of which, what happened with Yvette? You've been giving me the third degree, and you haven't told me anything."

"She's hot! Had me a couple of good ones before I left last

night." Sam paused to light a cigarette, then took a long drag before continuing. "Remember that miniskirt she had on? She didn't have a stitch on under it. When we got in the room, she turned on the radio and started to dance. Goddamn, Buck, I about creamed on the spot."

"Yeah, me too. Simone put on black stockings and a garter belt." Buck gestured toward the east, in the general direction of the United States. "I'm tellin' ya, they don't make 'em like that in Georgia."

"Not in South Carolina, either." Sam stopped for a moment and looked across the water, almost like he could see the States. Then he abruptly turned back to face Buck. "Oh, *y'all* might like to hear this. Yvette passed on an interesting piece of news. When I told her where we were earlier, she told me both her and Simone had worked at Le Club de Plaisir before they came to Madame Séduisant's."

"Shit, that's an entry in the small-world book."

"Surprised me, too. That's why they speak English better than the rest of them. They had to speak it at the club."

"Think they know Giselle?"

"I'm sure they do." Sam continued walking toward the cargo derrick. "When I talked to Giselle last night to arrange everything, she told me she's the assistant manager there, and has been for a few years now."

"Pete told me Simone has been at Madame's house for about a year, so she should know Giselle."

"How does Pete know that?"

"Because he had her last year, right after she started. Madame introduced them."

Sam flicked his cigarette butt over the railing and into the water. "So what's the deal with Pete, anyway? Does he have a thing going with the madam?"

"Don't know if you'd call it a thing, but he's slept with her before, and probably will again. She seems to have a hankerin' for him."

They had reached the work area. The derrick stretched high above them, with an ugly twist in the middle section that made it inoperable. Sam pointed to the bent metal. "Can you believe how fucked-up this thing is?"

"How the hell did it happen, anyway?"

"The operator raised it when he should've lowered it. He tried to reverse direction too damn quickly. The gears locked and bent the living shit out of it."

"Glad I wasn't the one running it."

"You and me both. It's costing a ton of money to have it fixed, but we're dead in the water without it. What good is a ship if we can't load and unload cargo?"

"Do you need me to do anything this morning?"

"Nah. I'll keep an eye on things here until Pete shows up. Why don't you get some shut-eye while you can?"

"Thanks, buddy. Oh, and, Sam, sorry I did an about-face last night. I know I pissed you off."

"Hey, you got laid, didn't you?"

"You bet I did, and then some."

"Hell, I've done a lot worse to get some pussy. Don't worry about it."

"Thanks, Sam. I'm going to catch some shut-eye now. I'll see you later."

Buck left Sam on the deck, then went to his cabin. He did need to sleep for a few hours, before getting ready to meet Giselle.

The information Sam had shared about Simone working at Giselle's club stayed on his mind. Last night, he wondered about having Giselle and Simone at the same time. If they did know each other, maybe, just maybe, they could work something out. With the thoughts of two women in bed with him floating in his mind, Buck fell asleep.

Thankfully, he'd had the presence of mind to set his alarm for eleven o'clock. He started awake when it went off. After a shower and a shave, he put on some clean clothes and stuffed a few more condoms in his pocket. Then, for the first time since coming on board two months earlier, he ventured into a foreign port city by himself.

# 5

---

Buck took the same route they had the night before, walking up La Canebière to the club, then finding Giselle's street from there.

By the time he found her building, he had made up his mind to broach the subject of Simone at some point that afternoon. Considering the proclivities of both women, and knowing they had probably worked together, he figured he'd strike while the iron was hot. The odds were in his favor. Maybe he could talk them into a threesome.

Before he went inside, he double-checked the address. He definitely had the right building. The front entrance wasn't locked, so he went in. Giselle had written *1D* on the paper. He found the number on a door at the end of the hall. Gathering himself up to his full height, he knocked.

Giselle opened the door. "Monsieur Buck, you came!" She seemed surprised.

"Sure I did, Giselle. You invited me, remember?"

"*Oui*, I remember well. But I did not know you would accept."

"Shoot, ma'am. If it isn't a good time for y'all, I can leave."

"Oh, no, monsieur! Do not leave. Come inside, *s'il vous plaît.*"

Buck reached up to take off his ball cap, then remembered he didn't have it. He followed Giselle into a dimly lit vestibule. "Do y'all live here alone?"

"I am alone. Many times, I share my flat with other girls from the club. But there are none here now." Giselle led Buck into a small sitting room. She gestured toward a deep rose settee. "Be comfortable, please. I will bring some wine and cheese."

Giselle left Buck alone in the room. Before he sat down, he had a look around. The room looked like something from the movies. Both the settee and the matching armchairs had fancy, carved wood frames, and flowers imbedded in the upholstery. Even the stool sitting in front of one of the chairs had carved legs and flowers.

A large mirror in a gold frame hung on one wall, and a poster of a beautiful black woman dressed only in feathers hung on the opposite wall. The poster read: *Josephine Baker Est Aux Folies Bergère.*

Buck wandered over to the window and pulled back the burgundy curtain. From that vantage point, he could see the street sign. Giselle lived on the corner of Allées Léon Gambetta and Rue Lafayette. Simone and Giselle were practically neighbors.

"Monsieur Buck?" Giselle had returned with a tray. On it, she had a bottle of wine, two glasses, a baguette and a brick of cheese. "You are well?"

"Glory, yes, Giselle. I'm fine." He went to take the tray. "Let me help you with that."

Buck took the tray and set it on the table in front of the settee. Giselle handed him the corkscrew. "You will open? I will cut the cheese."

Buck couldn't help himself. He burst out laughing. He

forced himself to straighten up, but he still couldn't wipe the smile from his face. "Damn, Giselle, I'm sorry. I didn't mean to laugh."

Giselle appeared bewildered. "I do not understand. I misspoke?"

As much as he didn't want to explain, Buck owed her a reason for his reaction. " 'Cutting the cheese' means something else to Americans. It's what we say when someone breaks wind—you know, when someone farts?"

Giselle grinned. "You thought I meant to break wind at you? Oh, no, monsieur, I only meant I would prepare some cheese for eating."

"I know. But it struck me as funny, hearing a pretty lady say she would cut the cheese."

"I am glad you laughed. You are more relaxed now."

"Yeah, I guess I am." Buck set about opening the wine bottle. "Y'all drink a lot of wine here, don't cha?"

"It is what we drink with food. Wine in France is like Coca-Cola in America."

"Sure beats soda pop, that's for sure." He poured them each a glass.

Giselle sliced some cheese. "Let me show you the French style." She picked up the baguette and tore a piece of bread from it. Then she put a chunk of cheese on top of the bread. After taking a bite and swallowing, she sipped her wine.

"I think I can handle that." Buck sat down on the settee and repeated the process. He had to admit, the flavors blended beautifully. "This is really good. Now I know why the upper crust always talks about having wine and cheese."

"In France, common people eat wine and cheese, the same as the wealthy. Those with more money simply pay more for the wine."

"Hell, this wine is fine." Buck held up the glass and sniffed. "What do they call it? A fine bouquet?"

"*Oui.* The bouquet is the aroma." Giselle also sniffed. "This is sweet, but still with some scent of the vineyard."

"It smells good, like you did last night."

"*Merci*, monsieur." Giselle sat down beside him. "Do you like my perfume today?"

Buck leaned in close and sniffed Giselle's neck. Being this close to her again, and smelling her, definitely had an effect. His prick stiffened.

He sat back. "Ma'am, you smell better today than you did last night. That's mighty fine perfume you're wearin'."

Giselle's eyes lit up, the way they had the night before. "You are kind, Monsieur Buck." She tore off more bread and put some cheese on it. She held it up for Buck to take a bite. "You would like some?"

Buck wondered if she understood what she had asked him. His answer covered whatever she meant. "You bet I would like some!" He leaned forward and bit the bread in half. Giselle popped the rest of it into her mouth.

Giselle sipped her wine, then put together another bit of bread and cheese. "How long is your stay in Marseilles?"

Following her lead, Buck did the same. "Probably about a week. Depends on how long it takes to get the repairs done."

"That is longer than most seamen stay." Buck left the obvious joke pass by this time, not wanting Giselle to think he was making fun of her. He answered her seriously.

"We're staying longer because the repair is sort of complicated. They have to cut out the part of the derrick that is bent and put the two good parts on a jig. Then they have to put in a new piece between the other two, align the three pieces, and then weld them together."

Buck noticed Giselle's eyes glazing over as he spoke. "Sorry, ma'am. That's probably more than y'all wanted to know."

Giselle smiled a smile so open and warm Buck's heart fluttered. "I do not understand all they must do, but I do understand it gives you more time in Marseilles. That is good."

"Glad you think so, Giselle." The night before, Giselle had been in charge. She told him what to do. Today he had to decide if he would make the first move, or wait and see if she did. Buck decided he didn't want to wait much longer.

"You grow quiet, monsieur. Is something wrong?" It surprised Buck that Giselle noticed.

"No, nothing is wrong." He set his wineglass on the table. "Truth be told, everything is right. I can't believe I'm sitting here with you."

"And I am surprised you came. Of the few I have asked, you are only the second to visit my home. The others have not come."

"Then they're dumber than a box of rocks. Don't pay those fools no mind, Giselle. It's their loss."

"You are different, Buck. I could see the difference as soon as you looked at me. Your eyes are kind, and your manner gentle."

"Back home, my granddaddy used to say I was shyer than a mockingbird, and scared of my own shadow. That isn't so, but it did take going to sea to make me feel like a man."

Giselle slid closer to him. "Did you feel like a man last evening?"

Images of both Giselle and Simone flashed in his mind. "I felt like more of a man last night than I ever have before." He almost told Giselle about Simone right then and there. But not wanting to upset the apple cart, he decided later would be better.

Buck took a deep breath and focused on the things Simone had taught him last night. He wanted to impress Giselle with what he knew, but in such a way that she wouldn't know he had learned a healthy portion of it last night.

He put his arm around her shoulders and pulled her close. The softness of her breasts pressing against his side made his pulse race. She wasn't showing as much cleavage as the night before, but he could see enough. Giselle had the best tits he had ever seen. As beautiful as Simone's were, Giselle's took the blue ribbon.

He tipped her chin up with his other hand so he could look into her eyes. "Thanks for askin' me to see y'all off the clock. I'm glad I have more than half an hour today."

"You do. I can also do more here than I can at Le Club de Plaisir."

"Sam says you're an assistant manager there. You shouldn't have to entertain men if you help run the place."

"Monsieur, I do not have to see men. I only do so when I am moved by someone to do so."

"But you went into one of those rooms with me."

"As I have invited you into my home. You do not understand that you are, as they say, 'the pick of the litter'?"

Buck whistled through his teeth. "Not once in my life has anyone ever thought me to be the pick of the litter."

Giselle rested her hand on his chest. "You are. I am pleased we met."

"So am I, darlin', so am I."

Giselle flicked her fingernail under the button of his shirt. Buck thought she might open it. But she stopped and asked, "Would you care to see my bedroom, monsieur? We would be more comfortable there."

Buck grinned. "Lead the way, mademoiselle."

They went back out through the foyer and down a hallway. The toilet door was open. Buck made note of where it was, in case he needed to use the head later.

The door at the end of the hall opened into a spacious bedroom, with two double beds, one on each side of the room. A long curtain rod ran the length of the room, dividing it down the middle. The attached curtain was neatly tied and pinned to the wall on one side.

Giselle pointed to the bed closest to the door. "That is my bed. The other one is for someone to share. It has been empty for a few months now."

"You can afford this place yourself?"

"*Oui*. My wages are good at Le Club de Plaisir. I am able to support myself."

"Good for you!" As soon as he said it, Buck's face flushed. If it sounded stupid to him, it probably did to Giselle, too. "That had all the smarts God gave a duck's ass, didn't it?"

"Pardon, monsieur?" Again, Giselle looked confused.

"Sorry. I mean that sounded stupid, didn't it?"

"No, Monsieur Buck. It sounded sweet. Sweet is not stupid."

"That's good of you to say."

"It is true." Giselle wrapped her arms around Buck's neck. "What would you like today? We are alone and we have time."

Even after his night with Simone, Buck still found it difficult to say outright what he wanted to do. Giselle's perfume wafted into his nostrils. He closed his eyes and took a deep breath. "Christ Almighty, you smell good."

"*Merci*, monsieur."

No question, he knew what he wanted. He wanted her. Before he could talk himself out of saying it, he pulled her close. "Giselle, I want to touch you, all over. Then I want to sleep with you." There, he'd said it out loud.

"I would like to touch you, too, Buck, like we did last night, but without any clothes on."

"Hot damn! Now we're getting somewhere." Buck squeezed her breast. "If you don't mind my sayin' so, ma'am, your tits are prizewinners. You must have men pawin' at you all the time at the club."

"Some want to touch, but most only look. It is good for business. That is why I show more there."

"Excuse me if this is rude, but I really want to know. Are you wearin' anything underneath, I mean, like a bra or panties?" Just saying the words gave Buck a rush.

"I do not own a brassiere. When I need support, I wear a bustier. But I am not wearing one now."

Buck threaded his fingers through Giselle's thick hair. "And panties? Are you wearing some?"

"They are black, with lace."

Buck sharply exhaled the words, "Shit, yeah!"

"And you, monsieur?"

"Sorry, ma'am, I don't know what you're askin'."

"What do you have on underneath?"

"Nothing except a pair of B.V.D.'s. And trust me, mademoiselle, they ain't sexy ones."

"What is inside those B.V.D.'s is *très bien, n'est-ce pas?*" Giselle squirmed against his hard-on.

"It's like a poker, which is what I want to do to you."

Giselle laughed. "Poke-her. *Très drôle!*"

"You're catching onto my jokes. That's an eight ball in the side pocket."

Giselle closed her eyes and crinkled her nose. A moment later, she blurted out, "That is the game of pool, correct?"

"It sure is. Y'all can teach me French and I'll teach you American."

Giselle giggled. "*Oui!*" She feigned seriousness. "But, monsieur, it may take many lessons and many trips to Marseilles to learn."

"Damn straight it will!"

"Might we take off our clothes now?"

"Leave your panties on. I want to see them. Then I want to take them off."

"*Oui,* monsieur. But then you must allow me to take off your B.V.D.'s."

Buck unbuttoned his shirt. "You're on. Tit for tat."

Giselle pulled her blouse over her head, then squeezed her breasts together. "These are tits. 'Tat' is another word for them?"

Buck answered while staring at her glorious bosom. "No, ma'am. 'Tit for tat' means a fair exchange. I'll take your panties off and you'll take my B.V.D.'s off, when we get that far."

"Tit for tat. I will remember." Giselle tossed her shirt onto a chair, then threw Buck's shirt on top of hers. While she undid her skirt, he decided to say what had been on his mind all day.

"Giselle, do you know someone named Simone, who used to work at your club?"

"*Oui,* I know Simone." Giselle continued to fuss with the clasp on her skirt.

Buck didn't quite know how to continue, so he asked, "Are you two friends?"

"I have not seen her for a time, but she stayed with me for a few weeks after she left Le Club de Plaisir."

"No kidding." Buck sat down on the bed, waiting for Giselle to finish undressing. "Do you know where she is now?"

"She is with Madame." The clasp finally gave way and Giselle's skirt fell to the floor. "But I am sure you know that, do you not?"

Buck ogled the shapeliest legs he had seen in a very long time. "Yeah, I do. I met Simone last night, after we left the club."

Giselle kicked the skirt across the floor, next to the chair. Then she came over to Buck, straddled his lap and sat down. Wearing nothing but her black lace panties, she ran her fingers through his hair and cooed, "You like Simone more than *moi*?"

Buck grabbed Giselle's ass with both hands. "Hell no!" Then he buried his face between her breasts.

"Then why do you ask me about her?"

Figuring it was now or never, Buck told her. "I thought that if you already know each other, that maybe I could see you together." He kneaded her ass with his fingertips. "Seein' as how she lived with you for a while, you must know each other pretty well."

"We do. But she has chosen a different path."

With matter-of-fact honesty, Buck finished the thought. "Yeah, I know. She's a whore, you aren't."

"Many would say that what I do is no different."

Buck's spontaneous response hit the bull's-eye. "When was the last time you took a riding crop to someone's ass?"

Giselle locked her hands around Buck's neck, leaned backward and howled with laughter. Buck shifted his hands to the middle of her bare back to keep her from falling. When she pulled herself together, her eyes glistened with merriment. "Simone gave you the crop?"

"She gave it to me good."

Giselle smiled. "It might interest you to know she lost her job at Le Club de Plaisir for doing it there. The manager let her go because men came to see her, and not the show. That is when I introduced her to Madame."

"You did?"

"*Oui*. Simone wanted to do more with men than we are permitted to do at the club, as did Yvette. They both went to work for Madame at her house."

"How do you know Madame Séduisant?"

"She owns Le Club de Plaisir. I work for her as well, in a different way."

Buck couldn't hide his shock. "You have to be kidding! Aren't you?"

"No, monsieur. It is the truth."

"Holy shit! I had no idea." As it all sunk in, Buck realized something else. "Pete has known Madame for ten years. He sure as hell doesn't know, or he would have said something."

Giselle pushed Buck backward onto the bed as she said,

"Madame acquired the club only a few years ago. She does not speak of her ownership, and does not wish direct involvement in its operation. If you tell your friends from last night, I must ask that you keep this to yourselves."

"Of course, we will."

"We can speak more of Simone later. Now I wish for no words."

"Yes, ma'am. No words works for me."

Buck wasted no time filling his hands with tits. He squeezed and pinched them, letting the sensual pleasure of her supple flesh carry him away. While he caressed Giselle, she also stroked his body. She rubbed his chest, tweaked his nipples and then kissed his belly.

Nearly breathless with having her all over him, he remembered what he wanted to do. "Giselle, let me suck you."

"Monsieur Buck, I also wish to suck you. Shall we try *soixante-neuf* together?"

He knew she meant doing sixty-nine. He'd only seen pictures. He'd never tried it with anyone. "I'm game. Let's see if we can make it work."

Feeling more adventurous than he ever had, he tugged Giselle's panties off, leaving her naked. She pulled off his undershorts, then pushed him down on the bed.

Giselle turned around and straddled his chest. Then she slid backward and bent over. Before Buck had a chance to acclimate to all the sights and sensations, her mouth covered his prick. He moaned just as she lowered her pussy onto his face.

Her scent filled him. The fragrance of her womanhood made him heady. He wrapped his arms around her thighs and positioned his head so he could lick her.

At first, Buck had trouble concentrating on his end of things as Giselle expertly sucked him. The mind-blowing feel of her mouth pulling on him obliterated every other thought in his brain. Gradually he adjusted. For several minutes, they lapped at each other. By the time she released him from her mouth, he was giving as good as he was getting.

Giselle flopped onto her back, her chest rising and falling in breathless anticipation. "Monsieur Buck, I am ready, *s'il vous plaît.*"

"Goddamn! So am I, Giselle!"

He grabbed his trousers from the floor and fished a condom out of the pocket. After rolling it on, Buck practically fell on top of Giselle, the urge to penetrate her overwhelming all his senses.

Giselle spread her legs wide, giving him plenty of maneuvering room. Buck let his instincts take over. He didn't have to think about where to poke. His natural impulse guided him to the right spot.

When his prick popped in, Giselle groaned and grabbed his biceps. This French beauty wanted it bad, almost as much as he wanted to give it to her. He remembered when Simone told him to go slow, and let the woman set the pace as long as he could manage it.

Buck held back and waited for Giselle to move. Sure enough, she did. He followed her rhythm. He rode her slowly for several minutes.

She murmured, "Buck, *c'est bon.*" He knew enough French from last night to understand she liked what he was doing to her.

He whispered back, "Giselle, tell me when you want me to pick up the tempo."

"*Oui*, Buck, do it. I want more."

Buck hoped she understood what he meant to do. He thrust harder, his orgasm closing in on him. Giselle slammed her pelvis against his, shaking the bed. He pounded her with the force of waves crashing against a ship in a storm.

Suddenly the intensity of the sex exploded in a mind-bending orgasm. Buck shuddered uncontrollably. Giselle shouted, "*Mais oui!*" and clutched his back. His whole body burned with sensation as the waves washed over him, and submerged him in a sea of pleasure.

# 6

Giselle went to use the toilet. On the way back, she said she'd retrieve the wine and cheese from the sitting room. Buck glanced at his watch. He still had a couple of hours before he had to be back at the ship for dinner.

The last two days had been a real education for Buck. Not only had he experienced the best sex he could have imagined, but he had also discovered a whole new world. No wonder his shipmates told tall stories about the ports they had visited.

Although he knew sailors were notorious bullshitters, he'd come to realize over the past couple of days that maybe, just maybe, a few of them were telling the truth. Pete had. Neither Sam nor Buck had believed his stories about the madam he knew in Marseilles. Turns out, he'd been telling the truth the whole time. Buck had a few stories of his own to tell now, too.

Giselle came back into the bedroom, carrying the tray. It amazed Buck that she hadn't bothered putting on any clothes, not even a robe. "It doesn't bother you walking around naked, does it?"

She set the tray on the nightstand and handed him his glass. "No, monsieur, I do not mind that you see me with no clothes."

"Back home, girls are shy about such things. Even when you've been dating a girl for a while, she still wants to turn out the lights before gettin' undressed."

"I do not understand why." Giselle sliced them some more cheese and tore more bread from the baguette.

"Guess they've been taught to keep their clothes on, no matter what." Buck took the bread and cheese Giselle offered him. "It's what's called the 'battle of the sexes' in the States. Women try to keep their clothes on, and men try to take them off."

Giselle got back on the bed with Buck. "French women are not shy. We hope that men will look at us."

"Is that why y'all work at the club?"

"It is a better life there than many would have otherwise."

Buck wanted to know more about Madame Séduisant, but wasn't sure if Giselle would tell him anything else. He asked anyway. "How long have you known Madame?"

"Since she purchased Le Club de Plaisir."

"How the hell could she afford to buy a club?"

"Madame owns many properties. It is where she chooses to spend her money."

The whole thing baffled Buck. "She seems to be a nice lady, and she has money. Why does she have to run a brothel?"

"Why do you have to be on a ship?"

"Because it's what I wanted to do."

"Perhaps the same is true of Madame."

Buck couldn't argue with that. "Maybe it is. Speaking of brothels, that reminds me of a joke I heard one of the guys on the ship tell.

"This old geezer walked into a local brothel and announced that he wanted a shapely, young woman. The madam looked him over. She figured he must have been about eighty years old.

" 'Sir,' she said kindly, 'I think you've had it.'

" 'I have?' he said, real surprised. 'How much do I owe you?' "

Giselle giggled. "Buck, you are a funny man."

"Well, I know how to tell a good story. It's part of growing up in the South."

"Where is your home, monsieur?"

"Savannah, Georgia. Y'all haven't noticed I have an accent?"

"*Oui*. But I am not familiar with all the states in the United States."

"Know something? I don't think I could name all fifty states if my life depended on it."

Giselle had her hand on his chest, absentmindedly twirling his chest hair between her fingers. He had recovered sufficiently for the slight tugging on the short hairs to have a definite effect.

He suddenly realized he didn't know if Giselle had gotten off. The only way to find out was to ask her. "Ma'am, did y'all have an orgasm when I did?"

"No, monsieur. I did not finish."

Wanting to impress her with his new knowledge, he nonchalantly replied, "If y'all will let me, I'll play with *la praline*, and make 'er pop."

Giselle smiled. "You have learned much from Simone."

Buck handed Giselle his now-empty glass to put back on the tray. "How did y'all know she told me about *la praline*?"

"You forget, monsieur, we know one another well." Giselle stroked his growing erection as she continued. "During the time she shared my home, she also shared my bed."

Buck's hard-on became considerably harder. "Holy shit! You two slept together?"

"*Oui*. She is expert at making *la praline en délire*."

"Yeah, I know. She taught me how." Buck flopped back on the bed. "Damn! This is amazing! You and Simone are lesbians, too?"

Giselle followed suit. She lay down beside Buck and rolled over on her side.

"We are not lesbians, monsieur. We want men, but also enjoy the company of women from time to time."

Buck rolled over to face her. "Sort of like wanting a change now and again?"

"*Oui.* Women know better how to satisfy another woman. Men can be clumsy and touch too rough."

Buck put his hand on Giselle's shoulder and lightly pushed her onto her back. "I'll show y'all what Simone taught me. Let me know if I'm doing it right."

Buck waited for Giselle to get comfortable. She stretched out on the bed and opened her legs. He'd never had so much opportunity to look at naked women as he'd had the last couple of days. He couldn't get enough of it.

Simone told him to go slow, and be gentle. Giselle had just said men can be too rough. Buck gently parted the moist lips between Giselle's legs and slipped his middle finger inside. He found the small, fleshy nub. With only a bit of pressure, he rubbed it with a circular motion. The nub hardened under his finger.

Giselle sighed. She visibly relaxed as he continued his intimate massage. "That is good, Buck. You learned well from Simone. That is her way."

Buck watched Giselle closely. As he continued to rub, her pelvis rocked, almost imperceptibly at first, and then more forcefully. He hoped he could maintain and not jump her bones. A live sex show wouldn't be any hotter than this! His boner ached, he wanted it so bad.

But he persevered. Buck wanted to make Giselle come, and held on to that end. The more he practiced, the better he would get at it. Women would be dropping their panties for him when they realized he knew how to get them off.

Buck groped her tit with his free hand and pinched her nipple. Giselle moaned and pressed harder against his hand. It occurred to him to ask, "Giselle, what do you like? What makes you hot?"

"Tickling my pussy as you are makes me wet, monsieur. Can you not feel it?"

"Sure I can. But I want to make you crazy. What would make you crazy, Giselle?"

Her answer nearly made Buck shoot onto the bed. "Simone cropping me, and forcing me to lick you."

"Lord have mercy!" Giselle lifted her hips off the bed and rubbed harder. "Simone has used the crop on you, too?"

"*Oui*. We would play before bed. She would tell me to take off my clothes and bend over. As she does with men, she striped my buttocks."

Buck slid his middle finger into Giselle's cunt and rubbed her clit with his thumb. "Did she make you come?"

Giselle humped Buck's hand as she lost herself in the memory. "Simone tickled my pussy with the crop, and then would lash my derriere. Then I would do it to her."

"Jesus H. Christ, Giselle! You cropped Simone, too?"

"*Mais oui.*"

The thought of the two women going at it sent Buck reeling. He had to fuck Giselle. He couldn't wait any longer. His boner wouldn't let him wait.

There was no mistaking it, Giselle would climax any second. Wasting no time, he rolled on top of her. She had her eyes closed and yelped with surprise at the sudden movement. Explaining himself as much as he could manage, Buck hoarsely muttered, "I have to fuck you, Giselle, I can't wait."

Giselle blinked, suddenly aware. "Monsieur, the condom."

"Motherfuck! I forgot!" Buck awkwardly scrambled off the bed and grabbed his pants, now pushed halfway under the bed. He pulled his pocket inside out, and three condoms fell on the floor. He snapped one up, tore it open and rolled it on.

When he again focused on Giselle, he saw her masturbating. "Shit, Giselle, don't come yet! I want you to finish while I fuck you."

"*Mon Dieu!* I am close. Hurry!"

She didn't have to tell him twice. He crawled on top of her and bore down. His prick sunk deep into her body. Giselle raked her fingernails across his back. "Be rough now, monsieur. I want it hard."

With his balls burning with need, Buck rode her. He sometimes humped a pillow this hard, but never a woman. Giselle slammed into him and then shouted, "*Nom de Dieu!*"

Her pussy clenched around his prick. Buck continued his assault, showing no mercy. He growled, "Oh, yeah, darlin', you like that, don't cha?" as he harshly banged her cunt.

Giselle moaned loudly and writhed underneath him. Buck fucked her senseless, the sense of power catapulting him into a place he had never before gone. When his orgasm overtook him, he gave himself over to it, burying himself deeply into Giselle's body. He filled the tip of the condom with his white heat, then remained on top of Giselle as he drifted back to himself.

Giselle pushed at his shoulder. Now quite herself again, she complained, "Monsieur Buck, you are heavy."

"Sorry, ma'am." He rolled over and collapsed on the bed beside her.

They lay quietly together for a few minutes. Giselle spoke before he did. "You understand you will have to pay Simone for her time?"

It took Buck a moment to register what she had said. "You mean if we all meet?"

"*Oui.*"

"Then you'll do it?"

"I will, if Simone agrees."

Buck grinned. "I think she will. She kept my hat, and won't give it back until I visit her again."

"You are a popular man, it seems, if Simone wishes to see you again." Giselle sat up on the edge of the bed and reached for a phone on the night table. "I will call and ask if she wishes to make you happy once again."

Buck closed his eyes for a few minutes while Giselle called Simone. She asked for Madame Séduisant. Buck couldn't understand the conversation, but he did hear his name, and then Simone's. He also heard Giselle mention Monsieur Pete and Monsieur Sam. Then he heard her say, "*Très bien.*" He hoped the wind was at his back and things were moving in his direction.

Giselle put the phone down. "Madame would like to invite your friends as well."

"Shit, I'm not doing you and Simone with Pete and Sam in the room!"

Giselle grinned broadly. "No, no, no, monsieur! Madame will send Simone to my flat. She will entertain your friends at her house."

Buck smiled sheepishly. "Oh. That's different. I know they both want to visit again before we sail. When, and how much will it cost?" Buck hoped he could afford to pick up the tab for his friends.

Giselle relayed his question to Madame, and then answered, "Madame says she will again only charge for an hour, as she did before, if you come on Monday. It is the weekend now, a busy time. Monday is the slowest day, and she can give longer then, at a lower cost."

Feeling more like he was haggling to buy spare parts for the ship than arranging some female companionship, he agreed. "Tell Madame it's a deal. And tell her I want to pay for my friends this time." Buck remembered he didn't have French currency. "Oh, and ask her if she'll take American money. If she will, ask her how much it'll be in dollars."

The conversation seemed to go well, even if Buck had no clue what was being said. Giselle smiled, then said, "*À bientôt.*" She hung up the phone.

"Madame is most pleased you have accepted her invitation. She is able to change money if you need."

"That's great. How much is an hour?" When Giselle told him what Madame would charge, Buck knew he could easily afford to pay for all three of them. He owed Sam one for the night before, and he owed Pete one for taking them to Madame's house.

It occurred to Buck to ask something else. "By the way, did she say if Sam will get Yvette again? He liked her."

"*Oui.* Your friend Sam will be with Yvette." Giselle's eyes lit up when she added, "Your friend Pete will spend his time with Madame."

"Can you believe that? She must really like him. I know she doesn't have to entertain men unless she wants."

"What you say is true. Her clients are only those she wishes to see, no others."

Buck sat up beside Giselle. "I should be heading back to the ship." Buck picked up his pants and the condoms he'd dropped on the floor. "Shit!"

"Is something wrong, monsieur?"

"What time on Monday? I don't think we can come during the day. Pete and Sam have to be around to supervise the repairs. And I don't know if I can get another day pass."

"Madame expects them at seven o'clock. That is also when Simone will come. Is that a problem?"

"Don't you have to work?"

"No, monsieur. Le Club de Plaisir is closed on Mondays. I do not have to work."

"Fucking fantastic!" Buck knew they could all manage to

get off the ship Monday night. "How long will I have with you and Simone?"

"As long as you wish. Madame says Simone is floating on a cloud today. She expects Simone to squeal with happiness when she is told to come here with you."

"Does Madame always decide who Simone sees?"

"I do not know, monsieur. That is between Simone and Madame. It is not my business." Giselle casually traced the anchor tattoo on his bicep with her finger. "Do all sailors have tattoos?"

"Most I've met have some kind of tattoo. The old saying is a sailor without a tattoo isn't seaworthy."

"This one is big, and fancy!" Buck's anchor tattoo covered most of his upper arm. A golden rope twisted and turned around the large blue anchor. The rope widened in the middle of the anchor, with "BUCK" written in red letters inside of it.

"Yeah, I know. After I sailed the Atlantic for the first time, a bunch of fellas hauled my ass to a tattoo parlor in Copenhagen. They said I had to get an anchor, 'cause that's the one that means you've crossed the Atlantic Ocean. Didn't know tattoos had different meanings until then."

"What do they mean?"

"Let's see." He pointed to his arm. "Like I said, this one means a seaman has sailed the Atlantic. A full-rigged ship means he's sailed around Cape Horn, and a turtle shows he's crossed the equator. There are lots of them."

Buck made a fist and pointed to his knuckles. "Met a guy once with HOLD tattooed on the knuckles of one hand and FAST on the knuckles of the other. When I asked him what the hell that meant, he told me it reminded him how to hold the riggings."

Giselle giggled. "That's silly. He could not remember that?"

"Guess not." He pointed to his own. "Some of my buddies say it's a good thing I have my name tattooed on my arm. They say it'll be easier to identify the body when I get washed up on shore."

Giselle grimaced. "That is a terrible thing to say."

"Hell's bells. That's nothin'. You should hear some of the shit they say." Buck reconsidered. "On second thought, no, you shouldn't. No decent lady should hear that stuff."

"You think I am decent?"

"Lord sakes, yes! You have the kindest eyes I've ever seen. It sorta feels like I've known you my whole life. I enjoy talkin' to y'all almost as much as I like lookin' at ya."

"What about this?" Giselle pointed to the bed. "Do you like it as much as with Simone?"

"That's like comparing apples to oranges. You two ladies are completely different in the sack. Don't think I could pick one over the other."

"Then perhaps I must work harder." Giselle reached down and fondled his balls. "You do not have time for one more?"

"Giselle, I have to get back."

"It is not late. There is time to do some more." She continued to feel him up. When his prick began to harden, Giselle latched onto it and jacked him as she had the night before.

Buck glanced at his watch. He actually had more than an hour before he had to be back. He closed his eyes and savored Giselle's hand on him. He muttered, "Fuck, that's good! Work it!"

"You like?"

Buck opened his eyes. "Oh, yeah, I like it very much." He stroked Giselle's breast with the back of his hand before he squeezed it. "Fuck, your tits are good."

He now had a full-blown hard-on. She sure as hell knew how to jerk a guy off. Since he had her naked beside him, Buck sure as shit didn't want to come in her hand. He stopped her.

Giselle's brown eyes widened. "Are you leaving?"

"Not yet, mademoiselle. I just don't want to finish like this. We aren't in the club now."

"No, monsieur. We certainly are not." Giselle stood up. "I do not have a crop, but I have this." She went over to her dressing table and picked up a hairbrush with a flat wooden back. "Perhaps you would allow me to do to you what Simone did?"

Buck considered Giselle's proposal and realized he'd rather try his hand at it. "How about this, Giselle? Perhaps you would let me paddle your ass."

"Monsieur!" Giselle seemed genuinely taken aback. "You are serious?"

"Sure I am." Buck didn't want to scare her off. "But if you'd rather not, I'm happy to let you tan my hide."

"It has been some months since I have been spanked." Giselle handed him the hairbrush, then pointed to her dressing table. "If you please, I would like to do it there, by the mirror. Then I can see you and you can see me."

"Giselle, you're my kind of woman, hot and horny."

"More than Simone?"

Buck had played enough poker to not give away his hand. "We'll see, mademoiselle." Buck gestured to the table. "Bend over."

Using her hands to support herself, Giselle leaned against her dressing table. When she bent over, Buck could plainly see her pussy. He glanced in the mirror. Her tits dangled in front of her; her nipples hard, rose-colored buds.

Feeling horny as hell, Buck asked her, "Are you hot, Giselle?"

"*Oui*, monsieur." She opened her legs wider. "You cannot see how wet I am."

Buck did see the glistening dew between her legs. "Back home, you're the kind of girl we try to screw in the backseat of a Chevy. A girl with a pussy as wet as yours would have herself a real reputation."

"Do men spank girls with a reputation?"

Buck slid his middle finger down the crack of her ass, then shoved his finger inside. Giselle pushed back on his hand. "I'm sure plenty want to. Don't know how many actually do."

Buck watched Giselle hump his finger for a few seconds before taking his hand away. "The way you're reacting, it seems you have a taste for it." Buck swung the hairbrush. It connected solidly with Giselle's plump ass. "Do you have a taste for it, mademoiselle?" He smacked her again.

Giselle gasped. "*Oui*, Monsieur Buck. It is a good feeling."

"Didn't think I'd like it as much as I did. Simone is good at it." He deliberately mentioned Simone. He'd picked up on Giselle's jealousy, and wanted a reaction.

She didn't disappoint him. "If you want Simone, go to her!" Giselle tried to stand up. Buck stopped her.

"I didn't say I wanted Simone." He whacked her bum again. Giselle moaned. "But I'll tell you what I do want."

"I will do what you ask, monsieur." Buck had her right where he wanted her. He suspected she would do whatever he wanted just to please him.

"Beside Simone, has anyone else ever spanked you and really turned you on?"

She didn't hesitate. "*Oui.*"

"A man or a woman?" Buck swung the brush again.

Giselle practically whimpered. "A man, monsieur."

"I want to know what he did, Giselle." Much to his surprise, paddling Giselle really got to him. He had no idea spanking a woman would get him going like this. If she told him what the other guy did to make her hot, he could add that to his list that he started with Simone.

He stopped paddling her and caressed her red buttocks. When she caught her breath, he asked again. "Who was this man, Giselle? What did he do that turned you on?"

"The man who sold Le Club de Plaisir to Madame, he would take me over his knee."

"Your boss?"

"*Oui*. He would touch my breasts, saying he had to make sure I would let the customers touch me. Then he would take me into his office and close the door."

"Goddamn!" Just like when she told him about Simone, Giselle seemed to lose herself in the memory. Buck diddled her pussy and urged her on. "What the fuck did he do to you?"

"He would touch me some more. Then he would take me across his lap and spank my bare derriere."

"You let him?"

"*Oui*. He said I had a perfect bum. Once it got red and hot, he would rub himself against it until he finished."

Buck looked at Giselle's ass. Sure enough, it had gone from pink to crimson. "Did he fuck you, too?"

"Sometimes. He mostly wanted to finish against my buttocks."

Buck leaned in very close to her ear. "What do you want me to do now? Fuck you or rub against your ass?"

"If you please, rub against my derriere."

Buck saw hand lotion sitting on the dressing table. "Mind if I make it slick?"

"The cream would cool my cheeks. They are burning."

"Oh, baby, so am I." The end of Buck's prick looked red and angry. He squirted the silky lotion onto his hands. It made a squishy, wet sound that struck Buck as incredibly sexy. "Frigging hell, I want to hump your ass so bad!"

After coating her with lotion, Buck grabbed onto Giselle's hips. He positioned his cock between her ass checks and rubbed off. His prick glided against her slippery skin. He reached around and cupped her vulva in the palm of his hand.

"Get off with me, Giselle. Hump my hand."

Her hips undulated against him as Giselle rode his hand. Buck masturbated with more force, and, in turn, so did Giselle. Their lewd dance continued for several minutes.

Suddenly Giselle went rigid against him. Buck jammed his fingers inside her. Giselle's cunt gripped his fingers as the muscles contracted in orgasm.

Buck thrust between Giselle's clenching cheeks while watching her reflection in the mirror. A few seconds later, his cream coated her ass.

# 7

Buck made it back to the ship just before dinner. He had enough time to go to his quarters, shower and change before heading to the mess room. Sam and Pete would want a full report. Sure as shit, he didn't want any jokes about smelling like a two-dollar whore.

Before he left Giselle, Buck had to ask her a question. He wanted to make sure her opinion of him hadn't changed, considering everything they'd done together that afternoon.

She said her opinion had changed. She wished he weren't a sailor and could stay in Marseilles, where she could see him more often. Her answer reassured him. He hadn't been too pushy with her, and he hadn't messed things up.

Buck actually thought the same thing. If he could, he would stay in Marseilles. Compared to these women, the women he knew in the States were uptight and prudish.

He'd never thought of himself as a ladies' man. Considering how often he'd struck out, he'd always blamed his own lack of experience. It never occurred to him that it wasn't necessarily his fault.

After combing his wet hair, he hustled down the alleyway toward the mess room. He hoped to beat Sam and Pete, and grab the corner table for them to share. Not only would they want to hear about his afternoon, but he also had to tell them about the plan for Monday.

Buck did make it there first. After loading up his plate with beef stew and piling on several dinner rolls, he took his tray to the same table where they'd had breakfast. A few minutes later, he saw Sam and Pete come in. Sam spotted him before Pete did and waved. Buck pointed at the table, indicating they should join him once they had their food.

After the last two days of incredible sex, Buck felt like a new man. He couldn't remember ever feeling so relaxed and sure of himself. Six orgasms in forty-eight hours, divided between two women, amounted to a personal best.

He'd never jerked off that much, let alone done it with anyone. And the damnedest thing, he felt like he could keep going. He bit into a roll and waited for his friends to join him.

Pete edged out Sam getting to the table. As Buck expected, the conversation started with a wiseass remark. "So, lover boy, your pecker hasn't fallen off yet?"

Buck snapped it right back. "Hell no. Giselle took good care of it."

"Did she wallop your ass like Simone did?"

Buck chewed a mouthful of stew and swallowed before he answered. "Nope. She wanted to, but I took a hairbrush to her tush instead."

"Yeah, right."

Buck didn't try to defend himself. He didn't have to, since he had the truth on his side. Sam joined them and sat down. Pete still stood by the chair, staring at Buck.

Sam shot Buck a look, then said to Pete, "What the fuck's going on? Sit down and eat." Pete pulled out his chair and sat.

He didn't say anything. Exasperated, Sam growled, "Will someone tell me what's going on?"

Buck spoke up. "Pete asked me a question. I don't think he believes my answer."

"What did you ask him?"

"I asked him if Giselle walloped him like Simone did. Claims he took a hairbrush to her ass. Damn straight, I don't believe him."

"Did you?" Sam studied Buck closely, waiting for an answer.

"Sure did. Made her come, too."

"Damn! What are you going to tell us next, that you paid Simone a visit on the way back?"

"Nope, that happens on Monday."

"What?"

Buck hadn't enjoyed a conversation this much since he told his granddad he'd passed his driver's test. "On Monday, I'm seeing Giselle and Simone. Oh, yeah, and Madame Séduisant has invited you and Pete back to the house for an evening."

Sam muttered, "Fuck!" just as Pete pushed out his chair.

"You're frigging full of shit." He picked up his tray and turned to leave.

Calmer than he could have ever imagined while being in this situation, Buck yelled at Pete's back. "Hey, Pete, there's more, if you want to know."

Pete hesitated, then looked over his shoulder. "Son, I wouldn't dig myself in any deeper, if I were you." Slowly, deliberately, he put his tray back on the table.

Sam stood. "Enough! If you two want to tangle, take it up to the deck."

"It's all right, Sam." There was no reason to fight.

Buck stood and walked around the table. He didn't want to be overheard. More than that, he wanted to face Pete down, once and for all.

Sam put his hand on Pete's shoulder. "My friend, if you throw a punch in here, I'll have the master-at-arms haul your ass to the brig. You'll cool your heels there for the rest of the night." Then he said to Buck, "I think you've lost your frigging mind. Sit down!"

Buck held his ground. "There's something you fellas don't know. Giselle works for Madame Séduisant. Madame owns Le Club de Plaisir, and Giselle set the whole thing up with her for Monday."

Sam's shocked expression said it all. "You're fucking joking!"

Pete continued to glare at him, saying nothing. Buck noticed Pete's hand had rolled into a fist, but he didn't back down. He wasn't finished yet.

"Pete, Madame says you'll be with her, and, Sam, you'll be with Yvette. Oh, yeah, one more thing. I'm paying for all three of us. Y'all were right, Pete. She's giving us a special deal. Can't figure out why, but she's sweet on you."

Once he'd said his piece, Buck quietly went back to his meal. Sam also sat down. It took Pete another minute, but he finally did sit back down next to Sam.

Pete picked up his fork, but didn't eat. "If this is true, why didn't Aimee tell me?"

Buck sipped his coffee. "Giselle said she doesn't want folks to know she owns the club. Someone else runs it for her. Sounds like she's only had it for a few years."

Pete pushed a chunk of beef around his plate. "She did tell me once she buys up property when she can. Said she waits till the bank is about to foreclose, then jumps in and snaps them up cheap."

Pete still hadn't touched his dinner. Buck watched him poking holes in a potato with his fork. "Didn't your mama ever tell you not to play with your food? Eat your stew before it gets cold." Then Buck gestured to Sam with his coffee cup. "You told me this morning that Simone had worked at the club. Giselle hooked her up with Madame when they fired her."

The tension had broken. Sam wasted no time digging into his dinner. With his mouth filled, he mumbled, "Why'd she get fired?"

Buck leaned in closer to Sam. "She swung that crop once too often, and had customers coming to see her and not the show. They canned her sweet ass for it."

"If Madame owns the place, why did Giselle have to get involved at all?"

"Because Madame Séduisant keeps her distance. I doubt she knows many of the girls who work there. She knows Giselle because she's the assistant manager."

"You said you're seeing Giselle and Simone on Monday. How're you going to manage that?"

"Madame is sending Simone to Giselle's place at 1900 hours. I'll leave you fellas at the house and head over to Giselle's flat. It's close by."

Pete tore a roll in half and dipped it into his stew. "Let me get this straight. You're seeing both of them at the same time."

Buck grinned. "Yup. I might not survive it, but what a hell of a way to go."

Sam couldn't believe it. "How the fuck did you finagle that one? Two at once? Jesus Christ!"

"I asked, is all. Since Giselle and Simone know each other, it didn't take much convincin'."

Pete held out his hand. "I owe you an apology, Buck. Shoulda known a Georgia boy wouldn't lie."

Buck reached across the table and shook Pete's hand. "No sweat, Pete. I didn't believe it when you told us about the madam you knew in Marseilles. Turns out, y'all were telling the truth, too."

"Hell, we all bullshit so much, it's hard to separate the wheat from the chaff." He turned to Sam. "I know the Captain keeps the slop chest locked while we're in port, but you have a key, right?"

"Sure I do. Why?"

"If you'll open it up for me after dinner, I'll spring for a bottle. I could use a good, stiff one."

Not missing a beat, Buck chimed in as well. "Hell, buddy, mine's been stiff all damn day. Don't need another one tonight. But I'd be happy to drink with y'all, if you're buyin'."

"Since you're paying on Monday, I can afford a bottle, maybe two, if you're thirsty."

"This stew is so salty, I think they piped seawater into the galley. Damn right I'm thirsty."

"Buck's right, Pete. I think this may be a two-bottle night. Tell you what. You buy one, and I'll buy one. We'll get Buck good and drunk so he'll give us a play-by-play of his afternoon with Giselle."

Pete slapped Sam on the back. "You're on."

Buck knew he could deliver; they wouldn't be disappointed. However, he wouldn't tell them jack shit if they weren't going to believe him.

"Giselle is really something. She'll do anything, twice. I'll tell y'all whatever you want to know, if you're ready to hear it." He glanced at Sam, and then he addressed Pete directly. "But if you call me a liar again, I don't give a shit if y'all are bigger than me. I'll kick your ass so hard, you'll fart and cough at the same time."

No one said anything. Buck continued to stare at Pete. Then Sam said, "Pete, I think he means it. He's fired up. I'd put my money on Buck knocking you through yourself."

Pete grinned. "Fuck, this boy's crazier than a shithouse fly. If he's ready to take me on for saying he's lying like a cheap rug, what he did must be riper than a brown banana."

"You bet your Texas ass it is! And I intend to do more of it before we sail."

Sam took that opportunity to give them a schedule update; then he skillfully redirected the conversation in the process. "Damn good thing we're doing this on Monday. The Captain says they expect to have the derrick repaired so we can sail on Wednesday. The ship owners are losing money with the off-hire."

Pete interjected, "We'll sail Wednesday if we work our asses off."

Sam threw his napkin on the now-empty plate and picked up his tray. "Pete, I need to know what's left to do, so I can manage the schedule. Don't want anything to put the screws to Monday night."

They cleared the table. After grabbing some clean glasses, they made their way to the slop chest. While they wound their way through the ship, Pete recapped the day's work. He knew his stuff, and filled Sam in on what needed to be done before they could sail. Sam said he would make sure the three of them had Monday night free.

The ship's slop chest amounted to a large pantry filled with supplies that the crew could buy. Sam dug through some boxes and found them a couple bottles of Irish whiskey. Pete would have preferred Kentucky bourbon, but Buck reminded him beggars can't be choosy.

Before locking up, Sam picked up another carton of cigarettes for himself, then recorded the sales in the purchase log. Every sailor kept a slop chest tab, which would be paid off from their cash wages. Only after all deductions were paid would money go into their pocket.

It was the weekend, so most of the crew had gone ashore for the evening. They practically had the ship to themselves. Sam led the way to a place on the deck where some empty crates had been stacked.

The three men arranged the crates in a table-and-chairs configuration. A cool breeze blew off the water. On one side of the ship, the stars lit up the sky. On the other, the lights of Marseilles glowed in the distance.

As Pete poured them each a drink, Buck realized how comfortable he felt, not just with Sam, but also with Pete. Without knowing how he'd done it, he'd turned a corner with them.

Before they had a chance to grill him about his afternoon with Giselle, he asked them a question. "How'd you two get to be such good friends, anyway? You've never told me." He took the glass Pete handed him, then sat down.

"You tell him the story, Pete." Sam took his glass and also settled in on a crate. Pete poured himself twice as much whiskey as he'd poured for Sam and Buck. Sam noticed. "See that, Buck. He's giving us two-to-one odds."

"Yeah, two-to-one you tenderfoots will pass out, and I'll still be drinking." Pete capped the bottle and took his seat. "Remember, I told you I met Sam in New Orleans?"

Buck pulled his makeshift seat in closer. "You took Sam to a whorehouse in the French Quarter. Sure I remember."

"Hear that, Sam? Mention a whorehouse and he pays attention." Sam bolted back some whiskey, then swirled the liquid in the glass. "I need a drink to tell you this one."

Sam agreed. "Fuck, that's the truth. I need it to hear it again."

Buck didn't understand any of it. "What the hell are you guys talking about?"

"Sam and I hooked up a few times, when he docked in New Orleans," Pete continued.

"We made a regular run there. Unloaded cargo at the port every few months," Sam added.

"Sam knew I had my Chief Engineer's license, but stayed dockside doing inspections for a couple of years. Made good money at it, but after a while, I got tired of living there. Then Sam offered me a job on his ship."

"Yeah. The Chief Engineer on our ship got hurt pretty bad in an accident just before we sailed back to New Orleans. He had to be transferred home. Since we needed a replacement fast, I asked Pete if he'd like to sail again. He said yes."

"That's how I ended up on the same ship as Sam. Now jump ahead—what, Sam—about fourteen months?"

Sam put his glass down and took out a cigarette. "Sounds right. You came on board in August '61. The collision happened in October '62."

Buck had never heard any of this. "What collision?"

"The collision that nearly bought us all the farm." Pete bolted back some more whiskey.

"Shit! What happened?"

"Foggy night, tanker off-course and no one payin' attention to their radar."

Sam nodded. "We were in the North Sea approaching the Schelde River on the way to Antwerp. The fog was so thick, you could've cut it with a knife. We had about two-and-a-half-miles visibility when my watch ended at 2000 hours. I handed the watch over to the Third Mate and left the bridge to get some sleep."

"And that's when the fucking asshole Captain nearly got us all killed."

"I know Antwerp is one of the busiest ports in Europe." Buck rubbed his forehead. "But I'm not following, Pete. How did the Captain nearly get y'all killed there?"

Pete continued. "I was in the engine room, keeping an eye on things with my crew. We'd taken on a pilot at the Wandelaar Station to guide us into the Schelde."

"Just before we got to the entrance of the river, the pilot sent a 'slow ahead' message to the engine room, and the damn telegraph jammed. The Captain had to call us with the command. Then he told me to come up and fix the bell. That's how I ended up on the bridge—"

Sam interrupted. "If you hadn't been, we wouldn't be sitting here talking, that's for damn sure."

"I got the telegraph working and was about to go back to the engine room, when the pilot spotted the tanker on the radar. It had been hidden behind a blind spot and he hadn't seen it coming. The officer on watch looked though his binoculars. He couldn't see anything. By then, visibility was about two miles."

Buck leaned forward, resting his arms on his knees. "Did y'all raise them on the radio?"

"Our man tried to raise them. No one answered."

Sam snorted and exhaled cigarette smoke. "Sparky must've gone to take a shit."

Pete chuckled. "Who knows? He could've fallen asleep, or maybe he didn't speak English. Anyway, the pilot told the Captain we should take evasive action. The Captain barely glanced at the radar, then told the helmsman to hold her steady.

"He quoted the rulebook, saying we were the stand-on vessel, and to maintain course and speed. The pilot argued with him, and said the give-way vessel was too damn close for that. He checked the radar again, then said the vessel was heading straight for us."

Pete bolted back the rest of his drink and poured himself some more. "That's when all frigging hell broke loose. I saw the pilot stare at the radar and turn white as a ghost. He yelled at the Captain, and then at the helmsman, 'Hard a'starboard! They're not turning! They're going to fucking hit us!'

"The helmsman looked at the Captain for confirmation. The fucking by-the-book fool told him to hold steady, maintain course and speed. That's when the officer on watch rang the alarm and yelled, 'Jesus Christ! Hard a'starboard! Hard a'starboard!'

"I didn't need binoculars to see the lights. They had broken through the fog at just under two miles. They must have seen us at the same time we saw them."

Sam looked out at the water, the moon illuminating his memory of that night. "I was in bed. The all-hands-on-deck sounded, and I hit the ground running." Sam shook his head and raised his glass to the sky. "I nearly met my Maker in my skivvies. There wasn't time to pull on my pants."

Pete also looked at the water, seeing the same ghost ship as Sam. "The greenhorn helmsman froze. Someone had to do something. I jerked the lever on the telegraph to full ahead. Then I knocked that spineless jellyfish on his ass and took the helm.

"The Captain told me to freeze, and then he tried to grab me. The officer on watch came at me from the other side. I thought he meant to help the Captain." Pete grinned at the memory. "Instead, he tackled the Captain and took him down. Guess he figured being alive in the brig was better than dying at sea.

"The pilot repeated an urgent full-ahead to the engine room. My men were on their toes, and gave us the juice we needed. We got our asses out of the way as much as we had time to do. The other ship had also turned. Nobody knew if we'd turned enough."

Sam picked up the story. "I made it to the deck and saw the tanker coming at us. Fuck, I'll never forget it. When she passed, our hulls scraped. It sounded like the Devil opening up the gates of hell. I could've reached out and shook the hands of the crew on the other deck, they were that close."

"I can still see their faces." Sam didn't so much look at Buck, as through him. "They knew if they rammed us, we were all dead men. Their tanker had a full load of gasoline."

Buck whispered, "Jesus Christ." In his mind's eye, he saw the fireball if they'd hit. "That wasn't a ship, it was a floating bomb."

Sam raised his glass to Pete. "If not for this crazy son of a bitch, there wouldn't have been enough left of any of us to feed the fish." Then he emptied his glass.

"What happened to the Captain?"

Pete emptied the first bottle and picked up the second one. "He got a frigging slap on the wrist. They charged him with negligence and failing to take action on the basis of facts. He got his license suspended for six months. When the six months were up, they reassigned him to another ship."

"You mean he's still sailing?"

"You got it, Bucko!" Pete opened the bottle. "Enough about that fucking asshole." He poured Buck another drink. "It's about time *y'all* shit or get off the pot. What did you do with Giselle?"

Buck had been so absorbed in Pete's story, he'd completely forgotten about Giselle. "Christ, it's hard to remember after hearing what almost happened to y'all."

"Hell, son. The women are what we should remember. The rest of it is all water under the bridge."

Buck took a drink, then told them all about his afternoon with Giselle. Even though both Sam and Pete sat with their mouths open through most of his story, neither of them called him a liar.

# 8

Buck double-checked his cash. He certainly had enough to cover the evening for all three of them. Sam and Pete said they'd meet him on the dock by the gangway at 1830 hours. He had to get going or he'd be late.

The weekend had been a busy one for all three men. Buck hadn't seen much of Sam or Pete, since they'd spent the evening drinking on Friday. Buck smiled. He wouldn't see much of them tonight, either.

Sam made sure they would get Monday night off. Buck didn't know how he'd managed it with Pete, but Buck had to pull an extra anchor watch on Sunday to make sure he'd have Monday night free.

Buck had to laugh when he saw his buddies waiting for him. Pete had his hair slicked back and wore a new blue shirt. Buck recognized it as one he'd seen in the slop chest. He'd also put on his dress shoes. The crease in Sam's trousers was so sharp that the ship's cook could've used it to slice tomatoes. He had a piece of toilet paper stuck to his chin, where he had obviously cut himself shaving.

When Buck reached the dock, he had to poke some fun. "Are you sure y'all are going to a whorehouse? It looks like you're going to a church social." He got a bit closer to Sam and sniffed. "Aftershave? Jesus Christ, Sam, you'll smell prettier than she does."

Pete agreed. "I told him he smelled like he fell in a barrel of it."

"All right, you two, knock it off. I nicked myself real good." He gently peeled the paper off his chin. "I thought maybe splashing on more aftershave might help stop the bleeding. Did it stop?" He curled his lower lip over his teeth and jutted out his chin.

Pete lightly slapped his cheek. "Yeah, it's stopped. Let's hope you air out on the way." This time, Pete led the way up La Canebière. Sam and Buck followed.

Buck wanted to make sure Sam and Pete understood what he meant to do. "Pete, I'll give you the money to give to Madame. She's only charging us each for an hour, but we'll have all night if we want. Then I'm going to meet Giselle at her place."

"Damn straight I'm staying all night. What about you, Sam?"

"We'll see how it goes, Pete. I have no trouble fucking there, but I'm not real comfortable sleeping there."

"Who the hell said anything about sleeping?" Pete punched Buck's arm. "I don't expect you'll be getting much sleep tonight, with two of them working you over."

"I s'pose that's probably right. But, hell, once we sail, I'll have time to sleep."

"Me too, son. That's why I'm not worried about it."

They stopped in front of Madame Séduisant's house. Buck took out his wallet and handed Pete the money. "I never did get any francs, but Giselle told me Madame changes money."

"I haven't met a madam yet that couldn't change money."

Pete double-checked that Buck had given him enough and then put the bills in his pocket. "One thing you can count on, bars and brothels will take American dollars. The exchange rate is lousy, but who the hell cares?"

"That's the truth. There's not enough time to find a bank. Anyway, whorehouse money smells better, and the madam always delivers it with a smile." Sam flicked his half-smoked cigarette into the gutter, then touched his chin. He studied his fingers for a moment before he asked Pete, "Are you sure I'm not bleeding?"

"No. But if you ask me that one more time, you will be." Pete headed up the stairs to the double doors. He abruptly turned around, and said to Buck, "Sure you don't want to come in and see if Simone is ready to go?"

"Nah. I'll see her at Giselle's. I don't want her to think I'm rushin' her."

Pete grinned. "If I see her, I'll make sure she takes her crop."

"Thanks, buddy. She'll need it."

"Damn, son, you're a pistol!" Pete continued up the steps.

Before Sam followed, he gave Buck his marching orders. "You have to be back by 0600 hours, no later. Got it?"

"Got it. I won't be late. I'll see you at breakfast."

Sam followed Pete up the stairs. Buck walked down Rue Lafayette to the corner, and turned onto Allées Léon Gambetta. He didn't have to check the number. He knew Giselle's building by sight. He went in the front door and knocked on 1D.

Giselle opened the door so quickly, Buck wondered if she'd been standing there, waiting. "*Bon soir*, Monsieur Buck, it is good to see you again."

Buck kissed her on the cheek. "It's good to see you, too."

"Come in, *s'il vous plaît*."

Out of habit, Buck reached to take off his cap. Then he remembered Simone still had it. "I sure hope Simone remembers to bring my cap back. It's my Houston ball cap. Don't know when I'll get back there to get another one."

"Do not worry, monsieur. I talked to her earlier. She will bring the hat, and the crop."

Giselle said it so matter-of-factly, Buck wasn't sure he'd heard correctly. "Did you say Simone told you she's bringing the hat and the crop?"

"*Oui.*" Giselle led Buck into the sitting room, where she had a tray of wine and cheese waiting. "If you recall, I do not have one." Giselle's eyes twinkled when she added, "For your pleasure, we will need one, no?"

"S'pose we will at that." Wondering what he'd gotten himself into, he added, "Guess Pete won't have to remind her to bring it." Buck perched on the edge of the sofa, the way he had at the club. He tapped his foot, having an unexpected case of nerves. Giselle picked up on it.

"Buck, we will take good care of you. I have talked to Simone about what to do."

Rather than calming him down, Giselle only made him more jittery. "Y'all have planned out tonight?"

"Not so much planned as shared our curiosities about what to do. We are both fond of you and wish for you to remember us with fondness."

"Ma'am, y'all don't have to worry about that! I'll never forget either of you."

Repeating what she had done their first time together, Giselle put her hand on his thigh. "We will make sure that is so."

To Buck's utter astonishment, Giselle leaned over and kissed him. It wasn't a soft, feminine kiss, but a kiss that smoldered with intense passion. He reflexively wrapped his arms around her and returned her kiss. Her amazing breasts pressed into his side. He wanted nothing more than to bury his face between them.

The kiss calmed him, and bolstered his confidence. He lowered his head and nuzzled her breasts through her blouse. She whispered to him, "You will remember, monsieur, you do not have to pay to be with me. You are welcome in my bed whenever you come to Marseilles."

Buck understood Giselle meant he would have to pay to see Simone. Buck teased her. "What, missy, you don't want me to see Simone when I come back?"

Giselle ran her fingers through his hair. "Perhaps I should get a crop and have Simone show me what she does with it. Then there will be no need for you to see her."

"Damn!" Buck sat up. "You would do that just so I don't go to her for it?"

"*Oui.* Simone will show us how to give pleasure to one another." Giselle poured the wine, filling the third glass as well. "She will be here soon. It is good we will be three tonight. We can both learn new things, you and I."

Buck put his arm around Giselle's waist and held her close. "Mademoiselle, I don't think there's much Simone could show you that you don't already know."

Giselle lightly touched her lips to his. She pulled away just enough to say, "Simone knows many things. It is her business, just as being a sailor is yours."

Her breath warmed his face like stepping into the sunshine on a bright summer day. "Giselle, Simone doesn't know how to make me feel like you do."

Then Buck kissed her, more passionately than he'd ever kissed a woman before. He didn't think about it. The impulse to do it overwhelmed him and he moved with it. At that moment, he would have preferred an evening alone with Giselle.

But the arrangements had already been made. Before he wanted the kiss to end, they heard a knock at the door. Giselle pulled away, but he didn't let go of her.

"Simone is here. I must let her in."

Reluctantly Buck released her. "Yeah, I know." Giselle stood. Before she walked away, Buck grabbed her hand. "Giselle, before you answer the door, I want to tell you . . ." He hesitated, not knowing how to finish the sentence.

"Yes, Buck, what is it?"

"Ma'am, you are the most beautiful woman I've ever known, inside and out. I'm mighty glad to have made your acquaintance. I hope you meant it when you said you want to see me again, 'cause I'll be back."

"*Oui*, monsieur, I meant it." She squeezed his hand, then went to greet Simone.

Buck didn't want his imagination to run wild, but he couldn't help wondering if Giselle's fondness for him had grown into something more. He also wondered the same thing about himself. He'd never been in love, and had no clue what it might feel like.

Before he had time to reflect further on the what-ifs, Giselle came back, followed by Simone. Buck hardly recognized Simone fully dressed. She had on a short black skirt and a striped midriff top. The outfit looked familiar to him. Then he remembered. The dancer at the club had worn the same thing during the streetwalker number. Simone must have done that act when she worked at the club.

Buck stood up and reached out his hand to shake Simone's. He felt uncomfortable kissing her in front of Giselle. "Hello, Simone. Glad you could make it."

"*Bon soir*, Monsieur Buck." She looked at his outstretched hand. "Oh, monsieur, we know one another better than that!" Simone embraced him, then kissed him on both cheeks. "I am honored you asked to include me this evening. Giselle explained I am here at your request."

That's when Buck realized she'd come into the room empty-handed. Not wanting to ask outright if she'd brought the riding crop, he asked instead about his hat. "I hope y'all remembered to bring back my cap."

"*Oui.* I left it there." She pointed toward the foyer. "Your friends would not let me forget my bag."

"You saw Sam and Pete?"

"I had to speak to Madame before I left. They were in the parlor with her."

"Did Pete say anything to you?"

Simone didn't answer. She turned around and went to the foyer. When she came back, she had a canvas tote bag. Buck immediately saw the crop sticking out of the top of the bag.

Simone set the bag on the floor and took out the crop. "Your friend Pete said you told him to make sure I had this." She trailed the flat edge of the crop down his cheek.

Buck's cheeks flushed so badly, he knew they must have turned purple. "Simone, I swear to God, I never told him that. He's the one who told me he would make sure you had it, not the other way around."

Giselle came up behind him and wrapped her arms around his waist. He started so badly, he elbowed her breast. He blurted out, "Jesus Christ, Giselle! You scared the living shit out of me!" He took a deep breath, then blew it out of his mouth. "I'm sorry. I didn't mean to bump you."

She breathed into his ear, "It is all right, Buck." She lightly massaged his chest with the palm of her hand. "You must relax. Simone, get him his wine."

Still holding the crop, Simone picked up a glass from the tray. She stood directly in front of him and sipped it before handing it to him. "Shall we sit?"

Giselle agreed. "Perhaps that is best. We will have some wine and relax together."

As Buck sat down in the middle, with Simone on one side and Giselle on the other, he couldn't think of a more unrelaxing situation. Three people barely fit on the settee. The two women were right up against him. For one awful moment, he thought he might hyperventilate.

"Giselle, does that window open? I could really use some air."

"But, of course, monsieur." She put her hand on his thigh and squeezed it as she stood. Buck swallowed a moan as the sensation moved up his leg into his groin. A cool breeze soothed his hot skin when she opened the window. She handed Simone a glass and took her own before sitting back down.

"Is that better?"

"It sure is." Buck inhaled deeply, drawing in a potpourri of perfume. "You ladies smell real good."

Giselle sniffed his neck. "You as well, Buck."

In spite of his nervousness, he had to laugh. "I ain't wearing nothin' except Palmolive soap!"

"It is not soap. It is your skin that has the scent. It is a masculine odor, and quite pleasant. Do you not agree, Simone?"

Simone picked up her cue, and sniffed the other side of his neck. Buck thought she sounded genuinely surprised when she said, "C'est très bon! You have the scent of a man's musk, but mixed with herbs!"

"I expect I smell 'cause I'm nervous. Glad you ladies aren't offended."

Giselle kissed his neck. "Oh, monsieur, we are not offended! You do not know the smell of a man excites a woman?"

"Never really thought about it. It makes y'all hot?"

"Monsieur, you make us hot." Simone licked his neck at the same time that Giselle kissed the other side. Another surge of sensation moved through his groin, and his erection throbbed.

These two women meant to get things going. Once again, he had to prove to himself he wasn't a gutless wonder. If he ran away with his tail between his legs, he'd never be able to face Giselle again. Considering how much he wanted to come back, he gathered himself up by his bootstraps. He set his glass down, then plunged into the deep end of the pool.

He put one arm around Giselle and the other around Simone. "Ladies, maybe we'd be more comfortable in the bedroom. This sofa is mighty small." He nodded toward Simone's
bag. "Missy, we can go just as soon as you give me my ball cap
back."

Simone picked up her bag from the floor. She dug around
for a moment and pulled out his cap. Instead of giving it to
Buck, she handed it to Giselle. "It is Giselle's now. She can keep
it, or give it back, as she sees fit."

Giselle did not give it to him. She put it on her own head.
"Perhaps I should keep it, to make sure you come back to me."

"You don't need a hat for that, mademoiselle." Buck took
his cap off her head.

"You are quite correct, monsieur. A hat is not enough to
bring you back." He thought he glimpsed her eyes well up, but
she stood before he could be sure. She picked up the tray.
"Come, let us be more comfortable."

Simone stood. With her bag in one hand and her crop in the
other, she followed Giselle. Buck stuffed his cap in his back
pocket and brought up the rear.

When Simone and Buck got to the bedroom, Giselle wasn't
there. When he turned to look back down the hall, he noticed
the closed bathroom door. "Guess she had to use the toilet."

Simone tossed her things on the bed she had once used as
her own. "Monsieur, you know, of course, Giselle is attached to
you. She told me today when we talked."

"What do y'all mean, attached?"

"*Elle est dans l'amour.*"

Buck didn't know all the words, but he sure as hell knew
"*l'amour*" meant "love." "Simone, this is only the second time
we've seen each other."

"She has been drawn to you since that first night at Le Club
de Plaisir. You blushed when she touched you, and you won

her heart." Simone rummaged through her bag and took out her black robe, the same one from the other night. She laid it at the foot of the bed.

"Do you really think she's falling for me?"

"I am sure of it. Monsieur Buck, do not be cruel. If you will not come back to Marseilles, do not tell her you will."

"Damn straight I'll come back. We're sailing for Rio on Wednesday. The *Halifax Star* docks in Marseilles again on the return trip."

"How long, Buck, before you return?" He turned to find Giselle standing in the door, holding the tray. Her eyes were red.

Buck hurried over to help her. "I expect about six weeks, to make the round-trip. We have to load the cargo before we leave Rio." He took the tray with the wine and set it on the dresser.

No one had ever cried over him before. In the few seconds it took him to collect the tray and put it down, he made a decision. Not knowing where he found the courage to do it, he asked Simone, "Could y'all show Giselle how you used the crop on me so she can do it herself next time?"

Giselle's face transformed. The strain disappeared as a smile replaced the sadness. Without saying a word, she went to her closet. From the corner, she took out a riding crop nearly identical to the one Simone had. "I bought this today."

"Damn, Giselle. I didn't know you already got one." Buck wanted a closer look, and took it from her. The smell of leather filled his nostrils as he swung it through the air. "It's a beauty, too."

Simone interrupted his examination. "It will certainly do the job, monsieur." It caught him off guard to turn around and find Simone topless. "It seems it is time for you to take off your clothes."

Giselle took the crop. "*Oui*, Buck. You must undress, if Simone is to show me what you like."

With both women watching him closely, Buck unbuttoned his shirt and took it off. An odd mix of heat and embarrassment filled his belly. He sat on the edge of the bed and took off his shoes and socks. When it came time to unzip, he hesitated. "Do y'all have to watch me take off my pants?"

As though they'd rehearsed it, Simone and Giselle said simultaneously, "*Oui!*"

Obviously outnumbered, Buck unzipped. He took his pants off, but left his undershorts on. His erection nearly poked out of the fly.

Simone chastised him. "You do not think I meant everything?" In full view of Giselle, she lightly tapped his hard-on with the crop. "Take them off, monsieur."

Buck hooked his thumbs in the waistband and pulled his skivvies down over his hips. They fell to the floor and he kicked them off. His erection jutted out in front of him.

Simone had obviously taken charge. "Giselle, perhaps monsieur would enjoy seeing your breasts while you tickle his penis with the crop."

Just hearing Simone say it nearly brought him off. Noticeable drops of fluid had formed on the end of his prick. "Girls, I don't know how much of this I'll be able to take."

Simone showed no mercy. "Monsieur Buck, you are not a virgin. You have chosen the crop tonight." She tapped his prick with it, harder than she had earlier. "You know what to expect."

Giselle stood in front of him and pulled her shirt over her head. Her tits were a sight to behold. Buck didn't think he'd ever be able to look at them and not get hard. "Fuck, Giselle! I'm gonna shoot if you whack me with that thing."

"If you do, Buck, then that will be the first of many times tonight."

She didn't hesitate. She picked up her own crop and mimicked what Simone had done to him. When she tapped his dick, Buck groaned and nearly doubled over with the effort to sustain control. Simone grabbed Giselle's arm before she could tap again. "Wait. Let me get a cold cloth."

Buck closed his eyes and took a deep breath. He remembered the night at the club. He'd been nearly as bad off during the show. He wondered how hard his dick would have to get before it cracked.

Simone came back with a wet washrag. "This will help you last longer." He didn't have a chance to brace himself. She reached down and wrapped the ice-cold cloth around his prick. He yelped and tried to pull away, but she had him good.

"Jesus Christ, Simone, what are you trying to do, kill me?" He could feel his erection wilting.

"No, monsieur. That comes later. This is only to prevent you from finishing too soon."

"Fuck, don't have to worry about that now." Although not completely flaccid, he had measurably softened.

"We will make it hard again. You need not worry, monsieur."

"Simone is correct, Buck." While he watched, Giselle took off her skirt. She again had on black lacy panties. "You like?"

Buck stared at her. "Yeah, sugar. I like." His cock regained some lost ground.

Then Simone took off her skirt. She had nothing on underneath. She walked behind Giselle. Buck could plainly see both women. The only clothing left among the three of them were Giselle's panties.

With no warning whatsoever, Simone swung the crop and connected with Giselle's ass. Giselle moaned the way she had when Buck had smacked her with the hairbrush.

"She likes that. It makes her hot. I used a hairbrush the other day."

Simone again swung the crop. "*Oui*, monsieur. Her cream runs with the crop."

Buck muttered, "Yeah, so does mine." His hard-on had returned with a vengeance.

Before Simone could swing a third time, Giselle stopped her. "I want Buck inside. Will you lace his buttocks while he fucks me?"

"*Mais oui!*"

Giselle wasted no time taking off her panties and crawling onto the bed. She stayed on all fours and spread her legs wide. Simone handed Buck a condom. "Monsieur, you will do as Giselle asks." He wasn't sure if she meant it as a question or an order.

He rolled the condom on. "Yes, ma'am, I'll do as she asks." With her ass in the air, she reminded Buck of a dog in heat, except no dog ever looked so beautiful.

Buck mounted her the same way his old hound would have mounted a bitch. He had no sooner penetrated Giselle, when Simone striped his ass. The force of the blow made him lunge forward, burying his cock inside Giselle. She moaned loudly.

Buck gripped Giselle's hips. He knew to expect another swipe, but he didn't know when. Hoping to sustain his balance when it hit, he managed two more thrusts before the second swing landed. This time, he groaned, the sensation nearly taking him over the top. He hung on.

Simone allowed him to hump Giselle several more times before she swung again. The third one did it. His prick sprayed inside the rubber like a garden hose. He couldn't hold back. He pumped into Giselle as Simone gave him three more strokes in rapid succession. Buck had never felt such scalding heat in his life.

The intensity of his orgasm left Buck breathless and tired. He needed some recovery time. He pulled out of Giselle and flopped onto the bed beside her. Simone told Giselle to stay put. She meant to bring Giselle off, using the crop.

The two women gave Buck quite a show. Simone took the crop to Giselle's lovely ass. Buck could tell Giselle got hotter with every stroke. When Simone turned the crop around and fucked Giselle with the handle, Giselle's climax shook the bed.

After watching two naked women performing obscene acts right in front of his face, Buck really wanted to fuck again. Giselle insisted he do Simone while she rested. Once Giselle had caught her breath, she kissed and caressed Simone. Buck humped Simone at the same time.

They spent the rest of the night trading roles. By about two in the morning, they had all run out of steam. While Buck and Giselle had one last round, Simone fell asleep in the second bed. Buck fell asleep holding Giselle.

When the alarm went off at five in the morning, Giselle grabbed it and turned it off. Simone never stirred. Buck wanted to shower before going back to the ship. When he came out of the toilet, he found Giselle in the sitting room, waiting for him.

"You should go back to bed, sugar. You have to work tonight."

"I will, once you are gone." Her voice cracked and she quickly turned around.

"Giselle, I will be back."

"You say that now, monsieur. But you are a sailor." She wiped her face with her hand. "Is it not true that sailors have a woman in every port?"

"Some do, I s'pose. I sure as hell don't."

"There will be others like Simone."

"I won't lie to y'all. I expect there will be. But, Giselle, there won't be others like you."

"I hope that is true, monsieur."

"It is." Buck turned her around. "Know something?"

"What, monsieur?"

He pulled his cap out of his back pocket. "I think you need to hang on to this for me." He put it on her head. "That way, you know I'll come back. That's my lucky Houston ball cap."

"You will let me know when you are returning?"

"When we get to Rio, I'll send y'all a letter. I'll know better by then when we're heading back here."

"*Très bien!* How do I write to you?"

"You gotta send a letter to the head office. They forward the mail to the agent at the next port, who'll get it to the ship." Giselle got him some paper and a pencil, and he wrote the address down. He handed it to her and teased, "Y'all know, I'll probably be back here before a letter catches up with me."

"Then I will make a copy so I can hand it to you in person."

As much as he hated to leave, Buck had to go. "Giselle, I really gotta go. Sam will hand me my head if he has to cover for me." Buck kissed her good-bye. "Tell Simone I said good-bye and thanks for last night."

"I will tell her." At the door, Giselle hugged him. "*À bientôt.* I will take good care of your lucky hat."

"I know you will, mademoiselle." Buck kissed Giselle once more, and then he left. He hurried down La Canebière to the dock, and back to the ship.

Pete and Sam were already at the corner table when he got to the mess room. Pete looked tired as hell. "Good morning. How are y'all doin' today?" Buck put his tray down beside Sam and pulled out a chair.

"You seem damned cheerful this morning."

Pete grumbled, "I'm surprised he can still walk."

Buck nodded toward Pete. "What's wrong with him?"

"Not enough sleep. He's been up most of the night."

"So have I. I'm in great shape today."

"You're also younger than I am." Pete finished his coffee and took Buck's. "I need this more than you do."

"Help yourself. I'll get another one. When did you get back, Sam?"

"About one this morning. Yvette asked me to stay, but I sleep better in my own bed."

"Had a good time?"

"I had a frigging great time. I don't have to ask if you enjoyed yourself. You're glowing like a hundred-watt lightbulb."

"What about you, Pete?"

"Aimee took good care of me. She always does. The problem with fucking the madam is that she knows every goddamned trick in the book. I didn't stay soft long enough last night to have a piss."

"And you're complaining?"

"Ever hear of having too much of a good thing? What I got last night will definitely hold me until we get to Rio."

Buck got up to get another round of coffee. Before he left, he asked Pete, "Know any good whorehouses in Rio?"

"Sure as hell do. We'll go to Conchita's. Her house is the best in Brazil."

Buck whistled through his teeth. "Conchita's, huh? Sounds sexy."

Sam nodded. "I've been there. Those senoritas are definitely hot-blooded."

Buck grinned. Maybe one of Conchita's girls could teach him even more tricks before he came back to Marseilles, and to Giselle.

# MERCHANT MAUREEN

# 1

Maureen put her duffel bag down on the dock. She needed to catch her breath before boarding the *Honey Rose*. Never in all her days had she been so torn about going back to sea. Before her dad died, she couldn't wait to sail. Now she didn't know if she could sail without him.

One thing she did know, she couldn't sail on the *Atlantic Moon* with another Captain. Every time she looked at the bridge, she would see her father standing there. If she intended to continue as a merchant mariner, she had to do it on a new ship.

The *Honey Rose* appealed to her because her friend Grace had signed on as a deckhand a little over six months ago. She wanted to be with her husband, the Second Mate on the ship. Grace got sick of being left home alone for months on end, and decided if you can't beat 'em, join 'em.

Maureen's eyes welled up when she remembered how her dad had helped Grace get the job. He'd been good friends with the Captain of the *Honey Rose* for many years. When Maureen asked him to intercede on Grace's behalf, he convinced Captain McPherson that Grace could pull her own weight.

With that recommendation, the Captain agreed to let Grace sail on the *Honey Rose.* He gave her six months' probation; at the end of which, her performance, as well as her husband's, had been reviewed.

Three months after Grace sailed on her first voyage, Maureen's dad had a heart attack. There had been a bad storm during a transatlantic crossing. Her father's heart gave out while navigating the rough water. He died at the helm of his ship, in the middle of the Atlantic Ocean. He'd made it clear years before that he wanted to be buried at sea. Being his only living relative, Maureen honored his wish.

After taking a few months off, Maureen decided to try sailing again. Grace's probation period had ended, and she had come through it with flying colors. Maureen asked Grace if she thought she had a shot at crewing on the *Honey Rose.*

Grace drafted her husband, Vince, as a coconspirator to get Maureen aboard. He used his influence as Second Mate to talk the Captain into taking on a second female crew member, the same way her father had done with Grace. It worked.

They needed another Able Seaman on board. Captain McPherson already knew Maureen, and he knew she had been mentored by her father. It also helped that Grace had proven a woman could work alongside the men, pulling her own weight and not asking for special treatment. After reviewing all the facts, Captain McPherson accepted Maureen as a full member of the crew.

Now Maureen stood on the dock, considering whether she would actually board the ship. She could walk away, and try to lead a normal life, like other women. But what in the name of God would she do? Her father taught her how to be a sailor. She couldn't imagine making her living any other way. With the memory of her father vivid in her mind, Maureen picked up her duffel bag and headed for the gangway.

She stopped at the foot of the ramp to adjust her duffel bag on her shoulder. The ramp had a steep incline, and the choppy water made it sway. She didn't want to lose her balance boarding.

The man on watch saw her and yelled, "Miss, do you have business on this ship?" He came down the gangway and stopped in the middle, summarily blocking her path. "If you do, I'll need to see your papers."

Maureen knew the drill. "AB Murphy reporting for duty." She put her duffel bag down and pulled an envelope out of her pocket. "Here are my working papers, signed by Captain McPherson."

"The Chief Mate told me to expect a new AB named Murphy. He didn't tell me you're a woman."

"Guess he wanted it to be a surprise."

The young man sniggered. "I don't think he knows. He has you bunking with Preston. Don't think that's going to happen."

"Don't suppose so." Maureen wondered how it could be possible the Chief Mate didn't know, considering the Captain, Grace and Vince all knew. She figured it best to keep her mouth shut and let things unfold as they would.

The young man took the envelope. He checked her identification and her letter of introduction. "You're Captain Murphy's daughter, aren't you?"

"That's me." She wanted him to clear the gangplank so she could board.

He gave the envelope back to her. "Sorry to hear your father passed away. I never heard anyone say a bad word about him."

If there's one thing she'd learned working with men, it's that a woman can't cry in front of them. No matter what the reason, it's a sign of weakness. She couldn't afford to start her stint on this ship by bawling like a baby because someone mentioned her father.

She managed to get out, "Thank you. He was a good man." Then she hefted her duffel bag back onto her shoulder. "I'm ready to board."

"Follow me. I'll take you to the Chief Mate. He can figure out where to put you." The young man turned around. She knew better than to expect any help with her bag. Steep, swaying gangway notwithstanding, she had to manage it herself. And she did.

Even with a heavy bag hoisted onto her shoulder, she managed the ramp with little difficulty. Her dad always said she was as sure-footed as a mountain goat. She could climb ropes and ladders, and keep her footing on slippery decks with the best of them. She tried not to laugh when the less agile men would fall flat on their cans and she stayed standing.

Her new shipmate stood on deck, and monitored her progress. She'd been here before, and understood she would have to prove herself all over again. For some unfathomable reason, the men seemed to want her to fail. That fired up her Irish, and pushed her to try harder to be good. Being a woman on a ship, you had to be good to survive.

When she reached the deck, she had no apologies to make for a misstep. "What's your name, sailor? You know I'm Murphy, but I don't know you."

"I'm AB Eddie Shaw."

"Nice to meet you, Eddie. It's okay to call you 'Eddie,' isn't it?"

"It is if I can call you 'Murph.' "

"I've been called a lot worse. 'Murph' is fine."

Eddie led her across the deck to the steel staircase leading to the bridge. "Roger Trent is our Chief Mate. I think he's on the bridge right now." He put his foot on the first step, then abruptly turned around. Maureen almost bumped into him. "If it doesn't work out with Preston, you can always bunk with me." He winked at her, then gave her a once-over.

"Thanks for the offer, Eddie, but you should know, I walk in my sleep. Don't remember any of it, but they tell me I nearly castrated a man once who came into my room unexpected. Would hate to have that happen to you." If she'd learned one thing being a sailor, it was how to bullshit her way out of any tight situation.

Eddie pointed to a wisp of hair that had peeked out from under her wool watch cap. "You have red hair, don't you?"

"It happens when you're Irish."

"They said Captain Murphy had a temper to go with his red hair. Guess you do, too." Eddie still didn't move up the stairs, again blocking her path. "I may have to call you 'Red' instead of Murph."

"Let me know what you decide, so I'll know to answer when you yell."

"I'll do that."

He finally hauled his can up the steps. Maureen followed. Her stomach fluttered as she considered she didn't have her father's protection on this ship. On the *Honey Rose*, she had to hold her own, on her own. The privilege of being the Captain's daughter, with the respect afforded to the Captain's kin, didn't exist here.

Maureen shook herself out of the fearful thoughts that wanted to slice into her mind. Focus, she had to focus. She had a job, and intended to do it well. That's all she had to think about.

She followed Eddie to the bridge. The *Honey Rose* wasn't as old as the *Atlantic Moon*. The bridge had newer equipment. Maureen didn't know how she would react to being on the bridge of a ship again, but she felt the familiar itch to get her hands on the helm.

She smiled as she remembered hearing her father boast to

Captain McPherson that his daughter had become the best helmsman on his ship. She hoped the new Master would remember that, and give her a crack at steering his lady.

Before she had a chance to look around, Eddie yelled, "Roger, the new AB is here." He didn't say anything else.

The man he told had his back to them. He had a large nautical chart spread out on a wooden table, and he appeared to be studying it carefully. Maureen heard him say, "Just a minute, Eddie. If we can't get a pilot on board tomorrow, I have to figure out how to get us out of here." He had a pronounced British accent.

"I can do it." Maureen had navigated the *Atlantic Moon* out of New Bedford Harbor many times. "I've already done it at least a half-dozen times."

Roger turned around and stared at her. "Who the hell are you?"

Eddie smirked. "This is AB Murphy."

"I'm too damn busy for bullshit jokes, Eddie. We have to get ready to sail. Get her off the ship."

Maureen put her duffel bag down and took a few steps closer to the Chief Mate. "He isn't bullshitting. I'm AB Maureen Murphy. The Captain hired me. He didn't tell you I'm a woman?"

"He told me he hired a new AB. He forgot to mention you're a damn girl."

Eddie spoke up from behind her. "She's Captain Murphy's daughter."

"Jesus Christ, you're Ben Murphy's daughter?"

"Yes."

"He died, didn't he?"

Maureen set her jaw, determined to keep it together. "He had a heart attack on the bridge of the *Atlantic Moon*. We buried him at sea."

"Miss Murphy, I'm sorry about your father. But we're short-handed as it is. This ship is no place for a woman. We need an AB that can help with the heavy work, and with the helm."

Maureen never expected the introduction to the Chief Mate to go like this, but she wouldn't wilt the first time a man challenged her ability. "Mister Trent, it seems that if the Captain is satisfied that I can pull my own weight, you should be, too."

"With all due respect, Miss Murphy, I seriously doubt you can."

Trying to stay cool in more ways than one, Maureen pulled her hat off, letting her red hair tumble to her shoulders. She walked past Roger to the chart. "You can't see the currents and shoals on these. You either need a pilot, or someone who knows these waters to get you safely out of here."

"She's right, Roger." Maureen recognized the voice. "Hello, Maureen. Welcome aboard." With the authority of a Captain, he dismissed Eddie. "Shaw, isn't it your watch?"

"Yes, sir."

Maureen turned to greet her father's good friend, and saw Eddie hurrying back down the stairs. "Hello, Captain McPherson. It's good to see you again."

Much to Maureen's surprise, the Captain kissed her on the cheek, in front of Roger. "I am so sorry about Ben. I wish I could have been at his funeral."

Maureen took a deep breath and steadied herself before answering. "He'd told me if anything ever happened to him, he wanted to be buried at sea as soon as possible, with no fuss made. I did as he asked, except we had to wait a couple of days to arrange it because the weather was so bad."

That's as much as she could get out. Roger spoke up and tactlessly changed the subject. "Sir, why didn't you tell me AB Murphy was a woman?"

"Because I knew you'd fight me every step of the way. I want Ben's daughter on this ship. She's a damn good sailor and we're lucky to have her."

Maureen couldn't believe her ears. "Thank you, Captain."

"No thanks necessary, Maureen. I expect you'll work as hard for me as you did for your father."

"You bet I will, Captain."

"Roger, what's the status of getting us a pilot?"

"There's a shortage, Captain. We can't get one on board until day after tomorrow."

"We're scheduled to sail tomorrow." The experienced Master took a look at the charts. "Maureen, what were you saying about the currents and shoals?"

"Sir, I took the *Atlantic Moon* out of here at least a half-dozen times."

The Captain seemed surprised. "You were at the helm?"

"Yes, sir. My father taught me."

"That's right, I remember he told me how good you are." The Captain chuckled. "It figures. The Ben Murphy I knew would tutor his daughter on the bridge." He tapped the chart with his index finger. "The pilot who brought us in here almost hit a sandbar."

Maureen could guess where. She went to the table and had a look at the chart. "I bet it was right here, at the entrance to the Acushnet River."

Captain McPherson leaned against the table and crossed his arms over his chest. "That's exactly where it was. When was the last time you took the *Atlantic Moon* out of here?"

"About five months ago."

"Think you could get us out of here tomorrow—"

Roger interrupted before Maureen could answer. "Sir, I have to object to this. You could be putting all of our lives in danger by having her take us out."

"Nonsense, Roger. She's as qualified as any pilot we could get."

"But, sir, she's a woman!"

"Get over it, Trent. We will use Murphy's skills, just like we would any other sailor." Speaking to her as the Captain, he continued. "Maureen, I want you to get settled in, and then report back to the bridge with Roger. Before I give the all clear on sailing tomorrow, I want to make sure you can handle the helm on this ship. We have newer equipment than you had on the *Atlantic Moon*. Let's see what you can do with it."

Maureen glanced at Roger. She could see how pissed off he was. She figured it best to bring her sleeping requirements to the Captain's attention. "Sir, I haven't yet been shown to my quarters."

"Where did you assign her, Roger?"

"Sir, I put him in with Preston. There's a spare bunk in that cabin. That's before I knew the *him* was a *her*, and that AB Murphy was a woman."

"There's a single cabin open two doors down from Grace and Vince, next to the utility closet. Put her there." Before he left, the Captain added, "Just remember, your not knowing her sex is my doing, not hers. Don't blame Maureen because I didn't want any grief from you over her coming on board."

"Yes, sir."

Much to Maureen's dismay, he left her alone on the bridge with Roger. She would have preferred being shown to her cabin by the Captain, or having him tell Grace to do it. Instead, she had no choice but to wait on Roger.

He had gone back to the chart, continuing to study it. She considered going over and looking at it with him, then thought better of it. Rather than twiddling her thumbs waiting on him, she went to study the instruments at the helm.

Everything looked familiar, just a bit newer. If the Captain or Roger would watch the radar, she knew she could safely clear the harbor without a pilot on board. Her father had weaned her at the wheel. She knew how to steer a ship, and she knew this port.

Maureen lost track of Roger as she examined the equipment.

She hadn't noticed him standing behind her. When he spoke, she jumped. "You're sure you can do this? If you can't, you'd better damn well speak up."

"I can do it." Not wanting to get into an argument with him, she picked up her duffel bag. "Are you ready to show me to my quarters?"

"Yeah. Let's go."

Again, she hoisted her bag onto her shoulder. Roger trotted down the steps two at a time, which she couldn't do carrying her belongings. Falling down the stairs would only make matters worse. When she got to the bottom of the staircase, she saw him already partway down the deck.

She hustled and almost caught up with him before he disappeared down another flight of stairs. Repeating the care she had taken a few minutes earlier, she managed the steps with no mishap. Maureen saw him waiting for her outside a door farther down the alleyway.

When she got within earshot, he opened the door and brusquely barked, "This is the cabin the Captain told me to give you. I'll see you back on the bridge in half an hour."

Then he continued down the hall to what Maureen supposed must be his cabin. He disappeared inside and slammed the door.

Maureen wanted to ask which cabin belonged to Grace and Vince, but Roger didn't give her a chance. She'd have to find out the particulars from Grace, like where they kept the bed linens and towels. In the meantime, she had her own room. For that, she said a quiet thank-you to the powers that be.

After tossing her duffel bag on the bare mattress, she went to use the toilet. Relieved she had her own commode, shower and sink, she took a quick pee and then splashed some water on her face.

When she came out, she noticed a note tacked on the back of her door. The handwriting looked familiar. It said, *Welcome aboard. I'm glad you're here. See you later.* The perfect penmanship belonged to Grace.

Maureen put two and two together. The Captain intended for her to have this cabin all along, if Grace knew to put the note in here. He had kept the whole thing quiet so he wouldn't raise the hackles of the crew. It seemed from Roger's reaction to her being here, the Captain had made a wise choice.

Now that she had a few minutes to herself, she wondered what it would take to get Roger to accept her. It surprised her to even want that. She'd never cared whether the men on the ship accepted her or not. Maybe it had something to do with how good-looking he was, and that sexy British accent.

As soon as the thought entered her mind, she beat it back. If she wanted her seagoing career to end, that would be the way to do it. Her father had warned her from the get-go, no fraternizing with the crew.

Anyway, so what if she found him attractive? She had just met him and he already hated her. And what's more, he had the surliest disposition of any officer she'd ever met. As she yanked her clothes out of her duffel bag, she tried not to think about how Roger Trent bore an uncanny resemblance to Laurence Olivier's young Heathcliff in *Wuthering Heights*.

When she opened the closet door to put her clothes away, she found bed linens and towels. Grace must have left them. Maureen muttered, "Bless you," and thanked her in absentia. She quickly put her clothes away in the tiny closet, then made up her bunk. Just before she left to return to the bridge, she glanced in the mirror over the bathroom sink. Her hair wasn't the best it had ever been, but it wasn't bad.

She retraced her steps, and found her way up the two flights of stairs to the bridge. The Captain heard her come in and turned around. He had been studying the charts Roger had left on the table. Roger hadn't yet returned.

"Hello, Maureen. I trust you are settled in?"

"Yes, sir. The cabin is fine. I have everything I need."

"Splendid!" He cupped his chin between his thumb and forefinger. "Before Roger gets here, may I offer some advice?"

"Certainly, Captain."

"He's a good man, finest Chief Mate I've ever had. But he has definite opinions about women not belonging on ships. Don't let him get to you—I mean, if he needles you or is tough on you."

"Sir, I'm used to it. I know I have to be good at what I do to make it. This is no different than the *Atlantic Moon*. I earned the respect of the crew by pulling my own weight. I'll do the same here."

"I expect you will. You're Ben Murphy's daughter, after all."

"Aye, that I am, sir. That I surely am."

"Now, let's take a look at these charts. Show me how you would steer us out of here."

By the time Roger arrived on the bridge, Maureen had a chance to show the Captain how she'd maneuvered around the shoals to take her previous vessel safely out of the port. She also had a chance to tell him she'd looked over the helm, and had familiarity with the equipment.

The Captain called Roger over to the helm. "Maureen, walk us through navigating the ship out of this port."

"Yes, sir." Maureen knew this would be "do or die." She had to explain everything correctly, or they would pull the plug.

She took a deep breath, then went to the helm. Her father's voice echoed in her mind. He'd turn the wheel over to her and he'd say, *"Focus, Maureen. Watch the compass and the rudder angle, but more than anything, use your eyes. Listen to my directions and maintain a steady course."*

When she heard those words, her concentration kicked in. It was like remembering how to ride a bicycle. With quiet confidence, she took the helm. She explained to the two officers how she had taken the *Atlantic Moon* out of the New Bedford port. When she finished, no one said anything.

Not knowing quite what to do, she asked, "Will there be anything else, sir?"

"Only one thing, Maureen. Why don't you get your Mate's license? I'm sure you know they finally opened the door for women to become officers."

"I've thought about it, sir. I want to log more hours at sea before I try for it."

"Who knows, my dear? Maybe by the time you're ready to go for it, women will be more accepted in this industry."

Roger let out a grunt. "Don't hold your breath on that one."

"Mister Trent, did you see anything at all wrong with what AB Murphy showed us?"

"No, sir."

"If she can navigate the ship out of this port and keep us on schedule, I'm going to let her do it. Do you have a problem with that?"

"Yes, sir."

"Well, you can frigging get over it! And Trent, consider that an order!"

Roger muttered, "Yes, sir" as the Captain stormed off the bridge.

# 2

Roger hadn't lingered on the bridge. Before he left, he barked at her to be on the bridge at 0400 hours; the vessel would sail at first light. She watched his back recede as he again took the stairs two at a time. Any thoughts of a shipboard romance with that disagreeable man seemed ludicrous.

Maureen mumbled to herself, "That's probably a good thing." Even as she went back to the helm for one more run-through by herself, a wave of disappointment welled up in her.

No one told her where to find the mess room. When she left the bridge, she bumped into Eddie on the deck. His watch had just ended. Since she had no one else to ask, she took advantage of the chance meeting.

"Hey, Eddie."

He gave her a big smile, first one she'd seen all day. "Hi ya, Murph. Do you still work here?"

"Sure I do."

He winked at her. "I still have that extra bunk, if you need it."

"No thanks. I got a small cabin with my own bunk. That's all I need."

"Well, if you decide you need a little more, once we sail, come and find me." He lightly touched her hair with the back of his hand.

Maureen took a small step backward so she would be out of reach. Then she deliberately lied, to cut this impromptu conversation short. "I have to run back to my cabin and unpack before dinner. Could you point me in the direction of the mess room? I haven't had my grand tour of the ship yet."

"Sure." He pointed to the stairs that led to her cabin. "Go down those stairs and hang a right. The mess room is at the end of the alleyway."

"Thanks. See you later." Maureen wasted no time going down the stairs, back to her cabin.

When she got to her door, she paused and looked around. The Captain had said Grace and Vince were two doors down. But she didn't know in which direction.

Roger had gone into a cabin four doors down from hers. That's when she realized they had put her on the officers' deck. No doubt, all the seamen shared quarters below. Since she wasn't an officer, this already set her apart from the rest of the crew.

She looked down the hall once more, and wondered if Roger had gone to his quarters when he left her on the bridge. Again shaking herself free of those thoughts, she went into her cabin to freshen up. Hopefully, she would see Grace at dinner.

Maureen took a few minutes to sit quietly on her bunk and close her eyes before going to the mess room. When she made her first entrance, she fully expected glances and whispers. There really wasn't any way to prepare for that. All she could do was get through it.

Just before she meant to leave, someone knocked on her door. Then she heard a voice that made her smile. "Maureen, are you in there? It's Grace."

"I'm here, just a minute." Maureen scrambled off the bunk and opened the door.

There stood Grace in the alleyway, looking as happy as Maureen had ever seen her look. "Thought maybe you'd like some company for dinner."

Maureen gave Grace a bear hug. "Sweetheart, you have no idea how true that is."

"Sorry I couldn't get to you earlier. I had to finish my shift. They tell me we're sailing tomorrow, if we can get a pilot."

"We're sailing tomorrow whether we get one or not."

"I don't think so. We had a problem coming in, even with a pilot."

Maureen closed her door. "Let's get some grub and I'll explain it all to you."

Walking down the alleyway to the mess room, Maureen gave Grace the short list of the afternoon's events. When she got to the part about Roger's objection to her being at the helm, Grace laughed.

"Vince and I knew having another woman on board wouldn't sit well with him."

"Lord Almighty! That's an understatement! He's acting like I'm a siren hell-bent on destroying the ship."

"The Captain told Vince not to tell Roger about you ahead of time. He expected this reaction."

"Wish someone had warned me. I feel like I tripped on a wasps' nest."

They had just come into the mess room. Grace poked her in the side. "Don't look now, but your favorite First Mate is sitting with my favorite Second Mate."

"They eat in the mess room and not the officers' saloon?"

"Vince eats in here with me. Roger usually eats in the officers' saloon. Guess he's in here tonight because of you."

"What do you want to bet I'm the reason his face is so red?"

Grace giggled. "That's okay. It complements your red hair." Grace tugged Maureen's arm. "C'mon. Let's get some food and join them."

"You're joking, aren't you?"

"Nope. I think you two have more in common than you re-alize."

Maureen picked up a tray and followed Grace. "Yeah. He's British and I'm Irish. That's as far as it goes."

"We'll see about that."

"Grace, whenever you had that look on your face in school, it always meant trouble. Don't you go getting any ideas about fixing us up."

"What, you don't think he's gorgeous?"

Maureen couldn't lie to her best friend. "Yes, he's gorgeous. But he's also a miserable Brit. Not a winning combo."

"He's not so bad, once you get to know him. He has to ad-just to your being on board."

"I'd lay odds he'll throw me overboard, once we're on our way, and then claim it was an accident."

"Let's see if Vince can help with this. Maybe we can double-team Mister Trent."

Maureen knew Grace well enough to know that once she made up her mind about something, no one could change it. She'd always been as tenacious as a bulldog. She defied her whole family by running away and marrying Vince. Then she shocked everyone again when she announced she would be sailing with him on a merchant vessel.

Truth be told, Maureen secretly hoped they could smooth things over with Roger. At the very least, it would make her stint on this vessel an easier one. Grace interrupted Maureen's musings when she whispered, "You might like to know Roger has his sights set on getting his Master's license. He wants his own vessel."

Maureen filled a glass with water and set it on her tray. "No kidding. Think he can do it?"

"Vince says he really knows his stuff. Dollars to doughnuts, he'll be a Captain one of these days." Grace picked up her tray. "Let's go join them."

Roger and Vince had taken seats opposite one another at the end of a long table. Grace grabbed the empty chair beside Vince, leaving the seat open beside Roger. Maureen resigned herself to Grace's maneuvering and sat down beside Roger.

Vince took the conversational lead. "Well, Maureen! Welcome aboard. It's good to see you again."

"Hello, Vince. You're looking good. Being on the *Honey Rose* obviously agrees with you."

"That, and having my wife sail with me."

Roger gave the three of them a pointed look. "You know each other?"

Maureen and Grace said nothing. Vince answered the question. "Hell yeah. I cut my teeth under Captain Murphy. I met Grace through Maureen."

Grace picked up the ball. "Maureen and I grew up together on the Cape. We went to the same high school."

Roger asked Vince the question he'd asked the Captain. "Since you know her, why didn't you tell me AB Murphy was a woman?"

Vince gave it to him straight. "Because the Captain asked me not to tell you. He didn't want to argue about Maureen coming on board."

"Jesus Christ! Was this a bloody conspiracy to get Grace's friend on the ship?"

Maureen had had enough, and couldn't take any more of this nonsense. She stood up. Grace reached for her arm and missed. "Maureen, don't go!"

"Gracie, I'm not going anywhere, and I'm about to let everyone know it."

Vince asked Grace, "What the hell is she doing?"

Grace shrugged her shoulders. "I have no idea."

Maureen picked up her water glass and her spoon. She banged the glass the way people do at weddings to get everyone's attention. Then she shouted, "Hello, hello! May I have your attention, please?"

The mess room quieted, but not everyone stopped talking. She repeated the clanging and shouted again. This time, the whole room fell silent. Once she had their attention, she made her unrehearsed speech.

"Good evening, everybody. I'd like to introduce myself. I'm AB Maureen Murphy. I sailed on the *Atlantic Moon* with my father, Captain Ben Murphy. A few months ago, he had a heart attack during a storm at sea, and died.

"Today I joined the crew of the *Honey Rose*. Yes, I'm a woman, and, yes, I'm a sailor just like all of you. I'll pull my own weight just like Grace does. I'm proud to be the newest member of your crew." She held up her water glass in a toast. "Enjoy your meal." Then she sat back down beside Roger.

She heard Eddie yell from another table, "Way to go, Murph!"

Then she heard the Captain's voice from the doorway. She hadn't seen him come in. "I came to introduce our newest crew member, but it seems she's already taken care of it. AB Murphy is a welcome addition to the crew of this ship. I knew her father for many years. He taught her how to be a damn fine sailor.

"I've asked her to take the helm tomorrow when we sail. She knows the New Bedford port and will guide us out of here. During this voyage, she will be taking the four-to-eight shift at the helm. I trust there are no objections to that order?"

Roger kept his mouth shut, even though this meant Maureen would share the four-to-eight watch with him every day. No one else said anything.

The Captain continued. "Enjoy your dinner, and get some rest tonight. We sail tomorrow at dawn."

Maureen sipped her water. Her stomach had to settle before

she tried to eat anything. It took a few minutes for the dinnertime chatter and laughter to resume, but it gradually did. Not being the center of attention helped Maureen calm down.

Of the four of them, Grace spoke first. "Damn, Maureen! That was a gutsy thing to do!"

"It's the difference between a quick, sharp pain and an ache that goes on and on. I had to do something. Now everyone knows I'm here, and they know what my job is." She turned to Roger. "I'm at the helm on your watch, according to the Captain."

"It seems so. I'll have another helmsman on standby, in case there's a problem."

Again taking the bull by the horns, she told him outright, "Roger, you haven't given me a chance. At least stop hating me long enough for me to prove to you I can do the job."

"I don't hate you."

"To hell you don't! I haven't done a damn thing to you to make you be so ignorant to me."

He turned and stared at her. More accurately, he stared at her hair. "By God, you really are Irish. Your hair is fluffed out like a cat's tail."

"And you are the rudest damn Brit I've ever met!"

Vince interceded. "Before we have an international incident here, let's all calm down."

Grace concurred. "Vince is right. You guys have to make this work. The Captain put you on the same watch. You can't fight like cats and dogs while you're on the bridge. You'll get your asses booted off the ship."

Maureen spit back, "All I want is to do my job. That's all I've ever wanted to do. Tell Mister Trent to back the fuck off and let me do it."

In an infuriatingly smug voice, Roger said to Vince, "It's the red hair. There's fire in the furnace of a redhead, especially an Irish redhead."

"That's something you'll never have to worry about, with your arrogant British stiff upper lip."

"And you'll never have to worry about making anything of mine stiff."

Maureen muttered, "That's a blessing." She forced herself not to look at his lap. If she had gotten to him, that would be rich.

"You know, you two could sell tickets to this while we're at sea." Vince winked at Maureen. "The crew would put cash on the table to watch a few rounds."

Grace poked him in the side with her elbow. "Don't make matters worse."

Vince laughed. "How could it be frigging worse? They're ready to take each other out, and we sail tomorrow."

Grace tried her best to make peace between them. "All right, you guys, listen up. You're going to have to make the best of this. Maureen, watch your temper. Don't let him get to you. And, Roger, for once in your life, try to accept the fact a woman can do a good job. I'm lucky I don't have to work with you. If I did, I think I'd feed you your nuts."

Maureen muttered, "Can we toast them like marshmallows first?"

In his perfect British accent, Roger quipped, "You won't need a fire if you do. I could broil a steak over that red head of yours."

Maureen glared at him, but didn't respond. If she did, this could go on all night. She stuffed a forkful of cold mashed potatoes into her mouth.

Vince changed the subject. He got Roger talking about the cargo holds, and the maintenance they needed to do before they loaded the next fish cargo in the Mediterranean. They were sailing ballast to the next port. The ballast tanks would be filled with seawater once they were underway.

Maureen quickly finished her dinner, then excused herself.

"I'm out of here, folks. I need to get some sleep." She turned to Roger. "I'll see you on the bridge at 0400 hours."

"I'll be there."

Grace threw her napkin on her tray. "Maureen, I'm leaving with you."

The two women left the men at the table. Maureen really wanted to have some time alone. As they walked down the alleyway back to their quarters, Maureen tried to beg off. "Grace, I don't feel like talking right now."

"Oh, I know you don't. But I bet you'll want to hear this."

"What?"

"While you were introducing yourself, I heard Roger whisper something to Vince."

"All right, I'll bite. What did he say?"

"He said you must be a real pistol in bed."

"Just what I need! I have the four-to-eight watch with him, and he's wondering what I'd be like in bed?"

"What's wrong with that? I bet he's great in bed."

"Are you kidding? The Brits don't have sex. They're like amoebas. They reproduce by splitting themselves in half."

"I wouldn't be too sure about that." They had reached the door of Maureen's cabin. Grace glanced behind them. The alleyway was empty. "We shouldn't be talking about this out here. Let me come in for a minute."

As much as Maureen wanted to be alone, she couldn't deny that Grace had her curious. "You can come in, but only for a few minutes. It's been a long day."

"Don't worry. I'll haul my behind out so you can sleep. But first, I want to dish."

Maureen opened the door and turned on the light. "You always have been a first-class gossip."

"Just with you. There's no one around here to do girl talk."

"All right, then, dish."

Grace sat down on the bunk and patted the spot beside her. "Get comfortable. This is good stuff."

Maureen sat down. "Why is it I get the feeling you had this planned all along? You want to hook me up with Roger, don't you?"

"What's wrong with that? With your dad gone, you don't have anyone. All you've got left is that big old house your grandmother left you on the Cape."

"So you want me to get involved with some grumpy Brit who hates women. Nice, Grace, real damn nice."

"Oh, darling, he doesn't hate women! That's part of the problem."

"I don't understand."

"I'd been on board about a month. One day, out of the blue, Roger told Vince he wanted to stay as far away from me as possible, and that having a woman on the ship should be against the law."

"Why on earth would Roger say that to your husband?"

"I think because he got some bad news. He told Vince he got a letter from his fiancée in England. It caught up with him right after I came on board. She told him she couldn't take him being away for months at a time, and not seeing him. She didn't want to live that way. So she'd decided to marry someone else."

"He got a Dear John letter here, on the ship?"

"He sure did. Vince said he's been a sour asshole ever since. He's even bitched to Vince that we make too much noise in bed. He said he heard us."

"Oh, c'mon! I saw him go into a room down the hall. He's not next door to you, is he?"

"No. In fact, Vince asked the Third Mate, who is next door, if we bother him. He says he's never heard anything. The only thing we can figure is that he walked past the door and heard us."

"Maybe he pressed his ear to it and listened."

"Who knows?" Grace got quiet and glanced at the door. Maureen could see she had something else on her mind.

"Grace, there's more, isn't there?"

Quite unexpectedly, Grace's eyes teared up. "After my six months' probation, the Captain took Vince aside and had a talk. He told him the only complaint he got about me came from Roger. It had nothing to do with my work, which is why it didn't come up in my review. Roger complained my being on board is too much of a distraction for the crew, and creates a hazardous situation on board."

"Too much of a distraction for the crew, or for him?"

"That's exactly what Vince said. You know, technically, I shouldn't be here. The Captain is the only one allowed to sail with his wife. Captain McPherson is a special man, and believes women should be allowed to sail, so he bent the rules. Did you know his mother was a nurse on a hospital ship in World War Two?"

"No, I didn't know that."

"Anyway, the Captain is satisfied with my work, but told Vince that if Roger pushed his complaint, he could be forced to put me ashore." Tears slid down Grace's face.

"Damn, Gracie!" Maureen hugged her as Grace continued to cry. "Has Roger complained to the ship owners?"

Grace sniffed as her nose ran. "Not yet. Vince talked to him and smoothed things over as much as he could. But you can tell by the way he treated you today that he's still on a mission."

"You can say that again. He wants me off the ship."

"Me too." Grace got up to get some toilet paper to blow her nose. She yelled from the bathroom, "Vince thinks he just needs to get laid and he'll calm his ass down."

"I suppose that is why you want to fix us up."

Grace came out and leaned against the door frame. "Honestly, Maureen, Roger is a good guy, and one hell of a good sailor. He's just angry, and still smarting from being dumped. Vince says he wasn't like this before."

"You mean he wasn't always a son of a bitch?"

"When I first came on board, he treated me all right. He didn't go out of his way to be friendly, like he does with the guys, but he also wasn't rude. After he got that letter, he got nasty. That's when he started his campaign to get me kicked off the ship."

"So we're paying the price because he's prejudiced against women, and then got dumped?"

"That's what I think."

Maureen now understood what Grace had in mind. "You think if he gets involved with me, he'll call off the dogs on you and Vince."

"Then everybody wins, right?"

"Maybe. Except on my first day, he's already decided I'm a piece of shit. His nanny must've dropped him on his head when he was a wee lad."

Grace laughed. "Except for Mary Poppins, you're the only woman I know that won't let him intimidate you. Go ahead, Maureen. If you can do it, you'll keep both our female asses on the ship."

"Grace, I can't say yes or no right now. I'm too damned tired to think. Nothing's going to happen unless I can steer this lady out to sea tomorrow. I have to get some sleep."

"All right, then. I'll catch up with you later." Grace stopped after she opened the door and pointed down the hall. "Vince and I are two doors down, between you and Roger."

Maureen sighed and closed her eyes. "Funny how that worked out, isn't it?"

# 3

Maureen set her alarm for 3:00 A.M. so she'd have time to get herself together. After listening to the minutes tick away most of the night, she snapped it off before the alarm sounded. She had a shower, then dressed in the standard-issue blue work shirt and jeans. Afterward, she went to the mess room to grab a cup of coffee and a doughnut.

She'd hope to beat Roger to the bridge, but found him already there talking to the Captain. The Captain smiled when he saw her. "Good morning, Maureen. I trust you had a good night's sleep?"

"Slept like a baby, sir." She lied.

"Good. Let's go over this once more before we sail, to make sure we're all clear about the navigation."

Roger hadn't said a word to her. She deliberately spoke to him first. "Good morning, Roger. How are you today?"

"As good as anybody can be getting up at sparrow's fart."

"In Massachusetts, we get up at chickadee's fart. Did you know chickadees are our state bird? It's a little-known fact, but they fart louder than a sparrow."

Roger stood there, stone-faced, but she did get a chuckle out of the Captain. "That's what we need on this ship, someone to lighten things up. Ben always could tell one hell of a good joke. Maybe he shared a few with you, Maureen?"

"Yes, sir. But some shouldn't be told in mixed company." Giving Roger a pointed look, she added, "They're for an American audience."

Doing his best W.C. Fields impression, Captain McPherson surprised her when he said, "My little chickadee, there comes a time in the affairs of man when he must take the bull by the tail and face the situation." He glanced at Roger when he said it.

Maureen nodded. "Yes, sir, I understand."

"Good. Let's get to work."

Maureen relaxed into the work she knew. They did a complete rehearsal of the departure, then went over the charts to discuss their route to the Mediterranean. They would be sailing 4,580 miles to Piraeus, Greece, where they would load the next cargo. They'd sail via Europa Point, through the Straits of Gibraltar.

"Maureen, have you been at the helm at Europa Point?"

"Yes, sir. We regularly sailed to the Mediterranean."

Roger ran his fingers through his hair in exasperation. "Captain, you know a ship sank there last month. You're not going to have her at the helm in the Straits, are you?"

"If it's on your watch, I am. Maureen, do you know what happened there?"

"Yes, sir, I heard it on the news. They took on water during a storm."

"Young lady, I'm only going to say this once. You know what's at stake. If we run into bad weather, and you're at the helm, tell me if it's too much for you. I know you have the ability and the experience. That's not in question.

"I'm not going to mince words about this. Your father died at sea in a storm. If your memories overshadow your good judgment, you'll put all our lives in danger. Do we understand one another?"

"Yes, sir. I'll speak up, sir, if I can't handle it."

"I trust you will." He looked out at the horizon. "The sun's coming up. We'll be sailing soon. I suggest you take care of any personal needs, which is what I'm going to do now." The Captain left to use the toilet.

Speaking more to herself than to Roger, Maureen softly said, "No wonder he was Dad's best friend."

She didn't expect Roger to respond, but he did. "He's the best Captain I've ever sailed under."

She looked at Roger and smiled. "Yesterday he said the same thing about you, that you're the best First Mate he's ever had."

"I've never seen him miss the mark yet about people. He's usually spot-on."

"Meaning?"

"Meaning he's sailing close to the wind with this one, but he seems to know what he's doing. I sure as hell don't understand why he trusts you. I just hope you don't let him down."

"I won't." Maureen wiped her sweaty palms on her thighs. "I also won't let you down. I can do this, Roger."

He shook his head. "Bloody hell, you damn well better do it, or we're all in the drink." He saw the Captain coming back. "You'd better use the loo. I don't want you pissing yourself when we run aground."

Rather than being irritated by his crack, Maureen laughed. "You'd better have a whiz, too. I don't want you pissing yourself when the vessel departure is a cakewalk." As she turned to leave, she discreetly glanced at his jeans. She smiled with satisfaction when she saw a definite ridge against his leg.

On the way to the head, she whispered to herself, "Captain Murphy, your daughter has found herself a mate."

Once the Captain gave the order to leave, and she got the all clear to proceed, everything moved quickly. Roger monitored the radar while Maureen stayed at the helm. The Captain kept an eye on both of them. She had no problems.

Roger gave her a heads-up when they reached the point where they ran into trouble. "We're coming up on the place where the pilot missed the mark and scraped the hull on a sandbar. Watch yourself."

Maureen held her steady. She knew exactly where the shoal made the water shallow. Roger telegraphed "slow ahead" to the engine room. After again confirming an all clear, she announced as a pilot would, "I'm altering my course to starboard."

The *Honey Rose* cut through the water like a knife through soft butter. She swung her wide to starboard and kept the vessel moving. Maureen could see the open sea ahead. Roger sent a half-speed message to the engine room.

Within a few minutes the land disappeared and they were surrounded by water. Maureen confirmed their direction and made sure they were on course. They were headed for Greece. "We are underway, sir. I am keeping my present course and speed until directed otherwise."

The Captain congratulated her. "Well done. Your father would be proud."

"Thank you, sir." Sweat dripped off her face. She wiped her forehead with the sleeve of her now-damp shirt.

"Roger, take the bridge for a few minutes. I'm going to get some coffee."

"Yes, sir."

The Captain left her alone with Roger. They both had to keep an eye on things, but could relax a bit now that they had left the port.

"We still have over an hour before our watch ends. Will you be all right in that wet shirt?"

She looked down at her chest. "I guess I soaked it up pretty good getting us out of there. It's not a problem. I'll be fine."

"I don't know if I will be."

"Excuse me?" When she turned to look at him, she immediately saw the ridge against his leg had become more pronounced. He didn't try to hide it.

Roger made no pretense about looking her over. "This is why it's dangerous to have a woman on board. As you can see, I have a bit of a problem. I can't control this reaction. It just happens, and it's a serious distraction."

Maureen didn't know if she should be flattered or pissed off. She felt a bit of both. "It's not my fault you can't control yourself."

He matter-of-factly answered in his perfect British accent, "Yes, it is. That shirt is clinging to you like a second skin. Your hair looks like you just got out of bed." He lightly touched the bulge in his trousers and grimaced. "Now I have to finish my watch with this. It wouldn't be a problem, if I had a man at the helm."

"When the Captain comes back, maybe you should go take a cold shower."

"Even better, I think I'll go to the loo and have a wank. That won't take as long."

"What, you're also trigger-happy?"

He smirked and simulated jerking off. "Only when I want to be." They both heard the Captain coming up the stairs. In almost a whisper, Roger said, "We'll continue this conversation later." Then he turned to look at the radar, effectively hiding his hard-on.

The implication of that last remark rattled Maureen, but at the same time, it excited her. They would be at sea for over two weeks before they reached their next port of call. A lot could happen in that time.

Roger waited until the Captain had settled in with his paperwork before excusing himself to go to the head. On the way out, he caught her eye and made another wanking motion with his hand. She saw he still had a problem, and he intended to take care of it.

When he came back about ten minutes later, he acted as though nothing had happened. His cool British veneer had returned, and he went about his business, effectively ignoring her.

It seemed as though for the next week, Roger avoided her. Except for seeing him on the bridge during their shared watch, Maureen didn't catch a glimpse of him. He didn't go to the mess room at all, and ate all his meals in the officers' saloon.

They literally had to eat their evening meal and get back to their watch. They only had half an hour for dinner, from six o'clock to six-thirty. When their watch ended at eight in the evening, Roger disappeared into his cabin.

She didn't see much of Grace, either. They had different schedules, and were either working or sleeping. Grace had an additional time constraint. She wanted to be alone with Vince. Maureen suspected they made love whenever they could manage it.

One evening after Maureen finished her watch, she decided to see if Grace might be available. If she didn't make the effort to get together with her, the voyage would end without them having much of a chance to talk. Since Vince had the twelve-to-four watch, she thought they might be in their cabin.

Maureen went farther down the hall and stopped in front of Grace and Vince's door. She raised her hand to knock and stopped short. At first, she thought someone had been hurt, the groan loud enough to be heard in the alleyway.

Then it hit her. She whispered, "Oh, shit!" Her suspicion had just been confirmed. They were making love.

Maureen abruptly turned, intending to dash back to her room. She slammed right into Roger and nearly fell backward. He grabbed her before she went down.

"I followed you down the alleyway. I thought you heard me."

Trying to regain her balance, and her composure, she tried to stand upright. When she did, they were only inches apart. "I didn't hear anything, except that." She gestured toward the closed door with her thumb.

"Loud, aren't they?"

Maureen clearly heard Grace groan again, then heard Vince growl, "Oh, baby, that's good."

She stared at the door. "Jesus, Roger, do they do that all the time?"

"Bloody hell, yes! I expect Grace already told you I complained to Vince about it."

"She said the Third Mate can't hear them and he's next door."

"Miss Murphy, you've been on a ship long enough to know the Third Mate's watch is eight to twelve. He's not in his cabin when they do it. They go at it a few times a week, about this time, before Vince's watch starts at midnight. I hear it in the corridor when I walk by."

"Why don't you swap cabins with them, so you don't have to go past their door?"

"I suggested that to Vince. My space is smaller, I have a single and they have a double. Can't really blame him for not wanting to trade. I'd thought about taking the cabin you have, before the Captain put you in there."

"Do you want to swap with me? I don't care, as long as I don't have to bunk with Eddie, or what was his name, Preston?"

Suddenly Grace let out a loud yelp and moaned, followed by Vince saying, "That's it, baby, come for me, come hard."

Roger grabbed Maureen's hand. "I can't take this. C'mon, let's get out of here."

Rather than going back toward her cabin, Roger went down the hall toward his. He let go of her hand and opened the door. Maureen didn't move. "Well, are you coming in or not?"

"I suppose so." Not knowing what to expect, she went in.

Roger followed and closed the door. "You know, this is the first time I've ever had a woman in here."

"I'm honored."

"Don't be. This goes against every sense of propriety I have."

Maureen didn't want to argue with him, or defend her presence there. "Then maybe I should leave." She walked past him, back to the closed door. He grabbed her arm before she turned the doorknob. "I don't want you to go."

With her heart pounding in her chest, she challenged him. "I didn't ask to come in here. You pulled me down the hall and opened the door. So I came in. Then you tell me, I'm somehow violating your respectability by being here. Either shit or get off the pot, Roger. What do you want?"

Roger came closer. Maureen stood her ground. "What do you think I want?"

"How the hell do I know? You're running hot and cold. Since we set sail, more cold than hot."

"You're hot every time I see you." He reached out and touched her head. "It's this damn red hair. It's frigging driving me crazy!"

Forcing her voice to remain steady, she looked him in the eye. "You've been driving me crazy ever since I set foot on this ship."

"Then maybe it's time we do something about it." Roger came closer and kissed her hair.

"This could cost us both our jobs." She could feel the hard ridge in his trousers pressing against her leg.

"Too late for that argument, Miss Murphy. You should have considered the consequences before you came on board."

Maureen knew she should say no, but she simply couldn't. It had been a long time since she'd been close to a man, and even longer since she'd made love. She had told him the truth. This recalcitrant Brit made her crazy.

Just before his mouth covered hers, Roger's breath scorched her face. Much too far gone to consider how this would impact their ability to work together, she returned his ardent kiss with her own. She wanted him as much as he wanted her.

Roger pulled her shirttail out of her jeans and reached under it. He cupped her breast in his hand. "Don't you ever wear a bra?"

"I don't own one. My tits aren't big enough to justify spending the money."

He rubbed his erection against her leg. "Jesus Christ! They're plenty big enough. Don't you know what your hard nipples do to me every day?"

Maureen squeezed his pectoral through his shirt. "No, tell me what they do to you."

"They make me want to fuck you right there on the bridge."

"We can't on the bridge."

"Don't you think I bloody well know that? Why do you think I act like you're not there? I have to, or I couldn't get through my watch."

Maureen unbuttoned his shirt and exposed an impressive hairy chest. "I could ask the Captain to reassign me. He knows we don't get along."

"Damn good thing he thinks that. Don't want him to know I'm fucking my helmsman."

"Is that what you're doing?"

"Damn straight it's what I mean to do."

"I hope you have some condoms, or you won't be fucking this helmsman until you get some."

"Every self-respecting sailor has rubbers. I just haven't needed any for a while." Roger led her to his bunk. He reached under the mattress and pulled out a small box.

"I thought you said you've never had a woman in here."

He handed her the box. "Look at it. It's never been opened."

Sure enough, he told her the truth. Maureen looked at the

box. Both ends were sealed shut. "You might be a miserable Brit, but at least you're honest." She tossed the box on the bed.

He unbuttoned her jeans and pulled down the zipper. "I expect my temper will be much improved by our next watch."

Maureen reached between them and rubbed his hard-on. "You think so?"

Roger slid both hands inside her underpants and kneaded her bum cheeks. "The night you gave your little speech in the mess room, I saw you weren't the shy, retiring type. I figured then you must be a fireball in bed."

"I didn't think you ever had sex. After all, you're British."

Roger didn't waste time unbuttoning Maureen's shirt. He took hold of the tail and pulled it over her head. "We have sex. We just deny we did in the morning. That's in the Union Jack code of ethics."

Maureen pulled down his fly and opened his trousers. "Do you know, you're a hell of a lot nicer to be around when you're about to get laid?"

"That's quite perceptive, for an Irish American." Roger pushed her backward onto his bunk. "Is all your hair red?"

"What do you think?"

He untied her work boots and pulled them off. "Let's find out." He tugged at the legs of her jeans. "Lift your arse."

Maureen lifted her bum off the bed and pushed her jeans down. Her underpants went with the jeans. Roger stared right at her pubic hair as he pulled her jeans completely off.

"Bloody hell, yes! Your pussy is as red as the hair on your head."

Maureen wasn't the least bit embarrassed as she lay naked on his bunk. She liked the way he looked her over. She opened her legs just a bit. "How long has it been since you've had any?"

"Probably longer than it's been for you, from the looks of it," he snapped back.

"Has it been longer than two years?"

Roger sat on the edge of the bunk and took off his shoes. "It's been that long for you?"

"I've been at sea."

"So have I. But you've been on a ship full of horny men. That doesn't help me, but it sure as hell should've helped you."

"You don't screw the crew when your father's the Captain."

"You'll have to tell me sometime why you went to sea with your father, but not tonight." Roger finished stripping and opened the box of condoms. "Goddamn, it's good to need one of these again."

Maureen lay back and opened her legs wide. She wanted this ornery Brit inside her more than she'd ever wanted a man before.

He crawled on top of her. Without any preliminaries, he positioned himself between her legs and bore down. She didn't get a good look at his erection, but she sure as hell felt it pop into her.

The moan that escaped came from her throat. She'd clamped her mouth shut to stifle the sound, remembering how Grace's voice had carried. With his first thrust, she gasped. She wrapped her arms around Roger and buried her face in his neck. "Jesus, I'm trying to be quiet, but this is so frigging hot, I want to scream."

"Redhead, I'm going to fuck you till you come. Just remember, if anyone hears us, this may well be the last voyage we'll have on this ship."

Maureen understood. "All right. I'll be quiet."

Roger picked up the pace and humped harder. Maureen bit her lower lip, nearly drawing blood. Only a soft grunt escaped.

Roger banged her again. "You like that, don't you?"

"Jesus, yes. It's good. Do me harder."

Roger obliged. He harshly drove his rigid prick into her. "You want it, darling, you've got it." He rode her with unrestrained lust, venting his bottled-up frustrations in a heated frenzy.

Maureen had never felt so overpowered, and so free, in her entire life. The passion this man kept locked inside had finally erupted. She had poked a hole in his controlled exterior and had triggered an explosion.

She felt her own explosion building. "Roger, I'm close. God, I'm so close!" Maureen clutched his arms as he continued to pound her.

"That's what I want, redhead, I want to feel you come, just like your friend Grace did for Vince."

"Oh, God! Yes!" Time stopped for Maureen. Her entire body incinerated in a flash of light as her climax overwhelmed her senses. Roger maintained his momentum while waves of pleasure engulfed her.

Suddenly she felt his body go rigid. He grunted, louder than he should have, as his orgasm hit. His buttocks clenched, and his biceps hardened. Roger rocked his bunk as he erupted inside her.

It took both Roger and Maureen a few minutes to catch their breath. Neither one of them said anything. Roger came around first. He sat up and peeled off the condom. Then he went into the bathroom and threw it in the trash can.

Maureen scooped her clothes off the floor. When Roger came back, she had already started to dress.

She gave him the once-over as she pulled on her underwear. "You know, you aren't bad-looking for a Brit."

He flicked her nipple with his index finger. "Neither are you, for an Irish American."

"I suppose I should get back to my own cabin."

"I suppose you should."

Maureen unbuttoned her shirt and put it on. Before she could button it up again, Roger pulled her close. "You know, we can't let on there's anything between us."

"I know. On the bridge, it's business as usual. I hate you, and you hate me."

"That's the way it should be."

"Yeah, I know."

Maureen pushed at his chest. He didn't let go. "Roger, I have to get dressed."

"Pity." He reluctantly released her. While Maureen finished dressing, he picked up his trousers and pulled them on. "What would your father have said about this?"

"Are you kidding? It wouldn't matter that I'm his daughter. He would put me off the ship."

"I expect Captain McPherson would do the same. Seriously, we have to be careful."

"What, all of a sudden, you don't want me put off the ship? That's what you've been trying to do since I came on board."

"I've changed my mind."

Maureen yanked a strand of his hair. "I can't imagine why."

"Ouch! That hurt! You'd better watch yourself. I'm still your boss."

"That's going to be interesting after tonight."

"You got that right."

"Before you go out, let me make sure the alleyway is empty." He opened the door and looked down the hall. "All clear."

Maureen stepped into the hall. "All right, then. I'll see you on the bridge."

"0400 hours sharp." Roger gave her a good-night kiss.

That's when they both heard the door down the hall open. Before they could dart back into his cabin, they heard Grace say, "Oh, my God!"

# 4

If Maureen hadn't been so mortified, she would have enjoyed the moment more. The expression on Roger's face would have taken first prize in a photo contest. He muttered, "Jesus Christ," then went back into his room. She stood alone in the alleyway, outside his cabin.

For a moment, she thought he would slam the door in her face. But he didn't. He'd gone back in to get his shirt. When he returned a few moments later, Grace and Vince were coming toward them.

Vince's grin said it all. When he got close enough to be heard without shouting, he didn't even try to be delicate.

"Well, now! Will you look at this? Seems you two worked out your differences."

In mock chastisement, Grace scolded him. "Vince, be nice! After all, everybody knows they hate each other. Roger thinks she's an incompetent woman, and wants her off the ship. And Maureen thinks he's an arrogant Brit and wants to toast his balls like marshmallows."

Teasing notwithstanding, Grace still pissed Maureen off. "This is all your damn fault!"

Grace feigned indignation. "How the devil is it our fault?"

Maureen looked straight at Vince. "'That's it, baby, come for me, come hard'?" Then she glared at Grace. "We heard you two fucking your brains out! Jesus Christ, Grace, I came by to say hello and thought someone was being murdered in there. No wonder Roger said something."

Grace blushed, then giggled. "You heard us?"

Roger confirmed. "At least now I have a witness." Then he said to Vince, "Where the hell are you going, anyway? It's not even ten o'clock."

"We were going to the mess room to have a snack. We're a little hungry."

"It's no damn wonder."

Vince had never been known for his tact. "Well, hell, you and Maureen should be hungry, too, considering you just did what we did. Want to join us? I mean for some food."

Maureen never expected Roger to agree to go, but he did. "Let me put on my shoes. I'll be right back."

Roger disappeared into his room, leaving Maureen alone with Vince and Grace. Grace whispered, "What the hell happened?"

Maureen whispered back, "I'll tell you later."

When Roger came out, Vince played devil's advocate. He put his arm around Roger's shoulder. "My friend, Grace wants to know what happened. Maureen said she'll tell her later. Maybe you'd like a shot at it first?"

"Bloody hell! By tomorrow, this will be a headline in the *London Times*."

Vince laughed. "Let's get some coffee and see what's left to eat."

Grace and Vince led the way. Maureen and Roger followed.

Maureen caught Roger glancing at her. "What? Do I have lipstick on my teeth?"

"If you don't own a bra, I'm surprised you have lipstick."

"Smart-ass."

"Isn't that the point? Makes you hot, doesn't it?"

"Do you know you're a son of a bitch?"

"I know. That's why you're falling in love with me."

Vince and Grace had already gone into the mess room. Maureen stopped just shy of the door. "What the fuck did you say?"

"You heard me. Can you deny it?"

"Not only are you a son of a bitch, you're an arrogant one to boot. You've got to be the single most infuriating man I've ever met!"

"Your nipples are hard again." He flicked one through her shirt, then went to join Vince and Grace.

Maureen watched the swinging door move until it stopped. She saw Roger through the window. He gestured toward the door and shrugged his shoulders. Then Grace got up.

Maureen stepped back so the door wouldn't hit her when Grace came out.

"Aren't you coming in?"

"I need a minute." Roger had rattled her. She didn't want him to know that.

"What happened?"

"That's the second time tonight you've asked me that."

"Seemed like a reasonable question, both times I asked it."

"He's driving me crazy."

"I don't think as crazy as you're driving him."

"What do you mean?"

"What, you didn't notice?"

"Notice what?"

"Wake up, Maureen! I saw the bulge in his pants when he came in. Vince saw it, too. He poked me in the side with his middle finger to get my attention."

"Are you serious?"

"I don't know what just happened out here, but you both have steam coming out of your ears. You can't blame this one on Vince and me."

"Holy hell, Grace! We're on the same watch. We have to work together."

"That doesn't have to be a problem. He just has to wear looser pants."

"Very funny!"

Grace took her hand. "Let's go in."

The men were sitting at the same table where they'd all had dinner the other night. They had the mess room to themselves, it being between shifts. Maureen saw a cupcake and a cup of coffee waiting for her on the table, next to Roger.

Vince grinned when she sat down. "I took the liberty of getting us all coffee and cupcakes, unless you'd prefer a glass of ice water."

"I'll manage with the coffee, but thank you for the offer."

"Anytime." Vince peeled the paper away from his cupcake. "All right, fess up. I want all the gory details."

Maureen sipped her coffee, then looked at Roger. "I don't remember either of us saying, 'Oh, baby, that's good.' Do you?"

"Certainly not. We British don't say those sorts of things. But I do remember hearing it somewhere."

"You know, so do I."

Not easily thwarted, Vince tried another angle. "Well, Roger, I'll just have to wait until Maureen tells Gracie in one of their hen sessions. Then I'll get the details."

Unlike Maureen, Roger wasn't the least bit flustered by Vince's fishing expedition. "There's not much to tell. Our watch ended at eight. On the way back to our cabins, we heard odd sounds coming from your quarters. Correct me if I'm wrong, Maureen, but wasn't it when Grace climaxed that it really became too much for us?"

"Sounds about right." Maureen sipped her coffee again in an attempt to hide her grin.

"Anyway, I've been damned uncomfortable for several days now, and decided enough was enough. I invited Maureen to my cabin, and she accepted."

Roger didn't say anything else, nor did Maureen. Vince couldn't contain his frustration. "Holy balls! You've been at each other's throats for days, and now you're sleeping together. Roger, you just got laid, and you're describing it like you're talking to Parliament or something."

"I would never consider speaking to Parliament until I get my Master's certification."

Maureen jumped on that one. "Are you really going for it?"

"I've been studying for my examination to get my license. I'm scheduled to take it next month."

"No kidding! That soon?"

" 'That soon'? I've been working toward this for years. I went the hawsepiper route, logging sea time and teaching myself. I want my own ship."

Grace kicked Maureen under the table. "Told you."

"Why didn't you go to school, if you wanted to be an officer?"

"I did what the men in my family have done for generations. I climbed the hawse pipe up the food chain. I didn't go to university."

"My dad did the same thing. He started as an ordinary seaman and worked his way up. He knew more about a ship than anybody I've ever met."

Grace kicked Maureen again, then asked Roger, "When you get your own ship, think you'll need a good helmsman?"

"I might. Know where I could find one that's available?"

"I know one that's ready, willing and able."

Maureen muttered, "Grace, for God's sake."

"What?" Maureen didn't answer. "Hell's bells, you both

need to get over yourselves. Look at Vince and me. We figured out a way to sail together—that is, if Roger doesn't screw it up for us. You need to think about these things."

Roger took exception to that remark. "How am I going to screw it up for you?"

"You don't think I know you put the only black mark on my record?"

Vince shushed her. "Grace, this isn't the time or the place."

"Why not, Vince? We're alone in here. I've been sick over this ever since it happened."

"Let her talk, Vince. Ever since what happened?" Roger interceded.

Grace's eyes glassed over as they had when she told Maureen about the warning. "After my probation period ended, the Captain talked to Vince about your complaint. You said I create a hazardous situation on board just by being here. If you push your complaint, the Captain will put me ashore."

"I didn't know he did that. Vince, you didn't say anything."

"I didn't want to rock the boat. You already seemed pretty ticked off. I thought it best to leave well enough alone."

"So you all know, I'm not going to push my complaint, especially not now."

Grace wiped her eyes with her napkin. "You mean you aren't going to get me thrown off the ship?"

"Not unless you fuck up, which you haven't done yet."

Maureen wouldn't let him off the hook that easily. "Just how many fuckups does it take to get a woman thrown off a ship, Mister Trent?"

"It depends on how big the fuckups are, Miss Murphy."

"Just a few days ago, you told the Captain everyone's life would be in danger with me at the helm. My only fuckup was being born the wrong sex—"

Grace interrupted. "Maureen, he's coming around. Don't set him off again."

"Don't worry, Grace. She won't set me off. Everything she's saying is true. But there is another side to this that no one is mentioning."

"Okay, I'll bite. What's the other side?"

Roger shocked everyone at the table by what he did next. He took Maureen's hand and put it in his lap, over his hard-on. She tried to pull her hand away, but he held it there.

"This is the other side. It's a problem I've been struggling with ever since you came on board. Great, we humped like rabbits. Well, guess what? It's back."

"That isn't my fault." Maureen wrenched her hand free.

"How the hell do you figure that? I don't get a stiffy sitting next to Vince, or any other man on this ship. With all due respect to your wife, Vince, it's only happened a couple of times since Grace came on board, but with you, it's every bloody day!"

"And that's my fault?"

"It's really nobody's fault. It's biology. It's what happens to horny men when they haven't been with a woman for months. Except for Vince, that describes most of the poor bastards on this ship, including me. And it's a dangerous distraction for the crew to have."

Grace had been listening carefully to Roger, when she suddenly piped up. "I think you're wrong."

"Is that a fact?" Roger deliberately reached down and adjusted his erection. "Sit with one of these for a few hours and tell me I'm wrong."

Grace laughed. "Women get horny, too. Don't we, Maureen?"

"Without a doubt. Ours just doesn't show."

"But I digress." Grace picked up her spoon and used it as a pointer. "The real issue is that I've been on board over six months, and you've only had two erections because of me? Gee, Vince, am I that unattractive?"

Vince practically leered at her. "Gracie, you're the frigging sexiest woman I've ever met."

"All right, bear with me here. Vince, do you react to Maureen the same way you react to me?"

"No offense, Maureen, but I never have. Even before Maureen introduced me to you, we weren't an item. True, Maureen?"

"Absolutely true, Vince. You sailed on the *Atlantic Moon* for quite a few months before I introduced you to Grace. You were always a good friend, nothing more."

Grace stood up and paced like a prosecutor in a courtroom. "Then I offer this theory, there has to be *chemistry* for two people to hit it off. I saw it at dinner the other night. The way you guys snipe at one another, that's not about hating each other, that's about wanting to jump each other's bones!"

Vince agreed. "She's right. Roger, when Maureen gave her speech, I half expected you to fuck her right here on the table." He patted the table surface with his palm. "She got to you that first night."

Maureen thought for a minute. "Everybody knows I'm on board. The only interest I've had is from Eddie, who asked me to bunk in his room. That's it."

Grace clapped her hands. "Exactly! Roger, you're not seeing the forest for the trees. You're jumping to the conclusion the whole crew is reacting like you are. Don't you get it? That's not true! It's only you! You and Maureen have chemistry."

"Now there's a frightening thought." Roger peeled the paper from his cupcake and bit it in half.

Vince stood up. "I hate to interrupt this quarrelsome foursome, but I have to get myself together for my watch. Grace, you coming?"

"Of course, I am." Grace jumped up and batted her eyes at Vince. "Wherever you go, darling, I am sure to follow."

Vince put his arm around her waist, then said to Roger, "See what you have to look forward to? Life is good."

"Have another cupcake. They're good, too."

"Don't mind if I do." Vince grabbed another cupcake from the tray on the way out.

Roger seemed in no hurry to leave. He sat quietly drinking his coffee. Maureen glanced at the clock hanging over the table.

"It's getting late. Aren't you tired?"

"I sure am."

Maureen couldn't read his frame of mind, and didn't know if she should stay or leave. She chose the diplomatic middle ground. "If you're leaving soon, I'll walk back with you. If you need some time alone, I'll head out now."

He crossed his arms over his chest. "I still have a bit of a problem."

"Only one?"

"One hard one. I'm trying to decide how to handle it."

"I'm sure you'll manage. You've had lots of practice." Maureen stood, intending to leave.

"What if I asked you to handle it?"

She turned around and leaned against the table beside his chair. From that angle, she could see his lap, and his problem. "What do you have in mind?"

"Don't know. We both need to get some sleep before our next watch. But if I have a choice between handling the problem myself, or having your assistance, I'd prefer your assistance."

"That can be arranged."

He discreetly rubbed the back of his hand against her thigh. "Go back to your cabin and leave the door unlocked. I'll be there in a few minutes."

"Yes, sir."

"That wasn't an order."

"I know, sir."

Maureen left him sitting at the table. She didn't know why

he didn't leave with her, but she welcomed the few minutes she had to herself to freshen up.

For the first time ever on board a ship, she regretted not having a single piece of feminine clothing to wear. When a duffel bag is your only piece of luggage, there isn't any room for feminine frills. Even her pajamas were baggy men's-issue.

She only had a few minutes to wing it. As quickly as she could, she stripped and washed up. Then she grabbed a clean pajama top from her closet. She only buttoned it halfway and cuffed the sleeves. The top barely covered her bum. She had nothing else on.

With her back to the door, she bent over to fluff her hair. That's when Roger walked in without knocking first. As she stood up, she heard him say, "Jesus Christ." When she turned around, her hair fell around her shoulders, and did whatever it did.

"Sorry. I thought I'd get ready for bed before you got here."

"Do you always sleep with nothing on underneath?"

"Only when I'm expecting company."

He tossed some condoms on the bed. That's why he'd lagged behind. He'd gone back to his cabin for them. "I hope Vince has a stash of these. At this rate, I'm going to run out long before we reach our next port of call."

"Don't they have them in the slop chest?"

"Yes. But I can't have them recorded on my tab while we're sailing. It only makes sense when we're docked."

"Have Vince get you some if we need them. No one will question him buying them."

"That's true. Hadn't thought of that."

Maureen didn't know how to be anything but herself, even with her attempt to be sexy. She suddenly didn't know what to do. "Remember when you said earlier, you'd never had a woman in your cabin?"

"I remember."

"This is the first time I've had a man in mine, except for my father. What am I supposed to do?"

Roger made an uncharacteristic guttural sound as he opened his trousers. "My dear, you're already doing it."

With just as much immodesty as Maureen had shown, he exposed his erection. When he penetrated her earlier, she could feel he had some size. Seeing it bare and fully erect, she couldn't help commenting on it. "Damn, Roger, no wonder it's so obvious in your pants. You're hung!"

"Bloody Americans. It's obvious in my trousers, not in my pants! And if I say you have a nice fanny, I'm not talking about your bum."

"Do I have a nice fanny?"

"Do you know what it means?"

"Tell me."

"I'd rather show you."

With the confidence of a Chief Mate about to become a Captain, Roger approached her. Something about his demeanor made Maureen shiver, not with a chill, but with excitement.

He looked her in the eye when he lifted her pajama top. With no prelude, he shoved his middle finger into her vagina and wiggled it. Maureen gasped and leaned against him, his hot organ rubbing her thigh.

"That, my dear Miss Murphy, is your fanny. I don't expect you will ever forget the British use of the word."

Maureen buried her face in his shoulder as he continued to finger fuck her. She picked up his rhythm and rolled her hips with the motion.

With his free hand, Roger reached inside her top and groped her breast. His breath had become harsh and irregular. She wouldn't have thought it possible, but he seemed more aroused now than he had been earlier.

Roger leaned over and nuzzled her hair. "You are so goddamn hot! Doing this with you could ruin my career, but I have to have you."

Even in her hyperaroused state, Maureen tried to reassure him. "It won't ruin your career, or mine. We'll be careful."

"Remember that on our four A.M. watch, when we see the Captain."

"I hate you and you hate me. I'll remember."

Roger stepped away from her and picked up a condom from the bed. "Close the toilet door and put your hands against it."

"What are you going to do?"

"What do you think? I'm going to have a piece of fanny."

"The British one or the American one?"

"Bend over and you'll find out."

This was by far the most erotic sexual encounter she'd ever had. Every other man she'd been with had her on her back. No one had ever wanted it from behind. The very thought of it had her wild.

Maureen closed the door and put both hands against it. The ship rolled a bit as they hit some choppy water and she stumbled. Roger caught her. "Get your sea legs back, sailor."

"That sounds like something a pirate would say in this situation."

Roger tore open the condom. "If any did, I doubt they were talking to a woman." Roger lifted the tail of her shirt over her back. "However, they might have said this. Stick out your arse."

Maureen stepped back a bit and raised her rear end. "An American pirate would've said, 'Stick out your ass.'"

"Six of one, half dozen of the other." Not so gently, Roger used his knee to open her legs wider. "Do you have your balance?"

"Yes! For God's sake, put it in already."

Roger grasped her hips. Maureen braced herself. She didn't know where he would poke. It quickly became clear he meant the British fanny. His first thrust sunk into her belly. She involuntarily pushed backward. The sensation made her shudder.

She didn't have time to recover from his initial penetration before he pulled back, then slammed into her again. "You are so frigging tight."

"Yeah, well, good thing I'm wet. Your dick is thick as a damn salami!"

"Oh, yes, doll, you're plenty wet." Roger's thrusts became faster and more insistent. Maureen kept up with him, and kept her balance, even with the choppy water. She could tell it would be soon.

Roger banged her bum hard and groaned. He pulled out and banged her again, this time moaning, "Oh, yeah, baby, milk it!" His fingertips dug deeper into her hips as he slowed down, until he finally stopped.

Maureen stayed still, then waited for him to catch his breath. When he did, he pulled out of her and helped her to stand.

She glanced at the clock. "Mister Trent, we have to get some sleep."

Roger cleaned himself up and then pointed to the condoms scattered on the bed. "Stick those under your mattress, so we have a few here."

"Yes, sir!"

Roger smiled. "That one was an order." He kissed her good night, then opened the door. "See you in a few hours."

From the hall, Maureen heard Vince's voice. "You know, buddy, we have to stop meeting like this. We're like ships passing in the night." Vince waved at Maureen as he walked by, on his way to his midnight watch. "See you on the bridge at 0400."

# 5

---

Maureen rolled out of bed at three-fifteen in the morning. Her inner thigh muscles hurt when she stood up. It surprised her to feel a bit sore. She muttered, "Guess that's what happens when you haven't had sex in two years."

In an attempt to loosen up, Maureen did a few wide leg squats before she showered. If Roger saw her limping today, she'd never live it down.

While she let the hot water revive her, Maureen wondered how he would react to her today. She would follow his lead, no matter what he did. In no way did she want to send any signals to the Captain that something personal had happened between them.

As she dressed, she again considered her lack of any feminine clothing. Not that she wanted to be girlie on the ship, but the idea of looking sexy for an after-hours rendezvous really appealed to her.

She'd have to find out if Grace brought anything naughty on board to wear for Vince. Maybe she could borrow something until she could buy herself a few things. It would help if she could find out what might appeal to Roger. Maybe she should buy a bra, since he seemed to be obsessing about it.

On her way to the mess room to grab some coffee, something else struck her. If Roger got his Master's license next month, chances are he would be transferred to another ship and would be leaving the *Honey Rose*.

What if they really did have chemistry? On one hand, she wanted to fem up for future meetings with him. On the other, he may well be leaving soon. Quite unexpectedly, the thought upset her. Grace had a point last night. How would they manage it if, in fact, they had found something together?

She didn't like black coffee, but this morning, she drank a full cup of it. She had to be fully awake and alert on the bridge. More than the Captain, Roger would be watching.

When she got to the bridge, Roger and Vince were going over the midnight-to-four handover notes. The Captain hadn't yet arrived. Vince saw her before Roger did.

"Good morning, sunshine! How are you this windy day?"

She played it close to the hip. "Good morning. I'm fine today."

Vince grinned. "Sleep well? You look a little tired."

"Put a cork in it, Vince," Roger barked.

"It seems someone else didn't get enough sleep." Vince winked at Maureen. "I'll let the English bulldog fill you in on the weather. I'm outta here."

"Vince, could you tell Grace I'd like to catch up with her later? Maybe at lunchtime?"

"Sure, I'll let her know. See you both later."

Roger still hadn't spoken to her. With the resolve to be professional with him firmly in place, she took up her post at the helm.

From behind her, she heard him say, "There's a storm in the

south Atlantic that's kicking up the water. I'm making a slight course adjustment to keep us out of the worst of the wind."

"Understood." She said nothing else.

"I've also ordered the ballast water adjusted to keep the ship stable in the rougher surf."

"Adjustment noted."

"Why do you want to see Grace?"

Before she answered, she made sure the Captain wasn't coming up the stairs. "I have a question to ask her."

"I'd prefer you wouldn't discuss with her what happened."

"What? Do you think I plan on asking her advice because I'm rusty?"

"I don't know what you plan to ask her. I would simply like to keep my private life private."

"I have something to ask her that indirectly involves you." Maureen nervously glanced behind her.

"Don't worry, I can see the staircase. There's no sign of the Captain. What do you want to ask her?"

"Oh, for God's sake, Roger! I want to know if she has any lingerie with her that I can borrow. And we shouldn't be talking about this here."

"No, we shouldn't. But if you see Grace at lunch today, this is the only chance I'll have to run interference." He shifted his position. Maureen could see he had a ridge forming in his trousers. "You don't need lingerie."

"I know I don't need it. That's why I don't have any with me. But I . . ." She thought better of saying it out loud. "Never mind."

"Finish your thought. But you what?"

Where Maureen had a head of steam building, Roger seemed cool as a breeze off the water. The only evidence that this conversation had any effect on him was the bulge against his leg.

"If you really want to know, I'll tell you." She brushed a loose strand of hair off her face. "I want something feminine and pretty to wear for you." Then she muttered, "Damn Brit. Remind me never to plan a surprise party for you." She turned back to the helm, and to her job.

"I'll look forward to whatever surprise you're planning."

"Don't they teach you anything in British schools? That's an oxymoron."

"So is Irish American."

They heard the Captain coming up the stairs, and abruptly stopped talking. When he came onto the bridge, he noted the silence, and the tension. "You two pissed off at each other already? Isn't it a bit early for that?"

Maureen didn't have to pretend to be irritated. "Sorry, sir. Mister Trent is his usual pleasant self."

"And Miss Murphy needs a lesson in the King's English."

"Now, now, children, play nice. We have a ship to run."

With a perfect irascible inflection, Roger responded, "As you wish, Captain."

After getting a report on the weather, and an update on Roger's course adjustment, the Captain inquired about the deck work. "Is it too windy to replace the wire on the derrick today?"

"Once Murphy completes the course correction, we should be able to do the work. We'll know by 0800 if we have to change the schedule."

Maureen had been manning the helm, and watching the instruments. She hadn't been paying much attention to the conversation behind her.

"You should observe the replacement, Maureen." The Captain's comment caught her unaware.

"What replacement, sir?"

"The wire replacement Trent is overseeing today on the derrick. It's scheduled for 0900 hours, right after breakfast."

She defiantly stuck out her chin. "Is Mister Trent amenable to that, sir?"

The Captain shifted his focus to Roger. "Trent, is that all right with you?"

"Certainly, sir, as long as Miss Murphy doesn't distract the bosun and cause him to injure himself, or worse."

Maureen bit back the *You son of a bitch* that bubbled up inside her. Instead, she responded to the Captain. "I assure you, sir, I will in no way interfere with the work."

"Good. I want you to become familiar with the equipment on the ship. This is an excellent place to start. Trent, answer whatever questions she has about the derricks."

"Yes, sir."

Both Roger and the Captain settled in with paperwork, while Maureen made the course correction. The rough water gradually settled as the ship sailed out of the wind.

After double-checking they were on course, Maureen informed the officers, "Course correction completed, sir." She didn't designate which "sir" she meant.

The Captain shifted in his chair as though to stand. Roger stopped him. "I've got it, Captain. I'll make sure we're on target."

"Try to do it without arguing about it." He went back to the stack of requisition forms in front of him.

"Yes, sir."

Roger came over and stood beside Maureen at the helm. She knew he didn't need to be so close. Unwilling to appear intimidated, she didn't budge. If he wanted her to move, he could tell her.

Roger studied the instruments and noted the course. He also checked the wind speed. All the while, he pressed his leg against hers. He acted as though that was the most proper and normal position he could assume. It was neither.

Maureen didn't react, nor did she move. Two could play this game. He knew very well that his touching her would get her going. That's why he did it. She would be damned to let him know it worked.

"Captain, course successfully corrected, wind speed within safety margins for the wire replacement on the derrick."

Totally absorbed in his paperwork, he didn't turn around when he said, "Good job, both of you. Steady as she goes."

Roger repeated, "Steady as she goes, Murphy"; then he pinched her ass as he returned to his post. Maureen knew she had opened Pandora's box, and there was no going back.

The rest of the watch progressed without incident. At 0800 hours, their relief arrived for the next watch. Roger got up to leave. "Murphy, I'll see you on deck in an hour. Don't be late."

"Yes, sir." She watched him take the stairs two at a time.

Before she left, the Captain called her aside. "Maureen, may I speak to you for a moment before you leave?"

"Yes, sir."

Her heart pounded. God, what if he had noticed something? If he did, it was about to hit the fan.

The Captain led her to the side, out of earshot of the Third Mate and the helmsman. "Maureen, it's obvious Trent is getting to you."

"Sir?"

"You can't let him irritate you. I know he's a pain in the ass, and rides you more than he should, but let it roll off. If I speak to him about it, I'm afraid I'll make matters worse. It's better if you handle it yourself."

The irony of the Captain's comment almost made Maureen laugh. She forced herself to remain serious. "Thank you for your concern, Captain. I can handle Mister Trent. I'm getting better at it every day."

"I hope so. I want you to learn as much as you can from him before he leaves. Did you know he's going for his Master's certificate next month?"

"Yes, sir. He told me."

"Well, at least you've had one civil conversation. Now go get some breakfast."

Maureen left the Captain on the bridge and went straight to the mess room. She'd forgotten how having a sex life can make a person hungry. She felt like she could eat a horse!

She didn't expect Roger to be in the mess room with the crew, and he wasn't. He must have gone straight to the officers' saloon. However, she did spot Grace sitting by herself at what had become their table. Usually, Grace ate earlier, with Vince. She obviously wanted to dish.

Filling her tray with a hungry woman's breakfast, Maureen joined Grace, who seemed fresh as a daisy in May. Maureen sat down beside her. "You look bright-eyed and bushy-tailed this morning."

"You don't. Vince said you looked tired." Grace grinned. "Didn't get much sleep?"

"I've already been through this with Vince. I'll tell you what Roger told him, 'Put a cork in it.'"

"My, grumpy, aren't we?"

"Sorry. Don't mean to be. I'm just hungry."

"I bet you are."

Rather than responding, Maureen stuffed her mouth full of eggs and toast.

"Vince said you wanted to talk to me. What about?"

Maureen swallowed her eggs. "I said at lunch, not now. I don't have much time. The Captain wants me to observe the wire replacement at the mast house at 0900."

"That's under Roger's supervision. I'd like to be a mouse in a corner for that one."

"Where will you be?"

"On the aft end, painting the deck. I get all the glamour jobs."

"A nice, quiet paint job sounds good to me. Wanna trade?"

"No thanks. I wouldn't dream of coming between the two of you."

"Wise choice. You stay out of the line of fire that way."

Grace glanced at her watch. "I've got to run. At least give me a hint about what you want to ask me. I'm dying of curiosity."

Maureen lowered her voice. "I wondered if you brought any sexy nighties with you that I could borrow. You know, baby dolls or something. I don't have a damned thing with me. I don't even own anything like that."

Grace lit up like a lighthouse. "Oh, my God, Maureen!"

"*Shhhhhh!* For heaven's sake, Grace, keep it down! You should know by now that voice of yours carries."

Grace giggled, then whispered, "Sorry. This is just so flipping cool! I can hardly stand it! Of course, I have a few things. I'll dig out a couple. Stop by later, I'll have them ready for you."

"Thanks. The first chance I have to go ashore, I'll pick up some frilly things of my own."

"We'll pick up some things together, sweetie. I'm going with you."

For once, Maureen appreciated Grace butting in. "Lord knows I could use some help with it. I don't even own a bra."

"Bet he loves that."

"Don't know if he loves it, but he's definitely noticed it."

"That's one for our side." Grace leaned in close to her ear. "I think you're falling in love with him."

"Yeah, so does he."

"Are you?"

"How the fuck should I know? I've never been in love before."

"Wanting to look sexy for him is a definite symptom."

"So, if I got the disease, what's the cure?"

"Lots and lots of lovin'. From the looks of it, you're on the right track." Grace glanced at her watch again. "Jeez, I really do have to go."

"So do I. Don't want to hear it if I'm late. I'll see you later."

Grace left, and Maureen wolfed down the rest of her breakfast. After a quick trip to the toilet, she went to the foredeck and found Roger already there.

"AB Murphy reporting for duty, sir." She didn't have to be that formal and announce her arrival, but she wanted to make sure he noticed her.

He gruffly answered, "Fine, fine. Stand over there, out of the way." Roger pointed to a spot near the starboard bulwark, away from the mast house, but close enough to see what was going on.

There were already several crew members milling around, including the bosun. Maureen knew from the *Atlantic Moon* that part of the bosun's job as deck foreman was to climb the mast and replace any wires that were worn or rusted.

The bosun went up the ladder to the top of the mast house. Roger followed him. They seemed to be having a heated discussion. Roger pointed to the wires rising high above the deck of the ship. The bosun also pointed to them and shook his head no.

Maureen jumped when someone tapped her on the shoulder.

"Hey, Murph. How're you doing? I haven't seen you in a few days."

Eddie stood beside her. "Oh, hello, Eddie. Sorry, I didn't see you." She pointed up to where Roger stood. "They look like they're arguing. Do you know what's going on?"

"Yeah. The bosun doesn't want to replace the wire, and says it's good for loading the next cargo. He wants to wait until we get to the next discharge port to replace it. The boss man says we should replace the wire today because it's nicked. If it breaks, it could injure someone."

"Why doesn't the bosun want to do it now?"

"He says it's dangerous to be hanging from the top of the mast today. It's still too windy and rocky."

"Eddie, Roger checked during our watch this morning. He said the wind has died down enough to do the work."

"Well, the bosun doesn't think so."

Maureen stood on the deck, transfixed by the drama unfolding on the mast house. Roger looked angry as hell, and the bosun seemed about to throw a punch. She would have given anything to hear what was being said. Eddie interrupted her concentration. He obviously had other things on his mind.

"So, Murph, I still have that empty bunk in my cabin."

"Eddie, you know I have my own quarters."

"I didn't mean you should move in. But you could visit once in a while."

"No can do, sailor. You know the rules."

Eddie had distracted her. She'd looked at him for a few seconds, instead of watching Roger. When she again looked up, she saw the bosun coming down the ladder to the deck.

Roger still stood at the base of the mast. In fact, he was standing there, looking in her direction. He had seen her talking to Eddie.

Eddie startled her again. He put his arm around her waist and said, "Rules were made to be broken." She felt his thumb brush the bottom of her breast.

"Not these rules. Back off, Eddie!" Maureen snarled. She pushed his arm away and stepped to the side. Then she looked back up at Roger. He had seen the whole thing.

Almost like he did it just for her, he unbuttoned his shirt. The men often took off their shirts while working on the deck, especially on a sunny day. However, she never expected Roger to do it.

His shirt fell open and she glimpsed his bare chest. She wouldn't have cared if Eddie had stripped naked and danced the hoochie-coo in front of her. Nothing could make her look away now.

Roger tossed his shirt on the mast house platform, beside a narrow ladder, which extended up the mast. One of the deckhands handed him a bosun's chair. He threw it over his shoulder and began climbing the ladder.

Maureen said more to herself than to Eddie, "What the devil is he doing?"

Eddie took a few steps closer and looked up. "I think he's going to remove the block and thread the wire himself."

"Jesus Christ, Eddie. That mast has to be at least sixty feet above the deck!"

"Yeah, well, if Mister Boss Man says the cargo runner has to be replaced, it will get replaced. If the bosun won't do it, he will."

Maureen remembered what Roger had said, about her being a distraction and causing an injury, or worse. She wondered if she should leave. But she thought again. If he looked down, and didn't see her, maybe that would be even more unnerving. So, as she had earlier, she stood her ground with him.

She heard another familiar voice beside her. Vince had come on deck. "I came to check on how it's going with the derrick. Why's Roger climbing up there?"

"It looked like he had some sort of argument with the bosun. Eddie says he's climbing up the mast to do the work himself."

Vince's only reaction was "That figures."

"Why do you say that?"

"He's tough. If he gives an order, he expects it to be done when he says it should be done, even if he has to do it himself."

Eddie agreed. "I sure as shit don't mess with him. If he tells me to jump, I ask how high."

Several crew members rolled a drum of steel wire across the deck to the derrick. Maureen watched Roger scale the ladder like a monkey climbing a tree. When he reached the top, he leaned forward—more than she thought he should—to hook the bosun's chair on the pad eyes.

She knew what he had to do. Once he attached the chair, he had to swing free of the ladder so he could sit in it. It took all the control she could muster not to cover her eyes. When he did step off the ladder, she gasped and covered her mouth.

Vince put his arm around her shoulders. "Don't worry. He knows what he's doing. It's how he earned his stripes."

"He damn well better." She saw him swaying at the top of the mast like a child on a playground swing. "The wind's picked up and he's not wearing a harness."

Vince gave her a squeeze and whispered, "Steady as she goes, Sunshine. You're shaking."

"Hell, Vince, I can't help it." Maureen shielded her eyes from the glare. "What's he doing now? I can't see."

Vince squinted up at the mast. "He's releasing the old wire from the block. Once it's released, the crew has to pull it down and rethread the new one. He won't stay up there for that."

"Who'll attach the new one to the top of the mast?"

"I expect he will when it's ready."

"Damn!" Maureen braced herself. She couldn't let him see her be a wimp about this, even if her stomach felt tight as a sailor's knot.

A flurry of activity at the mast house indicated Roger had successfully released the old wire. Some deckhands pulled the old wire down, while others climbed onto the derrick to release it from the lower blocks.

She couldn't take her eyes off Roger. Sixty feet in the air, with the wind blowing and the bosun's chair swinging, he grabbed the ladder like a trapeze artist. He got one foot on a rung, then swung from the chair onto the ladder. The empty chair continued to sway as he climbed down.

Totally focused on the work, he set about helping the crew

rewire the derrick. He straddled the horizontal pole like it was a horse, then worked alongside the deckhands threading the new wire.

If Maureen hadn't been so worried about Roger climbing the mast again, she would have enjoyed this part more. With no shirt on, the muscles in his arms bulged every time he pulled the wire.

Even with the impressive view, she wanted them to finish this job sooner rather than later. She brushed the hair from her face. The wind had kicked up even more. The bosun's chair swung high over the deck, waiting for Roger's return trip up the ladder.

After the crew hoisted the new wire up the mast on the chain block, Roger threw a coil of rope over his shoulder and again climbed the dizzying height to the top. Repeating his acrobatic performance, he made it safely into the bosun's chair, even with the wind blowing it sideways. This time, when he stepped off the ladder, she heard Vince mutter, "Crazy bastard. It's too windy to be up there now."

That didn't seem to matter to Roger. He attached the new wire to the mast block, and then he took the rope off his shoulder. He held on to one end, then tossed the coil back down to the deck.

"What's he doing, Vince?"

"He needs the grease bucket. See, they're tying the rope to the handle."

Sure enough, a few seconds later, Roger hoisted the bucket they had attached to the rope. Hand over fist, he pulled it up the mast. Once he had it, he set it on his lap. Then he dipped his bare hands into the grease and coated the new wire.

He finally finished. After lowering the bucket and tossing the rope after it, he climbed back onto the ladder. This time, he also had to retrieve the chair. It took him a few seconds to grab it as it flapped in the wind.

When he caught it, he unhooked it from the eye pads and tossed it over his shoulder. Then he started down. Even from the deck, Maureen could see black grease on the white rungs of the ladder.

"Vince, how slippery does that ladder get?" He didn't answer right away. "Vince, talk to me."

Eddie spoke up. "I'll tell you, Red. Ever try holding on to a greased pig?"

Maureen held her breath. It was more than not wanting him to fall. The very thought of Roger not being in her life gave her the shakes. She didn't want to lose him—not now, not ever.

# 6

Maureen had wanted to leave. Watching Roger do a circus act sixty feet in the air made her more seasick than any ship she'd ever sailed on. But she couldn't. Even more than the Captain's order to observe the derrick wire replacement, she wouldn't let anyone—especially Roger—think she couldn't take it.

He didn't finish until after noon. Once he climbed down, he had a brief meeting with the deckhands. Both Eddie and Vince left to get some lunch.

Maureen waited until he gathered up his shirt, then closed the gap between where she stood and the mast house. When Roger came down the ladder to the deck, she was waiting for him. He had his shirt tossed over his arm, and he didn't seem to mind she had come to meet him.

"I didn't think Chief Mates got their hands dirty. You're filthy."

"I do when it's necessary." He held up his greasy hands. "Like today."

"I guess so." She couldn't help herself. She glanced at his bare chest. Even streaked with grease, he looked good.

"Go get some lunch. I'll see you on the bridge at 1600." Before he left, he quietly added, "Get some sleep this afternoon. It may be another late night." He didn't have to spell it out. She knew what he meant.

Maureen watched him walk the length of the deck with the authority of a Captain, checking in with the crew as he went. She had no doubt he would have his own ship soon.

Maureen didn't see Grace in the mess room, and she really didn't mind. A quick lunch and some wonderful sleep, that's what she wanted right now. Once 1600 rolled around, she would have to hit the ground running.

When she got back to her cabin, she found a note tacked to the door.

*I have what you need. Come by before your next watch to pick them up. There's one I know you'll love. It's perfect!*

*xoxoxo*
*Grace*

Maureen wondered if Roger had seen the note when he went to his cabin. Considering how he'd reacted to her pajama top last night, she knew she'd damn well better get some sleep.

She slept soundly. The nap did her a world of good, except she nearly overslept. When her clock went off, she hit the button and dozed off again. Her eyes popped open at ten minutes until four.

She ran down the hall to Grace's room before going to the bridge. When she knocked, Grace immediately opened the door.

"Yes, I know, your watch starts in a few minutes." She shoved a small bag at Maureen. "I'd go with the black one if I were you." Grace blew her a kiss and closed the door.

Maureen dashed back to her cabin, tossed the bag on her bunk, then literally ran to the bridge. She barely made it on time.

Of course, Roger had already arrived, looking cool, clean and coiffed. He stood at the helm, where she should be. "Running it a bit close, aren't you, Murphy?"

"Sorry, sir." Maureen pointedly added, "I had to pick up something from Grace before my watch."

"Then perhaps you should have allowed more time."

"I overslept, or I would have."

He sternly gave her a warning. "Murphy, I expect you to be at your post, on time, no matter what the circumstance. Is that understood?"

Maureen's temper flared. She almost blurted out, Why are you being so pissy? Remembering the Captain could walk in at any time, she answered politely instead. "Begging your pardon, sir, I wasn't late."

"Might I suggest that the errand you ran could have waited? Arriving at your watch, breathless and looking like you just rolled out of bed, is not good form."

Maureen hadn't taken time to check herself in the bathroom mirror. "Do I look that bad?"

"Miss Murphy, I never said you looked bad. Quite the contrary."

Roger turned the helm over to her, and accidentally brushed against her leg. That's when she understood the problem. Her tousled appearance on the bridge had given him another hard-on. She'd been too flustered to notice.

"I have the helm, sir, if you need to excuse yourself."

With the same abrasive tone he'd used to reprimand her, he growled, "The errand you ran, what color is it?"

Remembering Grace's recommendation, Maureen simply said, "Black."

"If the Captain arrives before I get back, tell him I had a

quick call, and will return directly." He left her alone on the bridge.

Trying not to dwell on Roger's reaction to her, Maureen reviewed the handover sheet. Fortunately, there were no problems. Roger's earlier course correction had spared them the storm.

The Captain came onto the bridge. "Where's Trent?"

"He had to use the toilet, sir. He'll be right back."

"It's that damn chili they fed us for lunch. I haven't been right since I ate it." He picked up the clipboard Maureen had just reviewed. "Anything happening?"

"Everything's quiet, sir. It's smooth sailing at the moment."

"If I leave you two alone tonight, will you be all right?"

"Of course, Captain. If you aren't feeling well, you should go lie down."

Roger came up behind them. "You aren't feeling well, sir?"

"Same problem I expect you have." Roger shot Maureen a look that nearly made her burst out laughing.

Stifling herself, she quickly explained. "The chili at lunch didn't agree with the Captain, either."

Roger's British aplomb kicked in. "Oh, of course. Sorry to hear that, sir. Lethal, wasn't it?"

"Damn right it was. I have to speak to the cook, and tell him to tone it down next time. Are you feeling well enough to hold the bridge?"

"Yes, sir. I'm feeling much better since I visited the loo."

"You and Murphy won't kill each other if I leave you alone?"

With classic tongue-in-cheek Brit sarcasm, Roger retorted, "Sir, I promise you, there will be no homicides on the bridge. We'll wait until our watch ends to kill each other."

"Well, then, if you're both still alive, I'll see you in the morning."

Maureen waited until the Captain was out of earshot before she said, "We're going to kill each other tonight?"

"We might. You almost did me in, a few minutes ago."

"Didn't mean to."

"Tell it to the judge at the trial."

Since they had some time alone, Maureen decided to speak her mind. "Why are you always so pissed off at me? I haven't made a single mistake since I came on board last week. For Christ's sake, I wasn't even late today and you yelled at me."

"I never said you made any mistakes, and I'm not always pissed off at you."

"Then I guess you're just pissed off at women generally, because your fiancée called off the wedding."

"How the hell do you know about that?"

"Grace told me."

Roger muttered, "Fucking Vince. I told him to keep his mouth shut."

Maureen defended Vince. "He told his wife. That's what married people do. They talk to each other."

"I'll probably never know." He smirked. "Of course, neither will you, since you're married to the sea."

"Grace and Vince found a way to do it."

Roger leaned against the counter and crossed his arms. "All right. Let's assume for a moment they'll be allowed to continue this arrangement. What happens if she gets pregnant and has a baby? They can't raise a child on a ship."

Maureen didn't have an answer. "I don't know if they want children. If they do, and don't want to be separated, Vince will have to go ashore. Otherwise, Gracie will have to stay home alone and raise their kids."

"Some choice. It's better to stay single if you're a seaman. Then those problems don't exist."

"You were going to get married. How were you going to handle it?"

Her question hit a nerve. "Fecking hell! It's not like I didn't tell her what my plans were. She said she wanted to be the Captain's wife, and we'd manage it together."

"Maybe the dream and the reality were too far apart for her."

"I guess they were. She married a banker, instead of a sailor." Roger changed the subject. "What about you? Don't you want a home and a family?"

"My take's a little different on that from most people. I've always been alone, except for my dad and grandma. He passed his love of the sea on to me. His ship was our home."

"What about your mother?"

"She died in a car accident when I was little. I hardly remember her. My grandmother raised me."

"The one Grace mentioned, on Cape Cod?"

"That's the one. Since you're such a Brit, I don't know if you ever saw the movie *Tugboat Annie*?"

"I'm familiar with the story."

"Well, that was my grandma. She cooked on a fishing boat. That's actually how my father learned about the sea, and being a sailor. When he wasn't in school, she took him with her, the same as she did me."

"But you were a child."

"Didn't matter. I helped her in the galley when I went along. I grew up on a boat, the same as my dad."

"How did you end up on a merchant ship with your father?"

"My senior year in high school, Grandma had a stroke and passed away. When I graduated, my father let me spend the summer on the ship with him. He wanted to send me to college in the fall. But once I got on board, I never left."

Roger scratched his head. "Jesus, you've had more sea time than I have, if you count the time on the fishing boat."

"Yup, and I'm just as good as you are, too, except maybe at climbing sixty-foot masts."

Roger grinned, the first time he'd smiled at her. "Don't push your luck, Murphy. Like Grace said, I'm coming around."

"Yeah, I'll believe that when you stop being a pain in my ass."

"If I stop being a pain in your arse, you'll know I've lost interest. I can assure you, that's not the case."

Not prone to flirting, Maureen couldn't seem to help it. "Is that a good thing or a bad thing?"

"Both." He pointed to the helm. "Now get to work, sailor. Your performance is being monitored, on the bridge, and off."

"Yes, sir." Maureen kept the *So is yours* part to herself. She focused on the helm, and doing her job. Maybe if she stayed busy, eight o'clock would come around faster.

Roger didn't talk much more to her during their watch, except to update the handover sheet. He had the cargo manifest form with the bills of lading from the last discharge port to review. Maureen thought he took longer doing the paperwork than was necessary. Again he seemed to be avoiding her.

Just before their relief arrived, he asked the question she'd been waiting to hear. "Your flat or mine?"

She'd already thought about it. "Mine." It would be easier for her to change in her own cabin.

"It's black, huh? How short is it?"

"Don't know. I didn't have time to take it out of the bag." She looked him in the eye and added, "Or I would've been late."

"Well, then, I guess we can both look forward to the surprise, can't we?"

"I suppose so."

Maureen let his needling about the oxymoron slide. She clammed up, not wanting to risk being overheard. A few minutes later, the eight-to-twelve watch arrived on the bridge. There was still no sign of the Captain.

Maureen and Roger went down the stairs together. "You go on ahead. I'm going to check on the old man and make sure he just has a bellyache."

"Good idea." Maureen certainly understood the consequences if the Captain went down. Roger would have to assume command of the ship.

She hurried back to her cabin. At least this gave her a few minutes alone to freshen up and change. After making sure she'd left the door unlocked, she grabbed the bag she'd left on her bunk and went to take a quick shower.

After standing in the sun earlier that morning, she didn't want to worry about being sweaty. Taking care not to get her hair wet, she rinsed off. She still hadn't seen what Grace had given her to wear.

When she opened the bag, she saw something black and something dark red. She pulled out the red one first. The black one made her nervous.

Maureen shook it out and held it up to the light. The knee-length satin nightgown had spaghetti straps and a deep V-neck. She could tell just by looking at it that the material would cling like Saran Wrap.

Then she took out the black one, which was the one Roger expected her to wear. When she unfolded it, she blushed. Vince had to have bought this for Grace. It looked like a man's fantasy come true.

The black chiffon baby doll had fur trim around the bodice and bottom. Maureen could see straight through the rest of it. A pair of frilly black panties fell on the floor when she shook out the wrinkles. They were also transparent.

Again she faced a put-up-or-shut-up situation with Roger, this one personal rather than professional. She pulled the baby doll over her head. It fit, what there was of it. The fur trim on the bodice almost covered her breasts. The fur on the bottom tickled the top of her thighs. Roger wanted to know how long it was. The disconcerting answer: *not very*!

Maureen pulled on the panties, the comfort of wearing a bit more clothing more psychological than practical. They didn't hide anything. She glanced in the mirror and fluffed her hair. She didn't have any makeup, and really didn't need it. Her pink cheeks said it all.

She whispered, "Well, here goes nothing" as she opened the bathroom door.

Roger stood by her bunk. She hadn't heard him come in. He held a picture of her and her father, taken on the *Atlantic Moon* a few months before he died.

He'd already partially undressed. His shoes and socks were on the floor and his shirt lay across the bunk. Maureen's heart thumped in her chest as she stared at the reddish tint on his back and shoulders. He'd gotten sunburned while on the mast. She almost ran back into the toilet.

Before she could bolt, he turned around, with the picture still in his hand. He didn't say anything when he saw her.

She tried to act naturally, even though she looked like a pinup from inside a sailor's locker. "How's the Captain feeling?"

"He's all right. A good night's sleep will help more than anything. He said he'll see us in the morning."

"I didn't hear you come in."

"You were in the shower, so I made myself at home." He held up the picture. "This is your father?"

"That's him."

"You resemble him. He had red hair, too." When Roger said that, he studied the hair on her head, then looked farther down. "That outfit is obscene."

"I know. Maybe I should take it off and put something else on."

"Don't you dare." He came closer. "Wish I had a camera. You're hot as Hades in that black number."

She lightly caressed his shoulder. His skin felt warm under her hand. "You're hot, too. Looks like you got sunburned this morning. That's what you get for working on the mast without your shirt."

He grasped the back of her neck in his palm, then lifted her hair. "I saw Eddie getting fresh with you today. Maybe I should speak to him about that."

"That's not necessary. I can handle Eddie."

Roger put his other arm around her waist. "I don't want you messing around with him, or any other man." He nuzzled her red hair.

Maureen kissed his sunburned shoulder, then whispered, "Is that an order, sir?"

"That's an order, sailor." He slid his hand up her waist to her breast. "Your nipples are hard again."

Maureen reached between them and caressed his erection. "So is your dick."

"Seems we're a matched set."

"Maybe we are."

With his hand still behind her neck, Roger turned her head and tilted it back. "You know, you're driving me bloody crazy."

"Nice to know that's a two-way street. I about had heart failure watching you swing from that mast today."

"What, you didn't think I could do it?"

"I know you can do it. You've proven that beyond a shadow of a doubt."

"And I'm about to do it again." He wrapped his arms around Maureen and kissed her, a kiss that threatened to devour her. His tongue filled her mouth as his hands explored her body. He groped and caressed her, roughly bunching the fragile chiffon in his hands. Then he tugged at her panties, trying to pull them down.

She broke the kiss and hoarsely whispered, "Roger, don't tear them. This isn't mine."

He stepped back and gruffly answered, "Take them off."

While Maureen stepped out of the sheer briefs, Roger took off his trousers. Again she had a chance to see his impressive erection as his penis dangled from his groin.

Maureen unconsciously licked her lips as she ogled his manhood. He saw her do it. "Go ahead, redhead, lick it. I won't mind."

She hadn't given anyone a blow job since high school. "It's been quite a few years. Don't know if I remember how."

"You remembered how to fuck. I expect you know how to suck just as well."

She heard the challenge in his voice, and responded with one of her own. "I'll suck you, if you suck me."

The expression on his face was somewhere between a smile and a leer. "Now that's a proposition I don't get every day. You're on."

Maureen wanted to lick him. What better way to get an up close and personal view of the equipment? He'd taken off his trousers and left them in a crumpled heap on the floor. She bent over to grab them.

When she stood up, Roger had his dick in his hand, rubbing off while he checked her out. "If you ever give up sailing, you could pose for men's magazines. With that arse and fanny, you'd make good money at it."

She made a mental note. Seeing her bend over made him hotter, just like it had last night. The view from behind appealed to him.

"Thank you for noticing." She kissed his cheek. "You're the

only man that's seen my rear end in a long time. And that's how it's going to stay."

"Does that make me special?"

"I would say so."

She dropped his trousers on the floor at his feet. Before she knelt on them, she asked, "Any pointers before I give this a go?"

"Just watch the teeth. Other than that, have at it."

She couldn't remember the last time she'd been so horny. This man got to her like no other ever had. She'd already fallen in lust with him. Maybe love wasn't far behind.

Maureen knelt in front of him. The musky scent of his genitals made her head swim. He smelled like he had on some sort of exotic cologne. She knew better. His body made its own perfume, and she loved it!

Using his beefy thighs as support, she leaned against him. He didn't budge. She wrapped her arms around his ass and licked him. Roger grabbed her head to balance himself.

She stopped. "Do you want to lie down?"

"No. Keep going." He spread his legs a bit farther apart. "I have my footing now."

She smiled up at him. "Yes, sir."

He threaded her hair through his fingers. "Sailor, this is hardly a time to stand on protocol."

Maureen grinned. "I bet you say that to all the sailors."

Completely unperturbed by her insinuation, he coolly replied, "No. Actually, you're the first one. I've never been blown by a sailor before."

"Well, first time for everything." With that, she went at him full throttle. Maureen opened her mouth and took in as much of his length as she could manage. Then she sucked, hard.

Her technique might have been clumsy, but his reaction confirmed she'd done something right. He groaned loudly, then clutched her hair in his fists. The bit of pain from having her hair pulled didn't slow her down. She lapped at him like a thirsty cat drinking a bowl of milk.

Maureen felt the muscles in his legs ripple under her hand. He growled at her, "Jesus Christ, that's good! Suck it, red-head!"

She did as he said, taking her commanding officer to a place far removed from the bridge. He suddenly stopped her. "Bloody hell, you're going to take me over the top if you keep that up. I want to fuck. You can swallow it another time."

Maureen wanted to fuck, too. She'd gladly take a rain check on him going down on her to get to the fucking part. She wondered if she had the nerve to ask for what she really wanted. She realized she did.

Roger had already retrieved a condom from under the mattress. Maureen stood up and wrapped her arms around his neck before he put it on. "So, sailor, have you ever had an American fanny?"

"The only fanny I've ever had is the British variety."

"Want to try something new?"

"I might. Did the chili clean you out the way it did the rest of us?"

Maureen laughed. "How terribly delicate of you to put it that way. Yes, I went earlier."

"You aren't shy about this, are you?"

"Why should I be?"

"My former fiancée didn't have the inclination to be adventurous like you are."

"Yeah, well, that's probably because you Brits don't have sex."

"And you Americans are oversexed. Have you ever had it in the arse before?"

"No. I'm an arse virgin."

Roger stepped back and rolled on the condom. "You know, I'm going to drill you."

Maureen thought she might come, just hearing him say it. "If you take it slow until I get used to it, I'll be all right."

"All right, sailor, assume the position. Bend over and put your hands on the door, like you did last night."

With the tantalizing expectation of being sodomized at sea, Maureen bent over. She had never been so hot in her life. "Fuck, Roger, no wonder men do this. My asshole is twitching, I want it so bad."

"My dear, seeing your arsehole makes me want it, too. No way in hell am I interested in seeing a man's arsehole, no matter how hard up I am." He lifted her nightie and kneaded her ass cheeks with his fingertips. Then he gave her a good swat.

"Ouch! What was that for?"

"I've been wanting to smack your arse all week, on principle." He swatted her again. "I've also heard it loosens things up for what's to come."

Maureen flinched, but the second one felt sort of good. "Who told you that?"

He continued to massage her bum. "I may not have a taste for it, but some that I've sailed with have. I've heard a few things over the years." The flat of his hand connected again. She knew her ass must be getting red.

"I hope you're enjoying the view back there."

"Without question." He shoved his finger into her anus.

Maureen moaned and pushed back against his hand. "Fuck, that's good!"

"You're ready. Sailor, you're about to take it up the arse."

With no more preliminaries, Maureen felt him poke at her bumhole. The tip of his penis popped in. Again she pushed back. He didn't move. The force of her backward push made him sink in deeper. She shuddered.

Roger stood still. "Are you doing all right? Let me know if it's too much."

Maureen clenched her buttocks and rocked. The sensation took her breath away. She wanted him in deeper. "I'm okay. Push it in more."

Roger obliged, again giving her time to adjust. "Good?"

"Jesus, yes!" She wiggled, testing the waters for a real fuck. Satisfied that she could handle it, she gave him the order this time. "Go ahead, drill me."

She didn't have to tell him twice. He pulled out and pushed back in, holding her hips the way he had the night before. Within a few seconds, he gave her a full ahead and sustained a constant speed.

Never in her life had she been fucked like this. He pounded her ass with a vengeance. She didn't care if this was his way of punishing her for what she did to him. She never wanted him to stop.

Her orgasm hit like a wave breaking on the shore, slamming into her and drowning her in sensation. She couldn't contain the sound that erupted from her throat. Roger's grunts blended with hers as they rode the next wave together.

# 7

Maureen wanted Roger to spend the night with her, but he said no. "If I stay here, Murphy, we won't get any sleep." He put on his socks and shoes, then stood up. "In a few hours, we're back on the bridge."

"You're right, but that doesn't stop me from wanting it."

He laughed. "I know you want it. You've made that clear enough."

"Bloody Brit! Don't you ever get tired of being sarcastic?"

"Haven't yet, and don't expect to anytime soon." Just then, the ship pitched and rolled slightly to starboard. The picture of Maureen's father fell off the shelf and onto her bunk. "Looks like things are getting bumpy again."

"Either that, or Dad's turning over in his grave."

His seriousness belied her bad joke. "We're coming up on the coast. Entry to the Straits will be on our watch."

"Your point is?"

"You'll be at the helm in rough water."

"Isn't this mixing personal and professional, Mister Trent?"

"Yes, it absolutely is. I want to say this off the record. I want your word—if it's too much for you, you'll hand the helm off to me."

Maureen didn't care that she stood in front of him nearly nude. She'd be damned to let him get away with this. "You still don't think I can manage it, even after I got us out of the port and across the frigging Atlantic, course change and all!"

"I know this water. The tide will be coming in, and the rip currents will be coming out. This isn't a place to cut your teeth at the helm."

Maureen's temper exploded. "You frigging son of a bitch! I told you my first day on board that I've navigated the Straits before. How fucking dare you say I'd be cutting my teeth at the helm!"

"We'll see how rough it is at 0400." He turned to leave, then picked up a piece of paper lying on the floor in front of the door. After reading it, he handed it to Maureen. With no other comment, he left.

Maureen stared at the closed door. This isn't how she wanted tonight to end, not at all. It hadn't even occurred to him to apologize. Not only that, the bastard left without saying good night.

She made a fist, and inadvertently crumpled the piece of paper Roger had given her. When she opened it, she immediately recognized Grace's handwriting.

*Jesus Christ, that's good?*
*Suck it, redhead?*
*I want to fuck?*
*You can swallow it another time?*

*You're right. You can hear in the alleyway.*
*Hope you both had fun. We sure did.*

*xoxoxo*
*Grace and Vince*

Maureen tore the note into small pieces and threw it in the trash.

Before going to bed, she rinsed out the baby doll set and threw it over the shower rod to dry. She hung the red one in her closet. Given how they'd just parted, Maureen wondered if she'd ever use it.

She woke up several times during the night. The ship's see-sawing motion made sleeping difficult. Just before she planned to get up, someone knocked on her door. "Captain requests the 0400 watch immediately report to the bridge."

Maureen bolted out of bed. The ship pitched again, and she fell back on her bunk. She steadied herself and dressed as quickly as she could.

Roger was running down the hall when she came out of her cabin. "What the hell is going on?"

"Don't know. C'mon, hustle!"

The alleyway became a moving target as the ship continued to roll. When they got to the bridge, Vince and his junior helmsman were with the Captain.

When the Captain saw them, he didn't mince words. "We have a serious situation developing. The wind is coming from the east at Beaufort 7, sustained at thirty-five miles per hour. The weather report we just received says they're already close to Beaufort 9 in the Straits, and there is a gale warning in effect."

Roger stepped forward. "Captain, this is a bloody levanter, isn't it?"

"It certainly is, a classic one. It's being reinforced by a depression to the south, the same one you avoided yesterday. It's going to blow hard before it blows out—"

"Sir, asking for relief at the helm, sir!" the man at the helm interrupted.

The Captain barked, "Maureen, take the helm and hold her as steady as you can."

She snapped to. "Yes, sir!"

The sailor she relieved grabbed a bucket he'd stashed by the wall. He barely made it before he puked. Vince went to help him.

Maureen focused on the instruments, but she heard what the Captain said. "He's been sick for the last half hour. Vince, get him to his cabin—then get your ass back up here."

"Yes, sir."

The Captain turned his attention to her. "Maureen, have you navigated gale force winds before?"

"Yes, sir."

"You know about the levanter in the Straits?"

"Yes, sir. It's particularly bad when it blows hard against the current. It makes for a sharp, high sea and can take a ship down."

Roger spoke up. "Sir, might I remind you, a ship took on water and sank here last month in a similar weather pattern?"

Almost as an exclamation point to what Roger said, the ship pitched again. "Trent, that's why we're going to wait this one out." He turned back to Maureen. "We're not going to force our way through this. We're going to take evasive action."

Vince ran back up the stairs. "How're we doing?"

Roger made his way to the helm and stood beside Maureen. "Steady as she goes, Murphy?"

"Steady as she goes, sir."

Roger reported back to the Captain and Vince. "Murphy is holding her, sir. What are your orders?"

"We're diverting to Portugal. The closest port that might be able to accommodate our request is at Faro. Radio ahead, Trent, and request permission to put up in the harbor until this thing blows itself out."

The Captain approached Maureen. "Can you get us there in one piece, Murphy?"

"Aye, Captain. Feed me the course, and I'll get us there."

Maureen invoked the spirit of her father as her stomach tightened. She'd been in rough water before, plenty of times. More than proving to Roger she could do it, she owed it to her father's memory to get them out of this safely.

Roger radioed ahead to the port. A few minutes later, he reported back, "Permission granted to wait out the gale at Algarve Harbor, Port of Faro."

Vince shouted, "On it, sir."

"Trent, get over here and help him calculate the course correction. Murphy needs it, pronto!"

A wave unexpectedly caught the port bow of the ship, and it rolled starboard. Anything that wasn't tied down hit the floor. Maureen kept her balance, and responded, by the book, holding the rudder steady. The ship rocked; then it righted itself. It continued to plow through the foamy water toward the Straits.

Along with the clamor of things falling off the counters, she'd also heard a thud, but she didn't turn around to see what made the noise. Her full concentration had been on her job. Then she heard Vince yell, "Roger's down! He fell when she pitched."

The Captain growled, "I'll take care of him. Get Murphy the new course so she can get us the hell out of here."

Maureen knew she had to focus and didn't turn around. Gripping the wheel until her knuckles turned white, she yelled, "How is he?"

"He hit his head. He's unconscious."

She glanced in the direction of the Captain's voice. Roger lay on the floor, a puddle of blood pooling beside his head. "Sir, he's bleeding!"

"He cracked his head on the corner of the chart table."

Vince intervened. "Murphy, do you need me to take the helm?" Vince knew what the Captain didn't. Her concern went far beyond seeing a shipmate injured.

With her stomach pushing into her throat, she swallowed

the fear, and the vomit. "I have the helm. Get me the course we have to keep, so I know where we're going."

"You got it, Sunshine."

She checked their current position and direction. "Captain, with your permission, we should reduce speed and turn her to the northeast, right into the wind. If the bow takes on the waves, the swell won't cause as much damage. I'll adjust the course when Vince has it for me."

"Do it, Murphy. Heaving her northeast will get us closer to the coast, which is where we want to be. Vince, signal the engine room slow ahead."

While Vince telegraphed the engine room, she again glanced at Roger. The Captain had the first-aid kit. She saw him rip open a gauze bandage and press it against Roger's head. "Take good care of him, sir. I don't want to lose him." She didn't care what the Captain might think. She had to say it out loud.

"He'll be all right. He has a hard head."

"I know that better than most do, sir." Then she slowly turned the ship northward.

Vince fed her the new course, and she adjusted accordingly. Roger remained unconscious for about fifteen minutes, when she finally heard him groan. She'd never heard a more beautiful sound.

Vince heard him, too. "He's coming around."

Maureen couldn't go to him. The waves continued to toss the ship. She had to hold her steady and maintain their course.

Roger must have tried to get up. He moaned. "Christ, my head hurts."

"Trent, stay flat on your back. That's an order!"

"What happened?"

"You cracked your head like a walnut. You probably have a concussion."

"Bloody hell!"

The Captain seemed satisfied he'd fully regained conscious-ness. "Trent, I'd ask you what day of the week it is, but I'm not sure I know myself."

"It's Thursday, sir. Murphy's been my helmsman for nine days."

Maureen heard Vince chuckle, then mutter, "Interesting way to remember what day it is."

Even flat on his back, Roger still gave her a hard time. "Mur-phy, can't you keep this damn ship still? Every time it bumps, my head pounds."

"I'm doing my best, sir. We haven't taken on water yet. Something to be said for that."

"Yeah, well, keep it that way."

"I plan to, Mister Trent."

He continued to grouse. "Where the hell are we, anyway?"

Maureen answered before anyone else could. "We are on course for the Port of Faro, ETA at current speed, three hours twenty minutes. Wind speed is Beaufort 8, with sustained gale force winds at forty miles per hour. Gusts are reaching Beau-fort 9, at fifty miles per hour. Wind speed is expected to drop as we approach the shelter of the Algarve Harbor." She refrained from adding *So there!*

"You've manned the helm through the course change?"

"Yes, sir, I have."

"Even with me out cold?"

"Yes, sir, even with you lying there bleeding."

"I was bleeding? And you stayed at the helm? What the fuck?"

"Sir, with all due respect, might I suggest you need more practice with your sea legs before you get your Master's li-cense? It doesn't matter that you can climb a sixty-foot mast. If you can't stand up on the bridge, I don't know how you expect to be a Captain."

"Don't change the subject. I could have been lying here dying, and you didn't turn the helm over to Vince? Bloody hell!"

At that point, Vince burst out laughing. "For crying out loud! Pardon me, Captain, but do you listen to this every day?"

"Every day, twice a day, for the last nine days."

Vince continued to chuckle. "I told them over a week ago they should sell tickets. They would've cleaned up by now."

"I only hope I get to perform the wedding before they throttle each other."

Maureen ignored all of them, and continued to do her job. "Wind speed down to Beaufort 7, sustained at thirty-five miles per hour, and continuing to drop. We are maintaining course to Port of Faro."

"Vince, I'll take over the radar. Go find a few men to carry Roger back to his cabin."

Roger objected. "Sir, request permission to remain on the bridge until we reach Faro."

"Trent, you're relieved of duty until a doctor checks you out. We'll radio ahead to tell them we have an injured man on board and request medical assistance."

Roger persisted. "Sir, if they bring a cot to the bridge, I can lie here with a headache, just as well as I could in my cabin." He touched the bandage on his head to emphasize his point. "With this, maybe I shouldn't be left alone there . . . anyway."

Captain McPherson was nobody's fool. "Trent, will you go back to your cabin when Murphy can go with you?"

"Yes, sir."

"Very well. Vince, get a cot and put it next to the helm. Mister Trent wants to keep an eye on things for the remainder of his watch."

"With pleasure, sir." As Vince walked by, he whispered to Maureen, "I think the cat's out of the bag."

Vince came back in a few minutes with a cot and a couple of blankets. Together Vince and the Captain lifted Roger onto it. As they did, he grumbled, "I could get on the damn cot myself."

The Captain sternly replied, "Trent, you are confined to bed until you get medical clearance to resume duty. Head injuries can be serious, and there are insurance liabilities involved."

Vince tucked a blanket under Roger's head and threw the other one over him. "The Captain's right. Murphy will have to make sure you behave yourself and stay in bed." Maureen caught the subtle dig. After all of Roger's bitching about Grace, Vince deserved to rub it in.

Roger shot back, "I don't need a nanny, thank you."

Maureen also took a shot. "I have a theory his nanny dropped him on his head. That must be why he doesn't want another one."

Vince took a look out the window. "The sun's coming up. It's quite a scene out there. Too bad you can't see it, Roger." The first light of day brought with it their first view of the churning water. White foam streaked the blue surface as the sea seemed to boil all around them.

"What's the wind speed, Murphy?"

"Thirty-three miles per hour and dropping, sir."

"Looks like it's starting to quiet down. You still all right there, Maureen?"

"Yes, Captain. I'm fine."

"Glad we'll have a day or two at anchor waiting this out. We're down a mate and a helmsman."

Vince went back to the radar. "Sir, looks like we're not alone. I see another ship headed toward the coast. They're bobbing around as much as we are."

"Make sure they see us. Don't want them getting too close."

"I'll give them a holler on the radio, just to be sure they have a bead on us."

For the next few hours, Maureen maintained course and speed. Although the water remained choppy, the ship stabilized as the wind slowed down.

Even though the Captain obviously suspected she and Roger had feelings for one another, Maureen didn't want to compromise their situation any more than it had been. That being the case, she kept her mouth shut. She quietly kept an eye on Roger, just as he did on her, until he fell asleep.

By the time Maureen maneuvered them into the port and they dropped anchor, her watch was over. For being the worst weather she'd ever sailed, this gale was second only to the storm where she'd lost her father. It occurred to her that she could've lost Roger on the bridge, just as she had her dad.

The Captain interrupted her unsettling thoughts when he relieved her and gave her new orders. "Murphy, a tug is on the way with a doctor. I want you and Vince to stay here with Roger until the doctor comes on board. We won't move him until he's looked over."

Roger was still asleep. Maureen asked, "Should we wake him up?"

"Go ahead. He'll want to know we're at anchor. You can also tell him, on my authority, you are to stay with him and make sure he obeys doctor's orders. Understood?"

Maureen couldn't hide her smile. "Aye, Captain. Understood."

"Murphy, you did a good job today. Don't let him tell you otherwise."

"Thank you, sir. Don't worry, I can handle Mister Trent."

"I know you can." Then he spoke to Vince. "I'm going to check on any damages. With Trent down, you'll have to oversee whatever repair work we need before we sail."

"Not a problem, sir. I'll work on the report later this morning." The Captain left, leaving Maureen and Vince alone on the bridge with Roger. "Sunshine, I'm going to take a whiz. Go ahead and wake him up."

"Thanks, Vince. I'd like a few minutes alone with him."

Vince winked at her. "I knew that."

Maureen knelt by the cot. She lightly touched the blood-stained bandage taped to the side of Roger's head. Tears welled up as the impact of what could have happened sunk in. Using the edge of the blanket, she wiped her eyes. No way in hell did she want him to see her cry.

She brushed the hair back from his forehead. "Roger, can you hear me?" She gently shook his arm. "Roger, wake up."

He groaned, then opened his eyes. "Maureen?"

"Do you know that's the first time you've called me Maureen?"

"I have a fucking concussion, what do you expect? And why aren't you at the helm?"

"We're anchored at Faro. There's a doctor on the way."

"We made it?"

"Well, the ship made it. You almost didn't."

"It'll take more than a bloody bump on the head to take me out."

Maureen stroked his hair. "It was a bloody bump. You'll probably need stitches. The bandage the Captain put on your head is soaked through."

He crossed his arms over his chest, just the way he would have standing up. "How come you didn't give Vince the helm when I fell? You should've been the one to patch me up."

"How the hell do you figure that? The Captain is our medical officer."

"The Captain's not in love with me."

That one cut a bit too close to the bone. Maureen adjusted the blanket under his head, a little too roughly. Roger groaned. "Watch it! That hurt."

"Sorry." She gently finished re-forming his makeshift pillow, then tucked the blanket around him. "What makes you think I'm in love with you?"

"Aren't you?"

"I could ask you the same thing."

"I'm British. We don't fall in love."

"Is that a fact?"

"That is indeed a fact."

"What about your old girlfriend? You remember, the one who dumped you? Did you love her?"

"That's no question to be asking me now. My head already hurts."

Maureen played her ace. "That's fine. I'll have time to ask it again. The Captain has ordered me to stay with you, and to make sure you obey the doctor's orders."

"Bullshit!"

Right on cue, Vince reappeared. "She's telling the truth. I heard him give her the order."

"I'm not going to lie here and be treated like a bleeding invalid!" Roger tried to sit up, groaned and slowly lowered his head.

Vince grinned. "You wrote your own punch line. You are a bleeding invalid, whether you like it or not."

"Don't know if you remember this, but the Captain relieved you of duty until the doctor says you can work again," Maureen added. "It's my job to keep you in bed."

"And from what Grace and I heard last night, I don't think that part will be a problem." Vince got in another jab.

"Shut the fuck up, both of you. When does the frigging doctor get here?"

"Jeez! Having a concussion makes him even grumpier, doesn't it?"

"Cheer him up, Sunshine. I'll go check on the tug." Vince trotted down the stairs to the deck.

"What's the wind speed out there now?"

Maureen checked. "Tucked away in this harbor, it's down to eighteen miles per hour, just enough to rock you to sleep."

"Did you have any problems getting us here?"

"I managed it. We're here in one piece, aren't we?"

"You are." He pointed to the chart table. "I left a piece of my head over there."

It wasn't funny, but she couldn't help laughing. "Jesus! There's hair and blood on the corner of the table. You really did whack yourself good, didn't you?"

"Told you."

"If you can't keep your balance in a high wind, how the hell do you expect to be a Captain?"

"Maybe I'll have someone with me to keep me erect."

"What the hell does that mean?"

They heard Vince coming up the stairs. "He's up here. We think he might have a concussion."

Roger smiled. "Thought you might like a bit of something to suck on."

She didn't care if he did have a concussion. Just as the doctor came onto the bridge, she cuffed the top of his head and muttered, "Arrogant asshole."

# 8

"For God's sake, I'm all right!" Roger hadn't stopped complaining since Vince left to round up a few crew members to carry him to his cabin. "My frigging leg isn't broken. I can walk to my cabin." He tried to get up. Maureen stopped him.

"You heard what the doctor said. You are on complete bed rest for the next two days."

"Yes, and he also said that was a precaution. Unless blood starts shooting out of my nostrils, I think I'm going to live."

Maureen unfolded the piece of paper the doctor had given her. "Blood shooting out of your nostrils would be a definite setback. So would headache, nausea, vomiting, dizziness, irritability, crankiness." Maureen grinned. "Don't think I can use those last two. You're always irritable and cranky." She studied the rest of the list. "Here's a good one, change in libido. That one I can use."

"Fuck you."

"If you're a good boy and listen to doctor's orders, we'll see."

Roger frowned and crossed his arms. "You're enjoying seeing me flat on my back, aren't you?"

"Of course, I am! I'm only human." She stared down at him and scratched her head.

"What's your problem now?"

"Just thinking. When I came on board, I thought you looked like Laurence Olivier. I think I made a mistake. You look more like Winston Churchill right now. Your British jowls are showing."

Roger responded with a grouchy harrumph, but he didn't try to stand again. Maureen won that round.

Vince returned to the bridge, carrying a stretcher, followed by three other men. Eddie was one of them. He immediately came over to her.

"Hey, Red. Vince says our Chief Mate has a concussion. What happened?" Roger glared at Eddie. It tickled her silly to see Roger get jealous of him.

Maureen pointed to the table. "He fell and hit his head on the corner when the ship pitched." Turning to Vince, she added, "Someone really should clean the blood and hair off that thing. It's disgusting."

Roger didn't let that one pass. "Why don't you do it? It'll give you something productive to do."

"The Captain already gave me my orders." She shook the symptom list over his face. "Here they are."

Vince backed her up. "I'll have the table cleaned up later. Maureen, you do what the Captain told you to do." He winked at her.

"Thank you, sir. I intend to obey my orders to the letter." Roger harrumphed again.

Vince directed the operation. "We have to get you down two flights of stairs. Since you're a big son of a bitch, we're going to try to carry the stretcher two abreast, even if it's a tight squeeze on the steps. I sure as hell don't want to drop you."

"I will say it again, I can frigging walk!"

Vince gestured for two men to go on the other side of the cot. "Maureen, tell him again why he can't walk."

"Don't bother," Roger snapped.

The four men slid their arms under Roger and grasped each other's forearms. They created a cradle and shifted Roger onto the stretcher. "The doctor said to keep his head elevated, so it's feet first down the stairs."

Each man grabbed a corner of the stretcher, with Vince taking one of the bottom corners. "Maureen, I'm walking backward. You'll have to be my eyes and direct me down the stairs."

"Will do."

One careful step at a time, the impromptu medical team got down one flight of stairs to the deck, then a second flight of stairs to the cabin level. Maureen ran down the alleyway to open Roger's door. Using the same cradle technique as they had on the bridge, they hefted Roger onto his bunk.

Vince folded the stretcher. "Do you need anything else right now?" he asked Maureen, not Roger.

Maureen looked around. "Do you think a cot would fit in here if we moved the desk out into the hall? The doctor said he's not supposed to be alone."

Roger flared. "You're not fucking moving into my cabin!"

Vince ignored him. "Not a problem, Sunshine." Under protest from Roger, the men moved the desk outside the door; then Vince dismissed them.

Vince eyed the empty space. "A cot will fit, and you'll have a walkway. I'll bring it in directly."

"And how many frigging regulations are you breaking by putting a woman in my quarters?" Roger was fuming.

"As long as the Captain says it's all right, absolutely none." Vince kissed Maureen on the cheek. "Good luck, Sunshine. You're going to need it."

"Thanks, Vince. Tell Grace I'll catch up with her later. Oh, and tell them in the galley to bring us some food. I'm starving, and I can't leave him."

"Yeah, I'm pretty damn hungry, too." Vince took one last shot before he left. He shook his finger at Roger. "Better behave yourself, or she'll give you a spanking."

"Fuck you, asshole." Vince left and closed the door. Maureen heard him laughing in the alleyway. So did Roger. "Bloody hell! This isn't a goddamned joke! I don't want you in here!"

"Why not, Mister Trent? At least you'll have someone to talk to while you're lying there."

"The Captain could have assigned a deckhand to babysit, if that's what he needs for the insurance. He must be bats to put you in here with me."

"Captain McPherson is one smart cookie. He knows I'm the only one on this ship that can keep you in bed for two days."

"Well, sweetheart, if he knows that, our careers are shot to hell."

"Says who?"

"Says the rule book."

"The rules are changing, Mister Trent. It's about time you accept that." Maureen untied his shoes.

"What are you doing?"

"I'm taking off your shoes. You're not allowed to sit up until tomorrow, except to relieve yourself."

"Are you going to hold my dick while I piss?"

"Maybe, if you want me to." Maureen took off his shoes and socks. Just then, someone knocked on the door. Maureen answered. "Captain McPherson! Hello! I thought it was Vince."

"I passed him in the alleyway. He's gone to get you a cot and some fresh bedding." The Captain approached Roger's bunk. "I understand our favorite patient is a tad out of sorts."

"I have a headache," Roger grumbled.

"I think Murphy has one, too." He turned to Maureen.

"You are assigned to Mister Trent. The doctor spoke to me before he left, and he told me he put you in charge. You are to carry out his instructions, forcefully, if necessary. Understood?"

"Yes, sir. I understand."

"Mister Trent, I trust you have no objection to your assigned nurse?"

"Of course, I do! But that's not going to change your order, is it?"

"No, I can't say that it would. Murphy, if you need assistance, Vince and Grace are down the hall. Call me if you need anything more."

"Yes, sir."

"Trent, she's the best thing that's ever happened to you. Don't screw it up."

Roger grunted. "That's a matter of opinion, sir."

Before the Captain left, he said to Maureen, "I'll be damned if I understand what you see in him."

"Beats the hell out of me, too, sir."

The Captain leaned over and whispered into her ear, "Your father would approve."

Hearing that from one of her father's closest friends meant more to Maureen than anything anybody else could have said. She couldn't help it. Her eyes welled up as she whispered back, "Thank you, Captain." He squeezed her hand, and left her with Roger.

She tried to wipe her eyes, without Roger seeing the tears. In such a confined space, that proved impossible. "What the hell did he say to you? You're crying, for God's sake!"

Maureen couldn't quote him exactly, so she fudged. "He said my father would be proud."

"He's right about that."

"Don't bullshit me, Roger. This isn't easy." She went to the bathroom to blow her nose.

"I'm not bullshitting. You did a brilliant job today."

She yelled back, "Brilliant job? Jesus, I need to write that one in my diary." She came out of the bathroom to find Roger raised up on his elbows. "What the hell are you doing? The doctor said not to raise your head today unless you absolutely have to."

"That's going to make it awfully hard to fuck, unless you're on top."

"You drive me crazy! One minute, you're telling me to get out—the next, you're telling me you want to fuck."

"Isn't that the point?"

"Isn't what the point?"

"What we do together. I think they call it a love-hate relationship."

"With you, it seems there's more hate than love."

"And with you?"

"Why is it you keep trying to get me to say that I'm in love with you?"

"Aren't you?"

"So what if I am? What difference is that going to make?"

"Could make a big one. Think about it while I have a piss." He tried to sit up, and didn't quite make it. "Jesus, my head still hurts. When I lie still, it's not that bad."

"The doctor said it would probably feel like you have a bad hangover today. Let me help you."

Roger didn't object. "If I don't get in there soon, I'm going to piss my pants."

"Can you hold it for two more minutes?"

"Why?"

"I'll run down to the utility closet and get a bucket. You can go in that."

"Do it."

Maureen wasted no time. She bolted down the alleyway and grabbed an old metal bucket someone had stashed in the closet.

When she got back, Roger had already unzipped his trousers. It was the first time she'd seen him completely flaccid.

"We'll have to repeat the libido test later. Right now, you don't have a passing grade."

"Enough with the jokes. Help me up."

Maureen sat down beside him. He put his arm around her shoulders, and they slowly stood up together. Maureen held the bucket for him while he aimed his dick inside and pissed. She could tell from his expression his head hurt. When he finished, he shook it off over the bucket and tucked his business back into his undershorts.

"All right, nurse, while I'm standing, take these damn trousers off. I'm not going to sleep in them."

Maureen carefully set the bucket down. "You're not going to throw up, are you?"

"Not if you hurry up. My head is pounding."

Maureen quickly pushed his trousers down until they cleared his ass; then she pulled back the blankets on his bunk. "All right, slowly sit down." After he sat, she tugged his trousers off and unbuttoned his shirt. "Tell the truth, Mister Trent, would you really want a deckhand doing this?" She took his shirt off and helped him lie back down.

"I'd prefer my wife be doing it."

"Well, since you don't have one, I guess you'll just have to settle for me."

"Have you thought about it?"

"Thought about what?"

"Jesus Christ, Murphy! What I told you to think about while I had a piss."

"Oh, that. No, sorry, I've been too busy to think about it."

"This might help you to give it some thought. After my fiancée sent me that letter, I got to thinking. We'd been seeing each other on and off for over two years before we got engaged, and were six months into the engagement when she told me to go pound sand. In all that time, I can't remember her telling me once that she loved me."

"Had you ever said it to her?"

"Can't remember. Probably not."

"Then why were you going to get married?"

"Because that's what civilized people do."

Maureen sat down on the edge of the bed. "Even though you didn't say it, did you love her?"

"I thought I did, until now."

"I don't understand."

"Think about it." Roger closed his eyes, obviously in pain. "Dump that bucket. I may need it again."

As quickly as she could, Maureen cleaned out the bucket, dumping it and washing it out. When she came back, Roger still had his eyes closed. She set the bucket beside his bunk and sat down next to him. She lightly rubbed his stomach. "How are you feeling?"

"Better since I'm lying down. What you're doing, keep doing it. It's helping my stomach settle."

Maureen didn't mind continuing. In fact, rubbing his belly probably made her feel better than it did him. "Too bad you're out of commission. This is making me horny."

"Sorry, Murphy. Can't get it up right now."

"I'm watching. When it does, I'll jump on it."

Even in pain and nauseous, Roger chuckled. "Murphy, you're one for the books."

"So are you, Mister Trent."

Grace yelled from the alleyway. "Maureen, open the door. I have food, and Vince has a cot."

"Just a minute." She pulled the blanket up to Roger's waist.

"Thank you for protecting what little dignity I have left."

"You're welcome."

Maureen opened the door for Grace and Vince. "Hi, sweetie." Grace set the tray down on the floor. "How's he doing?"

"So-so right now. He's really not up for visitors."

"I can see that. Vince will set up the cot, and we'll take a hike."

Vince put the cot parallel to Roger's bunk, leaving a narrow walkway between. "Gracie, you left the bedding in the hall."

Grace went to retrieve it. When she came back, she set a stack of stuff on the cot. "Maureen, I stopped in your cabin and picked up a change of clothes. If you need anything I missed, give a holler."

"I will. Thanks for helping out."

"Hey, Sunshine. Like Gracie said, yell if you need us."

Roger hadn't said a word while Vince and Grace were there. "Do you want any food?"

"No."

"What do you want?"

"You know, we can keep this back-and-forth going for months. I don't have months. I go back to London next week."

"What are you talking about?"

"Remember? I have to take my exam for my Master's license."

"You said that was next month."

"Murphy, in ten days, it is next month. I don't have time to sail out again. From Piraeus, I go back to England. I thought you understood that."

"No, I didn't understand that! I thought we had more time. Jesus Christ, I fucking fall in love with you and you're leaving?" Her voice cracked and she ran into the bathroom.

"Murphy, come back here." She couldn't answer. If she had, a sob would have broken free. "Goddamn it, Maureen, come back here and talk to me." Roger didn't say anything else. Then she heard him retch.

A split second after she mumbled, "Oh, shit," her instincts kicked in. Not caring she had tears streaming down her face, she went to help him. He sat on the edge of the bunk with the bucket wedged between his knees, violently gagging.

She held his head, to try and keep it still. "Shhhhh, now. It's all right. I've got you. Relax and try not to gag." She felt him inhale deeply from his belly. "That's right, deep breaths and relax." He retched again, but not as forcefully. "Take another deep breath."

He managed three deep breaths without gagging. Maureen gently released his head and put the bucket on the floor. "Listen to me, Roger. I want you to very slowly lie down. I'll help you." Roger tried to say something, and started to cough. "Don't try to talk until your stomach settles. Just lie down."

Maureen helped him, and got him settled back onto the bunk. When she turned to go back to the bathroom, he grabbed her arm. "Don't leave."

"I'm just going for a washrag to wipe your face."

While she had the chance, she splashed some water on her own face and blew her nose. She came back with a wet cloth and a towel. "Doing better?"

"A bit."

"Good." She knelt beside the bunk and gently wiped his face. "You tried to stand up, didn't you?"

"You wouldn't come out of the loo. I have something I need to say, and wanted to say it to your face."

She didn't so much wipe his lips as caress them with the cloth. "I'm sorry I didn't come out. I couldn't."

"Why?"

Tears again stung her eyes. "Because I didn't want you to know I was crying."

"You said you've fallen in love with me."

The tears slid down her cheeks. This time, she made no attempt to hide them. "And you said you're leaving."

"Come with me."

"I can't come with you. I've signed on to sail with this ship. When she leaves Piraeus, I'll be on her, and you won't." This time, the sob did break from her throat. She tried to get up. Roger grabbed her arm.

"Marry me."

Maureen would have laughed, had the lump in her throat not been so big. "Yeah, right. Just like that." She picked up the towel and briskly rubbed her face, hoping the tears would stop. They didn't.

"If I could, I'd kneel. Maureen Murphy, please marry me. For the first time in my life, I'm really in love."

Maureen wiped her face again. "You're serious, aren't you?"

"Hell yes! I don't have time not to be serious. I'm leaving in a few days, and probably won't be back on this ship." In a strained voice, he echoed what she had said to the Captain earlier. "I don't want to lose you."

Roger winced and put his hand on his head. Maureen could see the pain etched in his face. "You need to rest. Let's talk about this tomorrow, when you're feeling better."

"No! I want an answer now. Will you marry me?"

# 9

Even with Roger's insistence, Maureen wouldn't give him an answer. He wasn't happy about that. She wanted to say yes, she really did. But she had to be sure they understood each other.

He'd been on the verge of heaving again when she finally got him to close his eyes and try to sleep. With a promise that they would talk about it when he woke up, he agreed to try and nap. She rubbed his stomach, and softly sang him a lullaby to help him relax.

Roger had fallen asleep, listening to her sing, *"Hush little baby, don't say a word. Mama's gonna buy you a mockingbird. If that mockingbird don't sing, Mama's gonna buy you a diamond ring."* The sound of her voice seemed to soothe him. She saw his facial muscles relax as the pain eased. His stomach muscles softened under her hand as he drifted off.

She watched him sleeping. How she could've fallen in love with a cantankerous Brit baffled her, and the ornery son of a gun wanted her to come with him. That astonished her!

It would have been enough for him to ask her to transfer to

his ship, once he became a Captain. She would be thrilled to serve under him, as his helmsman and otherwise.

But, for Christ's sake, he wanted to marry her! He hadn't said a single word about her sailing with him. That had to be part of the deal. Maureen knew she could never be a sit-at-home wife.

To try and talk to him about her concerns, with him in so much pain, would have been out of the question. He had to get some rest. Then they would discuss their future, and on what terms that future would unfold.

The doctor told her to wake him up every few hours, to check his symptoms. She had the laundry list he'd given to her memorized. Roger had already been sleeping well over two hours. She knew he would want an answer when he woke up. She figured she'd let him sleep a little longer.

She finished the sandwich Grace had brought and drank the now-cold coffee. A thermos pot of tea still sat on the tray for Roger. Maybe she could get him to drink some later.

They'd moved the desk and the chair into the alleyway, so the only place she had to sit was the toilet. She made good use of that, taking her time finishing her business there.

For the life of her, she didn't know what to do if she had to choose between Roger and the sea. She wanted to stay with him, but on a ship, not as a landlocked housewife. What if he didn't want her to sail anymore? What the fuck would she do?

Maybe she could think better lying down. She muttered, "I really am going nuts. That makes no frigging sense." Nonetheless, she decided to make up her bed and try it.

The cot didn't look very comfortable, but it was better than the floor. When she picked up the stack of bedding and clothes, she noticed a sliver of red sticking out.

Maureen whispered, "Gracie, you've got to be kidding!" She pulled out the slinky satin nightgown Grace had loaned her. She'd left it hanging in her closet. Grace must've seen it and thrown it in with her clothes.

"What's that?" Roger reached out and tugged her shirt. "And what makes no frigging sense?"

"You're supposed to be asleep." She turned around, still holding the nightie. "How long have you been awake?"

"Not long. You farted in the loo and woke me up."

"Lovely, Roger. Your tact is only exceeded by your sensitivity."

"What's that you're holding?"

Maureen held up the gown for Roger to see. "It's the other nightgown Grace loaned me yesterday."

"Are you going to wear that tonight?"

"Don't know. Depends on how you're feeling." She tossed it back on the cot.

"Why should how I'm feeling stop you from wearing that sexy little number?"

"You just answered your own question. Don't want you throwing up on it." Maureen changed the subject. "How're you feeling? Can I get you anything?"

"Not too bad, considering. And a glass of water would be spot-on. I'm dry as the Sahara."

"How about a spot of tea?" Maureen's attempt at a British accent failed miserably.

Roger chuckled. "You bloody Americans. You've never been taught to speak properly. It's 'How about a spot of tea?'" Roger repeated the phrase, his pronunciation and British accent an elocutionist's dream.

"Oh, for God's sake! Do you want tea or water? The tea's in a thermos. It should still be warm."

"I'll have some tea, thank you." Maureen went to pour it. "You never answered me. What makes no frigging sense?"

"I thought I might think better lying down. I'm all fucked-up." Maureen brought him his tea. "How's your head? Can you sit up without getting sick?"

"Let's see." Roger slowly raised himself up. "It's not too bad now. Still hurts a bit, but nothing like before."

Maureen handed him the cup. "Hold this. I'll fix your pillow." She fluffed his pillow and put it against the wall behind him. "Lean back."

"Thank you. That feels fine." He sipped the tea. "Have you thought about it?"

Maureen hedged. "I'm supposed to ask you the list of questions."

Before she could continue, Roger rattled off, "Today is Thursday. My head hurts a bit, but I'm not nauseous. I'm in reasonably good spirits." He threw back the blanket, exposing his groin and legs. "As you can see, my libido is returning, thanks to the thought of you in that sexy red nightgown. And, a few hours ago, I asked you to marry me, and am still waiting for the answer."

Maureen saw the obvious bulge in his undershorts. "You've got the stamina of an Angus bull. How the hell can you have a hard-on with a headache?"

Roger casually sipped his tea, deliberately raising his little finger in mock gentility. "I'm British. We don't have sex, but we do excel in fertility."

Maureen pointed to the nightgown. "So, when I wear that tonight, you're ready for it?"

"I do believe I will be. I'll have some dinner. If I keep it down, I think we're good to go."

Maureen shook her head. "You said I'm one for the books. Mister Trent, so are you."

"Which is why we belong together. Are you going to marry me or not?"

With the blanket thrown back, her heart beat faster at the sight of him. No question this man stood head and shoulders above any she'd met, both in looks and in intelligence. She respected him, as much as she loved him. But she couldn't be all starry-eyed and just blurt out yes.

"We have to talk."

"All right, let's talk."

"You haven't said a word about my sailing with you." Maureen decided right then and there she would give it to him straight. "I want to marry you, but I can't if you expect me to sit at home. Either I sail at your side, or we say our good-byes in Piraeus."

"Playing hard ball, Murphy?"

"No, Mister Trent, I'm not. This is my career, as much as it is yours. You can't ask me to give it up to be your wife. I won't do it."

"I haven't asked you to give it up."

"Not yet. Since you haven't discussed it with me, I have no idea what your intentions are. I have to know before I give you an answer."

"You've stated your case—now I'll state mine."

"I'm listening." Maureen braced herself. She knew this would be the deciding moment.

"You were forced on me. Had anyone asked for my opinion, I would've told them not to let you on this ship. When the Captain made you my helmsman, I figured I would sit back and wait for you to fuck up. Then I'd have cause to get you thrown off at the next port."

That remark piqued Maureen. "Mister Trent, this isn't helping your cause."

"Miss Murphy, let me finish. I've watched you closely since you've come on board. Your experience is obvious. Today you proved you can keep your head when shit hits the fan. To be an officer, you have to have that."

"I'm an Able-Bodied Seaman, not an officer."

"Well, my dear, if you're going to sail with me, you'd

bloody well better get your Mate's license. I'll be damned if I'll eat my dinner in the mess room like Vince does. A Captain takes his meals in the officers' saloon."

Maureen stood, dumbfounded. "You want me to become an officer?"

"You're a sailor, Murphy. You have the qualities and talent to be a damn fine officer." Roger handed her his teacup. "I'd like some more, please."

Grateful for the brief distraction, Maureen refilled the cup, then gave it back to him. "Here. Take it slow with this."

"I'm all right. My stomach is holding its own."

She glanced at the ridge in his skivvies. "So is your libido."

"Always happens with you around. At least if we're married, I have an excuse for having a boner."

Maureen sat down on the edge of the bunk. Still not sure she had it all straight, Maureen repeated what he'd said. "You're saying you'll let me sail with you if I'm an officer?"

"Yes, and if we're married. If you don't agree to both, I withdraw my proposal."

"What about children?"

"That will have to wait. We can't have a family while we're both at sea." He studied her for a moment. "Is that acceptable to you?"

"Hell yes!"

He grinned. "Don't mince words. Murphy, tell me how you feel."

"What made you change your mind? I never thought you would ask me to sail with you. I thought if it happened at all, I would have to fight for it."

"Want the truth?"

"I have to have the truth. Otherwise, I can't make a fair decision."

"That's exactly it! You've hit the nail on the head."

"Roger, don't fuck with my head. Just tell me the truth."

"You stayed at the helm with me out cold and bleeding. You didn't know how seriously I might be hurt, but you didn't leave your post."

"I thought that pissed you off."

"It did, royally! But you didn't let your emotions cloud your judgment. You had a job to do and you did it. And now, you're not letting me force you into a decision you're not ready to make. You're pissing me off again, and you don't give a shit."

"You got that right."

"I know I do. You're going to make one hell of an officer. I pity the sailor who thinks he can get one over on you. I gave it my best shot, and ended up falling in love with you."

Maureen took his empty teacup and set it on the floor. "Do you want some food?"

"I want an answer."

"What if they won't give me my Mate's license in the U.S.? They've opened the doors, but they're not posting any welcome signs."

"Once we're married, you can apply in the U.K. I have contacts there. We'll work something out."

"And in the meantime?"

"You'll be on the ship with me as an AB, until you get your Mate's license." Roger took her hand. "I will ask you once more. Maureen Murphy, will you do me the honor of becoming my wife? Will you marry me?"

This time, Maureen didn't have to think about it. "Yes, Roger Trent. I'll marry you."

Roger opened his arms. "Come here." Maureen scooted down the bunk. He wrapped his arms around her, and said simply, "Thank you." She could feel his heart thumping in his chest.

"I want Captain McPherson to marry us."

"So do I. But we will have to do it again in England, with all the paperwork and legalities. We'll have a real wedding there."

"I have no family left since my dad died. I've never asked you. Do you have family in England?"

"Jesus, yes, hordes of them. Wait until you meet my parents and sisters. Then there are my aunts, uncles and cousins. Most of them are in the shipping business." Roger tugged her hair. "And they all hated Angela."

"Don't tell me. She's the cold fish that dumped you."

"To quote my mum in the last letter I got from her, *Good riddance to that bit of business. She wasn't the one for you.*"

"Will she think I am?"

Roger laughed. "Are you kidding? I'm bringing home a red-haired Irish lass with a temper, who wants to sail with me. My seafaring family will love you!"

Maureen couldn't tell if that was sarcastic, or if he meant it. "Well, sure as hell, I'm not a passionless Brit!"

Roger nuzzled her hair. "Oh, no, my dear, you certainly aren't passionless." His breath on her neck made her shiver.

"All right, you've passed the libido test." Maureen stood up just as he reached for her breast. "I'm going to get you some food. Can I trust you to stay in bed until I get back? I'm not supposed to leave you alone, but you need to eat."

He pointed to the red nightgown on the cot. "I won't move if you promise to put that on after dinner."

"And what happens then?"

"You tell me, nurse. What am I allowed to do?"

"Not much. But I don't expect that's going to matter, is it?"

"Probably not."

"Damn mulish Brit! I'm supposed to make sure you follow the doctor's orders." Even issuing the obligatory slap on the wrist, she had to smile. "Just don't throw up on the night-gown."

Roger grinned. "At least if blood shoots out of my nose, it won't show."

"Small comfort." Maureen squeezed Roger's bare foot on the way to the door.

When she passed Grace and Vince's cabin, she heard them inside. They hadn't yet left for the mess room. Maureen paused, then knocked.

Grace answered. "Sweetie, is everything all right?" Then she yelled at the closed toilet door. "Vince, it's Maureen."

Maureen opened her mouth to answer and choked up. All she got out was "Roger . . ."

"Vince! Get out here. There's something with Roger."

Maureen waved her hand and managed to say, "He's all right. That's not it."

Vince came out, with his trousers still open. "What's wrong?"

"I don't know. Maybe you should check on Roger."

Maureen blurted out, "No! He's fine."

Grace pulled her inside and closed the door. "Maureen, you're not making any sense. What's wrong?"

Maureen forced herself to breathe. "Roger's fine. In fact, he's rallied." She took another deep breath. "He asked me to marry him, and I said yes."

Grace let out an ear-piercing squeal. "Oh, my God! I can't believe it!"

Maureen wiped her eyes. "I can't, either." She turned to Vince. "He's going to help me get my Mate's license, so I can sail with him as an officer."

Vince ran his fingers through his hair. "I'll be goddamned!"

Grace hugged her so tightly, Maureen could barely breathe. "Of course, I'm your maid of honor."

"You know you are. We're going to have the Captain marry us, and then do it again in England, with Roger's family."

When Grace let go, Vince grabbed her. "Sunshine, tell our esteemed Chief Mate that I'm available to do the honors as best man."

"I'll tell him." Maureen glanced at the clock. "I can't stay. I'm going to get us some dinner. I have to get back so he's not alone."

"I could get it for you," Grace volunteered.

"Thanks, but that's not necessary. He really is doing better. I'll grab us a tray and come right back."

Grace hugged her again. "I'm so happy for you. You're going to be great together."

"Yeah, if we don't kill each other first."

Not wanting a flood of questions about Roger, Maureen avoided the mess room and went straight to the galley. The Captain had already told them to deliver dinner. They had a cart with two trays almost ready. Maureen took it herself.

When she got back to the cabin, it surprised her to find Captain McPherson there, talking to Roger. She knew by the smile on his face that Roger had already told him.

"Hello, Miss Murphy, or should I say, the future Mrs. Trent? I understand congratulations are in order."

Maureen wheeled the cart in and parked it beside the toilet door. "I can't believe he told you without me."

Roger jumped in: "You told Grace and Vince without me. I heard Grace shriek clear down here—"

"I knew that locking you two in the same room would either result in an engagement or a murder," the Captain interrupted. "Glad to see no one will end up in the brig."

Maureen stared at him in disbelief. "You planned this?"

"Let's just say I saw an opportunity and took it. We'll do the shipboard ceremony once we're back in international waters. I see it on deck, surrounded by the crew. Is that all right with both of you?"

Roger answered for both of them. "Yes, sir. That will be splendid."

The Captain lifted the lid on the dinner plate. "Beef stew

tonight. Much better than chili." Turning back to Roger, he said, "I'll stop by tomorrow and go over the sailing schedule."

"Yes, sir." Roger held out his hand to shake the Captain's. "Thank you, sir, for everything."

"You're welcome, Trent. Take good care of her, or you'll answer to me."

"Yes, sir!"

Captain McPherson kissed Maureen. "Be happy, Maureen. That's what your father would want."

"I know. I think he's smiling right now."

"So do I."

The Captain left them alone. Maureen put the tray on Roger's lap. He ate like a champ. "You know, you should slow down."

"I'm frigging hungry. I haven't eaten since dinner last night."

"How's your stomach and your headache?"

"Stomach's fine. My head is getting there. The headache is nearly gone. It just feels sore where I hit it."

"Then I guess you're ready for this." Maureen pushed the cart out of the way and picked up the nightgown.

"I'm definitely ready for that." He stuffed the last forkful of stew into his mouth and handed her the tray. "Here, get rid of this."

Maureen took the tray and put it back on the cart. "I'm going to jump in the shower. Then I'm going to give you a sponge bath." She picked up the negligee.

"With that on?"

"Yup."

Roger closed his eyes and muttered, "She may kill me yet today."

Maureen quickly rinsed off, dried and put on the red nightgown. As expected, it clung to her like the peel on an apple. The plunging neckline exposed most of her breasts. Unlike the night before, when she felt nervous wearing the scanty baby doll, tonight she felt positively sizzling.

She'd scrubbed up the bucket earlier, anticipating Roger's sponge bath. What she hadn't planned earlier was to make it foreplay. Maureen knew he wouldn't take no for an answer tonight, but she didn't want him to overexert himself. This should satisfy his needs, and her concerns.

When she came out, she burst out laughing. Roger had taken off his undershorts. He lay, sprawled on the bunk, completely nude, with a full erection.

"What's so funny? I'm ready for my sponge bath, nurse." He gave her a thorough once-over. "Except for holding that bucket, you look smashing!"

Maureen set the bucket down beside the bunk, then threw the towel on the cot. She reached into the warm water and fished out the washrag and soap. "Just relax. I'm going to take care of you."

"Goddamn! I would say you already are!"

Maureen had never tried to be sexy. Quite the opposite. She'd hid her sexuality and her femininity under men's clothes and masculine work. Now, with Roger, that had changed.

She saw him trying to see down the front of her gown. Without being obvious, she deliberately bent over to wipe his chest, making sure her bodice gapped enough to give him a good look. The soft but guttural sound he made told her she'd succeeded.

Gently, even tenderly, she wiped his face. His breath warmed her cool hand. She continued to wash him, cleaning his arms and legs.

When she scrubbed his thighs, he raised his ass off the bunk. "You're driving me frigging crazy, Maureen. Wash my dick before my bollocks explode."

"Maybe I want them to explode," she quietly purred.

He reached for her, attempting to pull her on top of him. "I want to fuck."

Maureen dodged his hand. "So do I. But not quite yet." She dunked the rag again and squeezed it out. "I have to clean you first." With that, she enveloped his erection in the warm cloth. He groaned and thrust into her hand.

Roger pushed upward into the cloth, giving Maureen a clear indication of what to expect. "Mister Trent, would you like that to be me?"

"Fuck, yes! Mount me."

"Are the condoms still under the mattress?"

"Down there." Roger pointed to the bottom corner. Maureen found the box and tore one open. "Be careful putting that on me."

"Not to worry, sir. I know what I'm doing."

"You'd damn well better, if I'm marrying you."

Maureen laughed. "Having second thoughts already?"

"To quote your eloquent response, 'Hell no!'"

"Good. Neither am I." Maureen rolled the condom onto his prick. Roger's chest rose and fell, his breath coming from deep in his abdomen. "You're sure you can handle this?"

"I'm sure. Ride it."

Roger's eyes burned into her as she straddled him. She tugged her skirt up her thighs. "Do you want this on or off?"

"Leave it on, but pull it up so I can see the red hair between your legs."

She did as he asked, and then aimed his prick directly into the center of her flaming bush. At the moment when she bore down on him, his grunt blended with her moan.

With Roger fully inside her, Maureen stopped, allowing them both time to adjust. She saw Roger grimace. "Are you all right? You're not sick or anything?"

"I'm bloody fine, but you'd better damn well get down to it. My dick is about to crack in half."

That's what she needed to hear. Using all the strength in her legs, she rode him like a cowhand riding a bull. He bucked and she held on, slamming down on him as he arched to push into her.

Roger held on to her thighs as they fucked. "I'm getting close, Maureen. I want you to come first. What do you need?"

"Diddle me, Roger. Use your finger and rub my clit."

He pushed two fingers between her legs and found the nub. Just as she came down on him, he rubbed her, hard. The sound that erupted from her throat didn't sound human. Her whole body shook as she gripped his prick inside her.

Roger growled, "Oh, yeah, Murphy, come for me, baby. Show Papa that mockingbird, and I'll give you a diamond ring."

Even in the throes of her climax, Maureen hissed back, "Fucking Brit!"

"You'll be fucking this Brit from now on. Get used to it." With that, he pushed upward, lodging his prick deep inside her. He pushed again, then shuddered.

As Roger continued to pump into her, he moaned, "Oh, yeah, sweetheart. That's good! Ride me."

He gradually quieted and settled back on the bunk. Maureen gently rolled off him, then disposed of the condom.

Not bothering with the cot, she snuggled beside Roger. "We're really getting married, aren't we?"

"Absolutely! Someone has to keep an eye on you."

Just before she fell asleep, she murmured, "Captain Trent. That has a nice sound."

"So does the Captain and Mrs. Trent." Roger kissed her hair. "You used to be the Captain's daughter. Now you'll be the Captain's wife."

In an almost inaudible whisper, Maureen corrected him. "You're wrong. I'll be the Captain's mate."